ASHES
TO
ASHES

CHRISTOPHER I. THOMA

Angels' Portion Books

Text © 2025 by Christopher I. Thoma

FIRST EDITION

Angels' Portion Books
AngelsPortion.com
ChristopherThoma.com

Scripture quotations are from the King James Version of the Bible (public domain) and the ESV Bible ® (The Holy Bible, English Standard Version ®), copyright © 2001 by Crossway Bibles, a publishing ministry of Good News Publishers. All rights reserved.

Cover art and design by Angels' Portion Books.

Publisher's Note: This novel is a work of fiction. Names, characters, places, and incidents are either products of the author's imagination or used fictitiously. All characters are fictional, and any similarity to people living or dead is purely coincidental.

ISBN 978-1-955355-05-6

Printed in the United States of America.

For Jennifer

who cannot shake the
concern that readers will
see autobiography where
none exists.

PREFACE

It was my daughter who told me of an emerging trend among fiction writers. She noted that many are now including music playlists—artists and their compositions that reflect the work's inspiration or tenor.

At first, I thought the idea was somewhat silly. I considered it a limiter to the listener's imagination. Much of the fun in fiction is that, even as the author presents the story, ultimately, the reader fills in the mental cracks. The characters, objects, locations, and such materialize distinctively as the reader sees them, not necessarily as the writer does. This dissonance in this exchange becomes tangible when a book is developed into a motion picture. For many readers, there is disappointment, if only because the director's vision was too far apart from their own.

I never wanted to direct in this way. And yet, strangely, I should be forthright enough to share that this book was born of a song.

If I'm listening to anything, it's usually talk radio, podcasts, or rock—AC/DC and such. That said, during a trip to and from Mackinac Island, my son introduced me to a love I hadn't yet discovered for cowboy balladcering, sea shanties, and Appalachian-rooted folk sounds—bluegrass, old-time, and mountain gospel.

It didn't take long before I was hooked.

Sometime later, I was out and about on visitations when I happened upon Johnny Cash's *The Man Comes Around.*

Listening intently, I recognized it as a distinct mixture of scripture put to music—an apocalyptic meditation stitched together from Saint John's Revelation, parables of Christ, and Old Testament prophecy. I noticed Cash wasn't merely leaning on the Bible as casual source material. Its words haunted the song, threading through every verse with an otherworldly weight. And Cash employed it viscerally, painting a slow march toward judgment, both external and internal, with the grit of his voice evoking both the voice of God and the voice of human conscience.

Perhaps more distinctly, the song doesn't sit comfortably in categories like "sad" or "happy." Its tenor is solemn, more reverent. It evokes the awe and dread of divine judgment, not through despair or celebration, but through the plainness of "It just is and will be." With that, the song dares the listener to consider the weight of justice, the inevitability of consequence, and the fragility of the human soul.

Attuned to these melodic contours, and being a writer, I suddenly had an idea for a book.

The only clear image that came to me while driving 77 miles per hour on I-96 through Novi, Michigan, was of a pastor who suddenly wakes up to find the person he was visiting now dead. It came in a flash. And then that was it—*for about ten months*. And while I didn't act on the thought during those months, the time between the idea's birth and my first taps on the keyboard was not misspent. Cash's song became a favorite. I listened to it often, and others like it. As I did, each song's lyrics offered elements of atmosphere to the story. Each tugged a little here and there, laying bare a series of questions.

What happened? What would I do? More pressing—what crimes could land so near, so personal, that they'd shove a man across a line you'd never expect him to cross?

What could turn him into a man who *goes around taking names*?

So, returning to where I began, I suppose I'm willing to share the songs that were playing in the background as this narrative began to coalesce. Cash's is obvious. But some of the others are mentioned in the story on occasion, too. Nevertheless, I've decided to provide them here.

They tell different stories. But together, they form a kind of heartbeat, an earnest cadence that pulsed beneath my laptop's keys as Reverend Daniel Michaels went about doing what he does. Sometimes the rhythm was faint, like the murmur you'd hear while resting your head on another human's chest. Other times, it boomed like a drum—irrefutable and insistent. I have a sense that these songs echo Daniel's questions, mirror his doubts, and underscore his eventual choices relative to something ancient and inescapable.

I've provided a playlist below. It is by no means comprehensive or in any particular order. But it does share the undeniable ones. When you have a moment, take a listen. Or don't. That part's up to you—it was my daughter's idea, after all. As for me, I only hope you enjoy the story. I certainly enjoyed writing it.

Cheers,
Christopher I. Thoma ☩

> Johnny Cash
> > *The Man Comes Around*
> Poor Man's Poison
> > *Hell's Coming With Me*
> > *The Woods*

Hey Mister
Long Way Home

The Band of Heathens
Hurricane

Goodnight, Texas
The Railroad

Brent Cobb
Black Creek

Corb Lund
Dig Gravedigger Dig

Colter Wall
The Devil Wears a Suit and Tie
Sleeping on the Blacktop

Tyler Childers
Hard Times

PROLOGUE

But who can endure the day of his coming, and who can stand when he appears? For he is like a refiner's fire and like fullers' soap.

Malachi 3:2

There was a time when Daniel thought the Prophet Malachi preached of God purifying his people. Cleaning them up.

After Claire, he sensed something more—an element of burning.

Burning away the rot.

The lies.

The veneer.

God doesn't clean things with silk. He purges with ash.

He's sacramental. He uses things.

"Speak, for your servant is listening."

Daniel has become the ash.

He wears his clerical collar when he does it.

Always.

Not because he thinks it sanctifies the act, but because it's who he is. A called and ordained servant of the Word. A sheepdog protecting the Shepherd's flock. A man now walking a narrow corridor where conviction blurs with fury, a shadowed line between justice and wrath.

And he needs the wolves to see—*needs* them to know—who's bringing them to account.

He prays before.

He prays after, too.

The words are always crisp.

Strangely, through it all, *The Man Comes Around* plays in his mind like a psalm of fire. Johnny Cash's voice, a cracked prophecy in the chapel of his conscience.

The song was playing on his car radio before the first. It was bizarrely fitting, almost motivating, nearly approving.

The timing was just too right.

"There's a man goin' 'round takin' names…"

He keeps his work secret.

He keeps it sacred.

There's a list. Each name on it is a bruise on his soul.

As the road grows darker, as names rise and then disappear like unclean spirits from the list, heaven is silent.

But is it really?

Still, in the quiet, the bruising deepens.

Daniel knows all too well that refinement and ruin come from the same flame.

CHAPTER ONE

The first thing he noticed was the smell. It was familiar. It was the way her house always smelled. There was a sense of old iron, wood, and dust, and something faintly floral, like potpourri left too long in a bowl. Every time he visited, he remembered his grandmother's apartment and how the antique store in the town where he grew up smelled just like it.

But she was no grandmother. She was young. Barely thirty, if that. She lived alone, having no apparent interest from suitors. It's not that she wasn't pretty. She was. In truth, it concerned him sometimes when she'd call him to come for a visit. People have a way of twisting innocence, of creating narratives, even in the church. Especially in the church.

The second thing he noticed was the pain.

Reverend Daniel Michaels stirred from the floor, his body sprawled across her round living room rug that colored the hardwood between the chair he would always occupy and the couch where she would welcome his company. His shoulder was pressed against the coffee table atop the rug. His clerical collar was twisted and bent. Its edges were damp. A sharp ache radiated from the back of his head. His hand moved to touch it and came back slick with red.

Lifting himself from the floor, he blinked against the morning sun cutting through pale curtains. The light fell across scattered books on the table, across a spilled coffee mug, across a toppled picture frame, across the couch. It stopped at her. She was lying at the foot of the stairs. Face up.

Her long, sandy brown hair was in a tangled spray around her. Eyes wide.

Claire Madsen. Choir alto. Quiet. Faithful.

Now dead.

Daniel tried to be swift, but the world tilted as he took in the scene. Nothing but his coffee and the picture frame was out of place until, in his imbalance, he bumped a lamp from a side table. Passing the front door, it was barely open. But it was springtime, and she always left it open in the spring. There was no overturned furniture. There was no visible wound. Just her, still and staring, a sheen of pooled blood near her head and a single thin stream of blood from her nose.

He stumbled forward, one foot catching something on the floor. A sharp crack sounded as a solid object skidded across the wood and bumped softly against the baseboard. He glanced down briefly. It was one of the porcelain birds she kept on the side table near the stairs, now chipped and speckled red along its wing.

Staggering toward her, he dropped to his knees.

"Claire…"

His voice came out thin, trembling in the quiet room. Instinctively, he reached forward to touch her wrist, but even as his fingers made contact, he already knew there was no pulse waiting there. Her skin was cool and dry, as though she had already begun to slip quietly away into memory.

Daniel fell backward, breathing sharply. The pain in his head moved to his shoulder, which he now realized had struck the coffee table when he fell. Thoughts spun inside his aching head, fragmented and chaotic, as though each attempt to think clearly was being shrouded by a haze forming behind his eyes. He'd been hit hard. Still, he tried to recall something—

anything—that might explain the scene before him, but the images were strewn like puzzle pieces thrown carelessly across a table. They refused to fit together.

He remembered Claire greeting him at the door. She was bothered but not unwelcoming. He remembered sitting down and reaching for a cup of coffee. The memory stopped abruptly at the cup touching his fingers, warmth spreading briefly against his palm. After that, there was nothing. He replayed the last and clearest memory he had. It was Claire's voice on the phone, calling him last night just after he'd walked in his front door. Her voice had trembled slightly. He'd asked her if everything was okay. She'd paused, a hesitation he now wished he'd questioned further.

"Pastor," she finally said, "there's something I need to tell you. Something important."

He remembered thinking how tired he was, and how he just didn't have it in him for one more moment of pastoral care. All he wanted was a two-fingered dram of something expensive and then his pillow.

"Can you come by tonight?"

"Can it wait?" he asked, even though he knew the question might cost him later. Parishioners lose sight of a pastor's humanity, sometimes seeing him as a genie in a bottle to be conjured rather than a flesh-and-blood person who eats, sleeps, and, like everyone else, sometimes reaches the end of his ability to care. Glancing at a bottle of The Balvenie he'd already stretched into his cabinet to retrieve, he was willing to give a little.

"Or can we talk right now by phone?" he offered.

"Please," she said, a quiet urgency in her voice. "It really can't wait. Could you come by tonight? Or I could meet you at the church. It won't take long. Please."

She'd always been so respectful, so reluctant to impose. Still, it was late, and he'd only just gotten home from two hundred miles gathered between multiple hospital visits. Metro-Detroit hospitals are, by no means, near one another, and his church members never choose the same one. With that, he was tired. And yet, there was something in her voice. Pastors have those senses. Over time, they learn to hear beneath the words. They hear beneath the tones. Sometimes it was the pauses that said more than the spoken word.

Still, the exhaustion was too much.

"Claire," he said, "I don't think I can come by tonight. But I promise I'll be there first thing in the morning."

A moment passed. She did not speak.

"I'll come by your place before I go to the office," he added to the quiet. "I could probably get over to you by eight o'clock. Will that work?"

✝ ✝ ✝

Daniel's eyes focused again on Claire's still face. Her eyes stared upward from the floor as though fixed on something he couldn't see, perhaps something beyond the ceiling itself. His gaze shifted to the small trickle of blood from her nose, drying now into a brittle crimson streak. A small detail, but it troubled him. He'd seen death before. It was a tangible specter. When death was near—at hospital beds, at accident scenes, beside the quiet grief of hospice—the space would change. Death wasn't new to Daniel, but this was something else. It felt wrong. Claire's passing was unnatural. Her life had been taken. He knew it without needing evidence.

Slowly, painfully, Daniel pushed himself up. His shoulder stung. Once to his feet, even with the slight change in altitude, he staggered to find his balance, his head throbbing and his collar even wetter than before. He reached into his pants pocket, pulling out his cell phone. He dialed emergency services, his voice hollow as he relayed the address, the situation, his name.

The dispatcher instructed him to stay put and not to touch anything. Daniel hung up, his eyes—and eventually himself—wandering back to Claire's coffee table, the overturned picture frame, the broken lamp on the floor.

Don't touch anything.

But he did anyway, as if the dispatcher were a voice in an uncertain dream, his actions guided by a numb instinct, an automatic attempt to restore some sense of normalcy to the chaos around a parishioner he still cared for deeply. Sitting back in his chair, gingerly, he picked up the frame, noticing for the first time the smiling faces it once contained—a much younger Claire, her parents, the sister she rarely spoke about. It was a simple image, a backyard somewhere bright and beautiful. A long time ago, the framed memory was now distorted by spider-webbed glass.

His heart tightened. Claire had always seemed profoundly alone, rarely speaking of family, never mentioning close friends. She volunteered for everything at the church. She was always around. She was always serving. Everyone knew her. And yet, among the social busyness, she'd sit quietly, an unassuming presence, whether serving soup at the Lenten supper or sitting in the pews on Sunday. She was an equally meek presence in the loft when the choir would sing. She was devoted to the choir. She loved to sing. And the congregation knew it. Daniel knew it, too.

The distant wail of sirens grew nearer, forcing him quickly back into the moment. Without fully understanding why he'd picked up the frame, he used a nearby book, *Waterfalls of Michigan*, to brush broken glass from the table to make space for it. Standing it upright, he brushed more glass and then rearranged the books. He was told not to touch anything. But he was doing it anyway. The feeling was new, frighteningly instinctive. Pastors try to do right. They try to help. But this would not help an investigation. And yet, it was as if tidying this one part of Claire's life might somehow restore a certain dignity to the scene.

A car screeched to a halt, startling Daniel to attention. He moved to the doorway, breathing deeply, his back stiffened against its frame. Morning sunlight brightened the street, highlighting neighbors cautiously peering from behind curtains or stepping warily onto porches, drawn by the approaching sirens. Two squad cars had arrived, their red and blue lights strangely muted but still unsettling in the morning's brightness, casting uneasy flickers across her well-kept yard.

Doors opened. Uniformed officers emerged. So did plainclothes volunteer officers. The uniformed men moved purposefully up the walk, grim and professional. The others remained behind among the people near the street. Daniel knew the uniformed men, if only because the town of Linden was so small. He'd seen them around town. One attended his church. Well, his family did. He rarely showed his face, except for Christmas and Easter. The other had visited his church on occasion when called, once to investigate vandalism and another time to help direct traffic around an accident near the church's driveway. It was a hot day, and Daniel had given him a bottle of water.

Daniel's heart sank when the police chief, Jeffrey Stern, stepped from an unmarked vehicle at the curb. Stern was different. Stern had always been different. An occasional visitor to church functions, if only to be seen in the community—always affable, always polite—Daniel had never been able to shake the feeling that there was something profoundly off about him. Something hidden beneath a practiced veneer. It was nothing overt, nothing Daniel could put his finger on, but it had always been there, harassing him.

Stern's dark eyes fixed immediately on Daniel, appraising him carefully, his expression neutral and unreadable. He walked steadily up the porch steps, nodding slightly as he reached Daniel's side.

"Reverend Michaels," he greeted calmly, extending a hand that Daniel took reluctantly, the grip firm and cool.

"Chief."

"What happened here?" Stern asked, glancing past Daniel into the home, eyes calculating, probing already.

"I don't know," Daniel said slowly, carefully choosing each word. He pointed toward Claire, his voice trembling slightly. "I found her like this when I woke up. I—I don't remember."

"Woke up?" Stern's eyes narrowed. "What exactly was the nature of your relationship to Ms. Madsen?"

Realizing Stern's misconception, Daniel insisted, "No, it's not that at all."

"Then what happened? Were you injured?"

Daniel touched his head, showing Stern the sticky red smear of blood on his fingers. "I think someone hit me. I don't recall what happened. I stopped in this morning for an early visit. Claire wanted me to come by last night, but I couldn't."

"Did she call you, or did you reach out to her?"

"She called me. And like I said, I couldn't stop by last night, so I scheduled with her for this morning. I only remember setting my coffee down, and then I woke up on the floor by the coffee table. And then I found her."

Stern nodded, watching Daniel closely. "She say *why* she wanted you to come by last night?"

"She didn't. She just asked to see me. That's it."

"Did she seem bothered?"

Daniel hesitated, the urgency of her call now hot in his chest. "No," he lied. Pastors don't hide things. They don't deceive. "She just sounded like Claire," he added.

"Anything else?" Stern asked casually, though Daniel sensed a sharper intention behind the Chief's cool eyes. "She didn't mention any trouble, anything else she might be worried about?"

Daniel paused. His mouth opened, the words nearly slipping out—about Claire's pleading—but something stopped him. A quiet instinct, deep and primal, like the one that had made him reset the picture frame and rearrange the books.

"No," Daniel said finally, firmly. "Nothing else."

Stern studied him a moment longer, perhaps sensing Daniel's uncertainty, his withholding. "We'll need you to come down to the station to make a formal statement."

"Of course," Daniel replied. "Whatever you need."

"Good." Stern gave a tight-lipped smile, a pale imitation of sympathy. "Reverend, this is probably a new one for you. But trust me, we'll get to the bottom of it."

Daniel nodded politely, feeling an unseen weight pressing heavily against him.

Trust.

Trust was something Daniel reserved carefully. A fellow pastor's wife once told him, "Friends are friends until they aren't"—what she said came from experience. She knew from her husband—from being immersed in a pastor's life—that people are generally okay with you, that is, until their deeds require confronting. Then it's all too easy for longtime friends to become enemies. Daniel knew this, too. In his fifteen years of ministry, he'd learned plenty. He could sense genuine character beneath a person's polished exterior. He could discern intentions beneath smiles. Stern's kindness always felt trained, his sympathy strategic.

"Stay here," Stern instructed quietly, his voice gentle yet commanding. "Someone will drive you to the station shortly."

"I can drive myself," Daniel said, almost rebelliously.

"You sure?" Stern asked. "If you were hit hard enough to lose consciousness—"

"I'll be fine," Daniel interrupted, even as the world tilted slightly again, a wave of nausea briefly surging. He swallowed hard, determined to hide it.

Stern gave a look, then a nod, and moved decisively into the house, already taking command of the scene, issuing quiet orders to uniformed officers and investigators who had only recently passed him and Daniel on the porch. The street pulsed with activity, neighbors murmured anxiously, and Daniel stood alone, no longer noticed. Closing his eyes for a moment, he breathed deeply. With the oxygen came a startling moment of regret. The dim light of his living room. The whisky bottle. Claire's interrupting call. She needed him. She genuinely sounded concerned. But he was too tired. He was just too tired to help.

Whatever happened, he failed her.

The weight of the memory filled him, even as an officer approached, gently touching his arm. "Reverend, let's head over to the station."

Daniel nodded, his heartbeat steadying. He went back through the front door toward the coatrack to retrieve his jacket. He put one arm through the sleeve, then the other, as he followed the officer outside and down the porch steps. Reaching into his pocket to fetch his keys, his fingers brushed against something unfamiliar. He drew out a small flash drive. Without hesitating, he put it right back. It hadn't been there before. His fingers tightened around it as he turned to see Stern directing officers around Claire's living room. The Chief's gaze shifted back to Daniel, lingering just long enough to be bothersome. He gave a half-wave before Daniel looked away, pulling his jacket closed and zipping it up.

His eyes settled again on Claire's peaceful yard, now swarming with onlookers. Daniel stepped onto the driveway, pulling out his keys as he headed toward his car. A volunteer officer standing near his driver's side door raised a hand, blocking his path.

"Chief Stern said someone would drive you," the man stated firmly. Before Daniel could protest, Stern emerged from the front door, calling across the lawn, "It's alright, he can drive himself. Just follow him." With a curt nod, the man stepped aside. Daniel climbed into his black two-door Wrangler, started the engine, and backed out onto the street, eyes momentarily fixed on the police cruiser in his rearview mirror that immediately fell in line behind him.

CHAPTER TWO

Daniel was not at the police station for long. The report was as simple as the story he gave Chief Stern on the porch. A cup of the station's day-old coffee in his belly, Daniel drove home in a daze, every street he passed bathed in springtime light.

The tulips near the Mill building were already open. A kid on a scooter passed him near Broad Street, zipping through without concern. Another rode her bike and carried a fishing pole. The bakery's marquee read, "Raspberry muffins today!" Three moms pushed strollers past the fire station's open doors, the trucks freshly washed and gleaming. The gas station beside it bustled. A flag snapped crisply in the breeze. Every corner of Linden whispered peace. Every window box bloomed with naïve joy. It was almost insulting. It should have been pleasant. But it wasn't. It was unsettling. His head throbbed sharply, each pulse a reminder of the violent, unexplained events of Claire's home. In the rearview mirror, the police cruiser remained a steady, looming presence, an oppressive reminder that his life had changed irreparably. However, the cruiser wasn't meant to be that. The officer only followed him home because of his injury.

Upon reaching his modest house of little more than a living room, kitchen, bedroom, and study, Daniel parked the Jeep and lingered in the driver's seat, hesitant to move. The officer who followed gave a wave as he passed by. The flash drive, now in his pants pocket, pressed against his thigh, heavy with dread. With a steadying breath, he finally climbed out and went inside.

The moment he crossed the threshold, he slid off his jacket, hung it on a hook near the door, and hesitated only briefly before retrieving the flash drive from his pocket. It was small, simple, yet it seemed to vibrate in his fingers with unseen intensity. Daniel went straight to his study. And though he lived alone, he closed the door behind him—something he rarely did—as if, just in case.

For only a moment, he thought he might open the drive on his laptop. But he didn't. Instead, he opened the side drawer and dropped it beside a box of freshly-sharpened pencils and an unused journal someone had gifted him during his installation service years ago. Against his doctor's advice—given during a phone call at the station—he went straight to bed. He slept hard.

The next morning, Daniel woke, still dressed in yesterday's clothes. His shoes were beside the door, and his jacket hung neatly on its hook, but he didn't remember taking them off. He only remembered falling into bed, his thoughts clattering too loudly to allow sleep. And yet, at some point, he must have slept. The pain in his shoulder was worse than the ache in his head now, but both were manageable, especially in comparison to what had settled in his chest.

The flash drive remained where he'd put it. He hadn't checked it. He wasn't ready.

His phone buzzed. Two missed calls. One from Chief Stern, one from Jeane Rittner, the church secretary. Jeane's voicemail was simple, her voice weary but gentle.

"Pastor, I heard about Claire. I… I don't know what happened, but if you need anything, we're all ready to do whatever you need. We're all ready to—"

She paused.

"Just say the word. Call when you can."

Stern's message was less caring and more clipped.

"Reverend, we've got a few follow-up questions. Nothing urgent. Give me a call when you can."

Daniel didn't call either of them back.

He showered slowly, wincing as he raised his arm to shampoo his hair. There were already ugly bruises on his shoulder and forearm. He could feel them deep beneath the skin.

After dressing in dark slacks and a simple button-up shirt, he stepped into the kitchen and started coffee, but it went untouched. Instead, he walked to the living room window, opened the curtains, and sat on the floor in the square of sunlight that landed just before the couch. The light caught the edges of his face and shoulders. He was relatively thin— around 185 pounds—and carried himself with the posture of someone used to standing before a crowd. His sandy brown hair was still damp from the shower, and the bruise on his shoulder throbbed beneath his shirt. Six feet and one inch, clean-shaven, late forties, with lines that etched themselves slowly over years of sermons, hospital visits, and graveside prayers—he looked tired in a way that sleep never really touched.

He closed his eyes and whispered a prayer, though the words came out hollow. It was the kind of prayer spoken more from instinct than conviction. He didn't feel like a man of faith in that moment. He felt like a man on a wire, one misstep from unraveling.

He canceled all the day's meetings and visitations. Jeane

handled the notifications with her usual grace. She didn't pry. She knew better.

The hours passed.

He read from the Psalms. He took a walk through the park across from the church but avoided eye contact with anyone who recognized him. Everyone had heard by now. Small towns are that way.

By late afternoon, Daniel found himself in the church nave. He hadn't planned to go there, but somehow, his feet led him to the front pew. The sunlight poured through the stained-glass windows, casting fractured hues across the altar and the surrounding tiled floor. The air was still and cool, as if the building itself was holding its breath.

He didn't pray, not in the traditional sense. He just sat there, silent.

"God," he said, as if beginning a conversation. But then he stopped. He left the word hanging lonely in the quiet.

That was all he had.

Time passed. It seemed to do so without his noticing. All the while, his hands were clasped and his head was bowed, as if waiting for someone to arrive—or reply. But nothing came. No voice. No whisper. Only the echo of his own breathing and the creak of the old wooden pew beneath him.

Eventually, he rose to his feet. "Amen," he said dryly, before turning to walk down the center aisle toward the narthex. Passing straight through, he locked the old wooden door behind him, the soft clunk of its latch oddly final.

On his walk home, he took the long route through the cemetery behind the church, where several of his former parishioners were buried. He paused at the headstones of people he'd ministered to in their final days. Claire's name would be on one soon. The thought made his stomach turn.

The next day brought food. Not from neighbors, but from church members who took it upon themselves to treat their pastor with care. Lasagna. Chicken and rice. A rhubarb crumble from Kit Gunderson, the same recipe she brought to every funeral luncheon.

He put them all in the fridge. He wasn't hungry.

Instead, he read the draft of Claire's obituary he'd scribbled. It was thin, barely a paragraph. No mention of suspicious circumstances. No cause of death. No service date listed—because there wasn't one. Not yet.

Daniel called Claire's sister, Margaret. Well, he started to, but didn't finish dialing. Instead, he sat with the phone in his lap for a long while, staring out the window. It began to rain—a gentle, steady drizzle that muffled the usual sounds of the neighborhood. He watched it bead and run down the glass, every drop a silent metronome to his guilt.

Later that evening, he returned to his study and opened his Bible again. He reached into the side drawer for a pencil, assuming he might do what he always did, which was to underline, make notes, jot sermon ideas. But this time, the words didn't reach him. He closed the Bible as gently as he opened it and laid it on the desk. He opened the drawer to return the pencil. He stopped. He stared at the flash drive. He dropped the pencil in and closed the drawer.

He took a chance on checking email, hoping to distract himself with church business. Dozens of unread messages: committee updates, prayer requests, volunteer schedules. Among them was one from Claire, sent the evening before her death. The subject line was blank. The body contained only the words, "Dear Pastor, I'm sorry for pestering you tonight.

I look forward to seeing you tomorrow. Blessings."

He closed the laptop.

The third day brought something else: fear.

He was sitting at the desk in his study, fingers resting on the closed drawer where the flash drive lay hidden, when his doorbell rang.

Through the peephole, he saw Chief Stern. Daniel opened the door slowly.

"Just checking in," Stern said, holding up a to-go cup. "Jeane said you're a coffee drinker. Figured I'd help you get started right this morning."

Daniel accepted it but didn't drink. "Thanks."

Stern glanced past him into the house. "Mind if I come in?"

Daniel hesitated. "Now's not a good time."

Stern nodded. "Fair enough. You doing okay?"

Daniel gave a polite smile. "You were right. Murder is new to me."

The Chief studied him for a moment longer. "You know, it's funny," he said. "Every now and then, I meet someone who keeps a secret so well, they almost convince themselves it doesn't exist. But then something changes. And it's not the secret that gets 'em—it's the weight of carrying it."

Daniel kept his face neutral. "Is that what you came to say?" he asked. He could feel the frustration stirring. "Are you saying I'm a suspect?"

"That's not why I'm here."

"Then why are you here?"

Stern smiled. "Just coffee today, Reverend. Just coffee."

He turned and left.

Daniel closed the door slowly. The coffee cup, still warm,

sat untouched on the kitchen counter for the rest of the day.

That night, sleep was impossible. He tossed. He rose. He walked circles in his living room. At one point, he moved to his study and opened the laptop, hand hovering above the USB port.

But he didn't reach for the flash drive.

He poured a glass of water. No sooner was it full than he poured it out. Then he poured another. He stood at the sink staring into the drain for longer than he could explain. His house, once an anchorage, now seemed like a place where things were waiting to pounce—memories, consequences, truths.

That night, Daniel stood in the backyard, staring up at the stars. He'd spent the evening rereading Claire's last few text messages to him. He didn't like talking by text. He told her as much. He told the whole congregation. But no one listened. Still, he didn't mind so much when Claire sent them. She was lonely. And they weren't dramatic, like you might expect from a lonely person. Just normal things. Some were passing notes about choir practice. Others were about an email newsletter article he'd written or a hymn she liked. But now, they read like hidden messages, like something more was being said beneath the surface.

He looked toward the dark windows of his study.

Then back up at the stars.

There was no wind.

The flash drive waited.

But he still didn't move.

He wondered if someone was watching him. Not just Stern. Maybe someone else. From there, he wondered who hit him. He wondered what they used and how they did it.

He stepped back inside and locked the door. Then checked the windows. Then rechecked the locks.

The fourth day came. His forthcoming sermon waited to be written. He didn't want to write it. He drove instead. He had no destination in mind, just streets, just motion. He passed the gas station in the center of town. He turned and drove past the Mill Pond. He followed the road out of town. Doing a u-turn, he returned, but changed direction and passed the women's shelter at Linden's edge. He continued toward the neighboring town. He pulled into a Walgreens parking lot across from an apartment complex and sat in his idling Jeep for almost an hour.

He watched people living. He watched them coming and going. He watched people through the windows of a nearby diner. He saw them laughing. He heard honks at the nearby intersection. He saw a man pushing a stroller. A woman walked her dog.

When he got home, he didn't open the drawer.

Not yet.

He spent the daylight on the couch watching Netflix. He spent most of the evening at his desk flipping through a hymnal with no real purpose. Just hymns and their numbers. The titles blurred. The notes didn't rise from the page. He set it aside and opened Bonhoeffer's *Letters From Prison*. He read a paragraph three times and still couldn't remember it.

He stood and walked the perimeter of the house, checking every window, every door. Then, just to be sure, he checked them again. He turned off the lights. The darkness helped. It let him think.

The fifth day began with silence. It ended with resolve.

Daniel awoke before the sun. That was already typical for

him. He made coffee but didn't drink it. Instead, he went to his study, opened the drawer, and stared down at the flash drive for a long time.

Claire's voice echoed in his memory.

"There's something I need to tell you."

His hand trembled slightly as he took it out.

He set it on the desk.

He stared at it.

Then finally—*finally*—he opened the laptop and inserted the drive.

CHAPTER THREE

Daniel waited anxiously as the machine hummed to life in the silence. He had no family to disturb him. Daniel had chosen the solitary path, never feeling lonely in his solitude. At least, not until now.

Finally, the screen illuminated. His breath was shallow. A scroll followed by a few double clicks, and a folder appeared. It was labeled simply "Harbor." He hesitated, then double-clicked. Dozens more folders appeared. Claire had always been precise, organized, and methodical—qualities he appreciated deeply as her pastor, especially when it came to orchestrating the church's annual Vacation Bible School. Now, those very traits seemed oddly haunting.

The first folder he clicked, "Journals," was dated almost a year earlier. Within were individual text files by date. Skimming the first few files, Claire's journaling was stale. The secluded girl she was, it seemed her only goal was to document her regular nothings. Except, rather than do what normal women might—which is to buy a flowery diary—she chose the cold cathode style of a computer screen.

With the first file, Daniel learned that she had started volunteering at the local women's shelter. It was called Harbor. He knew it. It was operated by 737, the non-denominational church at the south edge of town. Harbor was on the north side. It had been the church's worship space until they converted it, ultimately building a new facility on Old U.S. 23. He'd visited Harbor after the renovations—met the founding pastor, David Graves, and exchanged polite introductions. Before that, they'd never met. Afterward, they crossed paths a few times. They weren't friends. But they also weren't strangers.

Daniel read Claire's words. She had saved each one in order by date. They were full and descriptive, some several pages in length. They sounded like her—dryly concise—something written by a person who listens more than she speaks, who watches more than you know. Indeed, it seemed Graves and his new ministry were a blessing. Claire clearly enjoyed the volunteer work.

After about an hour, Daniel encountered a particular portion in the March 12 file. He reread it. And then again.

> Something is not right. Women arrive. They are desperate and scared. As they should be. They're in really bad situations. I don't know what I'd do if I were in their shoes. But it's weird. Lately, some have only been here a few days, and then no one knows where they went. Pastor D was kind of evasive when I asked him. I'm not sure why.

Daniel didn't read any more from March 12. He clicked on the next file, and then the next, his eyes narrowing. Her entries gradually became shorter and tenser. Everything after April 17 was only a few sentences long.

> April 17 – Another one is gone. Gina. She was only here for three nights. I asked where she went. They told me she left "to begin her new life," but they couldn't tell me where. I asked if we ever follow up with the women. No one knew for sure. I was told to ask Pastor D.

Daniel continued scrolling and clicking.

> April 22 – I finally asked Pastor D why the shelter doesn't track the women after they leave. He smiled too quickly and said it's "a fresh start," that sometimes "cutting all ties" is healthiest.
> I don't believe him.

> May 2 – I met Mary today. Maybe in her early twenties, but it's hard to say. She has that look, like someone who's lived twice as long as her birth certificate claims. She is sweet, though. She sat with me while I folded sheets. She said she was from Grand Rapids, but I couldn't tell if she was telling the truth. I think it was the truth, but I'm not sure.

Daniel slowed his reading. The next few entries focused on Mary. Claire had grown fond of her.

> May 4 – I saw Mary laugh today. It was slight, but it was really genuine. I told a story about the time the choir robe rack collapsed and dumped robes everywhere. She laughed at the image of me buried in velvet. It was nice.

> May 6 – Mary asked me if Harbor was safe. It caught me off guard. I didn't know how to respond because I've been feeling really weird about everything for a while. I asked if everything was okay. She said she was fine, but I could see her hands were shaking. She ended up walking away. I plan to ask her more about it when I see her tomorrow.

> May 7 – Mary is gone. I came in for my volunteer laundry shift, and her bed was stripped. Her name was off the list, too. When I asked Carla, she said

Mary was placed in a job in Muskegon, but there was no forwarding info and nothing about the new job. Worst of all, I didn't get to say goodbye. I asked Carla for her last name. She couldn't remember it. She went to look it up in her file, but she couldn't find the folder.

May 8 – I found the shelter's original sign-in sheet for the day Mary checked in. Someone scribbled over her last name.

May 10 – I'm afraid. But I'm more angry than scared. Something is happening. I think something happened to Mary. I think Carla knows something but won't say. I'm going to keep looking around. I'll keep track of it here. Everyone who comes in. Every face. Every name.

The next entry was almost a month later.

June 4 – Women are here during my day shift, but then after I leave, which isn't usually until about 5:00, somehow they're transferred, as some keep calling it. I stayed last night. Well, not exactly. I parked down the way in the cornfield. I thought for sure I was going to get stuck. Thankfully, I didn't. I saw the shelter van, the one that Cameron uses to get groceries and things for us, it showed up at about 8:20. Usually, it's parked in the side lot behind the building. Tonight, it pulled in. I don't know if Cameron was driving it. I can't say for sure. I saw Pastor D walk to it when it arrived. Crissy was with him. He was kind of leading her. He talked to the driver, and then she got in the van. Pastor D went back inside. I thought I saw Mr. Keenan in the van, but again, I can't be sure.

Daniel sat back in his chair, his skin cold. His mind,

though already battered from the day's events, now reeled anew. He clicked on another folder—"Photos"—and saw file after file labeled only by date and time. Claire had taken pictures of the entry logs, staff schedules, and the facility security monitors when no one was watching. There were even shots of the white van with the worn "Harbor Ministries" logo on the door.

He returned to the journal folder.

> June 6 – I asked Pastor D again about Mary. I told him I wanted to follow up with her to see how she was doing. I figured it had been a month and maybe she was settled by now. He's so condescending. He's nothing like my pastor. Pastor Michaels listens. And he tries to help. Pastor D is dismissive. He said he can't tell me where she is and that it's for her safety. He won't tell me anything.

> June 8 – Cameron showed up with the van tonight at around 6:30. He and Ray unloaded a whole bunch of bed sheets and twin mattresses into the dumpster. They didn't seem happy about it. Ray sounded really mad at someone named Marty. He said something about how he was tired of doing his job for him. He said he was getting paid to be security, not cleanup, that his job was to make sure the place was secure, that the customers could get what they wanted in safety, and that Marty was supposed to be helping Cameron. I've never heard so many f-words in my life. They waited around for about an hour before finally leaving. I was just curious, so I went to look. Everything was disgusting. Every kind of stain imaginable. Blood, too. I took a lot of pictures.

> July 11 – I can't unsee what I've seen or unhear what I've heard. The photos do not lie. The

recordings don't either.

July 19 – I heard Mr. Topel and Mr. Keenan talking today. They didn't even notice me in the laundry room. Go figure. No one notices me. They said Dennis Anderson and Brett Durham made a mistake and gave someone the wrong girl. What do I do with this? Dennis goes to my church. Brett does, too. He and his family sit in my row. I feel sick.

Daniel felt sick, too. Dennis Anderson. A lawyer. Warm smile, firm handshake, a sociable grandfatherly figure who greeted members every Sunday, handed out bulletins, and laughed easily. Brett Durham. His grandmother, Elsie, was a founding member of the church. He visited her at least once every two weeks. Brett was soft-spoken, always neatly dressed. A thinker, for sure. He was a businessman. He owned an accounting firm in Waterford. He sat with his wife and children near the back in worship.

Daniel struggled to reconcile Claire's collection with the faces he knew so well. Dennis had served for many years as the congregation president. He ran the annual chili cookoff. He occasionally taught confirmation classes while Daniel was away at district conferences. Brett? He led the fundraising campaign for the new play structure in the church's side lot.

He opened another file, images Claire had discreetly captured on her phone. He knew some in the photos. Some he didn't. He certainly knew Dennis, his curly hair and button-up shirt barely hiding his rotund gut. There, as clear as could be, was an image of Dennis leaving Harbor at night, guiding a young woman into the supply van. And then there were more. There was no questioning Brett's image, either. It was him in the sequence of photos. He was exchanging envelopes and handshakes with unfamiliar men in each.

Daniel's throat tightened painfully. He reached for the desk's center drawer, withdrew an old, half-empty bottle of ibuprofen, and swallowed four dry, ignoring the burning in his throat. Leaning forward, he opened yet another folder marked "Financial." Claire had created a series of spreadsheets that tracked donations and government grants. Among them, she noted significant irregularities. Large sums had been given. But equally large sums had vanished, without notation.

She had done all the work. How she got any of it, who could tell, except to say, she was, as Daniel already knew her so well, an unassuming person. You'd never know she was near if she didn't tell you herself. In this instance, it was a skill. And so she collected everything, mapped everything, saved everything. She even took pictures of the diagrams she'd drawn. Lines with arrow heads at each end pointing to this thing and that, all showing a series of events that led to dreadful conclusions.

With trembling fingers, Daniel clicked another folder named "Suspects." It had only one text file. There were nine names on the list. Daniel knew only three personally—Pastor David Graves, Dennis Anderson, and Brett Durham. Pastor David was the first. Dennis and Brett were last on the list. The six others he knew only by name and reputation, or he didn't know them at all. Two were prominent community leaders— Steve Topel, the county commissioner and a construction company owner, and Bill Keenan, a member of the Linden city council. He didn't know the other four: Cameron Wexler, Martin Krill, Dr. Eli Webber, and Torrence Ray.

Daniel pushed back his chair abruptly, standing up to pace

the small room. His thoughts spiraled, tumbling over one another as he fought recurring nausea. Claire had discovered something monstrous, something she couldn't ignore. Daniel remembered her quiet, persistent demeanor. He whispered words into the quiet room that not even he could hear, the regret pooling in his chest. Claire had tried. She had called him. She needed him to know. Daniel sank back into his chair. The guilt had become unbearable.

He spent the next several hours absorbed in Claire's meticulous documentation, each new file deepening his horror and resolve. Daniel realized that Claire's investigation was thorough enough to be dangerous, and she'd likely paid the ultimate price for it. Someone realized what she'd been doing. Each file opened new doors into a dark and sinister world operating right under the surface of his community.

Outside his study window that overlooked his narrow driveway, the afternoon sun had begun its slow descent, casting long shadows over the quiet neighborhood. Daniel realized he had forgotten about lunch entirely, the gnawing emptiness in his stomach suddenly evident. But food felt insignificant in the face of what he'd learned.

He couldn't stop exploring. He couldn't stop reading.

And so, he didn't. He kept on, his eyes strained from the glowing screen. Claire had left detailed annotations on her suspicions about possible police involvement. She suspected they were providing cover, but she couldn't confirm it. Daniel's heart sank further as he read her careful, fearful words. He wondered if Stern was compromised. But she didn't say. And he wasn't on the list.

Daniel's eyes grew weary, but he forced himself to keep reading.

Eventually, he went to the kitchen for food. Before doing so, he opened yet another folder, discovering recordings Claire had made covertly. He pressed play and then turned up the volume, loud enough for him to hear it while making a bologna sandwich. But he couldn't eat it. He listened, stomach twisting, as conversations unfolded, hinting at transactions, threats, and worse. The voices he recognized haunted him, the betrayal cutting deeper with each familiar timbre.

As evening approached, Daniel stood abruptly, overwhelmed. He stepped away to his back steps, his mind racing with a thousand unanswered questions. His thoughts were chaotic, tangled between anger and profound sadness. Claire had known so much, endured so much, all alone.

He finally finished the hours-old bologna sandwich before making himself coffee, the bitter aroma grounding him momentarily. As he sipped, he moved back toward the study, drawn irresistibly by the gravity of the flash drive's revelations. The day's events replayed endlessly in his mind, each piece of evidence adding weight to his growing burden.

It was a tidal wash of awful information.

Night fell quietly, enveloping the house in darkness, save for the glow from the hallway light behind him. Daniel's concentration waned, exhaustion finally overtaking the seemingly endless stream of adrenaline. Still, he was determined to finish.

There was one final folder remaining. He'd been avoiding it, choosing instead to read as much as he could from Claire's journals about the players, the places, the transactions. He looked for things that would easily disprove it all, framing Claire as little more than a lonely young woman with too much time on her hands. But he didn't find anything. It was all so meticulously curated. Everything was in place.

And the audio recordings. That was Brett's voice. That was Dennis.

The last folder was labeled "Next Steps." Like the "Suspects" folder, only one text file was inside. He double-clicked it.

> Contact Pastor Michaels. He'll help me. He'll know what to do.

The words hit Daniel like a punch, leaving him breathless. He felt a heave of guilt so powerful it nearly crushed him. He pushed away from his desk again, snapping to his feet, a new and more frightful energy surging through him. His eyes caught his reflection in the bathroom mirror across the hall from the study—Reverend Daniel Michaels—a man he barely recognized now, ugly and burdened, growing pale.

He forced himself to pause, closing his eyes tightly, praying for guidance and clarity, his mind racing. He considered calling the authorities, yet the memory of Chief Stern's probing questions and unsettling gaze gave him pause. Again, did Claire think he was involved? If so, why was he not on the suspect list?

He stood and stared into the mirror. He was becoming weary and wrestling with uncertainty. The depth of betrayal was unfathomable. He knew what was expected of him—that Claire hoped he'd help—but the enormity of it left him paralyzed.

Outside, as Linden slept peacefully, Daniel remained wide awake. The bottle of whisky was still out from the night Claire called. He poured another dram. A little more than before. Some for himself, and a little extra for the person in the mirror he didn't quite recognize—the one who knew that somewhere within this small, deceptively tranquil town, evil moved freely. This person was sure Claire had been its latest victim, and it was growing easier to convince Daniel that it would also be its last.

CHAPTER FOUR

The church was full.

More than Daniel expected.

But this wasn't just any funeral. This was Claire Madsen's funeral—a quiet woman with no family in town, at least none who cared. Not even her sister, Margaret, attended. She had no real circle of friends. And yet, somehow, she had touched everyone there at Saint John Lutheran Church.

And so, they came. Out of guilt. Curiosity. Grief. Suspicion. All of it.

Daniel stood in the narthex, peering through the small beveled window in the nave's doors. The pre-service visitation was over, and people were gathering in the pews.

Daniel adjusted his stole. It was white. It was the Fourth Sunday of Easter, so everything was white—the paraments and banners. His collar was crisp and new. The previous one still stained faintly from blood—he couldn't bring himself to wear it. This one had arrived overnight from C.M. Almy. He'd ordered three, just in case.

He took a deeply slow breath.

The kantor had already begun his prelude. It was a sturdy weaving of *For All the Saints* and *I Know That My Redeemer Lives*, robust and occupied, the way Claire, a faithful Confessional Lutheran, would've liked it.

Jeane Rittner appeared from the church's hallway that led to the offices. Her usual brisk steps were tempered with solemnity.

"It's a full house, Pastor," she said.

Daniel nodded. "It is."

"I've never seen the nave this full for someone so—"

"Inconsequential?" he interrupted dryly.

Jeane gave a sheepish smile.

"She was always in the background. But maybe that's why she mattered so much."

"Maybe," he said. "People forget that those who move quietly are often the strongest among us."

Jeane nodded again, appreciating his words more than she likely knew.

He turned back toward the nave doors. His *Lutheran Service Book Agenda* in hand, the Funeral pages marked with a service ordo and a gold ribbon. His sermon was already in the pulpit.

But his heart?

His heart was elsewhere.

It was in the files Claire left behind. It was in the recordings. The photos. The names. The faces.

And now, some of those faces sat in his pews.

The prelude ended, and the nave doors opened. Their soft creaking caught everyone's attention. Heads turned. The congregation rose instinctively—not just in respect, but in a kind of desperate yearning.

The procession began, and the bell tower sounded its deeper tones.

The pallbearers—choir members who'd offered to help—rolled the casket along. A young crucifer carried the processional cross. Another youth carried the paschal candle. Daniel followed them, but led the pallbearers. Stopping first at the baptismal font near the door, where the service would begin, a pall was placed on the casket.

Daniel made the sign of the cross above the font.

"In the name of the Father and of the Son and of the Holy Spirit."

"Amen," the congregation replied, a whispering tide of voices.

Daniel led the congregation through the first portion of the funeral rite—the "Remembrance of Baptism"—before leading the procession the rest of the way to the chancel to the hymn *We Praise You and Acknowledge You, O God.*

Daniel walked slowly down the center aisle, passing row after row of solemn faces. Some nodded. Some smiled sadly as they sang. A few stared blankly. A child reached out to touch his robe and was gently pulled back by her mother.

Claire's casket was positioned at the front, simple and closed. A spray of lilies adorned it, white and pale pink. Her favorite colors, according to Jeane.

At the hymn's final stanza, Daniel ascended the chancel steps, turned, and faced the congregation. The liturgy carried him, insulated him. He moved by its commands, relatively unaware of the people in the pews.

He continued with the Kyrie and Collect, the readings— Job, Revelation, John—words he had spoken at a hundred funerals. But never like this. Never with this weight. Never with this fury simmering beneath. The Gospel text echoed in his ears even as he read it: "I am the resurrection and the life. Whoever believes in me, though he die, yet shall he live…"

He closed the lectionary.

He led the Apostles' Creed. Then came the Hymn of the Day—*Christ, the Life of All the Living.* His chest burned with the first stanza's words.

Christ, the life of all the living,
Christ, the death of death, our foe.

He looked up and over the congregation. And that's when he saw them.

Brett. Pulpit side. Second row. End of the pew. His wife, Marcie, sat beside him. No kids. His face slack with performative sorrow, a tissue in hand. Dennis. Three rows from the back on the lectern side. Arms crossed, face unreadable. His wife, Sherri, was elsewhere. She rarely came to worship. Why would she attend a funeral?

Nevertheless, Brett and Dennis had come.

They had dared.

Daniel swallowed hard. He tried to sing.

The kantor finished his final chords. A moment of silence. Then Daniel stepped into the pulpit.

He looked out across the faces again—some familiar, some strangers. But his gaze landed on Brett, and then briefly on Dennis. He did not look away. He had prepared a sermon like none he'd ever preached before.

"Saint Paul has called death the last enemy. It's a thieving foe. It steals breath. It steals laughter. It steals the next sunrise. It tears at the edges of what we believe to be good and just and true."

He paused.

"But sometimes death does not come uninvited. Sometimes it is summoned. Ushered in. Sometimes it is helped."

Murmurs shifted in the pews. A cough. The rustle of a tissue.

Daniel's eyes narrowed slightly, but he remained steady.

"Claire Madsen," he continued, "a servant of this congregation. Quiet, yes. Unassuming, certainly. But she was, without question, a servant of Christ. A woman devoted to serving his people. Youthful, and yet timelessly wise. A woman of order. A woman of… truth."

He let the word linger.

"She did not demand attention. She did not seek accolades. You all know this. She lived, instead, just as Saint Paul urged, a peaceful and quiet life, godly and dignified in every way."

Another pause. He would not preach as expected. He was not the same as before. Daniel gripped the edge of the pulpit. In between the sentences he'd already spoken, he felt like an impostor.

"'Vengeance is mine,' saith the Lord," Daniel called out. "'I will repay.'"

The words rang clear and cold across the nave.

Some heads tilted.

Daniel leaned forward slightly.

"You've heard that before. Many of you know it by heart. But too often, we hear it as comfort—as if God is only speaking to victims."

A subtle shift in his tone.

"But it's not only for the brokenhearted. It's a warning. The Lord, in his perfect justice, truly will repay. Not just in the end, but in time."

He let the silence grow.

"What if his vengeance is already on the move?"

The stillness was thick.

"In Psalm 94, the psalmist cries, 'O Lord, God of vengeance, O God of vengeance, shine forth! Rise up, O judge of the earth; repay to the proud what they deserve!'"

His voice grew sharper.

"Do not mistake God's patience for apathy. He sees. He knows. He does not sleep. He will act."

Daniel's gaze swept the room. He was becoming less Lutheran by the moment.

"And when he does, it will not be tidy. It will not be polite. It will not wait for any of us."

But even as he began drifting from his calling, another voice rang inside—softer, gentler, truer. It pulled him back to the moment.

"And yet, beloved, even as we cry for justice, the Lord's first desire is one of love, of mercy. He is the One who bore vengeance in his own body, nailed to the tree. He is the Lamb, silent before his shearers. He was led as a lamb to the slaughter—not so that we could become avengers, but so that we might become sons and daughters."

He paused.

His lips were speaking the Gospel. He could hear himself declaring Christ crucified, Christ risen, Christ victorious.

Still, a portion of himself and his heart—the other person in which it was beating—it remained behind.

Behind in the files.

Behind in the photos.

Behind in the recordings.

Behind in the blood trickling from Claire's nose.

He continued.

"And so, we commend Claire to her Savior, Jesus. She is not gone. She is alive with Christ. Her baptism is not undone by evil. Her life is not erased. Her name is still written in the Lamb's book of life. Death has not won."

He preached more of this.

A murmur of comfort rose from the pews. He saw tears. Nods. Relief. His call was carrying him convincingly.

But in Daniel's mind, the Gospel had already been eclipsed.

"Vengeance is mine... I will repay..."

The sermon ended, and the service continued—the Prayer of the Church, the Lord's Prayer, the Nunc Dimittis, Concluding Collect, Benedicamus, and Benediction.

It felt like forever. Even the final hymn and retiring procession took years. And the words that stayed with him were not "peace." They were not "mercy."

They were judgment.

They were fire.

Daniel greeted people at the narthex doors. Faces blurred. Hands blurred. Words blurred. Then Brett stepped forward.

"Pastor," he said, shaking Daniel's hand. "That was very moving. Claire would have appreciated your godly words."

Daniel didn't let go. Not immediately.

"I hope they were clear."

Brett smiled politely. "They were. God's people were comforted."

There was a pause.

Daniel studied him.

"Well," Brett said, withdrawing his hand, "if you need anything, just let me know."

"I will."

Marcie hugged and thanked him.

"Say hello to the kids," Daniel said.

"I will," she replied.

Daniel watched Brett walk away, the crowd folding

around him.

The last of the congregation filed through the front doors. All were making their way to the luncheon. Daniel turned back toward the altar. It seemed so far away.

He whispered a prayer. Not of peace. Not of comfort.

But of determination.

"Vengeance is yours, Lord. Here am I, send me."

CHAPTER FIVE

It was a Wednesday when he visited Elsie Durham.

She was ninety-three and nearly blind, but she always kept a plate of shortbread cookies ready for when "the good pastor" came to call. Her house smelled of lavender and liniment, and the record player in the corner was still loaded with Mahalia Jackson's *The Power and the Glory*. Elsie adored her voice, if only because they both hailed from the same city, New Orleans.

Daniel sat across from her in the same tweed armchair he'd occupied dozens of times before. He'd already served the Lord's Supper to her and was resetting his travel kit. Now it was time to chat.

But he didn't want to chat. He wanted to leave. He wanted to be alone.

The instant coffee she poured trembled in the cup, her hand shaking. She was telling a story, again, about her late husband, Walter, and the time he got lost in Detroit trying to deliver a ham to a shut-in.

Daniel wasn't listening.

Not really.

His eyes kept drifting to the crucifix on the wall. Cheap plastic. Faded. But it stared at him as though it knew.

A portrait of Brett and his family hung beside it, along with other images of cousins, grandchildren, and great-grandchildren from Walter and Elsie's wide-reaching life. All of it together, a collection of beauty, and yet for him, soiled by the one man, Brett.

"Pastor?"

Daniel blinked. Elsie had stopped speaking. Her wrinkled hands were folded in her lap, and she was watching him with eyes clouded by cataracts, yet impossibly clear.

"You're carrying something."

He hesitated. "We all are."

"But you're carrying something too heavy," she said meekly. "I can feel it in the room."

He said nothing.

"I remember Walter used to carry things like that. When he came back from the war. Before he could speak of it, his hands would shake. His heart would race. He said he felt like a fraud every Sunday morning when he went to Communion."

She paused. Then reached out and laid one frail hand over his.

"God doesn't forget the weight, Pastor. And he doesn't leave us under it."

Daniel felt something rise in his throat—grief or rage or maybe just the pressure of trying to stay human.

He forced a smile. "I should probably get going."

"You should pro'ly sit a while longer," she said, her New Orleans accent sneaking through. "Or you'll walk out with that same storm behind your eyes."

He hesitated, then set the travel kit down and sank back into the chair.

Elsie didn't press him. She sipped her coffee and looked out the window, her sightless gaze settled somewhere deep beyond the glass.

"I've been around a long time," she said. "I know things about things." A few empty seconds passed. "I sometimes think the Lord lets me linger," she said, "because old women say things others won't."

Daniel gave a soft chuckle. "Maybe."

"I know things about things," she said again. "I know people carrying things they don't like to talk about. Some with medals. Some with nothing. Some with reasons no one knows for sure. Still, my daddy always said, 'It's not what you do that ruins you. It's what you can't undo.'"

Daniel's smile faded. For anyone else, Elsie was rambling. But not for him. She was reading him.

Elsie leaned forward. "What happened with Claire was a hard thing, Pastor. I suppose it's clawing at you. It's right there in your silence. You think no one sees it. Let me tell you, I can't see it either. I can barely see anything anymore. But I can hear it. The devil can hear it, too. He does his best work in people's silence."

Daniel lowered his gaze.

"You preach about grace," she continued. "Remember, you need it, too. And grace ain't polite. It ain't soft. It's a hammer that breaks the chains, even the ones we make for ourselves. So, whatever's hoverin' in your silence, don't wait to talk to the Lord. He doesn't need it clean. He wants it honest."

He nodded slowly. "Thank you, Elsie."

Trying to sound normal, maybe even a little funny, he added, "Maybe you should help me write next Sunday's sermon." But there was nothing in the delivery. It was too plain. Too empty.

"You're welcome. Now help me up."

Daniel stood and took her hand. She rose slowly from her chair, her joints popping. She gestured toward the hallway.

"I want to show you something. Come."

He followed her, even though she needed him to guide her.

They entered a small room at the end of the hall. It was a kind of makeshift study—old wallpaper, faded books, and a cedar chest under the window.

Elsie pointed to it.

"In there. Walter's things. He wouldn't mind."

Daniel opened the chest. It smelled of dust and oil and time. Inside were neatly folded uniforms, medals, and various black-and-white photographs. Some of the images were of Walter as a child, and Elsie in what looked to be her early twenties. There were letters in there, too. And somewhat recent images of his children and grandchildren.

Daniel moved things around carefully, respectfully. Beneath the uniforms were three pistols, each partially wrapped in burlap. They clanked when he moved them.

Elsie winced slightly. "I never liked them. But Walter wouldn't part with them. They played parts in his life. I didn't have the heart to give them away."

Setting the uniforms on the floor beside the trunk, Daniel lifted one, careful and uncertain. It was cold, compact, and oddly elegant. The metal had dulled over time, but its lines were unmistakable—sharp angles, a squared trigger guard, and the slanted grip gave it a severe, almost surgical profile. It wasn't heavy, but it carried a certain gravity. The slide and barrel were long and narrow, the frame skeletal yet solid. A faint eagle stamp remained on the side—partially worn, but still visible. German. Wartime. The weapon felt more like a machine than a tool, something built with precision but meant for brutality. Daniel turned it over in his hands, his fingers brushing the grooved grips. He didn't know guns. But this one, even in its silence, spoke with menace.

"Which one do you have?" Elsie asked.

"I don't know," he said. "It has German on it."

"Oh, he took that off a dead Nazi, if I recall. Said it was just lying there, next to the body." She took a step into the room and leveled herself against a dusty dresser. "There are a couple more in there. One's a little smaller."

Daniel reached for the one she noted. It wasn't small exactly, just more compact, streamlined, even graceful in its design. The steel was dark and lightly worn, the bluing faded around the edges from time and maybe careful hands. The grip felt full in his palm, rounded in a way that suggested intent— a sidearm made not just to kill, but to fit the hand doing the killing. It was lighter than he expected. Balanced. Elegant.

"That one… that belonged to his friend. Killed at Normandy. Walter brought it back. Said it was all he could scoop of his friend from the sand."

"Why are you showing me Walter's things?"

Elsie's voice was low. "I know things about things."

"I know you do, Elsie, but—"

"You remind me of Walter," she said. "He took losing his friends very hard. I think you're standing at the same edge Walter once stood on. Different war. Same cliff."

Daniel didn't respond.

"He came out of those days with things he didn't ask for— memories and instincts… and habits, too. But also with choices. He chose me. He chose our kids. He chose life. He was a good man. He chose what to carry and what to bury. He loved his Lord, and he knew how to keep the darkness at bay."

She turned her head slightly toward him, her cloudy eyes unblinking.

"I know things about things. You strike me as a man wrestling with sadness. That trunk right there, it holds Walter's sadness. But also, a whole lot of his joy. Me and him courtin'. The kids. Our grandkids. There's sadness in there. But there's a whole lot of joy, too."

Elsie repeated herself. She only said what she felt was important.

"That third one," she said, "that was Walter's sidearm. The one the Army gave him."

The last pistol he lifted was heavier than the others. Its lines were simple but purposeful—blunt nose, squared slide, long hammer at the rear. The grip was checkered and worn smooth in places, darkened by decades of handling. It felt solid, almost blocky, but well-balanced in the hand. A relic, yes, but not fragile. The markings on the slide were still faintly visible: "U.S. Property" and a barely legible serial number. The finish had long since gone matte, the steel beneath showing age but no weakness. Daniel could feel the weight of history in it—standard issue, World War II, the kind of weapon a soldier wouldn't let out of his reach. It didn't look flashy. It looked final.

And he liked it.

Very much.

He felt something solemn radiating from it—weight and consequence pressed into steel.

He rewrapped all three in their oil-stained cloths, put the uniforms on top, and closed the chest.

"Strange things to hold on to," he said.

"Like I said, there's sadness in that chest, too. Walter once said those weapons reminded him of how close he came to being someone he didn't recognize."

She shifted her weight as though aching.

"Walter didn't have a choice in the war. But he still had to live with the part of him that came back."

Daniel opened his mouth to speak, but closed it again.

"You don't kill Nazis and come home clean, Pastor," she added. "Even when it's right, it still leaves a stain on you."

"But he still did it."

"Yes, I suppose he did," she said, sighing.

Daniel nodded. Of course, she didn't see it.

"Thanks for showing me Walter's things, Elsie. I should get going."

"Well," she said in a whisper, "okay, then. If you don't mind, help me back to my chair."

And so, he did.

He stopped at the front door. He looked back at Elsie and then down the hall to the room at its end.

"Elsie, do you mind if I use your restroom before I head out?"

"Yes, pastor. You know where it is."

Daniel went toward the bathroom but didn't go in. Instead, he closed the bathroom door and then made his way to the end of the hall.

Back to the chest.

He opened it again and lifted the uniforms. Carefully, he took the larger of the two American pistols—the one that had been Walter's sidearm. He studied it. It looked and felt solid. Like it could still work.

He slid it into the back of his pants at the beltline, then closed the chest once more. Passing by the bathroom, he opened the door and then reached in to flush the toilet, before pretending to wash his hands.

Elsie was relatively blind, but not deaf.

"Thanks again, Elsie," he said as he passed her. "I'll see you again in two weeks."

"I hope so," she said.

He left.

That night, at home, he poured two fingers of The Macallan Rare Cask and sat at his computer. He typed: *army side arm world war ii*.

It didn't take long for him to find it.

A Colt M1911A1, standard-issued .45 caliber.

He kept scrolling. He found the others, too. A Walther P38. A Browning Hi-Power, 9mm.

He sat back in the chair. The screen glowed. The Colt rested on the desk beside the near-empty glass, begging for another pour.

It was his now. But before he could use it, he'd need to learn.

Ammunition. Grip. Recoil. Cleaning. Discipline.

None of these things were beyond him. If he could learn Latin, Greek, Hebrew, and even a little bit of Spanish, he could learn this.

And he would.

CHAPTER SIX

It was Sunday morning, and the pews were full.

The light through the stained-glass windows swam gently across the chancel floor, painting the pulpit in ribbons of blue and gold. The worn wood creaked beneath Daniel's shoes as he stepped up to preach. As always, his sermon manuscript was already in the pulpit. He usually tried to keep to it. He knew that if anyone ever misconstrued something he said, the manuscript would be evidence.

Stick to the manuscript, he thought.

But another sermon had been written. It had been composed in the hush between midnight and dawn, hammered out like hot iron on an anvil of sleeplessness. He didn't know its words just yet, but he knew it was there, beneath the surface of his calling.

His alb was spotless. His stole—now green for the Trinity season—hung straight. Yet the collar felt tighter than usual, as though the fabric itself were judging him, maybe trying to restrain him.

He began, "In the name of the Father and of the Son and of the Holy Spirit. Amen." The congregation, still standing, now settled into the pews. No cough. No rustle. Crisp silence.

He did not look at the manuscript.

"In John fifteen," Daniel started, "our Lord says, 'Greater love has no one than this, that someone lay down his life for his friends.' We treasure those words. We inscribe them upon monuments. We stitch them into banners. We teach them to our children. Yet if we listen closely, we discover that our Lord is not sharing a gentle bedtime story. He is framing a very real battlefield, one so many know well."

His words lingered in the silence.

"Laying down your life," he continued, "doesn't always mean breathing your last. Sometimes it means breathing through what terrifies others, what kills others on the inside. It means carrying burdens no one else will shoulder, standing where others refuse to stand, bleeding in secret while the rest of the world sleeps."

Daniel's gaze swept the nave. He saw the Dorlan children whispering. He saw Cam Brimmer scrolling on his phone. He saw Carla Mays turning through the bulletin.

He saw Brett Durham in the sixth pew—listening but unreadable.

A wolf among the sheep.

"Too often," he said, voice becoming firmer, "the world mistakes Christian meekness for passivity. It assumes that turning the other cheek means closing one's eyes to evil. It believes that loving our enemies is the same as forgetting justice. But the Scriptures never confuse grace with cowardice." He turned a page of his sermon, even though he was not following it. "Our Lord turned tables. He rebuked rulers. He saw through veneers. He called the Pharisees whitewashed tombs. He called evil by name. He was gentle with the broken yet fierce with the wolves."

Inside his skull, Elsie's voice whispered, *Grace ain't polite. It's a hammer that breaks the chains.*

"'Is not my word like fire,' the Lord declared through the Prophet Jeremiah, 'and like a hammer that breaks the rock into pieces?'"

He let the statement breathe.

"The hammer will fall," Daniel said. "And you, God's people," he pressed on, "are not called to be numb to what you see. You are not called to make peace with wickedness. You are called to walk the narrow road, to carry the cross, to speak when silence fattens the darkness, to act when others won't."

He paused again, letting his words burn.

"The Apostle Paul didn't write his letters beside a lake at his cottage in the Upper Peninsula. He wrote them from prison. Jeremiah wept. Amos roared. Stephen died with stones at his brow. They didn't suffer for their silence. They were punished for truth."

He took a breath. "I wonder if we remember what truth sounds like anymore. It doesn't flatter. It doesn't stall. Truth has a weight. It demands something of us. It costs."

Staring into nothing and everything, he wondered, *Are they listening?* He turned another page of his sermon and then looked downward to read. He'd begin wherever his eyes met the page, whether it seemed fitting or not.

"And yet, hear the promise of Christ."

He managed only the one line before looking away from the sermon's pages again.

"Our Savior knows fatigue. He knows how heavy the cross can seem at dawn. For those of you who feel you're carrying something too heavy, remember: Christ does not leave you buried beneath it. His grace is not soft felt draped over sin; his grace is fire. It breaks chains, tears veils, and burns clean through your ugliness."

Another moment of silence lingered. He just couldn't get the words to come out of his mouth gently.

"Sometimes," he said quietly, "the Gospel feels like fire.

That does not make it less grace—it makes it purer."

He saw Mrs. Pritchard smile. Mr. Fischer lowered his head, eyes shut. A few rows up, Brett's wife, Marcie, reached for his hand. He didn't move.

Daniel's hands trembled slightly. Elsie's words echoed again—God doesn't forget the weight. He doesn't leave us under it.

And deeper still, beneath the memory of her voice, the unspoken confession: *Walter did what he had to do. He killed Nazis. And they deserved it.*

He let his tone drop.

"There is comfort, too, in obedience—in doing what the Lord places in front of you, no matter how strange the path may seem."

His voice became simplified and calm, as if reading to children.

"Our Lord died with a cry on his lips and rose with scars in his hands. Grace does not erase the cost; it gives what's needed to see it through."

His voice softened even more.

"Do not let the world convince you that grace and action, justice and mercy, are strangers. At the cross, they embrace. And when they do, the world shakes. It shifts."

He paused.

"Love acts. It responds. Sometimes, it takes up between the sheep and the wolves. And when it does, it rarely comes away unstained."

He was rambling. He looked down, hoping for an appropriate line.

"But Christ bears the deeper wounds."

A hush hovered in the nave. Daniel drew a breath that

tasted like prophecy and fear. Usually, he preached for fifteen to twenty minutes. And yet, he was done. He ended as he began.

"In the name of the Father and of the Son and of the Holy Spirit. Amen."

After the closing hymn, the congregation filed past him.

"Good sermon, Pastor," said Mr. Lewis. "Shorter than usual. I don't mind shorter."

Daniel smiled politely at his jab.

"That was to the point," said Carol, squeezing his arm as if to ground herself.

"I could tell you meant every word today," muttered Henry Dorlan, English teacher in the elementary school.

"You reached deep today," whispered Mary-Anne Fitz.

Daniel smiled and nodded to each, giving the polite acknowledgement they expected.

You understood nothing, he thought, and despised himself for the judgment.

He walked to his office, closed the door, and sat at his desk. His fingers still trembled slightly. He folded his hands in prayer. No words came. Just heat behind his eyes.

Grace is a hammer.

He stripped away his vestments before catching Jeane in the hallway.

"I'm not feeling so well," he said. "Let the folks in Bible study know I'm going home."

† † †

It wasn't long before Daniel was in his study at home. He changed from his clerical into jeans and a favorite *Fangoria* t-shirt. He laid Walter's Colt M1911A1 on the kitchen table. Its steel glinted dull and holy.

He opened his laptop.

Videos. Field manuals. Forum threads from collectors. He watched and listened. He read.

Thumb safety up. Slide stop lever. Barrel bushing.

He spent the afternoon field-stripping the weapon until the motions became rote. He memorized the recoil-spring weight and the magazine catch. He practiced press-checks, trigger pulls, and sight alignment. He dry-fired into a stack of phone books until the hammer drop no longer startled him.

He made notes. Cleaned the bore. Ran patches. Lubed the slide. He practiced racking it one-handed. Practiced drawing from his waistband, clearing the shirt with one motion.

He found himself talking aloud, quietly, as though to an old mentor.

"Safety off. Acquire sight. Controlled squeeze. Recover. Reset."

He studied the ballistics of the .45 round. Subsonic. Heavy. Reliable in stopping power. It wasn't sleek. It wasn't silent. But it ended all conversations.

He read testimonies from World War II veterans, those who carried it in mud and fire. It was the sidearm of last resort, a final and faithful option. He wondered how many men had whispered prayers while gripping one.

He wondered if Walter had.

He would need ammunition. Acquiring it would require caution. A purchase on record would betray him. But he already had a plan. Next Saturday and Sunday, July 26 and 27, was the Novi Gun and Knife Show. Of course, he would go on Saturday. General admission was ten dollars. The place would be crowded. He would go to learn, but more importantly, to listen.

There's something pastors know about sin. Not just the sin that gets confessed in the privacy of their office or whispered in a pew beneath a crucifix, but the kind that leaks out sideways in stories and sarcasm, in knowing laughs over coffee, in locker room boasts and deer camp legends. Shepherds spend their lives among the flock, but the work takes them to the underbelly. They learn the rhythms of addiction, the scent of deception, the way guilt grinds down the edges of a man's voice. Daniel had been listening for years. People had a way of revealing things. He knew someone at the Expo would say something in passing about how to get ammunition without retail or government intrusion. It would start as half a joke. However, it would then become a genuine request. When it did, he'd be ready. He'd laugh along, ask a question, maybe play dumb. But he'd hear what he needed. They always talked. Eventually, everyone talks.

And someone did.

✝ ✝ ✝

The weekend gun show buzzed with chatter and the smell of warm Michiganders. Daniel wore his black AC/DC t-shirt, cargo shorts, and a Ron Jon hat he'd gotten in Florida a few years back—anonymity by ordinariness. He handled nothing, bought nothing, merely looked and listened. At a surplus table, a bearded vendor wearing a Glock hat mentioned Kurt, a farmer outside of DeWitt, who sold ammo off-books. Cash only. Daniel memorized the directions given in fragments.

"Old U.S. 27 north to Pratt Road. Go East. After the dead

oak… green pole-barn… no sign. He's always in the barn."

He waited a week before going, just to be sure.

It was a Wednesday. The morning was gray, but it soon cleared. The drive took about an hour. Kurt—short, broad-shouldered, eyes like slate—was in the barn, moving where dust swirled in sun-shafts.

The conversation was dry, quickly steering toward its point after only a minute.

"Whatcha looking for?"

".45 ACP."

"How many?"

"Just a few boxes," Daniel said, his voice as plain as Kurt's expression. "Family heirloom. Grampa's Colt."

Kurt grunted before producing three battered military cartons—fifty rounds each, Lake City 1967 surplus. Daniel inspected.

Brass uncorroded, primers intact.

"Hundred fifty," Kurt said plainly. "Cash."

Money changed hands.

Kurt handed him a paper sack. "That all?"

Daniel nodded. "That should do it."

"Be careful out there," Kurt said.

"I always am."

✝ ✝ ✝

Daniel waited until the following Saturday morning to practice. A red sky bleeding into treetop silhouettes, Daniel parked his Jeep off an old track north of town. It was state land, too marshy for occasional hikers. He walked for a while, his boots sucking in damp earth.

He came to a relative clearing. He set the church's rusty mop bucket atop a fallen log. He put about twenty-five feet between himself and the bucket, even though he didn't expect to operate at such a distance. He loaded seven rounds. The magazine clicked home. He racked the slide. The .45 cartridge chambered with a satisfying clack.

He aimed.

The first shot cracked like judgment. The Colt leapt, startling and painful. A spray of dirt exploded behind the bucket.

He missed.

Daniel exhaled, his wrist throbbing. He corrected his grip—thumb along the frame, elbows bent. A second shot rang. He missed again. He breathed, took aim again, but did not fire.

He dropped his arms and stood still, feeling the posture he had practiced over and over in his bedroom mirror—the squared shoulders, the even stance, the steady breath. But it felt hollow, too mechanical. This wasn't where the weapon belonged.

He looked down at it, the dull steel heavy in his palm. The stance was wrong because it wasn't his. It was rehearsed, like an actor in someone else's scene. He wasn't here to play soldier.

After a moment, he slipped the Colt into his waistband, then closed his eyes.

When he opened them, he drew and fired in one motion. No hesitation. The shot was centered and clean. The bucket jolted, spun halfway around. He did not reset it. Another round—faster this time. The bucket was thrown again, a fierce dent and hole having bloomed on its side. The shots came without conscious thought. Then the fifth. The bucket twirled further away. His body didn't wait for permission. It just moved. The sixth. The seventh.

He wasn't firing with control; he was firing with purpose. When he leaned into the strange calm of doing what needed to be done—not fantasized, not dramatized, but simply done—the weapon responded as if it had waited for that clarity. The recoil no longer stung. The Colt felt like it belonged in his hand, like it had been waiting for the moment his mind would finally make peace with his intent.

He reset the bucket and reloaded.

He emptied the magazine one round at a time—no rush, no panic. Each squeeze was deliberate, steady, and clean. The steel sang with fire, the report echoing through trees that bore silent witness to the clergyman's unexpected skill. When the final brass casing spun to the ground and the chamber sat open, Daniel stood with a breath he hadn't noticed holding.

Seven rounds. Seven strikes.

Not perfect. But not uncertain.

He ejected the empty magazine, ran a finger along the slide, and whispered, "Let's go again."

In all, he reloaded three times. Twenty-one more rounds. Muzzle rise tamed, groups tightening. The bucket was all but shredded. The smell of gunpowder mixed with pine sap; the morning air tasted metallic, like almost anything made in the air fryer Margie Burrows bought him for Christmas.

He gathered casings from the mud. He'd leave nothing behind.

The sun was rising higher, and the air was getting hotter. Frogs chorused in the surrounding marshes. The weapon, still warm in his hand, he thought of Walter, of Claire, of Elsie's trembling hand reaching to his.

Grace isn't polite. It's a hammer.

The Colt now cooler, he holstered it in his waistband and walked back to the Jeep. Kicking the mud from his boots, he climbed in and drove toward the thin strip of road that would lead him back into Linden.

CHAPTER SEVEN

It was just after 9 PM on Monday. The house was quiet.

Daniel stood in the dim light of his study, the edges of his clerical collar catching the glow from a single desk lamp. The rest of the room was a shadowed hush, the kind that made even small movements feel large. The black shirt fit snug against his frame. He buttoned the collar carefully, the motions slow, almost reverent, as if preparing for worship. The stiff white tab slid into place like a key turning in a lock.

He exhaled through his nose.

The Colt lay on a blue towel beside him—clean, oiled, and ready. The slide, the trigger, the sights—he'd run his fingers over each like a priest preparing vessels for the altar. He took up a cloth and began wiping it down again, even though it gleamed already. He wasn't trying to clean it anymore. He was keeping his hands busy.

The sounds crackled from the laptop speakers.

The recordings had no introduction. No timestamp. No notes. Just raw sound—snippets of life Claire had somehow managed to capture, likely with shaking hands and a terrified heart. The first forty seconds were nothing. Static. Footsteps. Perhaps a refrigerator humming in the background. Then came a voice.

It was Brett's.

"Hey, hey—*shhh*—it's okay, just sit down. There. Yes, right there."

The tone was gentle. Fatherly.

A muffled sob responded.

"Mary," Brett said, the name barely audible through whatever device Claire had hidden. "You're okay. Everything is okay. But you need to stop crying."

The gentleness vanished by the next sentence.

"I said, *stop crying*, Mary."

Then again, softly, "You don't want to be a mess when he gets here. We can't have that."

Daniel's hands paused on the Colt. He stared at nothing.

He could hear Mary's breath hitching. A chair scraped. Something glass clinked against something metal. Claire had captured all of it—this controlled cruelty. Daniel sat still, listening with an ache behind his eyes, his teeth clenched tightly enough to pulse.

The voice changed again.

"You're a beautiful girl, Mary. Now, let's get you cleaned up a bit. And then we'll do just like we practiced."

Static swallowed the next few seconds. Then a door creaked. Then silence. The clip ended.

Still motionless, Daniel could feel what he'd heard settling on him like iron filings.

Claire had given him this. She had died for this.

He reached for the magazine, already loaded, and inserted it with a practiced push. It clicked into place like a final word.

He prayed as he chambered a round. He waited for a word, one of thunder or a whisper. There was nothing. The silence was his answer.

He holstered the Colt, this time inside the front of his waistband. He did not zip up his jacket. Then, moving with methodical calm, he unplugged the laptop, closed it, and placed it into the backpack at the foot of the desk. No sign of its use would remain. There was nothing on it, anyway. All the files, all the recordings, were saved on two separate flash drives—Claire's original, which he kept hidden in the spine of Volume 25 of Luther's Works, *Lectures on Romans*, and the other he was, even then, placing into a well-worn edition of Krauth's *Conservative Reformation and Its Theology*.

He glanced out the window. The neighborhood was asleep. Porch lights glowed like wicks in oil lamps. Somewhere, a sprinkler hissed to life.

He grabbed his keys.

The Jeep rolled slowly along Gilead Lane. Its headlights were off. The dash cast a faint blue halo across Daniel's face as he passed house after house—structures like teeth in a pristine smile when seen from the stratosphere. The houses were relatively far apart. No sidewalks. No wrong-side-of-town unease. Just money. Just fences surrounding curated lawns. Just darkness with string lights.

He pulled over and parked two blocks east of the Durham home. A few houses down, someone had left a garage television running on mute. It looked like a baseball game. He parked behind a dented Civic that hadn't moved in weeks. Likely a resident teenager's first car.

No cameras pointed this way. No smart doorbells. He'd already studied the layout during two separate visits under different pretenses—one as a pastoral call to a prospective family, one a few days later to bring church materials he'd conveniently forgotten in the first visit.

He smiled during those visits. Waved, too.

Now he moved in silence.

The Jeep clicked softly as he stepped out. He did not lock it. He tucked the key fob in his jacket pocket and then, before zipping up, he adjusted the Colt slightly in his front waistband. The air was humid. Fireflies blinked near a hedge.

He opened the door, got back in, and started the engine.

A moment passed. He turned on the radio. His phone synced to its Spotify application and played a song from his summertime playlist, which was always set to random.

"And I heard, as it were, the noise of thunder. One of the four beasts saying, 'Come and see.' And I saw, and behold, a white horse."

The guitar that followed this biblical reading was raw and clean—unregretful. The voice that came with it—Johnny Cash—was weathered wood and judgment. Even as he sat, he could see himself moving.

"There's a man goin' 'round takin' names…"

He passed under an oak tree and walked west.

The song continued. It described choices being made—who'd be set free and who'd carry blame.

He reached the driveway.

Cash sang of expired fairness, that some would be raised up and others cast down.

The house appeared ahead like a painted mask—nothing behind it but shadows.

The lyrics intoned a shining ladder stretching between heaven and earth, between the realms of God and men.

The porch light was on. A hanging fern swung lazily.

Cash preached Revelation's alarm with certainty.

Daniel's trigger finger hovered over the pause icon as he listened.

The Jeep's speakers warned of a dread so sharp it would raise the hairs on every arm, of a drink that carried terror with every swallow.

Daniel listened and waited.

The song pressed the choice: to take the final cup, or be cast away, disappearing into a betrayer's grave.

Daniel caught his own reflection in the rearview mirror as the refrain circled back—the reckoning when the man came around.

He paused the song. It's as if the world stopped with it.

Within moments, he was stepping out of the final shadow and into the streetlight spill near Brett's house. He climbed the porch steps slowly, his glossy black shoes firm on each board. He didn't knock right away, but instead looked through the front door's frosted glass. Shapes moved inside. Brett's shape, moving toward the kitchen. No children. No Marcie. Daniel knocked once. And then again. Easy and careful.

The door opened after a moment. Brett stood in joggers and a faded Central Michigan hoodie. His hair was damp. Maybe a shower. Maybe not.

He blinked.

"Pastor Michaels? It's late."

"I just need a moment," Daniel said. His tone was not aggressive. It was the tone of a man who had already been granted permission.

Brett hesitated but then stepped aside.

Daniel entered.

The foyer smelled like lemon cleaner and lavender. He saw a photo of Walter and Elsie on the wall—their arms around Brett as a much younger man. Another was up and to its left. In it, Elsie hugged Brett's two children.

"She loves you," Daniel said, pointing toward Elsie. "You're her pride."

Brett gave a weak laugh. "She's a good woman. Always

been a saint. She talks a lot about you, too. She's your biggest fan."

Daniel nodded and smiled.

"Can I pour you something, Reverend? You're a scotch drinker, right?"

Daniel nodded again.

They walked to the kitchen. The overhead light was soft and yellow. Marcie hated the LEDs. She wanted everything real. Granite countertops. A bowl of fresh apples.

In a moment, there was a glass of scotch before them both—a Laphroaig, the 2016 Càirdeas edition.

They sat across from each other at the kitchen table. Daniel left the Colt holstered.

"Why so late, Reverend? What's on your mind?"

"I've come to hear your confession," he said quietly and took a sip.

Brett swallowed a sip, too.

"And then to absolve you," Daniel added.

"I… I don't understand."

"You know why I'm here."

"No… I don't."

Something flickered in Brett's face—defiance, maybe, or panic pretending to be confusion.

Then he exhaled his realization.

"I heard what happened to you at Claire's place. Everybody knows. Whatever she told you, you don't know the whole story."

"She never got the chance to tell me anything," Daniel said. "Not while she was alive."

"Well, whatever you think you know—"

"Tell me, Brett. Make your confession."

"I don't know what you're talking about."

Daniel said nothing. He only looked down, keeping his right ear turned as if listening intently.

Brett shifted in his chair.

"They'll kill me," he said. "You think I wanted this? I didn't know what I was getting into. I thought… I thought it was just getting girls off the street. Helping. I thought—"

"Don't lie to me, Brett. You're talking to the one man who knows liars best."

There was no more wondering about Brett's face. He was panicked.

"Everything turned. It turned so fast."

"And you kept going," Daniel said, still looking down, still listening.

"There was money. There was—"

"How many girls, Brett?"

"I… I don't know. Fifteen or twenty so far. Not many."

"Not many," Daniel chuckled sarcastically through a whisper and gritted teeth.

"There are people running the operation," Brett continued. "People you wouldn't even—"

"I know who they are, Brett. I know all of them."

Brett took a nervous sip.

"But first," Daniel continued stoically, "I'll cleanse the Lord's house." He lifted his glass but did not drink. He smelled it. "You sat in Claire's row in that house, Brett. You prayed alongside her."

"I didn't touch her," Brett said quickly. "I swear to God."

"She's dead."

There was a long pause.

"What are you going to do, Reverend?" Brett asked, his

voice brittle, as if expecting the oncoming ruin that Daniel might bring by going to the authorities.

Daniel didn't respond.

He reached slowly into his coat. But he did not draw the weapon. Not yet.

He placed a folded piece of paper on the table. Brett reached out to unfold and read it. It was a copy of one of Claire's journal entries detailing Brett's involvement.

"There's more," Daniel said as Brett scanned the page. "I heard you say her name. Mary. She was crying. You gave her to someone."

Brett folded the paper and closed his eyes.

Daniel took another sip and leaned forward.

"You sent Mary into the darkness. You've sent others, too. You buried light."

"I didn't kill Claire," Brett insisted nervously.

"I believe you," Daniel said, sipping again, a much larger draw, as if he might swallow what remained. He was done talking.

Brett's hands trembled. "I can make it right. I can testify. I can give names."

Another long silence.

Brett looked up, tears forming. "Please, let me fix this. I have Marcie. I have the kids. Don't ruin their lives."

Daniel unzipped his jacket, drew the Colt, and set it on the table. Brett's eyes grew wide.

"What are you doing?"

Daniel said nothing, only stared.

Brett's lips trembled. "What are you?—Wait—Please—I can fix this—I can make things ri—"

"Maybe," Daniel interrupted and abruptly stood, taking

the Colt in hand. He turned his face upward before closing his eyes. He inhaled deeply, his chest expanding, and then exhaled slowly.

Brett held his breath.

"But not in this life," Daniel said, bringing his gaze squarely back to the man before him.

He raised the gun.

"You have to believe me, Brett," he said, almost apologetically. "I prayed for a different word."

Brett blinked. Daniel did not.

One shot cracked and flashed—barely softened by the weight of curtains and the suburban home's insulation. Then another. Both rounds passed through Brett's chest, striking the sliding glass door behind him. The tempered glass spiderwebbed around two neat, black-rimmed holes—clean entries punched through the pane, ringed by cracks that glittered like frost under the kitchen light.

Brett did not spin or get thrown back like the bucket. It was not like in the movies. Instead, his eyes wide, Brett gasped and then slumped, his arms twitching briefly at his sides before going still.

Red-stained flesh speckled the walls and glass behind Brett. Blood began spreading on the floor beneath him like a crimson shadow.

Daniel stared, but only for a moment. His heart was steady. His breath was easy.

He circled the table, being careful to avoid the pooling blood. He reached out and closed Brett's eyes.

"Kyrie eleison," he whispered.

Then he turned, grabbed his scotch glass, and finished the last of its contents. He took it with him on the way out, along with the casings, which had spiraled out and around near the refrigerator.

Upstairs, the sound of commotion. Marcie called out. She screamed out. Then a child's wailing.

Daniel didn't run. But he was gone long before Marcie had emerged from the hallway leading from the living room stairway to the kitchen.

Down the front steps. Past the hedge. Onto the driveway. His back straight. His face pale but dry, like a masked killer in a John Carpenter film. He walked with the chill of someone beyond concern or fear—something closer to determined inevitability.

He could hear Marcie's screams from behind him.

A block passed.

Then another.

He reached the Jeep and climbed in, but only after a momentary fumbling for its door handle. He hadn't realized until then that he'd walked the whole way with the Colt in one hand and the whisky glass in the other.

He didn't drive off right away. He didn't even start the engine. He stared into the rearview mirror, praying silently.

His thoughts were interrupted. There was Claire. Then Elsie.

"Oh, goodness," he said prudishly, having suddenly remembered something.

He pulled out his phone and scrolled through his calendar. *Tuesday, 10:00 AM — Elsie Durham (Communion)*

"I can't forget to go see Elsie tomorrow," he whispered, as if what had just happened was just another pastoral visitation.

He started the Jeep. Headlights off. His phone synced.

Johnny Cash's voice continued from where it had ended. He sang of pipes and brass, of a vast angelic presence, of multitudes trooping to the thunderous sound of drums.

He cruised beneath the subdivision's trees that reached across its streets, their trunks billowing high, but now seemingly darker than before. He could hear sirens, but he didn't cross paths with them.

CHAPTER EIGHT

The morning sun had more than crested the trees when Daniel pulled his Jeep to the curb outside Elsie Durham's white-sided ranch. The garden out front, though slightly over-grown, was still brimming with peonies and daisies, their tired petals catching the daylight. A bluebird darted from the feeder near the porch, and Daniel paused, one hand on the wheel, watching it disappear into the shadows of a maple.

He hadn't slept. Not really. The dreams were fractured and dry, like brittle film reels unraveling in his mind. In each one, Claire's voice called from somewhere out of sight—first from behind walls, then from under water, then from the back pew of an empty church, mouthing words he couldn't hear.

Now, as he sat staring at Elsie's front door, those dreams echoed in the tight space of the Jeep. He tapped the brake with his foot, not out of impatience, but as a nervous tic. Then, with a sigh, he stepped out.

Unlike too many among the clergy, he always wore his collar. Today was no exception. The black clerical shirt was crisp, the white tab square in place. The Colt stayed behind at home. He wouldn't need it here.

Elsie's short and shallow porch groaned as he mounted the steps. The door was open behind a mesh screen, and the smell of lilacs floated out on a slow draft of warm air. Daniel knocked lightly.

"Pastor?" Elsie's voice called from within. "That you?"

"It's me, Elsie."

"Come in. You're letting the air out."

He chuckled as he stepped inside.

The living room was unchanged—a few books stacked in short, uneven towers, lace curtains stained with years of sun, a framed portrait of Walter in uniform, and Mahalia Jackson on the record player, though the needle had finished its groove and was clicking softly in the center ring.

"Would you mind fixing that?" Elsie asked, pointing toward the record player. "Mahalia just finished."

Daniel lifted the player's arm to its cradle, and the disc stopped.

"Flip it over, please," Elsie added. "I'll have her sing for me again after you go."

He did. It seemed that besides Daniel's, Mahalia's voice was the only one Elsie had gotten to hear in these later years.

Elsie sat in her recliner, wrapped in a knit shawl of maroon and navy. Her four-legged walker stood beside the end table, next to a half-finished crossword puzzle and a mug with faint coffee rings along the rim.

"Well, the pot's on," she said with a soft smirk. "Go pour two if it's drinkable."

Daniel went to the kitchen, poured the burnt coffee into mismatched mugs. He added a little water to both and returned. He handed one to Elsie and took the chair opposite.

"You know," she said after a sip, "when I could get to church, when Brett and Marcie would take me, Claire always sat in our row. I can still hear her voice during the hymns. She didn't try to stand out. But, my dear, she sure had a beautiful voice. Enough to make the angels jealous."

Daniel nodded. "She served the choir well. She served us all well."

"She had a stillness to her, too. Most people fidget. Claire didn't. She was always so attentive."

He stared at the mug in his hands. "You've been thinking about her lately, huh?"

"Yes," Elsie said. "I don't know why. Just have. I didn't know her well, but I knew her well enough. I looked forward to seeing her."

Before either could say more, a knock came at the door.

Daniel stood.

"No idea who that could be," Elsie said, lifting her head as if to smell the presence rather than see it.

Outside, through the screen, Daniel saw Chief Stern and a second officer—Rhodes—standing on the porch.

"Morning, Reverend," Stern said. "Mrs. Durham. I'm sorry to intrude. May we come in?"

"Nothing but the screen door stopping you," Elsie said and motioned them in with a tired wave. Daniel opened the door.

"It's good you're here," Stern said to Daniel as he passed.

"Mrs. Durham," Stern continued gently, "I'm afraid we have some bad news. Your grandson, Brett, passed away last night."

Elsie sat very still.

Stern's voice remained careful. "We're still gathering details. The scene was… unusual. But Marcie and the children were upstairs at the time. They're okay. They're safe."

Daniel's breath caught as Stern spoke. The words were calm, but Daniel's mind had already fled the room.

He remembered.

He saw Brett's face again—bloated with confusion in the seconds before the trigger was pulled. In his mind, the hanging light above the table where they sat was flickering, casting twitching shadows across the walls. The Colt had bucked in Daniel's hand with a brutal jerk, louder than expected in the stillness of the house. Still, he was ready for it. He'd practiced it.

The first shot struck Brett square in the chest, dead center, punching through muscle and bone with a visceral thud. His body jerked. His mouth gaped. The glass behind him popped. Chunks jetted in a fine mist of blood.

Daniel fired again—lower this time, just beneath the sternum. The second round punched through and out, splattering crimson in a wide arc across the wall and floor tiles. Brett's expression was fixed, his mouth slack with disbelief, one hand reaching out as though he could still negotiate with what had already happened. He didn't even exhale. He simply dropped in position, like a marionette with its strings severed.

Daniel had stood over him, the sharp scent of copper filling his nostrils. His ears rang. He listened—really listened—for any movement upstairs. He heard something.

The hollowest part was the silence after. Not the screaming—Marcie had only started when Daniel was already down the walkway—but the quiet before. The moment between justice and noise. The breath of stillness in the wake of violent purpose. It was neither victory nor relief. Just necessity. And emptiness.

Now, standing in Elsie's living room, that emptiness bloomed again.

Stern added gently, "Marcie will be calling you later. She mentioned bringing the kids by this afternoon, if you're up for it."

"That'll be fine," Elsie said, her voice calm but quiet.

"I'm very sorry for your loss," Stern said. "If we learn anything more, someone will reach out to you."

He turned slightly to Daniel. "Reverend, a quick word before we go?"

Stern nodded to Rhodes to stay with Elsie.

Daniel followed Stern out to the porch.

They stood a few steps down, beneath the overhang, surrounded by birdsong and the distant hum of a lawnmower.

Stern folded his arms. "Long morning already."

"Yes."

"Actually, it was a long night."

"It sounds like you've been busy."

"You knew Brett. And Claire."

Daniel nodded slightly. "They were both members at Saint John's."

"It's been rough for your congregation lately," Stern said. "And you… you intersect with a lot lately. I'm not much of a church-goer, but I've sure felt the need to pray for you. You've got a lot on your plate."

There was a change in Stern's tone—a tilt from suspicion to something smoother, like an officer trying to charm a witness instead of interrogating him. Daniel recognized it instantly.

Pastors know these shifts. They sat across from cheating husbands and wives who swore everything was fine. They endured countless church council meetings where lies dressed as diplomacy hovered like smoke. They heard confessions in silence and watched body language collapse under the weight of half-truths. It wasn't magic. It was experience, intuition honed over years of shepherding people through shame and secrecy.

Daniel saw it now—the slight relaxation in Stern's jaw, the calculated neutrality in his voice. The man wasn't just making conversation. He was probing, but gently. Playing the long game. The "good cop" routine you might see on television.

Daniel played along.

"It's a small town," he said. "People's lives overlap."

Stern gave a slow nod, eyes never leaving Daniel.

"We're not jumping to any conclusions about anything. Linden hasn't seen anything like this before. Ever."

He took a contemplative stance. It looked rehearsed.

"We're close enough to Flint to be concerned. Still, small towns like ours can see their fair share of trouble."

Daniel didn't say anything.

"There's a lot of uncertainty. If anything comes to mind— anything Claire might've said, or anything odd you noticed with Brett—give me a call. Doesn't matter how small."

"Of course."

Stern studied him for a moment longer.

"For as long as I've known you, Reverend," he added, "you've been a steady man. The community appreciates you, what you do."

"I try," Daniel replied. And lest he sound less reverend-like, "By God's grace."

"I guess what I'm trying to say is—"

"I understand what you mean," Daniel interrupted, waving off the unnecessary flattery. "Thank you."

There it was again—a hint. A feeling that Stern knew more than he let on. That he suspected more. Daniel could sense it pressing beneath the surface, like a fault line shifting under calm earth.

They stood a moment longer. Stern glanced back toward the house, then returned his eyes to Daniel.

"Another funeral for you now, I suppose. Like you said, Brett was one of yours."

Daniel nodded. "Yes."

"That'll be a hard one, too," Stern said. "Just like Claire's. And so close to Claire's." He adjusted the weapon on his hip. "Preaching for someone you knew, especially when it's complicated, I imagine that can be tough."

"They're all complicated," Daniel said. "They're all complicated." He looked back toward Elsie's door. "But yes. This one will be hard. Everyone knew and liked Brett, too."

Then Stern offered his hand.

"Well, blessings, I guess."

Daniel took it.

"Thanks."

"Take care."

"And you."

Motioning to Rhodes through the screen, Stern turned to leave but then hesitated. He turned back. "You pastors probably see more grief than the rest of us. Hard not to wear it after a while, I bet."

Daniel nodded. "It stays with you." He made his way back toward Elsie's screen door. "But weddings are a lot harder on us."

Stern gave a cheap smile. "I'll bet," he said, and returned with Rhodes to the car.

Back inside, Elsie hadn't moved.

"You okay?" Daniel asked.

"I suppose. I knew something like this was coming."

"You did?" Daniel asked, betraying a deeper surprise. He

hoped—*he prayed*—she didn't know what Brett was doing.

"He changed. Years ago. Started visiting less. When he did come around, he was always… different. Not angry. Not sad. Just… removed. Like he was always halfway somewhere else. Like his mind was always occupied."

She took another sip of coffee.

"He started spending more time away in the evenings. Didn't say much about where he was. Marcie complained to me once. Maybe twice. Just little things—how the kids missed him. Or how dinner got cold more than once."

Her voice dropped into uncertainty.

"But I guess he seemed fine. Just… less kind. Less patient. The kids would be loud, like little ones can be, and he would snap at them. Oh, he snapped at them. He wasn't cruel. Just, well, too sharp for me. Not like the Brett I know. Not like this old woman."

She looked past him, her clouded eyes distant.

"He was here last week. Didn't stay for long. Brought me some groceries. Well, Pastor, I have to say, that was okay. I didn't want him to stay. He had a way of making a room feel cold without saying anything. You ever met someone like that? They smile, they nod, but there's something behind the eyes that just won't let you feel settled?"

Daniel didn't answer.

"I asked him once if everything was alright. He told me I was old and just getting worried again. He was right. I am old. And I do worry about him. But you know, Pastor, that stung a little. I should let go of things. I should. But I didn't ask him that question ever again."

They sat quietly.

"You know, Pastor," she said after a long pause, "I always

assumed he'd be the one standing over me in the end. Praying with me. Reading me the Psalms. He was there with Walter. I figured he'd be there with me, too. Instead, you're here. You'll be the one praying and reading, right?"

"You bet, I will," Daniel said. "I wouldn't be anywhere else."

"Brett's gone. But you ain't. I guess I'm okay with that."

Daniel took her hand. For a moment, he felt holy again. "I'll still be here. When the time comes."

Elsie smiled.

Daniel read the Scriptures, prayed, and served Communion.

They sat a little longer afterward.

"Can you stay for lunch?" Elsie asked.

"You know," he said. "I think I can." He wouldn't dare leave this woman alone. Not today.

She directed him to the freezer. Marcie had brought a stack of Lean Cuisines. He microwaved two of them, occasionally walking into the living room for more conversation while they cooked.

He stayed for another hour. It felt good. Elsie liked having him there.

Before leaving, he gave her hand a gentle squeeze. "Thank you, Elsie," he said.

She took his hand, her thinning, spotted skin like silk. "Get going, Pastor. I'll see you again soon."

✝ ✝ ✝

Daniel drove without a destination. His thoughts churned. Eventually, he parked at the church but didn't go inside.

Instead, he sat in the lot, windows down, letting the wind speak for a while. Eventually, he went inside and tapped away at a funeral sermon for Brett. He already knew what he wanted to say.

When the sun dipped lower, he drove home.

That evening, in the quiet of his study, he reached for Krauth's volume to retrieve the flash drive hidden inside. He opened the "Suspects" folder. He scrolled to the bottom of the list and deleted Brett's name. Dennis Anderson was now last.

"The last shall be first," Daniel whispered.

The Colt rested on the desk beside his laptop. He'd already cleaned it.

Planning began.

But prayer came first. Not much. Just a few words. He didn't ask for anything. He spoke.

"Not my will, Lord," he whispered, "but Yours."

He supposed his words were a request. But they weren't. And he knew it.

His eyes burned, and his clenched teeth ached.

He opened the side drawer and pulled out a small, dog-eared notebook with a push-button pencil already tucked between its pages as a bookmark. He'd already been charting Dennis's habits.

Another member at Saint John, a lawyer. Claire had discovered he had two addresses—his own, and the second, a duplex in Fenton. God only knows what happened there. And Daniel assumed Dennis's wife, Sherri, didn't know about the second. But why would she? He was a man in his late sixties. She was barely forty-something. As long as he kept gas in her Cadillac and water in the pool, she didn't pay him much attention.

Poor Dennis. But then he played the audio file.

Dennis's voice came through first—smug, slick, careless.

"I try not to think about it," Dennis said, his voice barely above the device's hum. "The money is good. It certainly keeps Sherri happy."

Brett's voice answered with a laugh. He was, by no means, being forced to participate.

The sound of clinking glass followed—ice in a tumbler, a pour of something.

The audio continued. Other names on the list were mentioned. Even Pastor David. His name burned the most. He knew why. And Daniel would get to him soon enough. The hammer would fall for all of them.

The hissed audio continued. A pickup time was discussed. Some girls would be dropped off at a hotel in Flint. A new girl had arrived at Harbor. Mary. She was pretty.

Daniel sat motionless, listening again to the cruelty embedded not just in their words, but in their ease. There was no shame. No second thoughts. Just routine—like this was nothing more than business.

Daniel flipped a notebook page while he listened. He scanned his notes. Monday and Thursday nights, Dennis closed his law office late, between 7:00 and 7:30. The lot was small, wedged between a bookstore and a title agency. Both closed at 5:00.

Daniel paused the audio. They complained about a young girl's blood and bruises, about how she'd been handled too hard and might not be of much use anymore.

It sickened him.

The alley behind the building, a narrow strip of asphalt with angled parking spaces where the businesses' employees parked, had no streetlights. Beyond it was an open field, farm-land separated from the asphalt by a rotting fence.

No one would be nearby. No traffic after dusk.

Daniel glanced again at the paused waveform on his lap-top—Dennis's voice still frozen mid-sentence.

This Thursday would be too soon, especially with Brett's forthcoming funeral. He wrote the word "Monday" and cir-cled it. Six days from now.

He stared at the circle.

A few moments later, the light was off, and he was in bed. No whisky tonight. Just sleep.

The house fell silent.

CHAPTER NINE

The fellowship hall smelled of pasta and fudge brownies. The air was thick with the quiet rustling of dark dresses and muted ties, the scraping of folding chairs and plastic forks. The food was laid out on long tables draped with white paper. A few ladies from the Altar Guild wore disposable aprons and whispered to one another as they offered second helpings with practiced gentleness.

Daniel stood near the punch table, a half-filled cup sweating in his hand. His collar was tight, tighter than usual, even though he hadn't gained a pound. The punch tasted like cold corn syrup and regret.

People came and went in waves. Marcie sat at a far table with the kids, the older boy, quiet and thin, and a younger girl who liked to braid her own hair unevenly. Marcie stared at her plate. She hadn't touched the potatoes.

He made his way over slowly, winding through familiar congregants murmuring kind things. When he reached the table, Marcie looked up and gave a worn smile.

"Pastor," she said softly. Her voice cracked from grief or fatigue—he couldn't tell.

"Marcie," he said, pulling out a chair.

The boy looked up at him, then quickly down. The little girl kept twisting her napkin.

Daniel leaned in gently. "I'm so sorry."

She nodded, blinking too quickly. "Thank you. It still doesn't feel real."

"No," he said. "It won't. Not for a while."

They sat quietly, the murmur of the room folding over them. Then Marcie spoke again.

"They released the house back to us already. The kitchen was… I just wanted to clean it. To keep the kids from… at least until we can get out of there."

Daniel nodded.

She nodded. "I bleached everything. Scrubbed it twice. I know they cleaned it already. I just had to do it myself… with the kids in the house… with the lingering smell. It still smelled."

Daniel exhaled gently, searching for something to say.

"You did what a mother would do," he said.

She gave a half-smile, but her eyes were glassy. "That's what my mom said, too. She's been calling a lot. We might go back to Missouri for a while. Just until things settle. The schools here in Linden, anyway…" Her voice caught. She was making excuses she didn't have to make. "I don't know. Everything reminds them of Brett."

"And of you," Daniel said softly.

She looked at him, startled by the weight of that statement. Then her expression softened. "That's why I haven't decided yet. I just don't know how to begin over."

"You don't begin," Daniel said. "You endure. And the Lord carries you."

She blinked and nodded.

"Thank you for the sermon, Pastor," she added after a moment. "I know it was hard for you, especially after Claire. Two funerals… two people in the chur—"

"I'm here if you need anything," Daniel interrupted.

They exchanged no more words. He touched the boy's

shoulder, then offered the girl a kind smile as he stood. She gave a faint one in return, her fingers still twisting the napkin into paper ribbons.

Daniel made his way toward the coffee urn. The line had shortened. The room, if anything, had grown louder—more awkward laughter, more conversation. The grieving had tipped into social routine, a pattern learned over generations.

He didn't stay long. He excused himself with a few warm nods and a few firm handshakes. Harry, the Board of Elders chairman, thanked him for "shepherding God's people." Someone else mentioned how strong Marcie had been.

"She's such a faithful soul," another said. "Real good woman. Shame about Brett."

Shame.

Yes. *Shame*.

He left through the west exit to avoid a crowd of choir members gathered near the coat racks. As the door closed behind him, the sunlight slapped his eyes. It was too bright. Too welcoming.

He got into the Jeep and didn't drive straight home. He drove to the cemetery. Not to visit Claire's grave. Not to stand over Brett's plot.

He just parked beneath the birch tree near the gravel path, killed the engine, and sat. The windows were down. Wind danced through the leaves. A distant lawnmower buzzed.

It was Saturday. Brett was now an urn of ashes destined for Elsie's flowerbed, or so Marcie suggested. Daniel hated cremation. He preferred burial.

He thought about Monday, which eventually came.

† † †

Three hours until dusk.

He'd eaten very little that day. He poured a glass of water and drank half before dumping the rest.

The Colt lay in its usual place on his desk. Oiled. Ready. Beside it, his notebook. Beneath the notebook, a pair of gloves. Black nitrile. Disposable. He'd already cut the fingertips off the right glove so he could feel the trigger.

He packed the gun in a small, zippered case—a repurposed satchel meant for a portable Communion kit. Ironic. But for Daniel, it was fitting. Still, he reconsidered. Removing the gun, he slipped it into his waistband. That's where he'd carry it.

His black shirt and pants were ironed. His clerical collar was crisply in place.

At precisely 6:30 PM, he drove.

The engine of the Jeep hummed like a confession withheld too long. Daniel didn't take the scenic route or loop the block to calm his nerves. He drove straight into the alley behind Dennis Anderson's office, turned off the headlights, and eased into a shadowed space between the dumpster and the faded brick wall. His view of the back door was unobstructed.

He waited.

The city slowed. It was quiet.

There was no music. Still, Daniel sang to himself in a murmur. Johnny Cash's voice—gravelly and apocalyptic—was Daniel's voice.

A sending and a reckoning all at once.

Daniel let what played in his mind come from his lips as he stared at the door. He didn't blink much. Didn't fidget.

He whispered the lyrics describing bridesmaids bent over

their lamps, flames readied for the bridegroom's approach.

He was coming.

He was here.

The door finally opened at 7:21 PM.

Dennis stepped into the amber cone of the doorway's overhead light. He was dressed like he always was after a long day of examining cases—shirt untucked, sport coat unbuttoned, phone in one hand and a set of keys jingling in the other.

Daniel rolled down the passenger window.

"Dennis," he called out, low and even.

Dennis flinched, then peered toward the voice. When he recognized the Jeep, he smirked.

"Well, if it isn't Pastor Michaels," he said, slipping his phone into his pocket. "What brings you out after hours? Lost a sheep?"

"You could say that," Daniel replied.

Dennis ambled closer, eventually resting his forearms on the open window. Scanning the Jeep, "Nice Wrangler. What year is it?"

"I need a word with you," Daniel said.

"Will it take long, because I need to get home. Sherri wants to put the boat out on the lake tonight with some friends. I need to—"

"It won't take long."

Dennis paused, still leaning on the open window.

"Yeah, sure, what's the good word, Reverend?"

Daniel got out of the Jeep. He put the nitrile gloves on as he did. The faint scent of the dumpster's souring garbage lingered in the air. Dennis carried a puzzled grin as Daniel closed the door and stepped around into the light.

Daniel met his eyes. "I came to hear your confession."

Dennis tilted his head and gave a slight chuckle. "What the hell are you talking about?"

Daniel didn't answer.

Dennis saw the gloves. And then he knew.

"You gotta be kidding me," he said. "There's no way."

Daniel remained silent.

"You're serious," Dennis said, reading the shift in Daniel's posture. "You're actually serious."

He took a step back, arms half-raised.

"Listen, I knew Brett's death was a wake-up call. People don't die like that in Linden." He gave a humorless laugh. "Call it instinct, or divine providence. After that happened, something told me I'd better be ready."

Daniel's expression didn't change.

Dennis took another step backward, slowly. "I'm not saying I'm guilty of anything. Hell, if I were, I know what sticks and what doesn't. No one would've had anything on me."

Daniel closed some of the space between them.

Dennis didn't step back. Instead, he relaxed. But he was pretending. And Daniel knew it.

"I figured someone… I didn't expect you, Reverend. Of all people, you? Is this about Claire? She was a good girl. Didn't deserve what happened to her. She must've really messed with your—"

Then his hand moved to the inside of his jacket. It was quick and practiced.

But Daniel was faster.

He lunged across the space between them just as Dennis's fingers brushed a pistol's grip beneath his coat.

They spun and slammed into the side of the Jeep. The car rocked from the impact. Dennis's hand was halfway inside his jacket when Daniel seized his wrist and drove his weight into him. The gun clattered to the ground, sliding beneath the Wrangler.

They rolled away from the fender and crashed into the building's cinder block wall. Dennis swung wild and hard. One punch caught Daniel's chest, straining his breath. He'd been hit before, but not since he was a kid. Time slowed in that moment. He considered how fighting as a child had been fast and clumsy, with no weight behind it, all flailing limbs and schoolyard noise. This was different. Adults didn't just swing—they meant it. Every punch carried mass. And there was no one to break it up, no bell to save you, only dreadful violence until someone finished it.

They continued—tangled, wrestling, fists flying. Dennis was still strong for his age. Much heavier, too. But Daniel was determined. He attempted the Colt, but Dennis kept his hands busy.

The door to the office was open behind them.

They fell through it.

The hallway light flickered overhead as they crashed into a metal cabinet. Papers scattered. Dennis shoved Daniel into the drywall, cracking it with a dull thud. Daniel managed a right hook that split Dennis's lip and rattled his vision.

Dennis fumbled for something on the counter.

Daniel followed, and the two men fell to the floor, grunting, limbs tangled.

A sharp metallic clang sounded nearby—a small letter opener, straight and silver, had tumbled from a desk and landed on the floor within reach.

Daniel saw it.

Dennis saw it too, and he was quicker this time. But

Daniel wrested his wrist sideways, driving the heel of his palm into the joint.

The letter opener dropped again.

Daniel grabbed it.

In an instant, the blade was in Dennis's side. But it didn't go deep. It scraped off a rib.

The second found meat.

The third went under the ribcage.

Each plunge gave a wet crunch, sending blood geysering onto the front of Daniel's shirt, speckling his white collar.

Dennis screamed. His body spasmed. Blood gushed in pulses.

The song pounded in his mind, Cash's image of a storm twisting through the thorns.

Dennis was still. His eyes were open, glazed and empty.

His lips twitched. Blood bubbled from the corners. He made a choking sound, a gurgling rasp.

Daniel leaned in close.

"You'll answer for every girl," he whispered. "The end has found you."

Then, slowly, deliberately, he stood. He left the opener in Dennis's chest.

Miraculously, the Colt had remained fixed in his belt. And so, he grabbed hold of it. Dennis was still gasping, somehow still alive. Daniel went back to his knees beside him. He put the Colt's barrel beneath Dennis's chin.

Dennis choked. "I didn't… Claire…" he gurgled. "But I know who—"

"Kyrie eleison."

The Colt roared.

The top of Dennis's skull blew out in a red and white

spray, painting the nearby wall with fragments of brain, scalp, and bone.

Daniel returned to his feet.

Smoke curled from the gun's muzzle.

The room smelled of cordite and blood and burned hair.

He retrieved the shell, pulled the letter opener free, and walked back to the Jeep. Stiff. No emotion. He left Dennis's gun where it was. The police could have it.

He drove home in silence. But in his head, the song played on. Its lyrics circled.

Alpha and Omega. The kingdom had come.

CHAPTER TEN

The call came in at 4:29 AM.

Stern was already awake and reading in bed, a history of Irish political conflict. It was one of those paperbacks with a dramatic subtitle and too many footnotes. He'd just finished a chapter when the phone buzzed against his nightstand. He blinked at the caller ID: Dispatch.

He was up before the third ring.

"Go," he said.

"Chief, Fenton PD is requesting assistance. They've got a scene on Monroe. Back entrance of a law firm. You're listed as contact by name."

"By name?"

"Chief Kress asked for you directly," the dispatcher said. "He said to tell you that if you're not too busy living the good life in Linden, he could use your help tonight."

Stern rubbed a hand across his jaw. "Call that idiot back and tell him I'm on my way."

He dressed in minutes, his mind already pulling together threads. Kress was a friend, and he didn't call for small things. He tucked his badge into his coat, slid his service weapon into the holster at his back—force of habit, not intention—and stepped out into the night.

By the time he pulled into the cracked parking lot in front of Anderson Law, the crime scene had long since taken shape. He tried to enter through the front door, but a forensic officer motioned through the window to go around to the back. A set of orange cones flanked the alley entrance. Two squad cars idled nearby, doors open, radios hissing with occasional chatter. Yellow tape was already in place. It hung lifelessly. There was no breeze. The back door to the building stood wide open.

Chief Tom Kress was already waiting. He stood beside the door with his arms folded, a half-spent pencil tucked behind one ear. He hadn't changed much since they served on the same task force in Detroit fifteen years ago—same hard jaw, same military posture, same eyes that never missed a thing. The only real difference was the thinning at his crown and a slight stoop in his right shoulder, a reminder from the Rosedale shootout neither of them liked to discuss.

"Jeff," he called, nodding as Stern approached. "Took you long enough."

Stern extended a hand. "Tom."

They shook like men who had known things together. Quiet things. Messy things. Dreadful things. Once, in Detroit, they'd spent three nights tracking a dismemberment case through frozen drainage canals. It had taken a month to thaw the horror out of their sleep. After that, Stern started considering small towns.

Kress gestured to the open door. "You ready for this?"

"I've probably seen worse," Stern muttered.

"Not in a while, you haven't."

They stepped inside.

The hallway was a mess.

Papers littered the floor like snowdrifts, some blood-smeared, others shredded along the edges. A folding table was broken in half, one leg snapped and splintered. Drywall had caved in along the north side of the corridor—obvious from where someone had been thrown or slammed. Two framed certificates hung crookedly on a wall. One had a crack running diagonally across the glass. The carpeting was stained dark from end to end from usual foot traffic.

A faint copper tang hung in the air, just enough to dry the back of the throat.

Stern paused, taking it in. "You woke me for a breaking-and-entering?"

"There's more, Jeff." Kress gestured down the hall. "The body's around the corner."

Stern could already see two feet in the flickering patrol lights, motionless and sprawling.

He took a step. But before going further, "Who found it?" he asked.

"Cleaning crew. They come late. Saw the door ajar, walked into this mess, saw the blood, and called it in. Smart enough not to go further."

Stern moved carefully down the hallway. Every step was a raspy crunch from debris. The fluorescent ceiling lights buzzed, flickering in sections. Shadows stretched and contracted.

The short corridor opened into the main office. A dim lamp glowed within, casting everything in a low amber haze. And just beyond it, on the floor to the left—

"Well," Stern muttered, betraying his surprise and halting in the doorway.

Blood coated the carpet in a wide radius. It had soaked into the base of the desk, pooled around a toppled chair, sprayed across the wall, and up onto a file cabinet littered with various community service awards. The air reeked—metallic and meaty, undercut by stale air conditioning. A fine mist had clung to the blinds behind the file cabinet, dotting them like rust. On the floor, crumpled in a lifeless sprawl, lay the body of Dennis Anderson.

His legs were twisted. His arms flared at awkward angles. One hand clutched his side like he'd tried to hold himself together, but the damage was too much. His shirt was stained from puncture wounds—plural. Crudely placed ones. Likely fast and enraged. A final, jagged entry wound bloomed just below his jawline—contact shot. The bullet had exited through the top of his skull, carving a gory crater into the drywall beside the file cabinet. Brain and bone clung to the surrounding landscape like someone had slung raw meat with a snow shovel. A portion of his face had gone with the top of his head, leaving some of his forehead hanging grotesquely over, making him barely recognizable from where Stern stood.

Stern tilted slightly for a better angle, then glanced at Kress. "Do we know who he is?"

"Yeah," Kress said quietly. "That's Dennis Anderson. He owned the firm."

Stern didn't flinch. But he exhaled slowly.

"No forced entry?"

"None," Kress said from behind him. "Front door was locked. Back door was wide open. That's how the cleaners got in. And get this—"

He led Stern back down the hallway to the alley beyond the open rear door. Just outside, the pavement shimmered from patrol car lights. Less than twenty feet from the door, in the center of a parking space near the dumpster, a pistol lay on the asphalt.

"Anderson's," Kress added. "Registered. .38. Not fired. Fully loaded."

Stern's jaw tightened.

"So, he was armed, but never used it," Stern said, crouching to look.

"Maybe he never got the chance," Kress replied.

"Or maybe he didn't think he needed to at first," Stern added. "Maybe he knew the guy."

Stern rose to his feet, and then, as if following a voice only he could hear, he made his way back inside and down the hallway, examining things as he went. He crouched beside Dennis's body, careful not to touch anything.

"They fought," Stern said. "All the way down the hallway. And it ended here." He scanned the space around him. "Did you find the stabbing weapon?"

"No. I figure he took it with him."

He scanned the scene again—his detective instincts kicking through the haze of early morning fatigue.

"Did you find his wallet? Any open cash drawers?"

"His wallet is in his coat pocket," Kress said. "Nothing was touched. No signs of robbery. No cash drawer tampered with. This wasn't about money."

Stern rose again to his feet.

"You ask me," Kress said, stepping inside, "this was personal. Whoever did this really hated this guy."

Stern stood. "Or needed it to look that way."

Kress raised an eyebrow. "You don't buy it?"

"I didn't say that."

Stern moved back outside to the handgun.

"We already have two deaths," he said. "Now three—inside of two months. Two likely knew each other. But this guy. This guy—"

"All three likely knew each other," Kress interrupted.

"What do you mean?"

"One of my guys recognized Anderson. Said he was a member at Saint John's in Linden. Same church as that Madsen girl."

Stern's eyes sharpened. "You sure?"

"Said he met him at his niece's confirmation. He was her elder representative, or something like that. Said he was a nice guy. Gave her a gift Bible and some money. He found out he was a lawyer and had him handle his divorce last year."

Stern exchanged a glance with Kress.

"Maybe reach out to the church," Kress said. "Ask the pastor if we can meet with the leadership. Ask some questions. Get a feel for the place."

"I'll talk to Reverend Michaels," Stern said. "Get us in the door. Maybe recommend some basic safety for worship—perp awareness training type stuff."

Kress nodded. "Nothing formal. Keep it low-key. We don't want to spook anyone. We just want to get some bearings."

A moment passed. Stern turned back toward the door. The morning was creeping in, deep blue, but paling at the edges. A cool wind stirred the yellow tape. Tech teams were still working quietly.

"Whatever happened here, it wasn't peaceful. It was rage."

"That girl, Claire, what happened to her?"

"The coroner found signs of blunt trauma. She was hurt pretty badly. Forensics said she was likely chased toward the stairs when she was hit from behind. Ultimately, it was the broken neck in the fall that killed her."

"Wasn't the Reverend there, too?"

Stern looked to the farmland beyond the alley. "Yeah, he was," he said. "He's a strange one. He's grieving. Took Claire's death pretty hard. But from what I've seen, it's what anyone would expect. He told us she was kind of a loner, and he made sure to pay attention to her. I think they were close."

"You think he knows anything?"

"I think he's wondering just like the rest of us," Stern said, before continuing. "If he does, he hasn't said." One more thought of Daniel, "He doesn't know anything," he concluded.

Kress nodded slowly.

The two men stood together in the quiet alley, the morning becoming more pronounced at the corners of the sky.

† † †

Back in Linden, the birds were stirring. A single robin trilled from the edge of Daniel's garage roof. The sky was purple at the edges. The town was still asleep.

Daniel stood in his backyard.

He wore jeans and a threadbare t-shirt. His hands trembled faintly in the cool air. It wasn't the temperature. It was the memory.

He'd already buried the letter opener. In his grip hung the bloodstained clerical.

He stared at it for a long time.

It had dried stiff—the fibers warped, the sleeves crusted. He didn't know how many times he stabbed Dennis. He only remembered the resistance of the flesh, the pressure of the blade, the final gunshot, the blood that sprayed up his sleeve and onto his collar. He remembered trying to catch his breath as the light went out of the man's eyes.

He hadn't meant to make it messy. It was supposed to be quick. It was supposed to be clean. But death had its own choreography. And now, he had far too much of Dennis on his shirt to keep it around.

He leaned over the fire pit, tossed the shirt in the center like an offering, and lit a match.

The flames took it slowly at first.

Then quickly.

The black fabric curled, whispering smoke into the morning air. The white collar blackened and snapped into flame. The dried blood turned to vapor. The edges of the shirt shriveled and folded inward, collapsing, like the man who had worn it.

And yet, Daniel's trembling stopped.

Sherri probably won't even want a funeral, he thought. *She'll take Dennis's money and go south. She always said the cold was the real sin around here.*

Without thinking, he whispered, "Ashes to ashes."

The fire crackled.

"Dust to dust."

He stared until nothing was left but embers.

Something clenched deep in his chest.

He'd prayed for clarity—long, aching prayers whispered into the dark, but the heavens offered no reply. It felt like speaking into a sky too vast for an echo, as if God had taken one step back for every plea Daniel sent upward. He told himself that justice was a holy thing, that it must be. But with Dennis—despite how satisfying it was to fight him, to invest in ending him, to stop the rot at its root—it hadn't felt sacred. It had felt brutal. And yet, somehow, disturbingly beautiful.

The moment lingered in his memory like stained glass—shattered, jagged, catching light in terrible colors. He feared he wasn't unearthing justice but digging a well with no bottom, each act sinking him deeper beneath the surface of who he once was.

Still, when he closed his eyes, he saw Brett's face, smug in the pew, chin lifted as if the cross on the wall meant nothing. He saw Dennis's shadow, long and slow, sliding across motel wallpaper like a predator. And he heard their voices—caught forever in those files Claire left behind—flat, cold, remorseless. Somewhere between the altar at Saint John's and their graves, between the language of forgiveness and the silence that follows justice served, Daniel had made a choice. It was not clean. But he had wanted it to be holy.

He walked back inside and poured himself a coffee from the pot that had already been simmering for hours. He didn't sleep well anymore.

The coffee was dark and bitter.

Fitting.

Dr. Eli Webber would be next.

Daniel sharpened his pencil and then opened his notebook and laptop.

CHAPTER ELEVEN

The call came mid-morning.

Daniel was seated in his office, Bible open, pen in hand, trying to draft a sermon about mercy—a word that had begun to look strange in his cursive. He stared at it for a long time before the phone rang. The screen showed an unfamiliar number. But the voice, when it came, was familiar.

"Pastor Michaels? Jeff Stern."

Daniel sat up straighter. "Good morning, Chief."

"I hope I didn't catch you in the middle of something."

"Just sermon prep," Daniel replied. "No worries."

Stern gave a small exhale that might have been a laugh, or maybe just a breath. "Then I won't take much of your time. I wanted to talk about Dennis Anderson. More specifically, about the church."

Daniel's pen stopped moving.

"Alright."

"We're hoping to meet with your church leadership. Nothing formal. Just a conversation about safety—basic things, protocols. Given the circumstances, you can probably imagine why we'd want to do this. It seems prudent."

Daniel didn't answer immediately. Outside, through his narrow office window, he could see the wind stirring the maple beside the sacristy entrance. The sunlight danced along the trunk, flecked with green and gold.

"Of course," he said finally. "When were you thinking? Would tonight work?"

"I've already got Chief Kress from the Fenton PD coming down this evening. If you're able to assemble your folks tonight, we'll make it brief and respectful. Again, we don't want to cause alarm. We just want to be diligent."

Daniel nodded to no one. "I'll see what I can do."

"Thanks," Stern said. "How about we shoot for six?"

"I'll call our congregation president and get the word out for six."

"I appreciate it. Again, let me know if that doesn't work."

"Just plan on it," Daniel said. "I'll get folks here. This is important."

Daniel waited a moment before adding, "And I appreciate the concern."

"And I appreciate the cooperation, Pastor," Stern replied. "It's helpful."

"See you at six."

"See you then."

The line clicked off. Daniel sat for a while, staring down at his sermon notes. He drew a thick line through the word "mercy."

† † †

The Church Council gathered a little before 6:00. The news of Dennis Anderson had been shocking.

The fellowship hall smelled faintly of floor polish and old coffee. The rectangular tables had been pulled into a square.

Everyone greeted one another as they entered, offering gentle nods and practiced small talk. Bob Vannert, the Council President, was first—broad-shouldered and deep-thinking. He was loyal to a fault. Daniel always thought he looked uncomfortable in his own tie, like a man halfway through confessing a secret he didn't mean to tell.

Carl Brandt, the Vice President, followed close behind—short, no-nonsense, hair clipped tight around his ears and glasses that clicked when he pushed them up to his nose. He always carried a pen, even into services, and tonight he had three.

George Kessler, the Treasurer, wore a jean jacket, even though it was still summer, and carried an accordion folder filled with insurance forms, meeting minutes, and at least one sermon critique from three months ago.

The rest trickled in—Trustees Chair, Elders Chair, Social Ministry, Christian Education, Youth Board. Daniel knew them all by name, knew their kids, their hurts, their anniversaries. They were good people. Ordinary people. People trying to steer the church without putting it into a ditch.

Stern and Kress arrived just as the Council settled. Stern wore a sport coat with a badge clipped at the belt; Kress came in full uniform—pressed, respectful, unreadable.

Daniel opened with prayer, his voice catching slightly when he reached the part about "peace in the midst of unrest" and "wisdom in all things." He closed with "your will be done," which suddenly felt more like resignation than faith.

Stern stood. "Thank you for having us. We want to assure you—there is no investigation into the congregation. This is not a criminal inquiry. We're here because we believe being proactive is part of good stewardship, for your people and your facility."

Stern had barely begun when Carl raised his pen. "You're saying we're not suspects, but we're... what? At risk?"

Carl's voice was annoying. But Stern was respectful.

"Potentially," he nodded. "We don't know. But the pattern, all three victims, they're members of this church. It's enough to merit caution."

"But we're the biggest church in town," Carl added. "Most folks in Linden are either members of this church or members of Pastor David's church up on old U.S. 23."

George leaned forward. "It is a bit odd, Carl, don't you think? Claire and Brett?"

"And Dennis," Kress added. "We can't say for sure what's going on just yet. But the connection is very real."

For several minutes, the meeting turned to logistics—doors and locks, Sunday traffic flow, childcare security. Bob asked about signage. The Youth Chair asked about training volunteers in de-escalation. George asked if he should check with the church's insurance company to see what was required for concealed carrying on the property. He also wondered aloud if installing cameras would violate insurance terms.

Kress answered with quiet professionalism, drawing on examples from other towns. "What works best is low-profile, eyes-on-site. Nothing tactical. Just present."

Daniel had already begun drifting away. Still, he spoke, suddenly.

"I've talked to Sherri."

The room quieted. The ceiling fan clicked rhythmically overhead.

"She doesn't want a funeral. She wants him cremated."

Daniel looked down at his feet.

"I asked if she needed anything. She told me no. Just the paperwork."

Someone shifted in their chair. No one spoke.

It was clarifying. Cold and out of place. But clarifying.

"You okay, Pastor?" Bob asked.

"I'm fine," he said, realizing he needed to cover his momentary strangeness. "Just don't worry about getting any of this together in time for a funeral. There won't be one. We have time."

The conversation resumed—protocols, liability, language for the bulletin. Daniel tried to listen. He really did. But Stern's voice blurred. The fluorescent lights above him dimmed in his mind. Thoughts from long ago crept in.

† † †

It was Joliet, Illinois. Summer. Blackstone Avenue.

He remembered it not as a movie, not as a story he'd told, but as something lived—something that still existed, as real as the chair under him now.

The concrete was hot, fractured in long pale webs. He could see the chalk lines of hopscotch on the sidewalk that his little sister, Annie, had drawn the day before, but now half-washed by a passing morning rain. He could smell the low boil of the neighbor's grill, the chain-link fence lining the side yard, the scent of sweet corn, hamburgers, and charcoal.

And he could also see Brent.

A huskier kid than Daniel, fifteen, maybe sixteen, with a tattered Blackhawks cap pulled low over eyes that never once looked uncertain. He walked like the world owed him a tax. He'd watched Daniel toss a tennis ball into the air and catch it. He crossed the street, walked through the yard, shoved Daniel to the ground, and took his baseball glove—like it was his right. Brent said nothing as he walked away.

Daniel was maybe eleven, twelve at most. Narrow-

105

shouldered, summer-skinny, no match for Brent in age or size. But the shame hit harder than the shove. The injustice, even more.

Daniel's friend, Joey, stood at the edge of the walk.

"If you want it back," he said, "go get it."

Daniel's stomach twisted. His glove—Rawlings, red laced, faded leather, his name scrawled in Sharpie—was slipping down the sidewalk, swinging at Brent's side like a trophy. Daniel had received it the year before from his grandmother, who spent some of her food budget to get it and told him to take care of it as if it were a good friend.

The cicadas screamed in the trees. The humidity clung like syrup. Daniel's breath came shallow. Joey didn't move.

Daniel ran.

The charge hit Brent awkwardly—more desperation than precision. They both went down. The sidewalk tore Daniel's arm, his whole body scraping the pavement. He swung. He missed. Then hit. Then missed again.

Brent grunted—low and wolfish. But he laughed, too. The first punch to Daniel's ribs made the world slope. The second put him on the ground. But he got back up. The third landed on his temple, making everything burst into white.

Daniel fell into the side yard's chain-link fence. The metal pressed into his back. He tasted blood.

He looked for Joey. Still on the curb. Watching. Not helping.

A few others had gathered—other kids, a woman on her porch, someone leaning against a car across the street. No one stepped in. No one called out. They just watched, like it was entertainment. Like it wasn't really happening.

Brent moved closer.

Daniel charged but ended up against the fence again. He tried to throw a punch. Then another. Weak. Maybe even pointless by comparison. But something in him had already decided he wasn't quitting. It was his glove. And Brent couldn't have it.

Brent shoved him into the fence, this time much harder than before. Still, Daniel got to his feet and charged, his head down to protect his face. Brent grabbed him around his shoulders and threw him to the ground. He huffed before kicking him in the side and tossing the glove on the ground near Daniel's head.

"My glove's better than this piece of crap, anyway," he mocked and walked away.

Daniel lay there. Breathing deeply. Bleeding. But not crying. One hand reached over to clench the glove. The other pressed against the ground to push himself up. His wrist bore a thin gash, which would later scab into a scar he still carried.

He had lost the fight.

But he had the glove.

† † †

"Pastor?"

Daniel blinked, his right thumb rubbing the scar on his left wrist. The room came back into focus.

Rick Vannert was leaning forward, elbows on the table. "Sorry," Daniel said. "Could you repeat the question?"

"We were wondering if you think it's appropriate to form a security team. Something official. A few trained folks. Quiet rotation during services."

Daniel looked around. At the Treasurer, still gripping his

folder. At Carl, one pen tucked behind his ear, another in motion. At the others around the table, uncertain but attentive.

Behind their faces, Daniel saw chain-link. Sweat. His friend, Joey, standing still.

"If we want to keep the glove," he whispered, "we have to fight for it."

A few heads tilted, confused. But no one asked what he meant. Lately, they'd been used to giving him a little space.

Daniel straightened.

"I think it's probably a good idea."

And no one in the room disagreed.

The words lingered longer than expected, stretching past the usual rhythm of closing remarks. Daniel sensed it—the silence thickening into reflection, even among those who usually rushed toward summary.

Stern, seated beside Kress near the back corner of the table, leaned forward and spoke carefully. "We can help you identify candidates for a security team if that's something you'd want assistance with—members who are already licensed, former military, off-duty law enforcement, that kind of thing."

Daniel nodded. "We have a few who fit that description. And some who don't, but who would still stand in front of a door if asked."

Rick Vannert rubbed his forehead. "I don't love the idea of armed guards in the nave, though."

"You won't have to," Stern said. "That's not what we're talking about. We're talking about watchers. Maybe one or two armed guards outside or in the lobby. But for the most part, more of a presence. Trained eyes. Radios."

"But if something does happen?" Carl asked, his fingers

drumming a rhythmic tap across his notepad. "If someone really does show up here with intent?"

"Then your best defense is already having a system in place," Kress replied. "The first ten seconds determine the next ten minutes."

Daniel spoke again, this time quieter. "After everything that's happened, the congregation won't resist if they understand it's not fear-based. We'll present it as stewardship. Of each other. Of the building. Of this congregation."

George Kessler leaned back in his chair, releasing a long breath. "I never thought we'd be talking about active shooter training in a church council meeting."

Carl nodded. "And yet here we are."

Kress broke the pause. "I worked homicide in Detroit for over a decade. You know what the one constant is, every time something truly terrible happens?"

Heads turned toward him.

He lifted one finger, holding it steady in the air—not to silence them, but to mark it plainly, unmistakably.

"There's always one sentence," he said. "One thing people say, every single time." He paused. "'I didn't think it could happen here.'"

He let the sentence settle like dust.

"And then it does."

The meeting moved into its final ten minutes with an air of reluctant determination. Assignments were made. Carl volunteered to draft a memo to the congregation. The Trustee Chair offered to walk the perimeter locks on Sunday mornings until someone more official was in place. George would call the insurance company.

When the meeting ended, some lingered to talk with Stern

and Kress. Others moved to the parking lot, making quiet remarks along the way about the state of things. Daniel thanked Stern and Kress at the door, offering a handshake with both hands, something he rarely did.

"Thank you for being gracious," he said to Stern.

"Thank you for not fighting it," Stern said. "That alone is rare."

After they left, Daniel wandered the empty hallway toward the sanctuary. It was dark. The stained-glass windows had gone black in the night, their stories unreadable without sunlight. He stepped inside and stood in the middle of the nave, staring down the center aisle.

He remembered preaching from this pulpit when Claire first came to Saint John's. She always sat in the same pew, always alone, always early. He had tried to preach words of belonging that day. He hadn't known yet how much she needed them.

He had the sudden urge to sit where she used to sit. So he did.

The wood was cold through his slacks. The silence seemed to hold its breath around him.

† † †

Back home, much later that night, Daniel stood once more in his backyard.

The fire pit was cold. Only a few flakes of ash clung to the grate—leftovers from the shirt, the collar, the dried blood that had once soaked his side. The wind had shifted, bending the tree limbs just slightly eastward, and for some reason, it made the entire yard feel turned at a new angle.

He crouched beside the pit and stirred the remnants with the fire iron.

Somewhere in the house, the coffeemaker clicked into its automatic cleaning cycle. He had forgotten to turn it off again. That, or his body had remembered something his mind had ignored.

The glove.

He hadn't thought about it in years—decades, really. But tonight, it felt near. Tangible. Like something tucked in the garage under a forgotten bin of Christmas decorations. He wondered if it was still around somewhere. If the Sharpie name had survived time. Or if it had faded away like everything else.

The fight had never left him. Not the pain, not the shame, and certainly not the feeling of being the only one willing to do what needed to be done. What had branded him wasn't the beating—it was the fact that others stood by. That the fence had felt like his only friend.

Some people were built to wait for rescue.

Others, like Daniel, had learned early that rescue wasn't coming.

He had the glove.

And now, years later, he had the gun. The blood. The names. The list. And the voice in his head that still prompted, "If you want it, go."

Back inside, the house was dim. He opened his laptop.

Dr. Eli Webber.

His profile photo stared back from an archived psychology conference. Clean-cut. Red tie. Smile too neat. Credentials listed like armor: trauma specialist, adolescent care, licensed in three states. A list of awards. Two academic publications. A church membership somewhere in Birmingham. Office in West Bloomfield.

Daniel narrowed his eyes.

Webber's name was next on the list Claire had created. And Webber's voice—the smooth, clinical timbre recorded in hushed conversations—still lived inside Daniel's memory like mold in a wall. He had spoken of the girls as patients. Of sedation protocols. Of fees.

Webber had not just been aware of what was happening.

He was making it possible. He was disarming the victims.

Daniel closed the laptop slowly, his fingertips resting on the lid for an extra second. He looked up at the cross hanging above his desk.

The lines of the crucifix were simple. Symmetrical. Wooden. Carved by a man from the congregation who had died six years ago. Daniel had preached a heartfelt sermon, ultimately burying him with a clean conscience. But his conscience seemed distant now. By no means quieter. It was always screaming, even from afar, keeping him awake. Like a bell in thick fog, it was still sounding somewhere.

But it no longer seemed capable of guiding him home.

CHAPTER TWELVE

Daniel stood in the church kitchen with Jeane, pouring water into the coffee maker for the second time that morning. She was at the sink rinsing a glass, her hair pinned up and back. The sunlight coming through the window gave her the kind of glow that made strangers assume she didn't age. But Daniel knew better. She carried things, too. Things only the two of them knew about. That's because she'd been his secretary for nearly fifteen years. It's hard to be together that long and not understand one another like family.

"I'm heading out for a bit," he said, casually.

Jeane glanced over. "I'm sure Dorothea is looking forward to the visit."

"She's at Henry Ford in West Bloomfield," he said. "I should be back sometime around noon."

Jeane nodded. "Give her my love. She's such a sweetheart."

Daniel smiled faintly and jingled his keys. "I shouldn't be more than a few hours."

Leaving the kitchen, his smile fell away.

The drive to Henry Ford was quiet. He kept the radio off and let the hum of the tires and the ticking of his turn signals fill the silence. He did visit Dorothea—sat beside her bed, heard her confession, and read Psalm 27. Well, he pretended to read it. He had it memorized.

He preached a short sermon and then served her the Lord's Supper. Afterward, he asked her to tell him again about her great-granddaughter's violin recital.

"You always listen like it's the first time," she said.

"Maybe it is," Daniel replied. He could joke with Dorothea. She was that way.

After an hour, he prayed with her again, hugged her frail shoulders, and left her half-asleep with the TV humming above her bed.

Then he headed east.

West Bloomfield was unlike Linden in every imaginable way. Linden wore its age with humility—fading signage, cracked sidewalks, secondhand stores that tried to pass as antique shops. West Bloomfield displayed its wealth the way a museum displays relics—climate-controlled, spotless, and meant to be admired from a distance. The homes were palatial. Lawns edged like military formations. Private driveways curled toward facades that looked more like institutions than homes. Daniel passed a black gate with gold inlay and an armed security kiosk. Someone on the other side of that fence probably owned a professional sports team.

His older model Wrangler, dirty and worn, felt like a trespasser.

Daniel turned from West Maple Road onto Orchard Lake Road. He headed north to where Webber's clinic was tucked into a two-story complex wrapped in mirrored glass. He parked across the street at a strip mall, took out a pair of readers with prescription lenses, and settled behind a copy of *Loci Communes*. He didn't need to read it. He just needed to look like he was reading it.

Webber's car—a charcoal gray Porsche 911 GT3—was already in its reserved space, sleek and dustless. A man with money, connections, and comfort. Daniel watched the front entrance and took notes in Melanchthon's manuscript.

Webber came out twice. Once to take a call, pacing the sidewalk. Another time to speak briefly to a woman in a navy suit, laughing before disappearing again. He didn't look behind him once.

Daniel sat still.

And then, without warning, a scent from Orchard Lake Road's busyness caught him off guard—warm pavement, oil, cigarettes, dirt. It carried him back. Hard.

† † †

Danbury, Illinois.

Not the sunny brochure version that most cities prefer to sell. Not even the modest Chamber of Commerce spin. The real one—the one where the air always seemed a little heavy, where the neighborhoods had overgrown alleys, where bugs crawled from the drains, and where peeing in the public pool is just what people did.

Daniel had grown up in a working-class home of barely a thousand square feet. It was a humble, older wood-frame structure fixed beside a tavern, with a gravel parking lot marked by old telephone poles. His bedroom window faced a giant tree that obstructed his view of the tavern but did not protect him from the smell of its dumpster on hot summer nights. Late-night shouts were regular. So were sirens. So were swollen-faced men sleeping on his front porch with their keys still in their hands. He would discover and step over them when he left for school in the morning.

The inside of their home was dusty and busy. The carpeting was stained. The wallpaper peeled at the corners. The linoleum in the kitchen had a permanent dark strip down the center from the refrigerator to the sink.

Every November, a thick Sears catalog would arrive in the mail. He and his sister would lie on the floor together in a narrow hallway leading to the bathroom, circling toys they'd never see, flipping through page after page with cheap pens and folded corners. Sometimes they made wish lists, just in case Santa might surprise them. He never did.

They kept their shoes on a shelf near the door—not out of neatness, but because bugs liked shoes. You shook them out before you put them on. Always. Without thinking.

Spiders. Earwigs. An occasional cockroach. They'd nestle in there during the night, dark and dry. When Daniel was eight or nine, he'd shoved his foot into his shoe beside his bed only to feel something crunch into his sock. When he pulled the shoe off, yellow bug guts coated his toes. He was surprised, but not really. It happened. It was Daniel's fault for not checking. That was the procedure.

He remembered a meaner boy in the neighborhood, Jeremiah, who once peed into a snow cone cup and offered it to Daniel's sister as lemonade. She didn't taste it. Instead, Daniel sent the kid home with a black eye and wearing his own dessert. He cried the whole way. He remembered hiding from Jeremiah's angry and cursing father in the alley bushes.

He remembered the bathroom door that didn't close all the way. He remembered the mold under the bathroom sink. The kind you didn't talk about.

Daniel remembered the way his friend Jay's live-in grandfather cursed at the television when the power flickered. He remembered the nearby elementary school's cracked and overgrown sidewalks, busy as ever, and yet, as if abandoned.

He remembered the filthy shack littered with pornographic magazines and stained mattresses in the woods next to the Hyster plant down the street.

He remembered too many things.

It wasn't until years later—college, and eventually the seminary—that he realized other people didn't live like that. Bugs in your shoes? Drunks on your porch? That wasn't a rite of passage. That was a sign you'd grown up below the line, somewhere between forgotten and ignored.

Someone sent him a link once, back when Facebook still felt like a living room instead of a marketplace. A friend from school who had moved to Chicago.

"Thought this would make you laugh," the message said.

It was an article from a travel blog—one of those half-satirical, half-cruel rankings of "The Worst Places to Live in the Midwest." Danbury had made the list. Number 3.

The writer called it "a rusting tribute to what happens when people give up."

He'd called the town "a bucket of cigarettes and gravel with train tracks running through it."

Daniel didn't read the whole article. He wasn't offended. Just... a little more hollowed out. Not because it was wrong. But because it wasn't.

† † †

Back in the car, Daniel shifted slightly. His hip was getting sore from the angle. Across the street, Webber reappeared—this time walking toward his Porsche, unlocking it with a flick of his wrist.

Daniel noted the time. 11:12 AM.

He waited.

Webber drove north. Daniel gave him a few seconds, then followed. The Porsche moved fast, weaving through traffic like it had somewhere to be. But it wasn't going to some run-down apartment or even a quiet cul-de-sac.

It was going home.

Webber lived in a neighborhood that didn't show up on real estate apps without a password. Daniel drove past mansions with fountains. One house had four garage bays. Another had a mailbox shaped like a bronze eagle with its wings outstretched.

Basketball courts. Flagstone walkways. Imported trees that died in the harsh Michigan winters but were reordered and replanted in the spring.

He passed one gate and saw the number on the stone pillar: 45.

Daniel gave it a wink.

He eased the car to a stop at the park entrance across from the neighborhood and shut off the engine. He opened a bottle of water he'd brought and stared at the house Webber had pulled into.

Big. Quiet. Safe.

Daniel took a long sip.

And then he whispered aloud.

"Probably no bugs in his shoes."

He had spent his childhood surviving. He'd learned not to accept survival as living. And now, here he was, pursuing a man who used anesthetics on girls to make them easier to sell.

Daniel opened Melanchthon's book and wrote something down.

"You carve your way out of the gutter. Or you rot."

He circled the word rot. Then he underlined it. Twice.

But he didn't close the book right away. He let it sit open in his lap while the wind shifted through the trees across the street. A jogger passed. Then a mother with a stroller. Neither looked in his direction. West Bloomfield was that kind of place—everyone had blinders. Wealth made privacy a muscle. People learned not to see what didn't concern them.

Daniel leaned back in his seat and let his eyes drift upward to the clouds. They were light and fast-moving, carried by a high wind he couldn't feel at street level. And yet, up there, things were already changing.

He thought back to the hospital.

He had sat beside Dorothea Connors in her beige room with the too-white sheets and the too-pink curtain dividing her from the room's second bed, which remained empty. She had smiled when he walked in, even though her eyes looked gray with fatigue.

Dorothea had been part of the congregation since before he arrived. She was one of those church women who never missed the potluck, never forgot a birthday card, always asked how your mother was, even if she'd never met her.

She didn't know what Daniel had done. She didn't know that the collar he was wearing was the one he didn't burn after Brett's death—that it had once been in a room soaked with a man's blood.

She had told him about her great-granddaughter again. How she played "Canon in D" on a little violin that looked like a toy. Daniel had nodded and smiled, and part of him had meant it. Another part had already left the room, already counting down the minutes before he could leave to follow Webber.

He had prayed with her. Said the words.

But when he reached the benediction's end—"the Lord look upon you with favor and give you peace"—he realized he wasn't sure who he was representing anymore. Was he in the stead and by the command of Christ? Was he something else?

He trusted what he learned. Lutherans were not Donatists. The validity of his work did not depend on him. The Word is efficacious. It's not the man. It's the Word.

This kept him sane during those moments.

Back in the car, Webber was on the move again.

Daniel followed at a distance, switching lanes only when necessary. He noted the ease with which the man drove—relaxed, no paranoia. He didn't glance in mirrors. He didn't look twice before changing lanes. He moved through the world like someone who believed the rules were always written in his favor.

Webber pulled into a high-end coffee shop—one of those chain-adjacent places that sold $8 lattes and vegan muffins that tasted like soap. Daniel parked two spaces down.

He watched Webber through the windshield as he stood at the counter, chatting with the barista. She laughed. He reached into his wallet—real leather, monogrammed, Daniel guessed—and pulled out a black card.

He stayed only five minutes.

Then it was back to the Porsche and back on the road.

Daniel kept following along with what had become for Webber a do-nothing, lazy day.

The doctor's home sat behind a thick stone wall topped with shrubbery trimmed as neatly as a hedge maze. The gate was wrought iron and motorized. The house itself—a wide, modern estate with huge front windows—sprawled across the lot with arrogant symmetry. The kind of home that had rooms no one used. The kind that had a fridge you didn't touch because it was for display.

Daniel parked farther down the street this time, just far enough to watch the front walk without drawing attention. He brought out *Loci Communes* again, writing down times, movements, and observations.

Webber walks like someone who's never been punched, like someone who's never found bugs in his shoes.

He doesn't check anything. He doesn't look behind him.

No dog. No wife and children. All about himself and his one-night stands.

The longer Daniel watched, the more he saw it: the carelessness. The lightness of Webber's steps. The ease of wealth that had never been challenged. He probably paid someone to cut his fruit. Someone else to sign his birthday cards. Maybe even someone to iron his pillowcases.

Daniel watched, eventually letting his hand drift to the glovebox, where the Colt rested. He didn't open it. Just felt its presence through the Jeep's plastic barrier.

He remembered his baseball glove. He remembered Jeremiah's snow cone. He remembered setting things right.

The drive back took longer. He took back roads, avoiding the highway. He wasn't ready to go back to the office just yet. He wasn't ready to explain his tardiness to Jeane, who'd already left him two messages.

Instead, he drove.

At one point along the way, at a stoplight, a car beside him at the light had its window down.

Music drifted out—soft, warm, and impossibly familiar.

Daniel's hands froze on the wheel.

Sister Golden Hair. America.

His sister, Annie, loved that song. She used to hum it while brushing her hair in the spotted bathroom mirror. Sometimes she'd sing it barefoot and loud in the kitchen, spinning like the stained linoleum was a stage.

He hadn't heard it in years. And just like that, Annie was there again. Alive in the passenger seat. Laughing. Young. Not pale and weightless beneath hospice blankets.

The light turned green. The song disappeared behind him. And his thoughts went back.

† † †

Danbury.

He must've been ten. Maybe younger.

It was summer, and their house's basement had flooded from a plugged sewage drain near the old washing machine. His mother had thrown towels down until they ran out. Then she'd used the kids' clothes. Nothing was cleaned up for two days. The stench betrayed it.

To escape the smell, Annie had gone outside barefoot. The back steps—rotting wood barely holding together—were slick with algae. She slipped and landed in a puddle of flies. She screamed. But not for the flies. For something else.

Daniel heard her and came running from the neighboring yard. And that's when he saw it—just beside the steps near the edge of the driveway's gravel, something moving.

He looked closer.

It was a baby bird. Or what had been a baby bird. Now it was a wet, matted carcass full of maggots, its eyes gone, its body already half rotted away.

He didn't say anything. He just acted.

He went to the shed, rusted and leaning. He moved a few bikes with flat tires and came out with a shovel.

"I'll take care of it," he told her.

Annie had already scrambled back.

Daniel didn't bury it. Not right away. Instead, he prayed over it, just as his grandmother had taught him. Then, he scooped it up with the blade, walked it out into the yard, dug a hole, and buried it.

Annie had followed along in the makeshift funeral. She bowed her head and prayed, too.

She died ten years ago from ovarian cancer. It took her fast. He didn't visit as much as he should have toward the end. He couldn't. He lived four hundred miles away. Sometimes, even now, he still sees her at the edge of his peripheral vision during prayer—like she's bowed beside him again, hands folded.

"The world won't clean itself," Daniel told her that day. "But God can use us to help. When He wants to."

✝ ✝ ✝

Daniel pulled into the church's parking lot a little before 3:00 PM. Jeane's car was already gone. He remembered she'd said she was going to her daughter's condo in Brighton for dinner. He didn't check his messages. Had he, he would've learned that she did.

He only stayed for a few minutes before heading home. He walked inside and poured a glass of water.

In the hallway, the cross above the door gleamed in the

dipping sunlight filtering through the sidelight window.

Daniel paused there for a long moment.

He thought of Claire.

Of Brett.

Of Dennis.

And now, of Webber.

Four names. The same path. He wasn't sure if its pavers were made from righteousness or rot, grace or judgment.

What he did know was that the world wouldn't clean itself, and that he'd do a little more research on Webber's home. Webber wouldn't see him coming. A short moment, as always, allowing for confession. But no monologue. No discussion. It would be quick, not messy, like Dennis.

For Daniel, the swiftness was grace enough.

CHAPTER THIRTEEN

The coffee shop on the corner of East Main and Ridge wasn't crowded, but it wasn't quiet either. The hiss of the espresso machine, the clink of ceramic mugs, and the low hum of indie folk music filled the space with a kind of low-frequency busyness. It was the kind of place where teenagers studied for exams they wouldn't remember in a year and retirees sipped while quietly judging everyone who walked through the door.

Stern and Kress sat in the back near the fireplace that hadn't been lit since March. Their table was small and circular, cluttered with napkins, two black coffees, and a notepad. Kress had brought the pad. Stern had brought the tension.

"I've been thinking about the timing," Stern said, reaching for the notepad and flipping it open. "Claire. Brett. Dennis. Roughly six weeks apart."

Kress took a sip of his coffee and frowned. "And all tied to that church of yours."

Stern didn't correct him. "Not mine. But yeah. Saint John's."

"Three deaths. All within two months. Two in Linden. One in Fenton."

"No suspects. No viable witnesses. No clear motive."

"No evidence tying them together," Kress added, "unless you're looking through the stained-glass window."

Stern tapped the notepad. "I suppose we do have a pattern."

"Just the church," Kress said. "Not the killings. Not yet."

"One blunt force trauma and a broken neck. And two with .45 holes. All three were members at Saint John's. It's pattern enough for me. If you're okay with it, I'm sending it up."

Kress's eyes lifted. "To Lansing?"

Stern nodded. "Michigan State Police. I'm not dumping the case. But they need to be looped in. I don't want them looking over our shoulder three weeks from now, asking why we didn't call them sooner."

"You expecting them to take it over?"

"Not unless it gets worse."

Kress looked out the window. A mother was helping her son climb into a minivan with a dented bumper. He wore a Spider-Man backpack and held a half-eaten muffin in his hand.

"So, what's worse?" Kress asked. "Four bodies? Five?"

Stern didn't answer right away. "Worse is when we stop being surprised."

The waitress came by and asked if they wanted a refill. Kress said yes. Stern declined.

"Let me ask the question," Kress said, lowering his voice. "Maybe the FBI?"

"Not yet," Stern replied. "We're not across state lines. And we've got nothing to attract the feds—no conspiracy charges, no civil rights angle."

Kress chuckled. "But we do have a church. If it were Christopher Wray's FBI, we might have a domestic terrorism case."

They both laughed.

"Let's just stick with the State Police. They need to know. And they'd be the ones to invite the feds… if it comes to that."

Kress grunted in agreement. "You writing it up?"

"I already did. Sent it yesterday. I'm meeting with Lieutenant Green at the post in Flint on Monday."

Kress leaned back, chair creaking under his frame. "You got a theory?"

Stern looked down at the coffee. "Not a good one."

Kress waited.

"And it's probably the same one as you."

"We worked together long enough," Kress said. "But we'll see."

Stern continued. "It feels surgical. The pacing. The targets. Whoever this is, they're picking names from a very specific list. They tried it without a gun. But it didn't work out well. Claire was the first. Pastor Michaels was next, but he survived. After those two, the perp got a gun, a .45. Brett was relatively clean. But Dennis got out of hand. He wasn't expecting a fight. That one got loud."

"And messy," Kress added. "I think it's someone they all knew."

Stern nodded. "I think so, too. At a minimum, he knew about them. Knew where they'd be. When they'd be alone."

Kress took another sip of coffee and said nothing.

† † †

Across town, Daniel stared at the blinking cursor on his laptop screen like it owed him something. The Word document was still titled "Draft," but the page was blank except for a single phrase: Blessed are the merciful.

He'd typed it an hour ago.

And then he'd sat. And stared.

The office was still. The old wall clock ticked like a metronome, punctuating the silence. Outside, a lawnmower hummed somewhere in the neighborhood. Birds chattered in the trees beyond the parking lot. It was all normal. All safe.

Except for the weapon in his desk drawer.

And the notebook on his desk with paragraphs of planning.

He stood, stepped to the window, and looked out toward the street. A girl on a bike rolled by. A jogger followed behind her. No one looked toward the church. No one noticed him in the window.

He turned back to his desk. The words on the screen glared.

Blessed are the merciful.

He highlighted the line. Deleted it. Then typed: "Let justice roll down like waters…"

Then deleted that too.

He closed the laptop.

The sanctuary was empty. The lights were off. Daniel stepped inside and let the heavy air settle over him. The stained glass was dim, its colors muted by clouds. He walked down the center aisle and stopped at the pew where Claire used to sit—sixth row from the front, lectern side.

He sat.

He remembered her voice. Her laugh. He remembered her confession that she always hesitated before the Creed, like she needed to steel herself for something holy.

He closed his eyes.

Nothing came. No prayers. No comfort.

Just the image of Webber's face through the scope of his imagination.

He stood, walked to the chancel, crossed into the sanctuary, and laid a hand on the altar.

"Do you still hear me?" he asked.

The silence answered in kind.

Jeane found him back in his office later that afternoon. He was sitting at his desk, flipping through a hymnal without really reading it.

"Do you need anything, Pastor?" she asked, surprising him. "I'm going to leave a little early today."

Daniel looked up. "No," he said before a lingering pause. "I'm good. Thank you. Have a good night."

She leaned away as if to leave, but then immediately turned back. Putting her head back through his doorway, "We've worked together for a long time," she said. "You've never been a very good liar."

Daniel forced a smile. "If anyone would know that, Jeane, it's you."

"Yes, it's me."

"I'm just… heavy," he said. "Still thinking about Claire."

"Well," Jeane softened. "You were there. I would expect that."

"I suppose so."

"You need to know we're all still thinking about her."

She reached into her bag and pulled out a card. "We got this today. From her Aunt Sally in Texas. She said Claire had talked about the church often. Said it was the only place she truly felt safe, felt like she was at home."

Daniel took the card but didn't open it. The words only brought more heartache.

She felt safe. She trusted Daniel.

"Let the Lord comfort you," Jeane said. "Just like he

comforted Claire, like you tell us he's caring for all of us."

Daniel didn't respond.

"None of us is carrying this on our own. You don't have to carry it alone, either."

"I'm not," he said, betraying a tinge of discomfort.

But they both knew he was.

"I'm fine," he added. "Just tired."

† † †

Daniel made a surprise visit to Elsie Durham that evening. He should have worked on his sermon, but he didn't. His head was too clouded. He was too eager to get to Webber.

Elsie answered the door slowly, leaning heavily on her walker.

"Pastor Michaels," she said, voice rough but warm. "I wasn't expecting company."

"I was out walking," Daniel lied. "Thought I'd check in. See how you're doing. See if you needed anything."

"Well, you caught me watching *Matlock*. Come on in." The Mahalia Jackson album was playing on low in the background, as always.

They sat for a little while. She offered tea, which he declined, and they spoke quietly about the weather, about Marcie and the kids, and how Marcie couldn't bring herself to clear Brett's things from the bedroom just yet.

"Marcie is taking things hard," she said, more to the *Matlock* episode than to Daniel. "The kids, too."

Daniel shifted in his seat.

"He was a good boy," she continued. "Changed, maybe. A little lost sometimes. But a good boy."

Daniel nodded, unsure if he was agreeing or confessing.

Before he left, Elsie reached out and touched his sleeve.

"Thank you for not forgetting about me," she said.

"I could never forget about you, Elsie," he replied, and meant it.

When he left, he sat in the car for five minutes before turning the key.

At home, he changed into more comfortable clothes.

He lifted the Colt from the drawer and laid it on a towel on the desk.

He checked the magazine. Clean. Full.

He cleaned the weapon again anyway.

Then he retrieved the flash drive and opened the laptop.

He found the file he was looking for:

Webber_Clinic_Claire.wav.

With it, a readable twin:

Webber_Clinic_Claire.txt.

He double-clicked the text file.

Within, Claire explained the audio file he was about to hear.

> The other recordings are self-explanatory. This one deserved an explanation. I met Dr. Webber at Harbor. Pastor D introduced him to me. It seemed like he was just visiting. Like Pastor D was giving him a tour or something. He said he worked with high-risk girls, and that most of his experience was with trauma patients. He was a really nice guy. Good looking, too.

> He started doing sessions with some of the residents in the staff lounge. I helped decorate the room so that it was more comfortable. He really seemed like

a saint. Eventually he didn't, though. It was like he started feeling too polished, especially when he took an interest in me. He seemed really calculated.

After I learned something was happening at Harbor, I don't remember when that was exactly, I played along with Dr. Webber. I acted unsure about myself. I really played up the shyness. Which, if you know me, wasn't hard. He told me one day that he offered pro bono sessions. He said he could see me privately, if I wanted, and that I wouldn't have to pay him. He said it's what he was at Harbor to do. He wanted to help girls who needed it, and since I was there doing the same thing, he figured he'd offer the same to me. That's how he put it. I didn't have to have insurance. I wouldn't pay him. He was volunteering his time, just like me.

"Don't do it," Daniel whispered aloud before continuing to read.

I said yes. My plan was pretty simple. I'd keep letting him think I was vulnerable. I would let him think he had a possible target. Then I would try to find something. I already had a recorder hidden in the lounge. I would just need to hit record. But he scheduled me at his office in West Bloomfield way down on Orchard Lake Road. He insisted that we do it there, especially since I wasn't a resident at Harbor. I don't know why. But I couldn't say no, not after already agreeing. I mean, I really played up the loneliness, and he was persistent. He kept asking me to make an appointment with his secretary.

I ended up making an appointment that next week. It was a Thursday. His secretary took me into his office. The session, if you can call it that, lasted about thirty minutes. Before it really got started, he left to get a form. It was some kind of waiver agreeing to pro bono treatment. I planted the micro-recorder under the couch while he was gone. I definitely prayed the cleaning folks wouldn't find it. It only holds about five hours of audio. There was nothing obvious at first. Like I said, the first thirty minutes were basic crazy people questions. He asked me questions about my life. I was honest. My life sucks. And I figured if he was actually an okay guy, I'd give the therapy a shot.

Daniel sighed.

I went back for another session that next week. Thankfully the recorder was still there. He's not an okay guy. I'm putting him on the list. I got about four hours of him being himself when no one else was around. He took some calls. He said so much that I have no doubt. I heard him use Brett's name. I think he was one of the callers. They talked about how much a few of the girls weighed, and how much to give them without killing them. Dr. Webber asked what they had on hand. He gave dosages for Midazolam and Ketamine. I had to look those words up. Midazolam is used before surgeries to relax patients. It also causes amnesia. I'm guessing he gives it to reduce resistance and screw up a girl's memories. It acts fast, too. It sounds like he has both pills and injections. Ketamine causes disorientation. It can be used to subdue someone without knocking them out. It's a lot harder to get it legally, but it's not impossible for a guy like Dr. Webber. He can get it. And it looks like he does.

Daniel tapped his finger and looked toward the Colt.

One of the other calls shed some light on where they

take the girls. Unfortunately, I never found out where it is. It sounds like they go to the same place. From what Dr. Webber said, I'm pretty sure it's a motel somewhere in Flint. That's it. Either way, I know what he is and what he does. He's the one scouting the girls. He's even making referrals to Harbor. He's the one who decides who gets taken and who doesn't. And he's the one getting the drugs, making sure the girls do what they're supposed to. Some customers want a sedated girl. Some want one who at least seems alive. He can give them both.

The journal went on for another paragraph. Daniel quit reading and played the audio file. It opened with a light static hum. Then Claire's voice.

"Test, test, test… Okay, I guess we're recording now."

He heard a muffled thump and hiss as Claire put the recorder under the couch.

Daniel listened for a little while, his gut burning as he did. Claire told Dr. Webber things she'd told him, things he'd tried to help her reconcile.

He nudged the slider ahead forty minutes. He heard mundane sounds of an office—keyboard clacks, phones, pages turning. Then, at 1:12:47, it started. It was everything Claire described. He listened.

Webber's voice was clear. The others were muted, somewhat distorted. Brett's name. The drugs. A girl's weight and a dosage recommendation for each drug. Then another girl and some calculations. Rooms 144 and 213. An unnamed place on the north side of Flint.

"She's older," Webber said. "Sixteen. Maybe seventeen. Parents sent her to Harbor. They just wanted to be rid of her. Too much trouble for everyone. She's already on a mood stabilizer, so don't mess up the Midazolam dose. You don't want her dead."

More shuffling.

Then, as if bored, "Yeah, yeah, I'll meet you there. Don't come here. I just got it. I can bring it to you."

Daniel nudged the slider forward again through silence. Another call. Another reference. Another girl.

Listening, there was a surge of invigoration.

Daniel didn't plan like a killer. He planned like a pastor preparing a liturgy.

When a pastor presides at the altar, he does so passively. He stands *in persona Christi*—in the stead and by the command of Christ. The liturgy is not his performance. It carries him. He speaks, but the voice is Christ's. He moves, but the action belongs to another. That's why he wears vestments—to disappear into the office. To be veiled. The people are not to see the man. They are to see God. He is moving and working for them.

Daniel had said those words to confirmands. He had spoken them in Bible study. He had preached them from the pulpit. He believed them.

But lately—here, now—something else was happening. His planning and actions felt liturgical. They, too, were ordered and reverent. His words and thoughts sounded like rites. His deeds were as ceremonies. Together, they carried him the way worship did. They were precise, and when executed rightly, would deliver something. Not grace. Not peace. But something else.

Maybe—just maybe—he still stood in the stead of Christ. But the Christ in question did not come to suffer this time. He came as the Pantocrator. He came to judge.

He'd already labeled the top of a note page "EW." He opened a folder with the same name on his screen. It was a sequence of PDFs and screenshots: public property records, real estate photos, satellite images from Google Maps. Webber's house. Its layout. Fence lines. Driveway approach. Back entryway. He clicked through slowly, jotting in the notebook.

> The front gate is cameraed, of course. Probably high-resolution. Likely equipped with motion sensors. But the house itself, that's the real question. The front entrance is exposed, flanked by large, clear windows. Coming in through the front door wouldn't be a good idea.

Daniel zoomed in on a Google Maps image.

The side yard. A long, curving path lined with boxwoods. It ran the length of the house and ended at a small patio that abutted a wall. In the real estate photos, it was a wall with floor-to-ceiling windows, the kind of luxury that assumed you had nothing to hide and that your neighborhood was more than secure. The windows appeared to open in a quarter section at the bottom.

He scrolled back through the listing photos for a better image. There—small black tabs along the interior frame. Vent latches. They're meant to open inward for airflow. He jotted it down. These were older model casement windows, just like the office windows at the church. If unlocked, they'd swing open with a push. If locked—well, a painter's multi-tool could pry the latch open without much noise. He'd seen a YouTube video about it last year on his phone when he got locked out of his office by mistake. He had to work at it a little, but he managed to climb in without breaking anything. However, he did knock a few things from the file cabinet beneath the window.

That's where he'd come in. Almost too providential. And he was okay with it.

He scribbled more into the notebook.

> Get there before Webber. Be ready and waiting. Approach from the west. Park at the nature preserve lot. Walk east on foot, across the irrigation ditch. Enter the side yard and get to the windows.

He tapped the pencil against his chin.

Webber likely had cameras everywhere. At least one on the drive. Maybe one on the back patio. But probably not on the side yard—too narrow, too private, and obscured from street view. A blind spot, maybe. One Daniel planned to use.

If he could manage it, he'd go just after sunset. There would be enough light to find his way along the preserve trail. And if any unknown cameras were looking his way, there wouldn't be enough light for detail. But before doing any of this, he'd have to observe Webber's movements a few more times to get this right.

He continued scribbling.

> No visitations or meetings tomorrow. Watch him again. Where does he park in the garage? What time does he usually get home? Was the last time an afternoon excursion, or is it typical? Go back and watch again on Friday. Walk to the church and ask to borrow Jeane's car. Just in case.

Daniel wanted things to be clean this time. He wanted a clean entry with no mess. But also, no trace.

The man lives like he's untouchable, he thought. *But he isn't. He isn't alert. He isn't prepared.*

Daniel narrowed his eyes.

What if he sets off an alarm?

"Alarms have delays," he whispered aloud. "Ten, maybe fifteen seconds. Enough time to get in and get close."

Daniel expected to be inside, ready and waiting for Webber to arrive. But if he couldn't, if he had to break in and get out, he'd do it with Webber distracted—maybe watching TV, maybe cooking, maybe pouring another glass of whatever he used to celebrate another windfall from what he did to the girls.

Daniel would be on him before he even stood up.

He zoomed out on the Google Maps image. It was everything he needed in view.

The nature preserve lot and its trail.

The spacious neighborhood.

The way in.

The house.

He circled a word he'd already written.

Friday.

He would decide for sure that day. If it couldn't be quick and clean—no fight, no shouting, no mess like Dennis—he'd choose a different way.

But still, he'd choose. Webber would die for his crimes, and Daniel would bring the benediction.

He closed the laptop and turned out the light.

CHAPTER FOURTEEN

The knock came before 7:30 AM.

Daniel wasn't dressed yet. But he was awake. He was in his study when the sound at the front door startled him like a cold pinprick.

He moved down the hall, suspiciously, eventually looking through the sidelight glass.

Marcie Durham.

He hesitated, hand on the knob. He hadn't seen her since the funeral. She'd taken the kids to Missouri. But it seemed she returned.

He opened the door.

"Marcie."

She looked thinner. Paler. Hair pulled back in a loose knot. No makeup. No jewelry. Just a plain gray sweatshirt and jeans that hung on her like they didn't quite know her shape anymore. In one hand, she held a small envelope.

"Hi, Pastor."

"Come on in," he said, stepping aside.

She paused. "I won't stay long."

"Still—please." He gestured again.

She entered slowly, eyes scanning the house with the gentle unease of someone intruding where they didn't want to be. Daniel offered her the couch. She sat stiffly on the edge, like she was bracing for something.

He sat in the recliner across from her.

"I know it's early," she said, voice flat. "I should've called first. I just needed to do this in person. And I needed to do it today."

Daniel nodded, unsure of what "this" and "it" meant. He glanced down at the envelope in her hand.

"We're moving to Missouri," she said. "I already found a home. With Brett's life insurance, we can live debt-free just around the corner from my parents."

His brows lifted slightly.

"Back to Missouri," he said.

"The kids… they need something different. They need… less of this."

Daniel said nothing.

She looked toward the front window. "I love this town. Really. It's home, even after… everything. I thought maybe we'd stay. That we could heal here."

He watched her closely. Her voice wasn't accusatory. Just worn.

"But everything is just too much, now. Every street, every Sunday. Even the grocery store."

Daniel's stomach tightened.

"I don't think I can raise the kids in a house—in a town—where their father was murdered, where everyone around us says they understand our pain and then pretend to do so."

She turned back to him.

"Do you know what I mean?"

Daniel hesitated. "I think I do."

She studied him. "How can you stay here after being there?"

He didn't reply.

"You were there when Claire died. You were in the same room with whoever did it. What is that doing to you, Pastor?"

Daniel's lips parted, but he didn't speak.

"It has to be doing something to you."

She looked down at the envelope and placed it on the coffee table.

"I wrote a letter," she said. "For the congregation. You don't have to read it in church. But maybe post it in the narthex. Or the newsletter. I don't know. I just want them to know how much I appreciated them. Even after… everything."

Daniel reached for it. His hand trembled slightly.

She continued, quieter now. "This place, this church, is family. I'm guessing there are things I didn't know about Brett. I don't think people die the way he did without having secrets. But still, he was ours. He was my husband. He was a father. He was a son."

She paused.

"He was a little boy once," she continued. "And every little boy is worth mourning. Don't you think?"

Daniel nodded slowly.

"I think people forget that," she added. "It's easier, I guess."

She stood. "Anyway. We leave on Sunday. My dad's flying in tomorrow to help with the truck."

Daniel rose, instinctively reaching a hand toward her shoulder, but stopped short.

"I'll let the church know you're moving," he said instead. "We'll pray for the transition."

She offered a small, practiced smile. "Thanks."

He opened the door for her. She stepped out, but then turned, one foot still on the threshold.

"You're a good pastor," she said. "You've been so good to me and my family. Even when things were hard. You listened."

He felt that like a punch.

"Brett liked you a lot," she added. "If he were still here, he'd hope you were okay."

Daniel's throat tightened.

"I am."

He lied.

She studied him a moment longer, then nodded and walked to her car. He watched her pull away until the vehicle disappeared past the tree line.

He closed the door and leaned against it.

The envelope sat on the table like a dare. He didn't open it. He didn't even touch it. Instead, he stared at the rug beneath it, eyes unfocused.

The coffee pot clicked in the kitchen. Its burner shut down with a soft pop, like a period on the morning's punctuation.

Daniel moved back to the study, carrying the letter with him. He put it into the drawer, laying it on his notebook.

But something had shifted. Something was pressing on his lungs.

He slumped into the desk chair and let the silence crawl up the walls. Marcie's voice echoed, "He was a little boy once."

So was Daniel.

He thought of Annie and the shovel. Of the rot. Of the whispered prayers over dead things.

Of Brent and the glove. Of Joey, standing still on the sidewalk.

He stood and stepped across the hallway into the bathroom. The mirror was still fogged slightly from his earlier shower, the corners streaked from half-hearted wiping. He stared at himself, arms limp at his sides.

His face looked older this morning. Not tired—hardened. His eyes, once so easy and soft behind the pulpit, now held a kind of tempered cold.

He pulled up his shirt.

A large, ugly bruise was still darkening along his left ribs. Dennis had landed that hit just before dying. Daniel could still feel the sickening crack of elbow against bone.

He touched it gently, then let the shirt fall. It was still sore.

He gripped the edge of the sink and leaned forward, staring harder into the glass.

"I could stop," he whispered.

It wasn't a prayer. Not quite. But it wasn't *not* a prayer either.

"I could let the system catch up. I could pass the drive to Stern. I could leave it in their hands and believe that's the best place for it."

He went back into his study and dropped into his chair.

"But I don't believe it."

The whisper sharpened.

He opened the drawer and lifted the Colt, checked it with muscle memory, then laid it gently back down.

He thought about Missouri and kids starting over. He thought about what it means to build something new with broken parts.

He thought about Webber and the needle-thin voice on that recording.

He pressed his palms flat against the desk and closed his eyes.

"He was a little boy once."

There was a long pause.

And then his eyes opened.

"But he still had to die."

Daniel dressed deliberately.

The desk drawer still open, he looked again at Marcie's envelope. It was daring him to be the kind of man who'd read it, a man with a softer heart.

But he didn't read it. Instead, he closed the drawer and turned off the lights.

He locked the door and stepped into the morning light with the quiet certainty of a man who'd chosen judgment.

Today would be the last day of surveillance.

Soon, Dr. Eli Webber would meet him and be judged.

CHAPTER FIFTEEN

The lot at the preserve was empty.

Daniel pulled the Wrangler into the farthest corner, beneath a canopy of old oaks leaning eastward from wind and time. The engine ticked as it cooled. His eyes moved slowly across the dashboard, from the folded-up trail map wedged beside the console to the sealed water bottle in the cup holder.

He wore a black pullover. His clerical collar peeked above it, crisp, white, and defiant. The uniform of his office would go with him through branches and over lawns. It would climb into and through a window, entering the home of a man marked for judgment. It didn't just mark the man, Daniel Michaels. It communicated his ordination. He was called. Sent. A servant in the stead and by the command.

And now, he killed with the authority of office.

That belief was dangerous. He knew that. He felt its weight. But it didn't leave him, and he certainly didn't push it away.

He opened the glove box and reached for the Colt. It gleamed with maintenance, ready and patient. He tried slipping it into his front waistline. But still sitting in the Jeep, it pressed up and against his ribs. Whatever vein runs through the center of the human body, he could feel it pulsating from the pressure. For a moment, he couldn't tell if it was his pulse, or if the Colt was alive. He slipped it into his back waistline.

Daniel checked the trailhead again. Still empty. He locked the vehicle and moved out, his feet crunching into gravel. The preserve was quiet, save for a few songbirds and the rustle of distant branches.

Dusk was spreading.

He moved east along the narrow trail. It was an easy jaunt. Of course it was. This was West Bloomfield. There were no stones to trip him or fallen branches to avoid. And now, with dusk as his ally, his only concern was to get to and from Webber during that space between the day and its ending, after the retirees and before the teenagers.

It was a window carved for righteousness.

The air smelled of moss and cedar. Leaves crunched beneath him like fragile bones. He walked for five minutes before veering off toward the fence line he'd noted in his previous surveillance—a back corner of the neighborhood where the preserve's trail edged close to the property boundaries of the estates beyond.

Webber's home rose beyond the trees, its roof just visible through the thinning green.

Daniel reached the irrigation ditch and stepped across carefully. He slipped, but just barely. On the other side, he moved through a break in the brush and found the small side yard that skirted Webber's property. No gate. Just a hedge line and a narrow flagstone path curving alongside the house.

Even though he was entirely out of sight to the other properties, he moved low, glancing once toward the far windows—floor-to-ceiling glass polished to mirror quality. The house was lit from within, but sparsely. A soft glow came from the kitchen. A lamp glowed in the den. The rest of the home remained dark. It gave the house the strange quality of a jet-setter's wife being awake but alone. She wanted someone. Anyone. She wanted attention.

He reached the side of the house and crouched near the small casement windows he'd marked before. They were older—single-paned, framed in white vinyl, just like the church's office windows. A row of them ran beneath the line of the countertop on the far wall of what looked like a home office or study. From the listing photos, it hadn't been obvious. A person can get turned around in an unknown place, especially in photos. But now, just feet away, he could see the details—bookshelves, a desk, an armchair draped with a gray throw.

He touched the lowest window.

It was locked. As expected.

But he'd already been in this situation. A minute of quiet jostling, and the lock gave with a tiny click.

He opened the quarter window. It slid dryly, a sound easily swallowed by the giant home as well as the ambient hum of neighborhood sprinklers kicking on in the distance.

Daniel climbed through. One leg. Then the other. He fell forward lightly, landing in a crouch behind the desk.

He was inside.

He glanced around the room for tiny red lights—or anything that might suggest he tripped a camera's motion sensor or triggered an alarm. Seeing nothing, he waited anyway, remaining still for several minutes.

His breath was measured. His hands didn't shake. He waited for a dog's bark, a voice, a sound—any hint that someone knew he was there. Nothing happened. No one came. The house remained quiet.

Daniel moved slowly through the office, surveying his surroundings. Books on psychology lined the wall—heavy texts, like his theology books. And yet, not like his books.

These were mostly unread, their spines uncreased. His were well-worn.

Webber's were about trauma therapy. One was about body language. Another was on pharmacological ethics. Daniel shook his head when he saw it. For him, this was hypocrisy stacked and alphabetized.

He stepped into the hallway beyond.

The hardwood floor creaked beneath his soles. A central rug ran the corridor's length, masking his movement. A staircase rose to his left. Straight ahead, the open concept of the main living space unfolded—massive windows, stainless steel appliances, leather furniture arranged around a minimalist fireplace.

He found his position behind a wide structural beam in the hallway, just inside the threshold between the office and the den. It gave him a clear line of sight to the front entrance and a view into the kitchen.

He would wait here.

He checked his watch. 6:42 PM.

The three times he pursued Webber, he usually returned between 6:45 and 7:15. He was always alone. He was never in a rush. He parked his Porsche in the same bay in the garage. Sometimes he'd unload something from the passenger seat before closing the garage door. From the listing photos, Daniel knew he'd emerge from the mudroom that led into the kitchen.

The garage door sound came at 6:56.

Daniel tightened his grip on the Colt, drawing it low and to his side.

It took longer than expected. Still, and as expected, Webber entered through the mudroom. He wore a fitted charcoal blazer, unbuttoned, and carried a Styrofoam cooler in his hands. His shoes clacked on the tile.

He nudged the garage's interior door closed with his left foot and walked past Daniel's line of sight into the kitchen. He placed the cooler on the island and opened the liquor cabinet just below it. A bottle and a rock glass emerged.

Scoresby.

Seriously? Bottom shelf garbage? Not GlenDronach? Or Dalmore? Not even Glenfiddich or Glenlivet?

This man deserved to die.

Daniel moved.

Soft steps. Steady. Colt drawn and angled down.

He rounded the beam and stepped into the kitchen threshold.

Webber hadn't seen him yet.

Webber turned slightly toward the sink, added a little water, and sipped. His phone rang. A harsh buzz on the granite. He glanced at it with rolling eyes and a frown. He answered with a tired, "Yeah."

A muffled voice filled the momentary silence.

Daniel froze mid-step.

"What? Now?" Webber asked.

More of the voice.

"I can't get out there tonight."

A pause.

"Yes. I brought it home. I've got it here."

Another pause.

"What happened to what I already gave you?"

The voice on the other end was getting louder. Maybe angrier.

"That's too much. You're using too much. You have to let it wear off. Give the girls some food. Some water, too, and then put 'em in a room to sleep it off."

Daniel shifted in the darkness.

"All four rooms are being used? Then go ask Manny for another room. It's not like he's all booked up."

The conversation was getting heated.

"Just go ask… Yes… All four rooms?… That's a lot of girls… Yes… Yes… Yeah, but double. If so, I'll leave here in five. Otherwise, you have to tell those guys to come back a different night. Yeah… Okay… Make sure Manny has my money. I'll leave the stuff with him."

Daniel seethed. He knew what was happening.

"I'll be there in an hour."

Webber hung up, took another drink, and walked toward the hall.

Daniel stepped backward silently, returning behind the beam, the Colt steady at his side. But he no longer intended to use it. Not in that moment. His plan had changed.

Webber moved past him, oblivious, and vanished into a side room—likely the bedroom. A few minutes passed. Daniel heard a drawer open. A zipper. Another muffled sound.

Then Webber reemerged. This time, a black leather duffel swung from his left hand. The kind doctors use for house calls.

He moved back through the kitchen. He grabbed the cooler as he passed the island and made his way through the mudroom.

The garage door hummed again.

Daniel ran back to the office window, fell through it, leaving it open behind him. He ran as fast as he could, around hedges and through lawns, eventually getting to the trail. What took five minutes to walk took barely two in a sprint.

Webber had diverted. He was going to the motel in Flint.

He was taking a new batch of medications. They were in the cooler. Four rooms were being used at the motel. Not two, as Claire suspected. All four would be occupied tonight.

Four customers. Four girls.

The Wrangler came into view.

He started the engine and pulled out onto the main road. He turned toward where he'd hoped Webber would be.

If he's going to Flint, he thought, *he'll head to 75 and go north.*

He caught Webber's Porsche a few streets over, just as he was making his way toward the interstate onramp.

He followed from a safe distance.

Webber didn't drive like he was in a hurry. In fact, he drove slower—annoyed, deliberate—in his familiar untouchableness. Nothing would happen until he arrived.

Daniel stayed three car lengths back. He reached to the Wrangler's aftermarket JVC stereo, tapping at its screen, choosing a Spotify playlist.

Sleeping on the Blacktop by Colter Wall kicked in first. The slow rhythm matched the pulse in Daniel's hands as they gripped the wheel. He let it wash over him as the Jeep gained speed. Webber's Porsche moved ahead like a scalpel, weaving lazily through slower traffic.

Daniel kept steady.

The next track slid in—Brent Cobb's *Black Creek*. A backroads hymn. It reminded Daniel of Danbury. Not the rot, but the spaces in between. The soft, small mercies. Annie's laughter. Gas station lunches with neighborhood pals, a pack of boys rolling through on bicycles like a biker gang. Lighting and pretending to smoke incense sticks like cigarettes.

Traffic thickened around Grand Blanc. Daniel slowed

with it, tapping the steering wheel along to the drumline in *The Railroad* by Goodnight, Texas. It moved like an old engine climbing toward judgment. A song that didn't care if you were innocent or guilty—only that you were going to escape the chain gang, no matter what.

Webber hadn't checked his mirrors once.

South of Flint, a truck kicked gravel into Daniel's windshield. The road scarred over from construction. The Wrangler rattled harder, and the next song answered—*Dig Gravedigger Dig*. Corb Lund's voice was carried atop the steel guitar. Daniel could feel the weight building in his chest, pulsing with each mile marker.

Then came *Hurricane* by The Band of Heathens.

He hadn't heard it in a while. He didn't listen to music much anymore. He didn't need to. He already had a song in his head most of the time. A soundtrack of sorts to his blurring life.

But *Hurricane* filled the space for now. It spilled from the speakers with the weight of memory, slow and humid. Something was coming, whether anyone was ready or not.

He left it playing.

They drove north. Then slightly west. I-75 merged with U.S. 23. It wasn't long before the signs turned grimier and the roads were cratered more than usual.

The music lowered as Daniel's hand tapped at the steering wheel's volume control.

They exited at Pierson Road.

Daniel kept pace.

The streetlights flickered. The businesses grew bars on their windows. Webber's Porsche looked wildly out of place. They passed abandoned storefronts, boarded restaurants, a gutted Rite Aid.

Then, after a slight bend in the road, on the north side, a motel.

It was exactly as Daniel had imagined for the previous fifty-five miles.

Two stories. Peeling paint. Flickering sign.

"PINEVIEW INN — WEEKLY RATES — FREE WI-FI"

Webber turned in. Daniel kept going. He turned right just past the motel entrance, eventually finding his way into the rear lot, which was big enough for overnight semi-truck parking. About a hundred yards from the motel, he parked beneath a burned-out light beside a construction mound covered in tall grass. He shut off the engine.

Webber had parked near the front office and was already inside. Daniel could see him through the larger pane in the motel throughway. He was talking with someone, a man standing behind the counter.

Manny.

The cooler rested between them. Webber reached over and behind the counter for an envelope. Manny didn't move. They continued talking.

The Colt was in the passenger seat. Daniel glanced toward it and then back toward the men orchestrating evil.

The Jeep's stereo was off. And yet, another song played. He hadn't heard it since Dennis. He hadn't heard it in Webber's home. But here, again, Johnny Cash's voice echoed in his mind.

Whoever is unjust, let him be unjust still.
Whoever is righteous, let him be righteous still,
Whoever is filthy, let him be filthy still.

Daniel stepped from the Jeep.

He tucked the Colt in his waistline. Again, he could feel a pulse.

He closed the door.

CHAPTER SIXTEEN

Daniel circled to the front of the motel. Webber was gone.

Daniel stood alone beneath the dying neon buzz of the Pineview Inn sign. The flickering pink glow spat weak pulses of color across the cracked pavement. The urge to chase him was there, hot and immediate.

But no.

Tonight was no longer about one man. It was about many men.

He turned back toward the lobby. The cooler was no longer on the counter. He walked to the door and pushed it open.

An electronic bell above the threshold gave a weak ding, ignored by everyone but the stale air itself. The front lobby smelled of mildew, microwaved noodles, cigarette smoke, and Lysol that had long since given up. Beige paint curled at the corners of the ceiling. The carpet was the kind that looked like it was deliberately designed to camouflage stains.

Manny looked up from behind the desk with the tired indifference of a man who'd spent his adult life watching cars come and go, girls stumble in and out, and crimes bloom under cheap fluorescent lighting. His shoulders slouched in a way that suggested either hopelessness or apathy—it was hard to tell the difference anymore. He barely reacted to Daniel's entrance.

But then he saw the collar.

"Well now," Manny said, voice dry, lips twitching in the

shape of a smirk he didn't quite believe. "If it ain't the Lord himself."

Daniel didn't speak. He let the door shut slowly behind him. The lock clicked. It reminded him of the sound the offering plates make when he sets them on the altar during the Offertory. He stepped closer, raising the Colt and pointing it squarely at the center of Manny's chest.

"Whoa, whoa… Easy now, padre," Manny said, lifting his hands slowly, like someone who'd rehearsed this before.

Daniel cocked the hammer. The sound was distinct. For Daniel, it had become sacred.

Manny's hands trembled, his smirk faltering. "Okay. Okay. You're serious? You're really serious?"

"I've come to hear confessions," Daniel said, his voice flat as the city's name. "It looks like I'll be hearing yours first."

Manny blinked. "What?"

"Room numbers?"

"Wait… wha—?"

"Give me the room numbers."

Manny gave a huff that tried to be incredulous but came out panicked. "Man, you don't wanna do this. I don't care what kind of collar you're wearing, you ain't no—"

Daniel stepped closer. "You are wasting precious time, Manny."

"How…? You…? I don't know you."

"I know you."

Daniel kept the gun steady as he walked around the counter and pressed the barrel against Manny's cheek, hard enough to shove his face toward the back wall. Manny's eyes went wide.

"Okay! Alright! 144 and 146. Upstairs—213 and 215. That's it. Four rooms, man, I swear."

Daniel's eyes didn't shift. "Where are they? Tell me exactly."

Manny swallowed. "Out the door and to the right. The back side of the building. Two doors down, past the ice machine. That's 144 and 146. The other two are on the front side. Top floor, last doors at the end of the hall. Just around the corner from the stairs."

Daniel was silent.

Manny's voice wavered. "Look, I'm just the night manager, man. I don't do what they do. I just—"

"You just what?"

Manny's lips quivered. He opened his mouth to speak.

"You just make it possible," Daniel interrupted, eyes narrowing.

Daniel paused and looked away, as if deciding whether to stay or leave. Turning back to Manny, he leaned closer.

"I only came for the men on the list."

Manny's eyes darted to the gun. "List?"

"You're not on it."

Daniel's voice cracked slightly—just slightly—as if he'd left with himself to discuss what he'd do.

In a moment, he was back.

"But you arc now."

Manny's lips trembled. "C'mon. Please. Please! I got kids, man! I got a daughter!"

Daniel didn't flinch.

"No," he whispered. "You don't."

Manny's mouth worked, his eyes filling. But for Daniel, no sounds came out.

He pulled the trigger.

The gunshot cracked through the office like a lightning strike.

Manny's head snapped sideways, and a gout of blood sprayed across the calendar behind him—some tourist photo of Traverse City, now splattered with reality. The back of his skull struck the paneling with a dull thunk, and he slumped forward against the countertop. He slid to the floor, eyes still open, mouth agape. A slow, thick stream of red leaked from his nose.

His left leg twitched once.

Then again.

Then nothing.

Daniel stood there a moment, the Colt still extended. The scent of powder clung to the air, mingling with the motel's stale perfume. He could hear the hum of the vending machine in the corner.

No sounds. No commotion.

He turned to exit toward the back of the building, stepping over Manny's splayed legs, leaving a streak of innards on the cuff of his pants.

He'd start with the first floor. Opening the door, he looked both ways. "This city," he whispered, as if trying to be funny, "has heard too much gunfire."

Outside, the motel breathed like a dying lung—sour, thin air, warm and still. Daniel's steps were silent on the threadbare outdoor carpet that lined the walkway.

Room 144 was first.

He reached the door, stood to the side, and listened.

A man was laughing inside.

A girl moaned in between choking sounds.

Daniel knocked.

He heard a scramble of heavy steps followed by a thud.

Torrence Ray.

Claire's description had been dead-on. Ex-deputy. Thick neck and meaty arms. Tattoos on his arms and knuckles. A cheap gold chain at his throat. The stink of Drakkar Noir trying to cover his sweat.

Realization flashed in Ray's eyes—just as the Colt came up.

The first round punched into his chest, just below the collarbone. The second tore through his throat, spraying blood against the doorway.

Ray staggered backward, one hand flying to his neck, the other reaching for a weapon he didn't have time to draw. He gurgled something that sounded like what the f— before toppling into the room. He hit the table hard, snapping a leg, sending a lamp crashing to the floor where it burst in a corona of glass.

A girl screamed and covered her ears.

Daniel stepped into the room.

The girl—fifteen years old, maybe less—was already curled into the far corner of the bed, a blanket clutched to her chest, her eyes wild and unfocused. Her arm was covered in needle bruises. Her lips were torn. One of her ankles was cuffed to the headboard with a belt looped through a shackle.

She wouldn't look at whoever had just come into the room. She only screamed and looked away, shaking her head back and forth.

Daniel didn't say anything. He didn't linger.

He turned and left.

Room 145's door opened as he stepped into the hallway.

Martin Krill.

Skinny and smug. His man-bun sat too high on his head. He wore a vintage T-shirt with a cartoon fox giving a thumbs-up. The moment he saw Daniel—the gun and the collar—his smirk cracked.

"Wait—"

Two shots to the chest.

The first tore through his sternum. The second took a piece of lung and spine with it. Krill reeled backward like he'd been yanked by a wire. He hit the wall and slid down, his fingers clawing at the air. Blood gurgled in his throat as he died choking.

Daniel stepped over the body without pause.

The screams were starting now. Doors cracked open. Some slammed shut again.

He sprinted to and up the stairs, taking two of them at a time.

Room 202's door opened as he reached the top, but closed again as Daniel jogged by.

He stopped at 213. The door was already open, but only slightly. Daniel nudged it further with the barrel.

A man stood at the dresser, buttoning his shirt in a panic, belt still undone. He turned at the sound. The man saw Daniel. He saw the Colt.

Daniel stepped in. There was a girl on the bed, barely breathing.

"Wait," the man said, raising his hands before him.

Daniel only scowled.

"Wait—wait! What the hell are—"

One shot to the head.

The man's skull burst open like a melon, painting the

dresser and mirror behind him with viscera. His body slumped against the wall, smearing red down the paint. A toppled table lamp cracked beneath his weight.

Daniel moved to the bed. The girl's skin was pale, almost blue. Her lips were bleeding. They moved soundlessly. One of her teeth was missing. Her wrists were raw. She had no clothes.

He pulled the bedsheet up to her neck and knelt beside her, brushing a clump of blood-matted hair from her forehead.

"You're going to be okay," he whispered.

Her eyes rolled toward him, but she didn't respond.

He stood, intent on one more stop.

Room 215.

Back through the doorway, he turned just as 215's door burst open.

It was Cameron Wexler. Daniel recognized him instantly. He drove the shelter van. He taxied the girls from Harbor.

Wexler was running, barefoot, pants half-zipped, heading straight for the stairwell at the end of the walkway.

Daniel didn't follow. Instead, he vaulted the metal railing. The motion was surprisingly smooth. He gripped the top bar, swung a leg over, and let himself dangle for a moment—feet kicking above a garbage bin and a patch of gravel below.

Six feet. Seven, maybe.

He let go.

The landing sent a jolt through his knees, but he rolled forward, regained balance, and rose just as Wexler rounded the corner of the building—no more than five yards away.

"Cameron."

Wexler looked, startled by the voice. He saw Daniel— covered in blood, his white collar spattered with rubied spots that shifted in the Pineview sign's flickering neon glow. Wexler skidded to a stop, unsure whether to run or plead.

Daniel raised the Colt.

The blast echoed like a sermon in the nave at Saint John's.

The round hit Wexler low in the side, spinning him off his feet. The bullet exited in an explosion of hip bone, tissue, and blood that sprayed across the side of a faded minivan parked beside him. A scream tore from his throat as he slammed into the pavement. He rolled once and then began to crawl, clawing into the lot. Blood painted the gravel beneath him in thick strokes. His knees scraped raw. His foot slipped in his own fluid.

Daniel followed, looming over him, watching him struggle. He wanted Wexler to hear the footsteps. He wanted his final moments to be something of terror.

"No," Wexler groaned into the earth. "No… please… plea…"

Another round wasn't necessary. Wexler's body went still. He'd bled out in the lot, his sweaty face caked with gravel dust, one arm twisted beneath him.

Daniel looked down at him, death now interrupting Wexler's spasms of pain and fear. He glanced up at the motel windows. Some curtains were pulled back. Doors were opening now. Yells and screams and motion swirled. No one lifted a phone to record, betraying their dark reasons for being there in the first place. Everyone was dirty. No one was clean.

He could hear sirens in the distance. He needed to make his way around the building to the Jeep, and he needed to do it fast.

But before turning, he looked up and froze.

Webber was standing beside his car, just outside the

entrance to the lot, watching what happened.

The Porsche's headlights were on. The engine was running. Webber's phone was in one hand, and his key fob in the other.

He hadn't gotten far. Manny shorted him on the payment. And so, he came back for the rest.

Now he just stood there staring at Daniel, his mouth open.

Daniel raised the Colt. Webber was too far away, but he'd take a shot anyway.

Webber's eyes widened. His body stiffened. He didn't run. He couldn't—like a man trying to decide if sudden movement would trigger the predator in front of him.

Daniel's arm was steady. His breath was even.

He pulled the trigger.

Click.

The Colt was empty. All seven rounds had been spent.

Webber blinked, realizing his chance. He dove into the Porsche, the engine revved, tires squealed, and the car skidded from the lot in a serpentine arc of smoke and rubber. The 911's red taillights vanished into the dark.

Daniel stood alone in the buzz of the parking lot, the Colt still raised.

He didn't lower it for several seconds, not until the sirens grew louder.

He looked down at the gun. He looked at himself. Tissue coated everything. His hands. His pants. He wiped his left hand across his chest and ran his fingers near his neck. His shirt and collar were soaked, too.

He tucked the Colt into his waistband, turned in the Jeep's direction, and began to walk—slow, measured steps—praying as he did.

He wasn't fleeing. He was simply done.

But Webber had seen him. Others had, too, for that matter.

As he neared the Jeep, the first cruiser turned into the lot behind him, sirens dying to a low whine, headlights sweeping over scattering people and Wexler's dead body. Daniel didn't look back. He opened the door, slid behind the wheel, and closed it with care.

He didn't move. He didn't rush.

He wiped his palms on his pants and rested his hands at ten and two.

Another cruiser arrived.

He started the engine. It growled like a sleeping dog disturbed. Still, no one had seen him so far off in the darkness. Not yet. But someone would remember a man in a collar. Maybe whoever opened and closed the door on the second floor. Or the girl with the split lip and missing tooth.

He shifted into gear and eased the Jeep out of the lot, turning away from the hotel—north—with his headlights off.

No one saw him. No one stopped him.

He adjusted the rearview mirror to see the scene behind him. But he saw himself. Debris on his collar and shirt. He looked away from his reflection and simply drove.

But he also smiled.

It wasn't joy. It wasn't pride. It was relief. The motel was still standing, but the thing inside it—the thing that had been feeding there—was dead. At least for now.

CHAPTER SEVENTEEN

Stern didn't usually watch the news in the morning. He preferred the radio—AM 760 or 950, usually—something about the grain of voices on air made it easier to think while shaving or frying an egg. But that morning, the house was too quiet. The radio didn't feel right.

He sat down with a lukewarm cup of coffee, opened a package of strawberry Pop-Tarts, and flipped on the small kitchen television mounted beneath the cabinet. It buzzed to life with static and then resolved into the low-fidelity visuals of a local morning news broadcast.

He wasn't ready for what he saw.

"Scott, I'm live outside the Pineview Inn just off of Pierson Road here in Flint, where state and local investigators have confirmed a series of homicides. At least five people are confirmed dead at the scene. Sources inside the investigation are also using the phrase 'sex slaves' to describe several young girls found at the scene. They appeared to be drugged and were being held against their will. Another source tells me there are others in custody, some with known criminal associations."

The anchor's voice trailed off as the broadcast cut to a shaky camera view. Close-up shots of yellow crime scene tape fluttering. The Pineview Inn's cheap neon sign blinked tiredly in the background. Uniformed officers moved like shadows between parked cars. A body bag—partially obscured by a news truck—was being wheeled into the back of a coroner's van.

Stern sat up straight.

The screen cut back to the anchor, who looked visibly rattled. "At this time, investigators have not confirmed whether the killings are connected to recent incidents across Genesee and Livingston Counties—"

Stern didn't hear the rest. He was already reaching for his phone.

He hit the contact for Kress.

"Tom, it's Jeff."

"You watching the news, too?"

There was a pause. "Just turned it on."

"Pineview Inn," Kress said. "Last night in Flint."

"Yeah. Brutal. They said five bodies."

"I saw at least three confirmed on camera. One was a former Oakland County Sheriff's Deputy. They haven't identified the other two, yet."

"Did they say the names?" Stern asked.

"No," Kress replied. "But I probably know somebody who can get them for me."

"Yeah, they mentioned our situation—Genesee and Livingston. They know we're already working on something."

"I'll call a little later," Kress said. "I'll let you know what I find out."

"They're related, Tom," Stern said. "I know it."

"It's Flint, Jeff," Kress replied. "This could be anyone or anything."

"You know I know," Stern insisted.

Kress was quiet before eventually agreeing.

"You're good at this," he replied. "Your gut usually knows before everyone else."

Still watching the TV, Stern rubbed his jaw. "It feels… just like Durham and Anderson."

Kress grunted. "We don't have jurisdiction in Flint."

"Doesn't matter."

"How do you figure?"

"Doesn't matter," he repeated.

"Jeff, don't step on any toes or we'll lose our own investigations, too."

"I'll bet we're going to discover the bullets are from a .45. No one uses a .45 for this stuff, Tom. In Flint, it's a 9mm or an AK. In our towns, it's… well… it's nothing, because this doesn't happen in our towns."

"You're thinking revenge, aren't you, Jeff? Maybe a vigilante?"

"More like executioner," Stern replied. "These people all died for a reason. They're all connected somehow. They're all tied to something bad. And someone knows it."

Kress muttered something under his breath before adding, "You're saying what, exactly? That someone's targeting these SOBs one by one? Doing the job for us?"

"I'm saying someone's cleaning house," Stern said. "And they're probably not done yet."

There was a pause.

Kress exhaled. "I don't know, Jeff. We both know there are a lot of bad guys out there with lots of reasons to kill people, good and bad. It could be a gang thing or cartel muscle. We already know they're working as far north as Muskegon. Hell, they're doing stuff on Mackinac Island."

"Not this clean," Stern said. "Gangs don't pull this kind of hit and then take the casings."

"That was at our scenes, Jeff." Kress argued. "This one in

Flint was a mess."

"Wait and see, Tom. No spray, no tags, no phone pings, no stolen cars."

Kress sounded skeptical. "You've got nothing but a gut feeling."

Stern sipped his coffee and stared at what was now a muted Empire Carpet commercial. "My gut has solved a lot of cases, Tom."

There was silence again.

"I'll come by," Kress finally said.

"Yeah," Stern replied. "Bring your stuff. You have some pictures I want to see again."

† † †

They met later that morning at a little diner in Linden, right next to the town's grocery store. The waitress knew them both and poured coffee without being asked. Neither of them touched the menus.

Kress dropped a manila folder on the table between them and tapped it once. "That's everything on Anderson. Preliminary findings, autopsy summaries, scene photos, toxicology."

Stern opened the folder but didn't read. He just stared at the top photo—Dennis Anderson sprawled on the floor with most of his scalp missing. Stern already knew the Durham images better than his own family photos.

"Both scenes were brutal," Stern said. "But both didn't start that way. The person behind the weapon knew them both. Likely called them friends."

Kress took a slow drink of his coffee. "Whoever's doing this, they're prepared before they—"

"They're disciplined," Stern interrupted. "They plan. They control the scene."

"You sound impressed."

"I'm concerned. A controlled person is a lot harder to catch."

Kress leaned back in his chair. "If we suggest a connection to the State Police, they'll take it from us. You know that."

"I've already sent what we have to them," Stern replied. "If they make the connection, then fine. But I'm not suggesting we tell them anything else. I just want to know who's in their line of sight, if they even realize they've got something here."

"You think they don't?"

"I think they think this is a typical Flint mess."

Kress raised an eyebrow. "And it isn't?"

"It's ours, Tom," Stern said, stirring his coffee with his finger. "If anything, it's mine," he continued. "It started in Linden. Claire Madsen was the first."

Kress set his cup down a little too hard. "C'mon, Jeff, she—"

"She was silenced, Tom. You read that autopsy report. She'd been hit. And her neck was broken. Someone had a reason to kill her, maybe to shut her up."

"And what about the Reverend? He was there. Why didn't they kill him, too?"

Stern didn't reply.

"You still thinking about him?" Kress asked.

Stern looked out the window. "I'm thinking about patterns. Madsen dies. Her pastor gets hit in the same room. Then two of his church members turn up dead. Now, a motel full of traffickers gets exterminated twenty miles away. You tell me."

"You think Michaels is involved?"

"I think Michaels is either very lucky… or very unlucky." Kress smirked. "Your gut."

"He knows something, Tom. He may not even know what he knows. But there's something."

They both sat in silence, the kind that lets shared thoughts circulate without speech. The waitress refilled their mugs. Both acknowledged her.

Finally, Kress said, "Okay. Suppose he knows something. What's your next step?"

Stern folded the folder closed. "I'm going to keep watching. I've already got eyes on almost everything around town. Nothing usable, yet. But something still bugs me about his interview that morning at the station. He was genuinely sad when I first met him on the porch. I poked at him a bit to test him. He definitely passed. He was in shock. But at the station, it's like he'd already come out of it, like he was already over what happened. He was different. There was something he wasn't telling me, something he figured out between Claire's and the station."

"You're thinking maybe he remembered seeing the killer?"

"I don't know," Stern said and paused. "Something."

"He seems like a good man, Jeff," Kress said. "I've met him a few times, and I have the same cop sense as you."

"I think he was supposed to die that day, too. But he didn't."

Kress scoffed. "Come on, Jeff. He's a pastor."

"And that means what, exactly?" Stern shot back. "Pastors don't get murdered? They don't keep secrets?"

Kress hesitated. "He'd have come clean. For sure. He's no

ghost."

Stern looked down at his coffee. "Maybe he is."

† † †

Later that afternoon, Stern returned to his office in Linden. He didn't turn on the lights. He liked the natural dimness, the quiet hum of old fluorescent fixtures that buzzed like dying bees in the ceiling.

Stern's office was small, utilitarian, and dim even during the day. The blinds were almost always drawn. A thin layer of dust lay over the shelves that lined one wall, most of which were packed with thick binders. In the corner sat a cardboard file box containing a stack of commendations, service awards, and plaques that he had never bothered to mount. They were from Detroit mostly—before the shooting, before the therapists, before the divorce. He wasn't the kind of man to decorate with praise, and he didn't want to remember what shattered his family.

But he had placed a few photographs by the lamp on his desk: one of his ex-wife on a beach in Traverse City, her hair windblown and laughing; another of his two daughters, maybe ages nine and twelve at the time, with matching Detroit Tigers caps and ice cream smeared on their cheeks. They didn't speak to him anymore. After he was shot—during a drug raid gone wrong in a crumbling house off Linwood—something had changed in him. He'd become harder, more impatient, and more controlling. He knew it. So did they. But he loved them still, and he checked in quietly over the years—an anonymous bouquet on a birthday, a card with some cash, a donation to a school fundraiser. The ache for them never dulled. He just learned how to simmer in it.

He closed the blinds and opened his laptop. The security clearance from Fenton's database gave him limited access to Genesee County records. He searched for arrest reports, 911 call logs, and incident photos.

But what he really looked for was the silence between reports—the gaps. Incidents where nothing was caught. Bodies where no struggle occurred. Places where fear left no fingerprints.

Everything was always right there, if you knew what to look for.

Stern leaned back in his chair. He stared at the ceiling, as if the answers might leak from the cracked tiles.

Then, almost without thinking, he opened a new document and began to type:

> **Subject:** Possible Pattern – Extra-Jurisdictional Homicides
> **Suspected Motive:** Vigilante executions
> **Known Victims:**
> – Claire Madsen (Linden) – suspicious death, blunt force trauma and broken neck; no signs of forced entry; COD ruled inconclusive, but consistent with sudden cervical fracture likely caused by application of force
> – Reverend Daniel Michaels (Linden) – survivor, blunt force trauma
> – Brett Durham (Linden) – gunshots, no forced entry
> – Dennis Anderson (Fenton) – struggle, multiple stab wounds, gunshot
> – Pineview Inn (Flint) – 5 confirmed DOAs

Common Factors:
– Evening kills
– Minimal forensic trail
– No signs of struggle at first
– If patterned, increasingly messy in scale
– Flint victims have suspected links to
   abuse/trafficking
– No known witness accounts

Current Hypothesis:
– Single actor
– High intelligence
– Military or tactical training likely
– Same weapon (?)
– Targeting systematically
– May have personal motivation

Next Steps:
– Liaise with Fenton & Flint PD, and State Police
   (through Kress?) to obtain full motel scene
   report
– I have no idea

He sat back and stared at the last line. He gave an uncomfortable chuckle.

His phone buzzed. It was a text from an old flame, someone he'd recently asked for a favor. Jeane Rittner.

"Pastor Michaels just texted me to cancel all his meetings again this week. Says he's under the weather."

Stern stared at the message.

Another came. "I'm worried about him," it said.

He didn't reply.

Instead, he erased the last line of his "Next Steps" and replaced it with something else.

– Discreet surveillance of Daniel Michaels

He stared at Daniel's name. His eyes redirected to the previous mention beneath "Known Victims."

Survivor, he thought.

Stern rose from his desk and walked to the window. He cracked the blinds open with two fingers. Summer was ending. And so, the early sun was still hanging low. The breeze had picked up, lifting the flags outside the fire station into full salute. Eventually, he pulled the shades open completely.

He lit a cigarette—an old habit he usually tried to suppress—and let the smoke hang in the air like a question he couldn't yet answer. Nancy, his secretary, hated it when he smoked in his office. But she wouldn't be in for another twenty minutes.

"Reverend…" he said aloud.

He didn't finish the sentence.

Instead, he stood and watched the morning sun move higher. He saw Nancy parking her Buick and waving to him through the window. He hid his cigarette and waved back. He promised himself that if another body turned up, if the State Police didn't move, if Kress didn't get any information from Flint, he'd go on without them. He'd follow his gut. He'd stop reacting and start hunting.

CHAPTER EIGHTEEN

David Graves liked the sound of "Pastor D." It had weight. It had authority. More importantly, it kept him unquestioned. He knew the power of influence, especially the gentle cloak of religion that almost always cast suspicion away.

Doused in this confidence, David moved through the muted elegance of 737's upper conference room, pausing to straighten a stack of brochures on the table. His fingertips lingered briefly on their glossy surface, the words printed in gentle, reassuring fonts: "Hope, Renewal, Purpose." He smiled faintly, appreciating the simple art of persuasion. People believed words like these. They clung to them, as though the words alone could change their reality.

He walked to the floor-to-ceiling windows overlooking the parking lot, hands folded neatly behind his back, observing as church members and volunteers drifted into the building below. Each person represented something valuable—a resource to cultivate or influence to wield. David knew each of them by name and by face.

And by their vulnerabilities.

A shepherd always knew his flock. He knew their weaknesses. He understood their needs.

His cellphone vibrated in his jacket pocket. He checked the screen.

Bill Keenan.

He answered. His voice was measured and pleasant.

"Yes, Bill?"

"I just happened to stop in over here at Harbor," Keenan said, "and it seems Carla is having a small issue with the girl from Muskegon."

"Define small." David's tone remained very nearly paternal.

"Carla said she asked about calling her family. She said someone told her she'd get time on the phone with her father, but that she hadn't gotten any. Now the girl's panicked. And so is Carla. Carla's trying to settle her down, but it seems like it might be escalating. I just figured I'd call you before heading back out. I told Carla, if anyone could fix it, it'd be Pastor D."

David sighed, as if burdened by the inconvenience of other people's problems. "First of all, remind Carla we don't panic. That's not how we care for people. Then tell her I'll call personally. Give me five minutes."

"I'll let her know."

David glanced again at the brochures, their tidy promises neatly printed but entirely empty. He dialed Carla's number, pausing briefly to ensure his voice carried the appropriate warmth.

"Pastor D," Carla answered, sounding breathless and relieved. "Thanks for calling."

"Carla," he said, his gentle authority wrapping around her name. "What's happening?"

"It's Beth. She wants to call home. I wasn't sure how to handle—"

"Let me speak with her."

There was a pause, a rustling, and then Beth's voice. It was thin and worried.

"Hello?"

"Beth," David began softly, "I heard you're having a rough go of things today. Talk to me."

"I… I just want to call my dad. Someone told me I could talk to him. They said they knew how to get ahold of him."

"And they do, Beth," he soothed. "Everything is in good order. This isn't just about paperwork. You know that, right? It's about safety. Your safety."

"I don't understand why—"

"Beth," he interrupted with a fatherly voice, "you've trusted us this far, haven't you? Trusted me?"

A hesitant silence. "Yes."

"Good. Then trust me now. I promise you'll talk to your dad soon enough. For now, we need to get you situated. The best way to do that is to follow Carla's lead. She'll take good care of you. Can you let her do that, Beth? Can you do that for me?"

Another pause, longer this time. "Yes, Pastor D."

"That's good. I knew you would." He ended the call and returned the phone to his pocket, adjusting his tie as if he'd just resolved a world war. He made his way to the main worship hall.

† † †

David liked to rehearse in an empty room.

He told his staff it was for acoustics. "I like to feel the shape of the words in the space," he'd said once, waving his arm like a conductor. "The Gospel should echo through this place with relevance."

However, the truth was much simpler, and some of the staff members knew it, even though they'd never say so out loud.

David liked seeing the spotlight hit the stage with no one else in it.

The worship space of Seven Thirty-Seven Church—stylized as 737 Church—wasn't really a sacred space at all. It was a concert hall for performing. Worse, it was an arena for TED talks that sold the Gospel. A big-box performance space. Tiered seating in semicircles. A thrust stage with low fog and warm LED uplighting. The 16-foot digital wall behind the stage cycled softly through ocean imagery—waves, then waterfalls, then still lakes. There were no crosses anywhere in the building. That was by design.

Pastor D, as the staff called him, told the architects, "We don't want crucifixes or crosses. We don't want anything related to death. We want to be inviting. We want hydration for thirsty souls."

Apparently, he'd never acquainted himself with 1 Corinthians 1:23. And the whole place reflected the ignorance. The stage, most of all, was sleek, modern, and Christologically sterile.

Pastor David stood center stage now, a lavalier mic clipped to the collar of his fitted t-shirt. The jacket was tight and cropped. The jeans, tighter. His sneakers were spotless white, name-brand, and youth-coded. His hair was frosted gold in sharp contrast to the gray that crept beneath. His face was smooth, Botoxed, and caught the light strangely when he turned. His age—sixty-three—was camouflaged beneath styling efforts meant to place him in his early thirties.

It wasn't working.

But it wasn't failing either.

He was charismatic, and everything he said was syrupy

sweet.

David didn't care much for doctrine. Theological precision bored him. To him, truth was less important than tone. He believed what people needed wasn't substance, but sensation. Not creeds, but chemistry. His goal wasn't to preach Christ crucified—it was to engineer an experience. He wanted his listeners to feel something, anything, and to associate that feeling, not so much with Jesus, but with himself. That was the win. That was the brand. Pastor David, the local celebrity. The rest, the ancient stuff—confessional documents and the uncomfortable demands of Scripture—was just religious baggage. And it didn't sell.

He clicked the remote.

The LED wall lit up behind him.

WATER IN THE WASTELAND
Isaiah 43:19

David inhaled as the fog machines hissed gently, their timed release catching the first waves of uplight. His silhouette stood tall and theatrical.

"Behold! I am doing a new thing!"

He paused, took two confident steps forward. A hint of a grin played at the corners of his mouth, and his voice amplified only in the monitors.

"That's not just prophecy. That's promise. That's not just Isaiah talkin'. That's God talkin' to you. You've been stuck. You've been circling the same wilderness—but the water's about to break. Come on, somebody say it with me! Breakthrough!"

He reached his arms toward the empty seats, his voice

rising.

"You're not in a waiting room anymore. You're in a birthing room! Something new is springing forth! Do you feel the spirit? Do you feel it? That pain you've been dragging behind you—that's labor pain, child of God! You're not broken. You're becoming!"

His voice softened.

"And 737 Church—this house, this place—is the Lord's delivery room. It's Jesus's delivery room!"

He took two more slow steps forward.

"And the Jesus I know," he said, his voice warm and practiced. "He's no dusty theologian with a Latin lexicon. He's a savior with open arms and a well of blessings. He wants you. The real you. No matter who that real you might be. And he has nothing but goodness for that real you."

He let the silence breathe.

He liked silence. It made his listeners lean in.

"That's definitely tomorrow's vibe," he whispered, clicking off the screen. "Water in the wasteland."

From the back of the hall, his worship director lifted her hand.

"Five minutes," David called back. "I'll be ready."

He turned to grab a bottle of cucumber water from the stage riser when he heard footsteps.

Dr. Eli Webber emerged from the side hallway like a man being chased. His coat was half-buttoned, his dress shirt untucked on one side. His hair stuck out in the back. His face was pale and twitching.

David sighed and rolled his eyes. "What the hell—"

He noticed the worship team members in the back turn to look. His mic was still on. He smiled and waved, and then clicked it off.

Webber stumbled to the front row. "David—"

"I told you not to come here," David growled through a smile.

"I know, I know," Webber replied. "But we've got a problem, and I didn't know where else to go."

David opened his mouth to speak, but Webber kept on, except in more of a whisper.

"They're dead. They're all dead."

David blinked slowly. "I heard."

"From who?"

"Topel called. Gave me the basics. Torrence, Krill, and one of the clients."

Webber scratched his head and looked backward at the worship team. His brow twitched. "And Wexler," he said. "He bled out in the parking lot. I saw it."

David moved to the edge of the stage and sat, dangling his legs over the edge. The sound he made doing it betrayed his age.

"So, we need three new guys, then," he said coldly.

Webber hesitated. Something in David's tone chilled him. Not just the words, but the way they dropped from his lips—dry, flat, like he was talking about throwing away used plastic cups. Eli felt his throat tighten. He was shaken from the night's chaos, but now—suddenly—he was also afraid of the man in front of him. David didn't seem worried. He didn't seem human. Just efficient. Cold. Like something in him had long since gone still.

"I barely got away," Webber finally continued. He waited for a moment, hoping for a hint of gladness or concern. David didn't respond. "He aimed at me," Webber added, "but there was nothing. I think he was out."

"And the shooter? Did you see him?"

"It was dark. And he was too far away." He thought for a moment. "But there's one thing I did see. He was dressed like a priest. I could see his… priest neck shirt, or whatever it's called, in the motel sign's light." His frayed nerves made trouble for his words.

"Could you make him out if you saw him again?"

"Probably not. I told you, he was too far away. But he definitely saw me. He knew something about me. Enough to let others run and to aim his gun at me."

"This is funny."

"What's so funny?"

"You're saying a man walked into the Pineview and took out five people… with precision… and then he got away without a trace… and you think he's clergy?"

"I'm telling you he was wearing a priest neck thing!"

"A clerical collar?" David whispered, as if belittling his nervous forgetfulness.

"What?"

"A clerical collar. One of those white plastic inserts. At his neck. Black shirt. The works."

"Yes," Webber insisted. "He was wearing a clerical collar. I know what I saw. I don't know who he was, but I'm telling you, I know what I saw."

David folded his arms.

"Well, that narrows things down, doesn't it?"

Webber waited.

"There're maybe a dozen pastors and priests within thirty miles who still dress like that. I mean, Daniel Michaels here in town suits up in that off-putting stiffness every day."

Webber leaned in. "Could it be him?"

"Michaels?" David laughed. "No. No chance."

"Wasn't he the one at that Madsen girl's house when—"

Webber didn't finish his sentence. He knew better than to go any further.

"He was there," David said.

He thought for a moment and then waved it away.

"Doesn't matter. Point is—Michaels? He's not the guy. The man writes 3,000-word sermons, crafting them like he's writing Shakespeare. He's a nobody with no friends. He doesn't even attend the joint worship services in Fenton. We've been trying to get him into the inter-church network for years, but he never bites. The last time I saw him at a pastor's luncheon at the high school, he offended every pastor in the room. He said something about cooperation in the externals being okay, but altar fellowship was a no-go, as if we all believed in different Jesus's." He gave a short chuckle. "He's an ass."

David looked to the worship team circling impatiently at the top of the center aisle.

"But I'll look into him, anyway," he added. "Maybe have Bill arrange for some unexpected inspections. Water meter. Permit stuff. Whatever. Maybe they can get inside his house. That kind of thing."

"Anyone else they should look into?"

"There's a priest living over on Argentine Road. Father Mal. He serves a parish in Howell. But I don't think he wears the collar. He's a pretty good guy. He calls me for advice sometimes."

Webber swallowed. "You should move your operation, David."

David exhaled. "Yes. Harbor's compromised. I'll talk to the Board of Directors. I'll tell them intake numbers are far too low to justify Harbor, and that the answer is to consolidate with the Grand Blanc campus."

"You think they'll buy it?"

"I know they will. I've already been talking about it for a couple of months."

"What about new security?"

David's eyes flicked toward him. "You mean muscle?"

Webber nodded. "You need protection for this. You need another Torrence. If I'm going to continue in this, I need protection. I can't do what Krill and Wexler were doing."

"I'll make some calls."

Webber wiped his face. "You're not even rattled, are you?"

"I'm a preacher," David said. "Eyes are always on me. I don't rattle."

Webber turned to go.

David called after him. "Doctor."

He stopped.

"Just stay home. Lay low. Take a few weeks of vacation. Tell Kerri—that's your secretary, right?—tell her you're going to the Bahamas. I'll call you when things settle."

Webber nodded once, then disappeared through the hallway.

David motioned for the worship team before clicking his remote. The LED wall cycled back to tranquil waves, casting soft blues and whites across David's face. The fog machine came to life again. The lighting—angled from above and below—caught his jawline and cheekbones in strange relief, sharpening every edge. In that moment, with his arms spread casually and his silhouette framed against an ocean of projected grace, he looked like a messiah to the untrained eye. But to anyone with discernment, to anyone who still believed in evil, he looked like something else entirely—something hollow and hungry. A demon wearing popular religion like stage makeup.

CHAPTER NINETEEN

The sky over Linden was pale blue and thin—the kind of late-summer light that told the trees it was almost time to begin their slow dying. There was no wind. The bells outside Saint John Lutheran rang their usual summons, their tones slightly warped, not from disrepair but from time. The bells had hung there longer than any living member. They had moved at least three generations to kneel at their calling, some faithfully, some reluctantly, some only at Christmas and Easter, some only once and then never again.

Inside, the nave was full in that predictable, early-autumn way. School had started. Routines were solidifying. Families filled the pews in clustered formation. The stained-glass windows softened the late-summer sun into warm patches that spilled across the tile and oak.

Daniel stood in his office, vesting in silence.

The green stole—a shade somewhere between pine and tired grass—hung limply over his shoulders. It matched the chasuble. He touched the covering's fabric absentmindedly, adjusting it not out of reverence but to give his hands something to do. His eyes were hollow. He hadn't spent time on the sermon. He only wrote it that morning, and he was feeling a moment of guilt for doing so.

"Someone left a note," Jeane said quietly from behind him. "At the Elder's table in the narthex."

He turned slightly.

"Stan gave it to me," she continued, handing it over.

"Asking if we could pray for the victims in Flint."

Daniel took the paper and glanced at it. The handwriting was neat, detailing the sort of request that came from someone trying to make sense of the world in small, hopeful ways.

"You don't have to," she said, almost apologetically.

"I can add it," he replied. "No worries."

She hesitated. "You doing okay this morning?"

He gave her the faintest nod, which was neither lie nor truth. She read it as both.

Daniel exhaled. The choir had started the entrance hymn—*Lord, Help Us Ever to Retain*. The tempo was too slow, and it annoyed him. The organist played it this way, not because he was incapable or lacked confidence, but because he knew the architecture of Lutheran memory was built on patience and repetition.

The service began. The people confessed. The Kyrie was sung and the Collect prayed. The readings were offered. The Gospel—Luke 10:23–37—rested open on the lectern. As the congregation sang the final stanza of *Jesus, Thy Boundless Love to Me*, Daniel crossed the chancel and ascended the pulpit.

The hymn ended, and Daniel glanced toward his manuscript, making the sign of the cross.

"In the name of the Father and of the Son and of the Holy Spirit. Amen."

He paused, letting the invocation and the listeners who'd been standing for the Hymn of the Day settle in.

"I'll bet you think you already know what this sermon is about," he began, his tone calm but pointed. "The Good Samaritan—everyone knows this one. Even unbelievers. We've got state laws named after it. 'Good Samaritan Laws.'

Protecting people who stop to help. Encouraging us to be good citizens. And if I asked around, I'm sure I'd get confident answers. 'It's about how Jesus wants us to be good to our neighbors.' 'It's about being kind to people in need.' And sure… it works well when we're correcting our kids. 'Be nice to your sister. Jesus says to be a Good Samaritan.'"

He gave a faint smile. A few parents in the pews chuckled knowingly.

"But is that really all this is? An ethical tale with the lesson tacked on? Be nice. Be good. Try harder?"

He leaned slightly on the edge of the pulpit.

"Let me ask you this: If that's what Jesus meant—just be like the Samaritan—then why did he start and end the conversation with the words: 'Do this, and you will live'?"

His voice shifted, quieter now.

"That's not Gospel. That's Law. And Law has sharp edges."

Daniel scanned the nave instinctively. And that's when he saw him.

Stern. The last pew on the pulpit side. Suit jacket. Tie slightly off-center. Hands folded over his knees. Watching.

Daniel didn't flinch.

He continued.

"You see, when Jesus tells this story, he's not simply instructing. He's indicting. He's stripping away the smug self-assurance of a man who thinks the Law is a ladder to climb. He's talking to a lawyer who thinks righteousness is measurable—and achievable. And so, Jesus doesn't give him a checklist. He gives him a mirror."

He let the silence carry his words.

"He shows him a man beaten and left for dead. A priest

comes. Passes by. A Levite comes. Passes by. Why? Well, ritual purity, obligations, caution. Reasonable, really. They had justifications."

Daniel looked up slowly, meeting the gaze of a woman in the fifth pew who hadn't blinked since he started.

"You see, love is the fulfillment of the Law. That's what the lawyer says to Jesus. Love God. Love neighbor. Simple. Until you actually try it. Until the neighbor is inconvenient. Until it costs you something. Until they don't look like you. Until they scare you."

His voice lowered.

"And then Jesus drops the bomb."

He closed his Bible gently.

"A Samaritan."

A shift ran through the congregation, subtle, almost imperceptible.

"Not just a stranger. An enemy. And he stops. And he binds wounds. And he pays the cost. And he promises to return. The one who, by every cultural measure, should have been the villain… becomes the savior."

He paused.

"And in that, Jesus does more than teach us to be kind. He reveals something deeper. He shows us the true nature of mercy. That it crosses boundaries. That it humiliates pride. That it takes on risk and filth and inconvenience and debt."

He turned a page slowly.

"The Law shows us how we should live. But also how far we fall. The Gospel? The Gospel shows us the One who didn't fall short. The Good Samaritan isn't just a parable about doing better. It's a picture of Christ."

Daniel's eyes moved across the congregation again.

"The Samaritan bandaged wounds, lifted the broken onto his own donkey, and walked while the dying man rode. He took him to a place of rest, not his home, but a place to recover. He paid the price. Promised to return. Sound familiar?"

He let the question hang.

"Jesus didn't just tell a story. He painted a portrait. Of himself. The One who comes to us, not when we're strong and upright and respectable, but when we're bloody in the ditch. Condemned. Enemies of God."

A rustle of movement. A few heads bowed.

"He picks us up. He carries us into the care of his Church. He washes us with water and the Word. He feeds us with his body and blood. And he promises: I will return—and I will settle all accounts."

Daniel looked back down at the manuscript he'd retrieved from his files. He couldn't look at his listeners when he spoke the next line.

"He's coming back," Daniel said carefully. "And he'll settle all accounts."

He paused again. Finally, he looked up.

"So if you hear this story and imagine yourself as the Samaritan—think again. You're the man in the ditch. And Christ is the One who didn't pass by."

He stepped back from the pulpit.

"In the Name of the Father, and of the Son, and of the Holy Spirit. Amen."

The liturgy continued with the Nicene Creed and then moved into the Prayer of the Church.

His voice remained steady.

"We give thanks, O Lord, for Your mercy that binds the wounds of sinners. For the Church, that it may be a place of rest and healing. For the nations, that justice would be done…"

He took a breath.

"And for the victims of the violence in Flint. Those who perished, and those left behind. Grant peace. Grant truth. Grant justice."

It was a line that cost him. His lips trembled. He felt he could cry.

He only said it because someone asked. But the words felt sour in his mouth. What would they think if they knew the justice they prayed for had already come and gone, dressed in black, carrying judgment in his waistband?

He finished the prayers. The Preface and Proper Preface were sung. The Lord's Supper was distributed. He noted, with professional detachment, that Stern remained in his pew.

After the benediction and the recessional hymn, Daniel stood by the doors in the narthex. Parishioners passed by with brief greetings. Most didn't shake his hand. They smiled, nodded, and murmured, "Thank you, Pastor." But they kept moving.

Stern approached.

"Pastor Michaels."

"Chief."

"I read the bulletin," Stern said. "About Communion. You asked people to speak with you first. So I didn't come forward."

Daniel nodded once.

"What do you believe about the Lord's Supper?" he asked plainly.

Stern shrugged slightly. "It's a remembrance meal… Like a holy reenactment."

Daniel didn't smile. "Had you come forward, I wouldn't have communed you."

Stern blinked once. "How would you have known what I believed?"

"Because I would have asked you."

"Right at the rail?"

"Yes. Right at the rail."

"I appreciate your honesty," he said after a moment.

Daniel crossed his arms loosely. "Most people don't these days. Americans think they're owed access to everything. Even God. They've lost the sense for holy."

People were still passing by, avoiding eye contact, sensing the conversation's weight.

Stern took a step back, then forward again.

"You free for coffee after this?"

"I have Bible study after this."

"After Bible study?"

"I've got a few things—"

"He doesn't," Jeane said, appearing at his side like a stage cue.

Daniel turned. Her tone was light, but her eyes were serious.

"I checked his calendar," she added. "It's clear until Tuesday." Turning to Daniel, "You should go. It'll be nice to just get out and do something."

Daniel glanced between them.

"Yeah, sure," he said. "Why not?"

† † †

The café across from the station was quiet. They sat by

the window. Stern drank his coffee black. Daniel did, too.

The early September breeze came through the open door.

"You ever wonder," Stern began, "what it takes to make a man cross the line?"

Daniel didn't respond.

"I mean… really cross it. Not just fantasize about justice. But act."

Daniel kept his eyes on the cup.

Stern continued. "I've been in law enforcement a long time. You learn to read patterns. Not just of behavior, but of heart."

He swirled his coffee and sipped.

"I'll bet it's the same for you," Stern continued. "You see some bad stuff, too. Ugly sins."

"I do," Daniel replied, but went no further.

"I don't know about you, but after a while, I can almost smell intent. The Pineview scene—someone wanted more than just to kill all those people. Maybe it was a mixture of stuff. Maybe justice. Maybe vengeance. Maybe some absolution, too."

Daniel's jaw tensed.

"You know what kind of man does something like that?" Stern asked.

Daniel set his cup down.

"Someone who's tired," Stern said. "Of excuses. Of red tape. Of watching people get away with things. He's not evil. Not insane. But he's broken. And he's convinced he's the only one left who can do what's needed."

Daniel's stare darkened.

"You came here to say something?"

Stern leaned back. "No. I came to drink coffee. And I

wanted some company. I wanted to bounce my thoughts off of someone who might actually be able to relate."

Daniel didn't respond at first. He looked past Stern to the edge of the café window, where a couple walked a golden retriever along the sidewalk.

"I don't know if I do relate," Daniel finally said.

Stern gave a slow nod. "No, probably not," he said. "Still, I think you're too much like me."

Daniel turned toward him.

"You strike me as a man who sees things," Stern continued. "Who actually feels the weight of them. Most pastors I've ever met seemed pretty shallow. Especially guys like that Pastor D fellow at 737—wannabe hipsters, fake smiles, preaching like they're pitching timeshares. It's all stage lights and slogans. No substance. No scars. Just a sales pitch with a Bible verse at the end. Others, the guys I've met, guys like you, guys in collars, they always seem to know what's holy and what isn't. But they can also keep things a little too clinical. They walk around, hands folded, quoting verses and such, and then they just seem to move on. But you don't look like you're moving on."

Daniel's voice was quiet. "Guys like me try not to get in the way of the Gospel."

"That wasn't what I said."

Stern sipped again.

"Jeane told me you'll mop the nave floor sometimes just to feel like you've finished something. Visits and sermons and more visits and meetings, there's never really a project that can be started and then completed."

Another pause.

"I lost someone once," Stern offered, eyes fixed on the

rim of his cup. "She didn't die. She just... couldn't do the job anymore. Couldn't carry what came home with me every night. I kept thinking I could shield her from it. Turns out, I was just getting better at being alone."

Daniel studied him. "Is that what you think I am? Alone?"

"I think you're tired. And I think you want to see things finished. I think you want to make things right more than you want for your own peace. I've been there. Hell, I still live there."

Daniel glanced away again.

Stern sipped. "There's something about our kind of work—yours and mine. People expect us to fix things. But no one ever really teaches us what to do when the fixing we do doesn't work."

Daniel nodded, almost imperceptibly.

"You don't have to say anything," Stern added. "But if you ever need someone to listen..."

Daniel finished his coffee and set the mug down with deliberate care.

"I'll keep that in mind," he said. "And I'll keep you and your ex-wife and girls in prayer."

Stern felt his words. Not as stinging, but as comforting. He didn't know Daniel knew. Perhaps, Jeane? But that Daniel offered to pray made Stern feel better, even if only for a moment.

† † †

That night, Daniel did some cleaning.

Behind the garage, the fire pit welcomed more ashes. The clothes were unrecognizable by the time he doused them with lighter fluid. The fire popped and hissed. He watched it all burn.

Inside, the house was dark. He opened his laptop and clicked on the list.

He scrolled and highlighted.

> Torrence Ray
> *Delete*
> Martin Krill
> *Delete*
> Cameron Wexler
> *Delete*

He typed two new entries.

> Manny
> Some unknown pervert

He immediately deleted them, too.

"For good order," he whispered.

He wanted to delete Webber's name, but he couldn't. It kept shifting higher while deleting the others. It stopped below Bill Keenan.

Four names remained: Dr. Eli Webber, Bill Keenan, Steve Topel, and Pastor David Graves.

Daniel stared.

Webber saw me, he thought.

He closed the laptop and sat in the dark, hands folded. He said a prayer for Stern and his family, as he had promised to do. He was deliberate. He asked for reconciliation. He asked for Stern's peace. For the first time in a while, he felt a sense of well-being.

He ended, "...through Jesus Christ, Your Son, our Lord, who lives and reigns with You and the Holy Spirit, one God, now and forever. Amen."

Then silence. Except for the hum of the refrigerator and the tick of the wall clock counting down to whatever was next.

CHAPTER TWENTY

The Mill building stood on Broad Street, giant and white, across from the mill pond—a piece of another era. Its only real additions were a screeching elevator installed in the 80s and Cat-5 network cabling.

The first floor still housed the Linden public library, though it had closed earlier that evening. Upstairs, behind tall windows and etched glass panels, sat the old Council chambers. The building had once served as a town hall, post office, and courthouse, depending on the decade. Now it bore history in its bones and dust in its corners.

The walls of the Council chambers were painted the same color as hospital corridors and resignation—something between tired cream and faint defeat. The folding chairs were arranged in imperfect rows, each leg scraping linoleum as late arrivals adjusted their angles. The air smelled like old coffee, aftershave, and ink from printed agendas no one would read. A small-town flag stood limp in one corner beside a picture of Governor Whitmer. Few in the room liked her. Even fewer voted for her. But they felt obliged to keep the image hanging anyway.

Daniel sat in the back, collarless, a civilian tonight. He hadn't come for the meeting. He'd come for Keenan.

He hadn't even known about the meeting until that morning. He heard someone mention it at the corner gas station while filling the Wrangler. It had seen a lot of miles in the last few days and needed the refreshment.

The station conversation was between two elderly men, the kind who'd be interested in a city council meeting. One lobbed to the other portions of the meeting's agenda: routine city business, the usual talk about zoning and facility planning. But one item caught his attention.

"Bill Keenan's going to recommend the city purchase that shelter up north of town."

"Which place is that?" the man pumping gas near a dusty black Chevy Tahoe asked.

"Pastor David's place. Harbor, I think it's called."

Daniel's breath had caught.

Now he was there, three rows from the door, black jacket folded across his lap. He lived close enough to walk. Still, he drove.

The room buzzed with mundane anticipation. Teachers chatting about parent conferences. One of the retirees he saw at the gas station was reading the minutes from last month's meeting. Neighborhood HOA presidents—residents of the neighborhoods they represented, fluttering among attendees, talking about drainage issues and a recent increase in vandalism.

Daniel scanned the room—not for exits, not for safety, but for signs of conscience. The council members wore their usual faces, a mix of fatigue and self-importance. A few smiled too easily. Others kept their gazes fixed on their notes, already planning how to make motions sound like wisdom. The audience wasn't much better. Parents who came for pothole updates. A couple of elderly ladies who treated this like television. No one here had the faintest idea what was happening— *really* happening—in Linden.

Keenan sat up front, preening.

Daniel's eyes rested on him with an intensity that made his fingers ache for the Colt. He'd heard his voice in Claire's recordings. Now, Keenan's posture, his expression, the small movements of his mouth as he whispered to the councilman beside him, stirred Daniel's trigger finger to tap on his lap.

The meeting began with a bland invocation, followed by the Pledge of Allegiance. The councilwoman beside Keenan led both, her voice steady but indifferent. Daniel had kept his eyes open during the invocation. Peering around and past the heads in front of him, he watched Keenan. He watched his breathing. He watched his hands.

The room was still standing when the mayor called the meeting to order. He was a heavier man, well fed, flipping through the printed agenda like a diner menu he intended to order from. Zoning issues. Tree trimming bids. Budget realignments.

Each was handled. It was slow. And Keenan was making it this way.

Daniel had been in enough meetings to know that if you want something to pass—a special initiative or purchase—put it at the end of the meeting when everyone's ready to go home. And if things move along too quickly toward the item, slow it all down with questions. Make folks want to say yes and move on.

Keenan was doing that. He wanted item nine's success.

Then, after almost ninety minutes:

"Item nine—recommendation to purchase the Harbor facility on Lahring Road. Councilman Keenan, you have the floor."

Keenan rose with slow ease, like he wanted every eye on him. His navy blue sport coat was too tight for his rotund frame. His tie, a perfectly bland diagonal stripe. His smile was the real event—wearing a thin mustache, practiced and wide, and just short of genuine.

"Thank you, Mayor. As many of you know, Harbor has been a part of our community for about ten years now—first as 737's worship space, and then after they built the new place over on Old U.S. 23, a transitional housing facility, all under the leadership of Pastor David."

He adjusted his beltline and then clasped his hands in front of him, almost reverently.

"But seasons change," he continued. "Pastor David has decided to consolidate operations to their Grand Blanc facility, which offers better proximity to long-term partners and better funding streams. And in doing so, he's graciously offered the Harbor property to the city—for a price well below market value."

He paused to let it hang. Daniel could almost hear the pageantry behind it: Look how benevolent we are. Look how generous.

"I've reviewed the appraisal. I've spoken with Pastor David personally. This isn't just a good deal—it's the right deal. The building is structurally sound, centrally located, and versatile. We'd be fools to pass it up."

A question came from the back.

It was Stern. He was standing in the doorway.

"Why would the city need the Harbor property?" he asked. "The last I heard, the budget was too tight for a new patrol car."

He moved from the doorway to an empty seat. A few murmurs of agreement rippled through the room. Someone in the front row whispered to Keenan, who then looked to a figure in the side aisle. He motioned the mayor's attention in the same direction.

It was Steve Topel.

He adjusted his sport coat and nodded toward the mayor. "If I may?"

The mayor gestured permission, and Topel stepped forward.

Topel had the swagger of a man who knew he was trusted, whose fortune had never been in question. His voice carried without strain, and he spoke as though he were simply clarifying the obvious.

"I'm not here as a commissioner tonight," he said. "Just as someone who knows this town." Smoothing his comb-over, he continued, "As you all know, I've worked in construction and development across Genesee County for three decades. My company's been a partner in school expansions, utility infrastructure, and public roadworks. I know what things cost. And I can tell you—this? This saves money."

He turned slightly, addressing the whole room, but in particular, Stern.

"We've been assessing properties for an auxiliary staging site for months. Somewhere to keep salt, plows, and backup equipment. The current site across from the high school is tapped out. We're due for expansion. Now we've got a facility—already standing, already zoned—that can be converted with minimal effort."

He gestured to Keenan.

"Bill's right. This isn't just practical—it's smart. Pastor David's offer is generous. And we'd be fools to let it go."

Topel smiled, as if he'd just sold the room a Cadillac with no engine.

Stern didn't reply. He knew better. The room held elected and unelected people who decided things, and he was still a few years from even thinking about retirement.

Daniel sat motionless. But inside, he was shaking. Not with fear, but with anger. He suspected what was happening.

Keenan and Topel were doing more than pushing a real estate deal. They were laundering a legacy. At Pastor David's urging, they'd fast-tracked the city's interest in Harbor under the guise of strategic consolidation. The story they pitched—publicly and privately—was airtight: Grand Blanc's facility had stronger infrastructure, deeper donor relationships, and more central access to partner agencies. That part was technically true. But what they didn't say, what they never would say, was that Harbor had also become a liability. It had hosted too many conversations, too many transfers, too many late-night van runs that didn't appear on official logs. So Keenan—leveraging his seat on the council—and Topel—pulling strings through his construction firm—arranged a swift reclassification. By the end of the month, Harbor would be rezoned, repurposed, and retrofitted into a public works annex. The cafeteria would become equipment storage. The intake office, a key room for plow drivers. The paperwork would say "community efficiency." But in truth, they were razing something sacred to bury something damning. If the Pineview investigation ever found its way to Harbor, it would all be gone.

Topel had been talking while Daniel thought. But even at half-attention, he heard enough. Topel paced slightly, just enough to give the air of thoughtful motion.

"Like I said, the city needs more space. Salt staging. Equipment garages. Backup storage for county and municipal assets. Right now, our options are limited. We were looking at building new off Lobdell, but the bids are double what this purchase and retrofit would cost."

He gestured toward Keenan again. "And thanks to Councilman Keenan's due diligence—and Pastor David's generosity—we've got a chance to solve two problems at once."

Daniel heard the words. "Three," he whispered.

"What's that?" the person beside him whispered back.

Daniel said nothing, giving a faint smile and waving the moment away.

A question came from the crowd.

"Again, like I said, we've reviewed the site. With minor structural reinforcement, we can have it ready by winter. Salt reserves, county vehicles, no disruption to traffic, and it stays in public use. Everyone wins."

The room bustled with commendation.

Topel returned to the side aisle like a man closing a deal.

The mayor was nodding. So were most of the council. One woman—Schilling—looked hesitant, but when she caught Keenan's glance, she gave a reluctant smile.

It was done. Just like that. No questions. No audit. No suspicion. The sound of the gavel might as well have been a shovel scooping dirt over something that had barely stopped bleeding.

Then, as if planned, but without ceremony, the back door opened and the mask of benevolence walked in.

Pastor David was dressed like a guest speaker at a leadership conference. He was playing the audience. On stage, he was young. Here, he was an adult—gray slacks, polished shoes, navy sweater over a white collared shirt. Warm and grandfatherly, giving the best rendition of rehearsed humility.

He stepped to the front and shook hands with the mayor.

Daniel felt the air change. Not colder, not warmer—just more theatrical. Like someone had opened the back of the stage and swapped out the script. People shifted forward in their seats, as if what they were about to hear would clarify their good fortune.

"I wasn't planning to speak," he said, "but I wanted to express my gratitude. To this council. To this town."

He looked around with careful, calculated slowness.

"737 is a joy to serve. And Harbor, one of its unexpected fruits, has been part of my life's work now for many years. I remember right after we moved to the new space and converted the old Lahring Road worship center. I remember the first beds, the first meals, the first woman we helped. But like all things, ministries evolve. Needs change. And so, we're moving forward—consolidating our operations to Grand Blanc."

He paused. It was measured and performative, as if at any moment the wall behind him might explode in LED wonder.

"I believe in stewardship. I believe in mission. And I believe that when the people of God make space for others—whether it's through shelter, or storage, or something as simple as a warm truck cab in winter—they're doing holy work."

A few people clapped. Others nodded.

Daniel stared straight ahead. Pastor David's voice was smooth, untouched by shame. Untouched by blood.

He thought of the girls at Pineview.

He thought of Claire.

The mayor turned to the council. "Shall we vote?"

"All in favor?"

Hands raised. Every one.

"Motion carries."

The gavel struck. Then the applause. The thing was done.

Daniel stood. His knees ached. Only then did he realize why. He's too old to climb motel railings and drop six feet. He didn't notice it then. The adrenaline. His goal. Wexler's terror at the Colt. He remembered how natural it had felt in his hands—the weight, the clean recoil, the way the hammer clicked forward like punctuation. He hadn't flinched once. Not at Pineview. Not at the law office. Not at the Durham house. The weapon didn't ask questions. It delivered absolution.

He turned to leave. Stern had already made his way closer. He leaned to grab Daniel's shoulder.

"Neither of us is in uniform," he joked.

He wore a long gray coat, collar turned up, one hand in his pocket.

"I didn't think you owned a uniform," Daniel turned and said with a half-smile. He didn't stop walking.

Stern didn't follow.

Outside, the Michigan cold was sharpening. Daniel pulled on his coat as he walked to the Jeep. He stood beside it for a moment, staring out across the narrow river streaming out from the city's dam beside city hall.

He didn't get into the Wrangler. Not yet.

Instead, he rested his hands on the hood, letting the wind bite his knuckles. He needed the cold to thin the boiling that had risen in him during the vote. There were too many names still on the list.

He had a thought.

Seeing Keenan, Topel, and David together had reminded him of something. For as nightmarish as Pineview had been—and continued to be—it was efficient. Ugly, yes. Messy and loud. But effective. In a single night, Daniel had handled three names, plus two more for good measure. He didn't even know they'd be there—not all of them—but when they were, the decision came easy. The Colt was steady. His motions were easy and liturgical. The event carried him.

Now he had Keenan and Topel still alive. And they were moving in tandem—appearing in public together, trading glances, circling the same story. If there were a way to bring them into the same space again, he'd find it.

Another council meeting, maybe?

No.

He didn't know how yet. But the opportunity would come. He'd make sure of it. And like Manny and the unknown pervert, if others got in the way, so long as he had enough rounds, they'd die, too.

† † †

At home, he sat in the dark of his office, the glow of his laptop screen reflecting on a two-fingered glass of the Bruichladdich Octomore 8.1.

"The Well," he whispered, opening the browser and searching for 737's Grand Blanc facility. The name alone was telling—part of David's whole theology of hydration, spiritual thirst, slick branding soaked in borrowed metaphors. Daniel clicked through pages of smiling volunteers, stock images of hands cupping water, a three-minute intro video with David's voice soft and sugary beneath an acoustic guitar. He closed it. He couldn't watch. Instead, he opened the list. Four names were still there: Graves, Keenan, Topel, and Webber.

The last one unsettled him. Webber had seen him. Not

clearly, maybe. It had been dark. The distance was long. But Webber hadn't gotten back in his Porsche right away to escape. He'd stopped. Looked. Hesitated. That hesitation meant something. And Daniel couldn't shake the feeling that Webber most likely would have talked to David by now.

He saw me, Daniel thought. "But he didn't see *me*," he said aloud and with emphasis.

David knew Daniel, but only in the way men like David knew anyone. If you were useful to him, if your platform could amplify his own, or if your name carried weight in a room he wanted to control, he'd shake your hand, say your name in front of others, and act like you'd always been close. If not, you were invisible. Not even worth a passing nod. That's how it had always been. Daniel had attended a handful of civic events through the years. He'd spoken to David plenty of times. David had even stopped by the office to introduce himself to Daniel—to size up Daniel's influence in the community. Daniel remembered asking a hard question at a clergy luncheon and receiving frozen smiles in return, the coldness led by David. Since then, David hadn't had much use for Daniel—not at community events, not even while passing one another in the grocery store in town. And tonight was no different. David had entered the council chamber like a man anointed, shaking hands with council members and clasping shoulders like a candidate on a campaign stop. He saw Daniel but didn't nod. He didn't even flinch. Which told Daniel everything he needed to know: Webber saw Daniel, but he didn't know who he was. If he did—if he knew it was Daniel at Pineview—then David would have known, and he wouldn't have dared walk into that room with a speech and a smile. He would've sent Keenan alone. Or maybe even left town.

But instead, he performed. Because in David's world, if you didn't matter to him, you didn't exist. And that meant Daniel still had the advantage. Even over Webber.

The phone buzzed.

It was Stern.

Daniel stared at the screen before answering. He didn't want to talk. Not tonight. But something in him said it was better to keep that bridge from burning—at least not yet.

"Hello," he said.

"Evening," Stern replied. "You busy?"

Daniel closed the laptop. "Just sipping a scotch and getting ready for bed."

"You slipped out of tonight's meeting pretty quickly."

There was a pause.

"Come to think of it," Stern continued, "I don't think I've ever seen you at a city council meeting before."

"I'm trying to get more involved," Daniel said dryly. And then it slipped out. "I'm even thinking about running for office."

He didn't mean it. He just wanted to sound legitimate, maybe even human.

"Well, I'd vote for you," Stern said.

"Can I help you with something, Chief?"

"I've been thinking about our last conversation. Wondered if you'd be up for coffee again."

Daniel didn't answer right away.

"Just talk," Stern added. "Nothing heavy."

Daniel didn't want coffee with Stern. He didn't want coffee with anyone. He wanted to be left alone to plan.

"Sure," Daniel said reluctantly, pressing himself to maintain a bridge he'd much rather douse in gasoline. "Same place?"

"Same place. Can you do ten o'clock?"

"How about eleven?"

"That'll work."

"How about I swing by to get you. I'll drive. You pay."

He knew Stern was attempting friendly humor, maybe even hoping for a friend.

"Sure," Daniel replied. "See you then."

He set the phone down and picked up his glass. The scotch was smoky and warm. He sipped and glanced at the list. Four names. Maybe more, if the timing was wrong. Or maybe right. But either way, they'd all be sent to the place where traffickers belonged.

It stung him to feel this way. To almost want it.

CHAPTER TWENTY-ONE

Daniel was always awake before everyone else in town. He preferred an early start. But he wasn't sleeping well, anyway. Getting up and getting started was always preferable to lying in bed. Today, he'd get away. Go for a walk before he met Stern for coffee later that morning.

Stern was pestering him. It probably wasn't to be friendly. He had a different reason. Something thick. Daniel wanted to recalibrate. Prepare. Relearn how to be normal, if only for the morning.

The first frost came light. Just a sheen across the lawns and windshields, gone by sunrise. But it was enough to shift the air, to make the cornfields breathe in a different rhythm and the earth crackle faintly beneath Daniel's shoes.

It was the end of September. He parked the Jeep to the side of Seymour Road. The fields outside Linden wore a dull golden tiredness. Crops hadn't been harvested yet, but you could smell their readiness—the dry anticipation of machines coming soon to reap what remained.

Daniel walked the perimeter of Miller's acreage, where a service trail ran between the cornrows and a shallow drainage ditch. Jed Miller, a widower with two sons, was a member at Saint John's and didn't mind his pastor wandering the property.

His collar was up, hands sunk into the pockets of an old brown Carhartt coat that had seen more winters than any sermon he could remember preaching. He walked not for exercise but for clarity. The air helped. So did the open space.

Fields don't talk back. Fields don't ask for an explanation. They wait.

Like cemeteries, Daniel thought. *Or God.*

His shoes patted rhythmically on the path as he walked, the soil firm and faintly dusted with chill. He liked it out here—away from the city limits, away from people. It wasn't far from town, maybe a seven or eight-minute drive from Saint John's. But the distance was more than the mileage. It was psychological. The town had its own heartbeat—news cycles, council meetings, holiday planning committees, whispered gossip that pretended to be concern. Out here, none of that mattered.

A line of maples stood along the fence line, their color just beginning to turn. The sky overhead was milk-gray, thick with northern cloud and the smell of burning leaves somewhere downwind. Someone was up as early as he was. He didn't know who, but the scent of their fire traveled easily on the cool air. Sweet and acrid. Like something dying gracefully.

Everyone at Saint John's knew Daniel hated Michigan winters. His preferred escape was Florida. He loved the heat. He craved palm trees. He disappeared there for two weeks every year in the summer, retreating to a house with a private pool in a gated community just outside Orlando. He didn't go to the Disney parks. A single man didn't do that. Not unless he was hiding something from his congregation. And Daniel certainly wasn't. He just appreciated solitude more than most. All he wanted to do was read long books with dog-eared pages, swim slow laps, drink scotch, and watch Shark Week reruns. Sometimes, on cooler evenings, he'd meet up with a pastor friend and his family for dinner—usually steak or seafood, always low-key.

He hadn't always gone to Florida. For years, he stayed closer to home. But eventually, he realized he had to be beyond reasonable driving range—far enough that if something ever happened at the church, he wouldn't be the first phone call. That kind of distance, he learned, was the only way to let go. To breathe. To not feel guilty for resting.

He hadn't gone anywhere this summer. Not after Claire.

And yet, as the calendar's pages changed, a quiet familiarity returned. There was something about autumn that he trusted. Florida gave him rest, but Michigan in the fall gave him something else—something that always slipped past his defenses. The trees turned without needing permission. The air cooled without apology. The dying of things didn't frighten him here. It soothed. It made sense.

In a way, autumn in Michigan was his mistress. Jed knew because he'd seen him out walking, and they had talked. He supposed Jeane might know. She knew more than she let on.

The road that bordered the farm was cracked and patched—never repaired fully, just managed. Like most things in the county.

Daniel passed an old barn on the right, the kind that leaned slightly from age and memory. Its boards were splintered and graying from weather, its roof patched with mismatched tin. A plastic chair sat out front, abandoned. Probably belonged to the old Miller who took breaks watching the deer emerge cautiously from the woods in the late afternoon.

As he walked, he found himself talking. Not out loud. But somewhere in the middle distance between silence and prayer.

He rehearsed the names again.

Brett. Dennis. Ray. Cameron. Martin. Manny.

He'd learned the name of the unknown man: Neil.

He stopped walking and looked across the cornfield. The stalks were tall but thinning, the husks dry, leaves curled like old parchment. In a few more weeks, harvesters would come, and then the land would go bare again. Then cold. Then snow. Then still.

That was the Michigan he despised.

September always fooled you. Warm enough to feel familiar. But one frost, and you remembered what was coming.

Daniel kept walking.

He decided he'd come out here more before the snows arrived. Maybe just enough to remind himself there was a world bigger than the one with sermons, hospital visits, never-ending meetings, and easily offended parishioners.

The wind picked up slightly, rustling the corn in waves. Daniel paused to listen. It was an eerie sound if you weren't used to it—a kind of dry whispering, as if the stalks had worse secrets than him.

He imagined Claire standing in the field.

He didn't picture her as she'd been found. He imagined her like an echo—a figure walking through the rows, brushing her fingertips across brittle husks, saying nothing but not needing to.

There was still no news. No leads on who killed her. He suspected it was someone on the list. But had he already handled it? Or was he still out there? Was it someone Claire didn't know about yet?

That's what haunted him.

The town was haunted, too. No arrests. No updates. Just speculation. The people awaited answers. No one pried. It certainly wasn't the topic of every conversation. Still, kids didn't wait at the bus stops alone anymore. Neighborhoods appointed chaperones.

And yet, somehow, the world kept turning. Stores in town hung up harvest wreaths. The high school prepared for the homecoming parade. The city council finalized October's trick-or-treat hours like it mattered. And all the while, two locals were dead. A third in Fenton. All three were burned into the corners of police reports and seemingly forgotten.

For Daniel, this was good and bad.

Daniel knew what was waiting at the edge of any discovery. He knew his quiet would be disrupted. Either he'd finished what he started, or… something else.

He turned from the cornfield and headed toward an old pump house near the tree line. It obviously hadn't been used in years, not since Jed and his boys put the new irrigation system in. But the stone foundation was still strong, and the place gave shelter when the wind rose.

He pushed the door open slowly. It creaked. Inside, the air was musty and cold. Dust twirled in the light that spilled through a broken slat in the wall.

He sat on the concrete lip that once supported a rusted-out tank. A bird's nest had been built in the rafters. The nest was empty now. He imagined it held life once. Most things do, for a while.

Daniel pulled a folded sheet of paper from his coat pocket. It was the agenda from the previous night's council meeting.

Keenan's name was there. Topel's wasn't. But it should have been. His role was pre-planned, a part of its orchestration—the vote that turned Harbor into a public works annex. Topel was helping with the sanitization, selling a lie as logistics and cost savings.

Nothing to see here, Daniel thought.

He folded the paper again and put it away.

A plane passed overhead, just a small one—maybe a commuter from the town's private airstrip, or a student pilot from Bishop Airport. He followed its arc through the slats in the wood. Then silence.

He said the names again.

Brett. Dennis. Ray. Cameron. Martin. Manny. Neil.

He didn't stay long. The chill was lessening, but it was still cold, and the walk back was about a mile.

Outside, the wind had shifted. The scent of burning leaves was gone.

Back on the trail, he saw a tractor working in the far field—just a speck, really. A silhouette rising and dipping along the ridgeline. Probably Jed. Or one of his boys. He wondered what it was like to live that way, measuring time in seed and harvest instead of meetings and lies.

He passed the barn again. This time, there was movement—a cat, striped and filthy, darting across the threshold and into the brush. Daniel paused, watching it vanish. Even feral things need sanctuary.

By the time he reached the Jeep, parked just off the road not far from the Miller mailbox, the morning had given way to something brighter. The clouds were thinning, streaks of sky cutting through the overcast. He didn't drive right away. Just leaned on the hood, hands braced, staring back toward the fields.

He hadn't been out here since his first go-round with the Colt. He forgot how quiet it was to walk without internal screaming.

Inside the Jeep, the cabin was cold. He turned the key. The

engine rumbled, then settled into its familiar hum.

As he pulled away from the shoulder, a group of crows lifted from the field and circled once before heading west.

He didn't go back to the church right away. He drove through Linden instead, past the high school, past the subdivision entrances, past the millpond, past the cemetery, and then back around toward Saint John's.

But he circled again. He stopped at the gas station for a coffee. He hopped back into the Wrangler and turned down Bridge Street, then left on Broad. The town was waking up slowly. A few folks waved. He waved back.

He didn't feel real. Not in the usual sense.

He felt like someone impersonating a pastor. Driving the speed limit. Offering small smiles. Nodding to people who didn't know the names that filled his thoughts every night.

They were dead. But they didn't leave him.

He'd made them answer for their crimes. But he was simmering in his own.

He pulled into the church lot but didn't get out. He watched the leaves falling across the roof. Watched the way they caught in the corners of the gutters, in the crevices of the bell tower.

Eventually, he stepped out.

Inside, the building was quiet, as usual. Jeane's voice would soon echo faintly from the office. She'd take calls and shout down to him who was on the line. She'd take another call or entertain a visitor. There'd be laughing. It would be genuine.

Daniel walked into his office. He let its stillness wrap around him. He should've started working on the sermon for Sunday. But he didn't.

Letting out a sigh, "I'll bet the nave could use a mopping," he said.

He didn't go right away. He reached for David Scaer's *Discourses in Matthew*. He turned the pages for an hour.

CHAPTER TWENTY-TWO

Daniel pushed the church door open with his shoulder, one hand still gripping the paper cup of gas station coffee from earlier in the morning. The mid-morning air hadn't yet given up its grip on the building. It was cool and still inside, the kind of quiet only old churches know—layered and settled, like the dust lying in its rafters. He took a sip and grimaced. It was bitter and burnt. And ice cold. But he sipped again, anyway, even though he'd be leaving in an hour for better coffee with Stern.

"You drink that stuff all day?" a voice said from behind him. Stern let the door fall shut. It echoed faintly through the nave.

"You're early," Daniel said.

"Cozy," Stern replied, looking around the place. "It even smells holy."

"It does," Daniel said without turning. "It didn't always."

The morning walk had helped him prepare for small talk.

"The guy before me," Daniel continued, "a boomer. He tried to make this place feel more like a concert venue than a sanctuary. He got rid of the hymns. He gutted the liturgy. Replaced it all with goofy praise band nonsense. He tried hanging screens—"

"No," Stern said, pretending to be horrified.

"But folks revolted. It nearly killed the place."

Stern smirked. "So, what—you just came in and put everything back?"

"I came in and listened," Daniel said. "People didn't want gimmicks. They didn't want trend-chasing. They wanted something holy. Real Lutheranism is just that. Stable. Familiar. Something that didn't change every four weeks with a new sermon graphic and branded hashtags. It's the same faith passed along for thousands of years."

"I take it that guy wasn't really a Lutheran?"

"He was," Daniel said, "but he wanted to be something else. I suppose I don't blame him entirely. A lot of mainline guys looked at the non-denoms and thought, 'That's the future. That's how you grow.'"

"Isn't it?"

Daniel shook his head. "No, it isn't. And besides, you ever read the stats on this stuff?"

"All the time," Stern replied, once again attempting sarcastic humor.

"Mainstream evangelicalism is hemorrhaging members, especially the non-denoms. It was inevitable. It was all built on novelty. But novelty doesn't anchor a soul. The truth is, churches like this—" Daniel waved his finger in a wide swirl, "creedal, reverent, sacramental—they're the ones still standing. And they will keep standing, no matter who's at the helm or standing in the pulpit."

Daniel paused for a moment, as if he'd spoken those words to himself.

Stern looked around again. "Like I said, it smells holy in here."

Daniel gave a faint nod. "And like mercy. If you know where to stand."

They walked slowly down the center aisle. Daniel carried the mop but left the bucket.

The pews were neat, hymnals arranged in the racks. The altar was still dressed in Trinity season's green. He stopped near the front and set his cup on the edge of the wooden Communion rail.

"You wanted to talk about something," Daniel said, turning to face Stern. "Do you still want to go for coffee?"

"I only wanted to step in and compliment this place's aroma," he said. He joked too much, as if brimming with dad humor he never got to use with his girls.

Daniel gave a false smile.

Stern exhaled and rubbed the back of his neck. He looked tired—more so than usual. His coat was open, his collar rumpled, and the thin skin beneath his eyes bore a dappled fatigue that came from more than just lack of sleep.

There was something else there, like a man who'd seen something he couldn't unsee, but didn't know what to do with. Maybe a flicker of moral exhaustion. Daniel had seen it in hospital rooms, too—family members at the edge of endurance, caught between knowing too much and doing too little.

"I got a call yesterday before the council meeting," he said. "Tom Kress."

"Who's Tom Kress?"

"The police chief in Fenton."

"Oh, right," Daniel remembered. "I know him. Met him at a fundraiser in Holly."

"He and I go back a while," Stern said. "He's a friend. Good man. He's been working the Anderson case. But he's backing off."

"Backing off?"

"Of the whole case. He said it plain. Said he can't help anymore." Stern paused. "Too many cooks in the kitchen.

Anyway, the State Police are looped in officially now, and someone higher up in Genesee County pulled a few strings. They told Kress to recuse himself unless formally invited back in. He assured me that the invitation would not be coming."

Daniel didn't respond. He folded his arms and looked past Stern to the stained glass. The light coming through was rich and flickering, coloring the freshly mopped floor with faint hues.

"But before he let go," Stern went on, "he sent me an email."

He reached into his coat pocket and pulled out a folded printout. He held it for a moment, then extended it to Daniel.

Daniel didn't move to take it.

"It's not classified," Stern added. "Not technically. Just… not public, yet."

Daniel took the paper and unfolded it slowly. It was short—from Kress's personal email account. He'd forwarded an official State Police notice containing three bullet points with terse descriptions.

Three names separated by grayed dividers.

"Victim identifiers," Stern said.

"Yeah, so?"

"Look closely."

Daniel did. Beside each name was a list of details—their social security numbers, individual cities of residence, past residences, phone numbers, spouses and children, employers, and other obscure details uncovered during an investigation.

Then Daniel saw it.

Each had the words "Harbor Transitional Ministry." That's not what the shelter was actually called, but Daniel knew what it meant. Beside each mention of Harbor was a note detailing the victim's role. Wexler was listed as the supply van operator. Krill and Ray were both noted as volunteer janitorial staff.

Daniel read it twice. Then he folded it neatly and handed it back.

"You already suspected," Stern said.

"I didn't know this until now," Daniel replied. The lie burned. He knew these things and more.

Stern gave a small, humorless smile. "So, you're not as good a guesser as I thought."

Daniel didn't answer.

"Kress also got a partial match on Anderson," Stern continued. "He was still waiting to confirm it when he called me. It looks like Dennis, your former member, did some of 737's legal work. That's not Harbor, but it's pretty close."

Strangely, Daniel liked where this was going. Everything was swerving right around him toward Pastor David.

Until it wasn't.

"You wanna know what I think, Reverend?" Stern asked without giving Daniel a chance to respond. "I think someone's after these guys. I think we're going to find out that something dirty was happening at Harbor. Something that involves the girls who went—"

"Have you reached out to Marcie Durham?" Daniel interrupted, attempting to steer away slightly. It was the first thing that came to mind.

"I have," Stern replied, "but she hasn't returned my calls. You know, she's in—"

"Missouri. Yes, I know."

"Either way, Kress was a little spooked, especially after he was essentially removed from the case. He thinks it all ties together. Harbor and Pineview."

"Then why back off?" Daniel asked. "If he believes there's a—"

"Because belief's not enough," Stern cut in. "And because his leash got shorter. He was told, more than once, that if he kept pulling at threads outside his jurisdiction, he'd find himself in early retirement. He's like me. He needs to keep working."

Daniel smiled, but there was no joy in the moment.

"What about the media?" he asked.

"Nothing yet," Stern replied. "At least nothing to speak of. Nothing's public. MSP's keeping it quiet for now. No charges. No leaks. A couple of reporters have been asking around, but they're watching the wrong things—grant irregularities, zoning stuff. Nothing has surfaced about the victims or their connections."

"So, then, it's just you," he said.

Stern nodded. "Sort of. I'm working in my town. And Kress gave me what he could from his. So, now, since Harbor's in my backyard, I figured I'd start with that Pastor David guy. I don't know him very well, but—"

An uncomfortable moment passed. Stern had trouble getting the words out.

"But you do," he continued.

Daniel tilted his head slightly. "He's barely an acquaintance. That's not the same."

"What can you tell me about him?"

"I can't really tell you anything about the guy."

"You think there's any chance he could be dirty?"

Daniel's jaw tightened. He looked away, toward the crucifix above the altar. For a brief, flickering second, he considered telling Stern everything. Walking him to his laptop. Showing him the list. The photos. Letting him hear the recordings that connected abused flesh to monsters. He imagined Stern's face as he examined it all—the shock, the slow nod, the sick realization that justice had already started to unfold without anyone's permission.

He thought about the Colt, too. Wrapped in a blue towel in his drawer at home. He thought about Brett's chest flowering open and Anderson's skull exploding. He thought about the others, too. Wexler. Krill. Ray. Manny. The formerly unknown sleazebag in the room, Neil. He thought about Claire's journals, her voice on the tape, her voice on the phone the night before she died.

He wanted to tell him.

But he couldn't.

Not yet.

Not until the work was done.

"I don't know," Daniel finally said, his voice level. "But that's why you wanted to talk?" He turned, giving Stern a skeptical glance. "To me?"

"You're a good man," Stern said. "An honest man, just trying to do God's real work. You're nothing like David, which means you're likely a good judge of people."

Daniel shook his head slightly. "That's generous."

Stern smiled. "You're not stupid. You read things. You listen more than you talk. And you were at that meeting the other night. One pastor observing the other, what's your sense of the guy?"

Daniel paused. He felt the answer form immediately—but he didn't speak it. Instead, he looked away. Back toward the altar.

"He's polished," Daniel said at last. "He's a glory hound. He knows how to read a room. He speaks the language of needs and hope, but it's transactional. Not pastoral."

"You think he's dangerous?"

"I think he's opportunistic. Which can be dangerous, depending on what you're hoping to gain."

Stern waited.

Daniel kept his eyes on the altar.

"I'll say this," he added. "If he didn't know what was happening in his organization, then he's the most negligent man ever to call himself pastor. And if he did know…"

He let the sentence drift unfinished.

Stern nodded slowly. "I just needed your gut. That was it."

A short silence followed.

Daniel turned and began walking toward the side sacristy. Stern followed, but slower.

"You know I have no authority to compel anything here," Stern said. "No subpoena. No warrant. No formal questioning. This isn't a probe."

"I know."

"I'm not accusing anyone. Yet."

Daniel turned and looked at him. "But you will be?"

"If the trail leads to it."

Daniel opened a small utility closet beside the sacristy. He pulled out another mop. The other had already lost too many of its worm-like strands in the bucket and under pews. He didn't say anything as he walked back to the nave's center.

Stern stayed where he was, watching.

Daniel fetched the bucket still resting near the narthex doors. It sloshed while Daniel returned. Stern noticed the smell of bleach.

Daniel dipped the mop slowly, wrung it twice, and began working from the front of the nave, only a few rows away from Stern.

"Do you still want to go for coffee?" Daniel asked, his arms moving this way and that way, guiding the mop on the tile.

"You always mop yourself into a corner?" Stern asked, trying to lighten the air.

Daniel didn't laugh.

"I do this because it helps," he said simply.

Stern watched in silence for a long moment.

"Well," Stern said, "I'll let you finish. I suppose we don't need to get coffee now if you don't want to."

Daniel looked up to speak, but didn't.

"Besides," Stern added, "you probably would've made me pay anyway."

Daniel glanced over. "You make more than I do."

"You haven't seen my divorce settlements."

They shared a brief silence—one that bordered on friendly. In fact, it was.

Stern walked back down the aisle toward the narthex. He pushed the door open halfway and paused.

"You know," he finally said, "Kress told me something else. One of the girls at Pinewood said she saw an angel. She was pretty out of it. But at the hospital, she said she saw someone holy. A man in black. He covered her. Whoever it was, he told her she was going to be okay."

Daniel paused mid-swipe, but didn't look up.

"God acts," he said. "He's never far from those who need him." Stern took it as a theological reflection. But Daniel meant it literally.

"I'll see you later," Stern said. "Of course, if anything comes to mind—"

"I'll call you."

"Right. You'll call me."

When the door closed behind Stern, Daniel stopped moving. He stood motionless, the mop dripping in place. Then he wrung it out again and worked the floor slowly—row by row—until the light through the windows began to shift.

He found solace in the work. The smell of bleach. The smooth pull of the mop head. The way the light refracted through the moisture illuminating the wood and tile. It grounded him. Every motion was deliberate and precise. And yet, his mind roamed even as his body stayed still. He could think clearly here.

He thought about Stern's words. He thought about the four remaining names getting exposed before he got his chance to delete them.

He rinsed the mop one final time. As he did, he noticed a small leaf, likely carried in on Stern's shoe. It was brown and curled at the edges. Daniel found it near the front pew, picked it up with his fingers, and put it into his pocket.

It was a message from autumn. Things outside were dying.

He finished the work. In the front of the nave, near the chancel, the light had turned cold. He felt it on his neck.

He sat in the front pew and looked up at the crucifix above the altar. The light hit it at a strange angle now—half the Christ figure in golden shine, the other in shadow. He folded his hands out of habit, not intention, and stared into the silence.

If Stern followed the trail too far, he'd trip over something sharp. Something still loaded. But if he didn't, if he stayed on the safe path, others might get away.

Daniel had stopped believing in clean endings a long time ago.

He stood again, smoothed his palms against his thighs, and reverenced the altar.

He had more cleaning to do.

CHAPTER TWENTY-THREE

Daniel sat at the desk in his study, elbows resting on its oak surface like he had fallen into prayer without meaning to. His dogeared notebook lay open in front of him, mostly empty, except for a few scattered lines he'd crossed out hours ago. None of them were plans. Not really. Just fragments. Half-thoughts.

The desk lamp was off. He preferred the softer light from the hallway behind him—just enough spill to shape shadows along the edges of the room. It made things feel older. Simpler. As if time might rewind if he sat still long enough.

The glass beside him—two fingers of Glenrothes—reflected soft amber onto the desk.

He was thinking of Topel and Keenan again. Webber was a problem. But he would have to wait. Now he wanted the ones who erased Harbor—the ones he couldn't seem to reach through planning. At least, not yet.

He wanted them together.

He pulled open the drawer for a sharper pencil. The Colt wasn't in its place. But he wasn't worried. It was in the Wrangler's glovebox. He'd been keeping it locked in there while he was out and around during the day. Just in case an opportunity for Topel or Keenan presented itself. He knew better than to leave it out there all night. He'd retrieve it before bed.

He closed the drawer and took a sip, then leaned back in the chair and let his eyes wander. The room was quiet, bare but familiar. On the bookshelf to his left, from behind an uneven stack of *Concordia Theological Quarterlies*, something was peeking.

It was his Detroit Tigers hat, the one he bought at the K-Mart in Danbury as a kid. Whenever he saw it, he thought how prophetic it was now that he lived in Michigan. Still, he only bought it to be like Magnum P.I.

He reached for it without thinking. It wasn't anything new to him. He sometimes wore it around the house. In fact, it was on his desk because he'd already been wearing it that day.

As he turned it over in his hands, the feel of it—thin and stiff with age—something jarred loose.

He blinked.

It wasn't just a flurry of memories. It was something deeper. Something placed into him. It was the kind of recollection that didn't rise on command. It was the kind that came like a whispered suggestion, as if a hand was placed gently on his back, and a voice had said, "Remember that one winter so long ago?" The hand, the voice, they weren't forcing but guiding.

Then, slowly, the present slipped away.

† † †

It wasn't even January yet, but the cold had settled early, and the furnace sputtered in its last dying efforts against the Illinois frost. The water heater, too. The windows in their house—thin, single-pane relics—wore frost on the inside corners. Daniel's breath came in clouds when he stood near them. The power was still on, but only so long as no one tried running the microwave and the space heater at the same time. Dad only had so many more fuses for the box—the porcelain kind you screwed in like a light bulb.

He was ten that year. Maybe eleven. It was hard to pin down. His memory didn't sort itself by age, but by events, especially the ones that ached. That winter ached. He remembered the sound of his sister crying in the bathroom. He had learned to endure bathing in barely room-temperature water in the middle of winter. He'd make up fanciful scenarios about diving down into a shipwreck in the northern Atlantic. He only had so much time to accomplish his mission—get washed up, if at all—before he'd run out of oxygen and drown. Keeping this cadence, he hardly remembers hating it. But not her. She was still too little to understand why the water was so cold and why her mother held her in it.

He hated the sound of Annie crying. He'd retreat to his room for as long as he could before feeling the urge to return and soothe her. Sometimes he'd be ready at the bathroom door with his black stuffed bear, even though the tear in its seam made its left leg flimsier than the right. Still, Annie felt better with his bear. Other times, after she'd gone to bed, he'd sit on the hallway floor and talk softly through the crack beneath her door, telling her dumb stories or making up plans for the spring—when they'd build a fort in the woods by the Hyster plant or hop one of the trains on the other side of Garfield park and ride it to the fairgrounds.

She never said much back, but eventually, the tears would stop. He learned to measure comfort not by smiles but by silence. He also learned that no one was coming to fix her sadness. If he didn't act, then no one would. And deep inside, without realizing it, a switch had flipped. He stopped waiting. Stopped hoping for help. And started acting.

That instinct would stay with him long after childhood

ended. Long after he was done being a brother in that house. It would become the part of him that knew how to build a plan when no plan existed. The part that could look at a broken thing—or a broken person—and decide not to walk away.

It could also look for solutions. It could find ways to win.

Three days later, the snow came hard and fast—thick flakes falling like ash, layering the streets with the kind of stillness that muffled sound and made everything feel both heavy and light. School was canceled. The roads were quiet. All of Danbury slowed, as if even the wind respected the cold.

That's when Jeremy called.

Jeremy was a good friend—a little heavier and half-wild with imagination. He lived in a two-story home on the north side of Danbury, the more affluent side. He had one brother, two dogs, and woods behind his house that stretched for what felt like miles.

Daniel's mother let him go. She didn't ask questions, didn't check his gloves. She just said, "Have fun," with a voice that showed more concern for watching *The Days of Our Lives* than frostbite.

The Tigers hat was the last thing Daniel grabbed before leaving.

Jeremy's dad picked him up in a Lincoln Town Car, its pearl white catching the gray winter light as it eased into the driveway, the neighboring tavern looming just beyond. Daniel always felt a flicker of embarrassment at the contrast—his crumbling front porch framed against that polished car, but it never lasted. The moment he slid into the leather seat, it meant escape. And warmth.

When they reached Jeremy's house, his brother was already standing on the porch with two other boys from Daniel's class: Matt and Kevin. They'd been invited, too.

"Wolverines!" they all shouted when the Town Car pulled in.

Daniel and Jeremy hopped from the car and yelled back with the same, punching fists in the air like characters from the movie *Red Dawn*.

They played war in the woods all day.

The forest behind Jeremy's house was thick with every tree imaginable, the kind of terrain perfect for imagined guerrilla battles. They had plastic pistols and rifles. The AK-47s and M-16s whirred when the triggers were pulled. Jeremy's mom let them cut up an old white sheet to wrap around their camouflage clothing, just like the kids in the movie.

They split into two teams—the Wolverines and the Russians. Daniel was always a Wolverine.

The war was a world unto itself. The cold didn't matter. Wealth distinctions didn't exist. The Wolverines built "bunkers" with fallen branches, tunneled into snowbanks like trenches, and called out orders. They could hear their enemies from across the dried ravine doing the same in fake Russian accents. They quoted the movie religiously. "Avenge me!" and "Shoot straight, for once, you Army pukes." Battle after battle, they made each other bleed a little, sometimes from roughhousing, sometimes on purpose. Either way, no one cared. It felt real.

That day, the last go-round before sunset, Daniel was outnumbered.

Three of the boys—Jeremy's brother Sam, along with Matt and Kevin—were the Russians. Daniel had Jeremy and a smaller classmate, Micah. But Micah had gotten captured earlier and was sitting in a prison camp at the end of the trail near the Vermillion River. Sometime before Micah's capture, Jeremy had twisted his ankle in a snow-covered rut and was back at his house drinking hot chocolate.

Daniel was alone.

They didn't call a timeout. That wasn't how war worked. You fought until the end.

So Daniel made a plan.

He doubled back through a thick grove of pines, using a game trail only deer and the boys knew. He crouched behind a split cedar and waited. He knew Sam and the others would come down the east ridge. It was the only high ground left, and they always used it when they thought they were close to winning. And they were. Micah was a prisoner, and Jeremy was "dead."

But what the Russians didn't know is that Daniel had come with smoke bombs and a Zippo his Uncle Frank had given him the previous summer. The smoke bombs were glorified fireworks—harmless, mostly—but they gave off thick yellow smoke when lit. He used the Zippo to spark the fuse, then tossed it low and far into the snow clearing below the ridge.

Then he ran.

He circled around, fast and low, cutting through the brush to flank them from the opposite side. The smoke was already rising, curling like fog, and the three boys were doing precisely what he hoped—running toward it, laughing, thinking they'd found the enemy's last stand. Even shouting, "Give up, Danny boy! We won!"

Daniel reached the tree house they'd built a few years ago, now abandoned, and scaled it with cold fingers and boots slick from snow. From there, he could see everything. He waited and watched. The three Russians reached the clearing and started arguing about where Daniel was. They didn't even look up.

Daniel aimed his rifle.

"Brrrrrrrtttt!" he said as loudly as he could.

All three were "dead" before they even knew where he was.

He dropped from the tree laughing, adrenaline hot in his chest. "You're all dead!" he shouted. He turned away from them and lifted his plastic AK, calling out in obnoxious victory, "Wolverines!"

Sam cursed. Kevin threw his gun in frustration. Matt laughed, but only a little.

"Dude," Sam whined. "You cheated."

Daniel grinned, still breathless. "This is war, man." Then he stepped up to Sam, pulled his plastic army pistol from his waistband, and pressed it dramatically to his chest. In his best imitation of Patrick Swayze's grim defiance, he declared with animated seriousness, "Because we live here!" and pulled the trigger.

Sam shoved him. "That didn't even make sense."

But Daniel and the others laughed.

Micah heard the noise and came up the ridge from the river. He high-fived his teammate.

Daniel smiled and wiped the sweat from his forehead with a muddy glove. His heart was pounding. His skin was cold, but he didn't feel it.

That night, as the boys sat around a wood stove in Jeremy's den, eating popcorn and bragging about the day's battle, Daniel stayed quiet. Not because he had nothing to say, but because he was still thinking about his victory.

It was three against one. He hadn't been bigger or faster. He'd been smarter. And ultimately, he made them come to him. Then he waited.

† † †

The memory ended in a slow fade—the kind that simply dissolves until you're back in the present, unsure of how long you'd been staring at the wall.

Daniel sat at his desk, the light from the hallway giving just enough light to see.

His Glenrothes was crisp. The house was silent. And for the first time in days, he knew what to do.

Topel and Keenan.

He didn't have to find them separately. He could be the boy in the blind again. Except smarter. And stronger.

He didn't have to stalk them one by one. He would draw them. Pull them in. Make them walk into the smoke and think they were about to win.

He scribbled a single sentence into his notebook:

They'll come to the smoke.

He took another sip, grinning now.

He'd need a place. He'd need a time. He'd need the smoke—*the bait.*

Then he knew what he'd do. And he knew the window for accomplishing it was already on the city council's calendar.

Then, from somewhere beyond the edges of the room—part memory, part shadow—he heard an old voice drift in. It was familiar.

All that hate's gonna burn you up, kid, said Colonel Tanner, *Red Dawn's* downed F-15 Eagle driver.

Daniel didn't hesitate, but laughed at himself and gulped the last of his scotch.

"It keeps me warm," he whispered back into the darkness.

CHAPTER TWENTY-FOUR

The last parishioner, Georgie, pulled away from the lot, her blinker clicking too long before she turned onto Main. Daniel wasn't leaving yet. He had only walked her to her car, talking about the snacks for next week's midweek Bible study. She planned to bring cherry cobbler and a coffee cake.

He stood beside his Jeep, watching her taillights disappear behind a grove of gold-leafed maples, their branches just beginning to surrender to October's slow, inevitable fade.

The lot was quiet now. Sunday stillness. It was the kind that crept into the bones of the church like incense after a high liturgy—dense and holy.

Daniel was always the last to leave. A small ritual, of sorts. He'd travel the facility, checking doors, turning off lights, checking the candles one last time. He didn't mind doing it. Like mopping the nave floor, it was something he could see completed.

The door to the nave clicked shut behind him. He fished his keys from his coat pocket and moved toward the driver's side door.

That's when he heard the purr of the engine.

It was Webber's charcoal gray Porsche, like a shark coasting along a glassy surface.

It pulled in with too much ease, as if it belonged there. As if the man behind the wheel already knew this road, this parking lot, this rhythm of Daniel's day.

Daniel didn't move.

The Porsche coasted into the space beside his Jeep and came to a halt. The door opened, and Webber stepped out. Daniel couldn't believe it.

"Reverend," Webber said, smiling like a man who'd rehearsed the moment.

Daniel shut the Jeep door slowly. "Can I help you?" He could feel himself getting warmer.

"You might," Webber said, offering his hand. "Dr. Webber. I'm a forensic psychiatrist. Or was. I've been consulting with the State Police—informally—for the last few months."

Daniel took his hand. He nodded once. "Alright."

Webber let his hand drop. "Sorry to show up without warning. But I was in the area, and I thought it best to speak face to face."

Daniel kept his expression calm. "About what?"

"There's a man—a priest—who lives in the Argentine area. He's got an independent Catholic church… not affiliated with the local diocese or any formal church body."

"Father Collins. Goes by Father Mal."

"Yeah, that's him. You know him?"

"Not really, no."

"From what I can tell, he's kind of a loner. His name keeps coming up in certain… conversations."

"What kind of conversations?"

Webber smiled. "The harder kinds."

Daniel said nothing.

"I'm helping with the profiles for the Pineview case. Did you hear about what happened there?"

Webber was reading Daniel. Daniel was reading Webber.

"Some think he might know something about what happened there," he continued. "I'm just trying to get a sense of who he is. Your name came up, too… as someone who might be willing to help us with the case."

"Who gave you my name?"

"Chief Stern here in Linden. He's really close to the case."

Daniel knew that was a lie. He also knew that if Webber was willing to lie about something that Daniel could easily verify, something was about to happen.

"What did Stern think I could do for you?"

"Actually," Webber said, "we both thought you could go with me to see him. You might not be besties," Webber laughed, "but you know each other, and he may open up to a fellow clergyman."

Daniel didn't move.

Webber went on, his voice light and confident. "You're welcome to say no. But you strike me as someone who might at least want to help in some way."

Daniel studied him. "Stern's a good man," he said, tapping at his door handle. "If he thinks I can help—"

"This is purely for truth-finding," Webber interrupted. "And he said the same thing about you. He said you're a good man and would be willing to help."

Daniel waited, watching his eyes. "I know Father Collins."

Webber's smile didn't break, but his pupils narrowed ever so slightly.

"Got time to go see him today?" he asked.

"When?" Daniel replied.

"Well, I'm here right now if you've got some time."

"I can take you to him," Daniel said. His stomach burned. "He lives back a ways, just off Argentine Road. A little gravel driveway leads up to the house. It's not too far from here, but it's hard to find unless you know where you're going. And your GPS will be useless. No one gets a good signal on Argentine Road."

"Sounds good," Webber replied, almost too eagerly.

"I'll lead," Daniel said. "You follow."

Webber gave a single nod. "Perfect."

They drove west, through the curling outer roads that marked the divide between Linden and nowhere. Past shuttered antique barns and collapsing fence lines, past deer blinds and rows of orchard trees leaning toward harvest.

Daniel kept a steady pace, never losing sight of Webber in the rearview.

He took them down Argentine Road, then further still, onto a narrower side road unmarked by signage. The pavement turned to gravel, then dirt. On the right, the silhouette of a cornfield climbed into the sky, gold and gray under the late-autumn light. On the left, a shallow access lane curved toward what had once been a barn—long gone now, only its stone foundation remaining. But the old farmhouse was still there, rotten and overgrown, hiding behind a grove of trees.

Daniel turned in. The Jeep rattled over loose gravel before coming to a stop near the center of the clearing. He prayed. At least, he thought he did.

Webber pulled in behind him.

Daniel climbed out and waited.

The corn husks scratched and scraped faintly in the wind.

Webber stepped out of the Porsche. He moved beside the Jeep, only a few paces from Daniel.

"This it?" he asked.

Daniel nodded toward the trees behind the clearing. "He lives back behind that grove."

Webber didn't move.

The silence stretched.

Then, without pretense, Webber lifted his coat and pulled a baby Glock from his waistband.

Daniel didn't flinch.

"This really was too easy," Webber said.

Daniel looked at the gun. "You've been rehearsing this."

Webber's smile thinned. "I spent the last three weeks putting the pieces together. I'm no idiot. The investigators might be. David might be, but I'm not. Everything pointed to you. Everything."

Webber spoke nervously. He said far too much.

"I got access to the same state files Stern's been using. More, actually. I've got a friend at MSP—in forensics—who owed me a favor. He gave me everything I needed."

Daniel was strangely at ease. His pulse was steady, not quick. Was this how it was supposed to happen? He wondered if this was a test. Something divine. To see if he'd continue. To see what he was willing to do—what he was willing to endure—to finish the work. A severe gunshot wound? Traumatizing fear?

Neither frightened him. There were still names on the list. Still blood in the soil—girls, somewhere—whose stories would never be known.

"And now?" Daniel asked.

Webber raised the pistol slightly. "I'm here to end whatever it is you think you're doing."

Daniel said nothing.

"You're not who you pretend to be, Reverend. You think you're better than me. I'm nothing compared to you. You've left more blood on the ground than all of us combined."

Daniel stared at him calmly. "What makes you think I—"

Webber tightened his grip. "I've planned this. I'm way ahead of you. I know people like you. I know what you're thinking. It's what I do."

Daniel slowly raised his hands, just slightly, palms out and measured. "What now?" he asked. "You shoot me in a field in the middle of nowhere? What if you're wrong?"

Webber stepped closer, shortening the already minimal distance between them. His overconfidence was showing, even as the gun trembled in his hand.

"I'm never wrong," he said, and meant it.

He shifted his stance.

"Tell me I'm right," Webber continued. "I want to hear it."

"You want a confession?"

"I want you to say what I already know."

Daniel took a shallow breath but said nothing. He wouldn't confess anything to this man.

Webber knew he was right about Daniel. How could he not be? And so, he rolled his eyes at Daniel's obstinance, looking away with a victorious grin. Just once. But that half-second—that flicker of ego—was all Daniel needed. If this was a divine test, he was ready to steer into it. He was going to get his baseball glove back, even if it killed him.

His hand caught the pistol, forcing it upward. It went off, startling Webber. It was obvious he was not practiced, not like Daniel, whose other fist was already snapping forward into Webber's chest. Webber wheezed, and the gun clattered as it fell to the gravel.

Daniel followed with another strike to Webber's head. The doctor dropped with an airless thud, barely enough for a groan. The world around him spun.

Daniel grew up in Danbury. You got in fistfights in Danbury. Webber had never known the colder things. Not the real cold.

"You're never paying attention," Daniel muttered and turned. *Even your scotch selections are ignorant*, he thought.

He left Webber there and walked to the Jeep. He heard Cash's melodic rasp with every step. It wasn't accompaniment. It was ceremony.

In his mind, the air filled as Cash described: with horns and pipes, a vast choir swelling, multitudes moving to a rhythm older than war.

He opened the glovebox. The Colt was there. He hadn't fetched it the previous night as he intended, but chose to go straight to bed instead.

The imagined chorus now broke into wails and summons, cries that rose and fell like an ocean surf.

He checked the magazine and chambered a round. By the time he returned, Webber was coughing into the dust and crawling toward the Glock. Daniel kicked it away, the song's vision splitting between birth and burial, arrivals and departures in the same breath.

He raised the pistol. The final note tolled in him—the beginning and end converging, the kingdom breaking in.

Webber sat up. He clutched at his chest while holding up a hand. "Wait—please."

Daniel's voice was low. "If you had really understood my mind... what I've done... you'd never have come out here alone."

"Reverend, wait! I—"

"I'm here for your confession."

Webber's eyes were wide.

Daniel took a step forward.

"I never touched anyone," Webber stuttered through welling eyes.

Daniel stared.

"I don't even keep the money!" Webber cried, waving his hands in defense. "I don't need it… Do you think I need it? I give it back! To help pay for things at the shelter!"

Daniel looked to the sky for a moment, shaking his head. For all of Webber's degrees, his ignorance astounded him.

He looked back down. Straight and steady. His face became like stone.

"Kyrie eleison."

Webber's mouth opened.

Daniel fired once. The round hit Webber square in the chest. The man pitched backward into the weeds.

Daniel took another step. One more round. It hit the side of Webber's neck just beneath the jaw, tearing a path through cartilage and spine. The man's head snapped sideways with a violent jolt. Blood burst in a bright arc across the weeds before his body went flat, twitching once, then going still—mouth still open as if trying to finish a final word that didn't come.

He stood over the body a moment longer, breathing through his nose.

Then he knelt. He said what felt like a prayer of thanksgiving before wiping the Colt with the inside of his shirt cuff and holstering it in his waistline.

He picked up the Colt's casings but left the Glock's.

The wind picked up again. The stalks moved like ghosts, whispering prayers over the man who'd thought he could outplay the simple-minded clergyman.

When Daniel returned home, he deleted Dr. Eli Webber's name from the list.

CHAPTER TWENTY-FIVE

Stern was pouring coffee into a thermos when the phone rang. He glanced at the clock on the microwave—5:43 AM. He answered without looking at the ID. Only the dispatcher called that early.

"Yeah."

A pause on the other end. Then a few words.

Stern closed his eyes for half a second and held his breath.

"Not again," he exhaled.

He hung up, twisted the thermos cap tight, and grabbed his coat from the peg near the door. He rushed out, forgetting the thermos.

A Linden cruiser's headlights cut through the predawn mist as it idled at the mouth of the access road off Argentine. The cornfields on either side rustled in the wind, brittle and tall, hiding everything beyond a few feet of the gravel lane. A lone deputy, Rhodes, leaned against the front bumper, arms folded, watching his breath coil into the gray morning air. He'd been the first to report it. He saw the Porsche while on his morning commute and got curious. Finding the scene, he called it in. It was just a little after five.

Stern's Explorer came to a stop in the gravel near the tape line. Stern didn't get out right away. Kress's voice was still in his ear, tinny on the speaker.

"I thought you moved out this way to get away from this stuff," Kress said. "Just like me."

"I did," Stern replied. "I thought I was done with this BS."

"We're never done, Jeff. We both know it."

Stern looked out at the field, the corn swaying like pale spectators. "That's what scares me lately."

He reached for the door. "I'll keep you posted," he said and ended the call. Pocketing the phone, he stepped out into the mist. He tugged the collar of his coat tighter. It was chilly. It wasn't the coldest morning, but it was the kind that suggested winter was rehearsing somewhere off stage. He looked toward the makeshift perimeter—tape strung between corn stalks, another deputy keeping the area clear, two Genesee County forensic techs beginning their slow, meticulous work in the brush. A state trooper stood a few yards off, speaking with one of them.

He nodded once to the deputy at the bumper. "What do we have?"

"Male, early to mid-forties. Gunshot wound to the chest and neck."

Stern moved forward, stepping carefully around the flagged markers that noted things he couldn't see so early in the morning. The ground was uneven, but Stern had walked worse. What struck him first was the silence. Even the birds were still. Only the stalks hissed. And beyond them, the faint clicking of camera shutters and discussion.

The body was flat but twisted, arms splayed, one hand still curled toward the chest as though pleading. Blood had dried into the weeds in a fan-like shape behind the head. A small Glock lay a few feet away. A single 9mm shell casing rested about fifteen feet away.

Stern crouched. "The neck shot?"

"Straight through," said one of the techs. "Took some of his jaw with it. Likely close range. We've already dug one of the rounds outta the ground."

One of the markers Stern had avoided.

"I can't be sure," the tech said, "but it looks like a .45 caliber. It's definitely not from that Glock," he said, pointing toward the pistol still resting in the gravel. Just then, another tech scooped it up and dropped it into an evidence bag.

Stern looked down at the man's face. His eyes were still open. Whatever had been in his mind at the end, it was locked there now. He didn't look local. The clothes were too sharp. The haircut too careful. A trim beard, expensive shoes— scuffed now by dust and blood. The Porsche they'd found parked nearby only confirmed the impression."

"Do we know who this guy is?" Stern asked.

"Deputy Rhodes ran the plate. Belongs to an Eli Webber. Lives in West Bloomfield."

Stern glanced around the scene. "You sure the Glock didn't do this?"

"Whoever did this," the tech replied, "took everything but the Glock."

Stern didn't respond. He stood and looked around. The clearing was secluded. No homes nearby. No cameras. The road barely existed anymore, likely unmarked on most GPS systems. It was a place only locals would know.

No one comes to this place by accident.

Stern glanced back at the tech. "Any signs of a struggle?"

The man shook his head. "He was probably disarmed first. Then shot here. Standing, most likely. Blood spray's low. Dropped where he stood. The second shot was to the neck, probably after he was already down."

"Who called it in?" Stern asked.

"Rhodes. He was on his way into the station."

Stern exhaled through his nose.

"Has anyone checked the car yet?"

"Not yet," the state trooper called back. "That's next. Your man, Rhodes, is keeping an eye on things."

He turned back toward the edge of the clearing, where the Porsche sat half-cocked on uneven gravel. The doors were unlocked. He gave Rhodes a slight wave before pulling a glove from his coat pocket and opening the driver's door.

Rhodes called from behind him, "Nice car."

Stern didn't acknowledge him.

He leaned in, one hand on his leg for balance. The interior was black and clean. It smelled like something Stern could never afford.

He noticed a manila folder in the passenger seat, a photo sliding into the seat's crease. He reached, but then hesitated.

He stood and closed the door. He walked slowly around the car as if examining it. But really, he was after the folder. He opened the passenger door. The driver door and the October gray obscured Rhodes. Stern knew it.

He leaned in and lifted the folder.

The first photo showed a man in a clerical collar, his face caught mid-turn, entering a building that looked like a church. The next few were of other men in similar collars—clergymen Stern didn't know.

But then Stern paused.

One of the photos near the bottom was different.

It was Daniel.

It was clearly him. The angle was off-center, a bit too close, like it had been taken in a hurry. He was stepping through the side door of Saint John, his collar visible and his expression neutral.

Stern's mouth tensed. He looked over his shoulder. None of the techs were nearby, and Rhodes was looking back toward the road.

He slipped the photo from the pile, folded it once—quickly, cleanly—and tucked it into the inside pocket of his coat. His pulse had barely changed, even though he'd just done something he shouldn't have.

He set the folder back and closed the door.

He gave the scene one final look, then walked toward Rhodes. Another State Police vehicle had arrived minutes earlier, parking on the shoulder. Two troopers were already speaking with the other trooper and one of the crime techs.

Stern adjusted his coat. "Looks like State's going to take point on this," he said to Rhodes. "No sense in me crowding the scene. Keep me in the loop, but let them run it."

Rhodes nodded. "You got it, Chief."

Stern didn't wait for a reply from anyone else. He turned back toward the Explorer, his hand briefly brushing the inside pocket of his coat. The folded photograph pressed lightly against his chest.

Stern was at his desk within the hour, stopping first at his home for a thermos of coffee he'd left behind in a rush. He made a call. He needed a favor.

A call came just before eleven.

"Jeff, it's Marcia," said the familiar voice on the other end. Dr. Marcia Combs. Genesee County Medical Examiner. "This isn't official. Just a favor. Because you asked."

Stern was standing, but sat down. As he lowered himself, he reached back with one hand to swing the office door shut behind him, stretching awkwardly to stay on the line without breaking the connection. The latch clicked just as he settled into the chair.

"Go ahead."

"The guy from this morning? Dr. Eli Webber. He's a psychiatrist. Lived in West Bloomfield. Had a practice on Orchard Lake Road."

Marcia cleared her voice. "That name mean anything to you?"

Stern hesitated. "No. Should it?"

"I don't know. We ran tox. He's clean. No signs of restraint. Single shot to the chest, clean kill. The neck shot was completely unnecessary, like what happened to some of the victims at Pineview."

Stern didn't speak.

Marcia sighed. "Just wanted you to have that before it gets into the system. My guess? Whoever killed Webber was making a point. It's almost…"

A moment passed between them.

"Almost what?"

"Ritual."

Stern tapped his fingers on the desk.

"Thanks, Marcia. I owe you one."

"No, you don't. We're even."

She hung up.

Stern sat back and stared at the far wall of his office.

Ritual.

His mind scattered to what he knew. But now he had something new. And it didn't make sense.

Dr. Eli Webber. Why was a psychiatrist from West Bloomfield driving into a field in Linden, Michigan? And why the hell did he go there carrying a Glock?

He reached into his coat pocket and pulled out the folded

photo of Daniel.

He studied it for a long while, but he wasn't ready to make anything of it. Not yet. But the question still pestered.

Why was Webber taking pictures of Daniel?

Across town, the day was moving on as if nothing had happened.

Daniel heard about the discovery the same way most people in Linden did: from newsfeeds on their phones. Although that morning, he'd been listening to News Radio 950 in his office. The station ran a news brief just before the noon hour. A body was found. Male. Local police were cooperating with state authorities.

They didn't say Webber's name. They gave no details.

But Daniel didn't need them, anyway.

He stood in the doorway of his office, one hand still holding a half-eaten apple, and listened to the broadcast end.

Then he dropped the apple into the trash can beside his desk and turned off the radio.

"I'm heading over to see Elsie," he called to Jeane. "I'll be back in an hour or so."

Jeane called back an acknowledgement.

Outside, the wind had picked up. The last of the maples on Main Street were losing their leaves.

Halloween was coming. It wouldn't pass quietly this year.

CHAPTER TWENTY-SIX

737 looked more like a corporate training center than a church.

Stern parked along the edge of the large asphalt lot and took in the scene. The building's façade was smooth and modern, its glass doors reflecting pale clouds that drifted across the October sky. A pair of tall banners flanked the entry, each bearing the 737 logo in bold, sans-serif font.

No crosses.

No stained glass.

No visible sign of anything ancient or holy.

The lot was full for a mid-morning Tuesday. Probably a staff gathering or a "leadership summit," if the buzzwords hadn't gone out of fashion.

He killed the engine, checked his badge in his breast pocket, and stepped out into a cold breeze. The air smelled faintly of mulch and asphalt sealant. The building had been added to recently. The glass looked new. So did the signage.

Inside, the lobby was vast. Bright wood flooring, exposed steel, and a coffee bar near the wall. A wall-mounted screen scrolled announcements for the upcoming sermon series: "Be Fearless and Flourish." One graphic had the words "Live Bigger" against the backdrop of a sunrise.

Stern muttered under his breath. "Jesus must be exhausted."

He approached a woman behind the welcome desk, early thirties, stylish, with a name tag that read Jenna.

"Morning," he said. "I'm looking for Pastor Graves. Is he in?"

Jenna offered a smile that didn't quite reach her eyes. "Oh, you must mean Pastor D. No one calls him Pastor Graves."

"Well," Stern continued, "Is Pastor D in?"

"Do you have an appointment?"

"No," Stern said. "Just passing through. Tell him it's Chief Stern. Linden police."

Her smile flickered. "Give me a moment."

She disappeared down a corridor.

Stern stood by the wall of TV screens and marketing slogans, wondering how many ways the Gospel could be boiled into a tagline. That's what the place felt like. A church where you could tithe with Apple Pay and walk away with a latte.

Jenna returned. "He's between meetings, but he said he had a few minutes for you."

"Lucky me," he replied.

Stern followed her through a wide hallway lit with recessed LEDs. The floor absorbed every footstep. She stopped beside a glass-paneled door.

"Right through here," she said, then vanished again.

Stern knocked twice and entered.

The office was sleek. A long window overlooked a manicured courtyard with concrete benches and potted trees. The walls were painted in soothing grays and creams. On one shelf sat a row of curated hardbacks. If there was a book written about church growth models or pastoral leadership, it was likely on that shelf.

There was no Bible in sight.

Framed photographs lined the wall behind his desk—David standing beside bestselling Christian authors, nationally known pastors, and even a couple of well-known worship leaders. Some were posed beside conference podiums, others at round tables during ministry banquets. The wall was a résumé dressed in spiritual authority, curated for anyone who might wonder just how far David's influence extended. It didn't surprise him that Daniel was right, that David was a glory hound. Guys like David loved proximity to celebrity. Faith was just the branding.

A low glass table held a tray with mineral water and stacked coasters branded with the church's logo. A single framed quote sat on the edge of the desk: "Excellence honors God." There was nothing else. Just a brushed-metal desk lamp, a spotless keyboard, and a small arrangement of dried eucalyptus that looked too perfect to be real. The room didn't speak of faith. It spoke of presentation.

Pastor David stood near the window, phone in one hand, eyes focused on something beyond the glass. He turned as Stern entered.

"Well now," he said, slipping the phone into his coat pocket. "One of Linden's finest."

Stern nodded. "Pastor Graves," he said intentionally. "Sorry, I didn't call ahead."

David smiled faintly. "That's alright. God sends visitors unannounced, too. And just call me David."

Stern didn't sit. "You got a few minutes?"

David gestured to one of the modern chairs arranged in a semicircle. "For you? Of course."

Stern lowered himself into the seat, which was too soft and too low. He felt like a teenager in a guidance counselor's office. David remained standing.

"I assume this isn't about parking violations," David said.

"No," Stern replied. "This isn't anything official. I'm just doing a little catching up."

David tilted his head. "I thought the State boys had taken the reins."

"They have," Stern said. "I'm not technically on the case anymore."

"So you're moonlighting now?"

"I call it nosing around," Stern said. "A lot of what's been happening across this county touches Linden, and I figured it wouldn't hurt to pull on a few threads."

David nodded slowly. "And which thread brings you here?"

"Claire Madsen," Stern said, watching David's face.

The pastor didn't flinch. He gave a thoughtful nod. "The name sounds familiar."

"She was a volunteer at Harbor."

"Ah. That might be where I've heard her name," David said. "We have so many volunteers doing the Lord's work, it's hard to keep track sometimes. Names just don't stick for me like they used to."

"She was also a member at Saint John in town," Stern added. "Pastor Michaels' congregation."

David's brow rose ever so slightly. "Interesting. I can't say I knew that."

"She spoke highly of her time volunteering at Harbor. At least, according to some folks."

Stern remembered a line buried in one of the early reports—someone had described Claire as "diligent but quiet," the kind who showed up, but didn't want anyone to know she showed up. It wasn't much. Still, most of the notes overlapped in this way. And something about the phrasing made Stern's gut respond. He wondered if she'd seen something. Maybe learned something. People like that usually did.

David stepped behind his desk, smoothed his coat, and sat. "We were grateful for all the help we received. Claire, was it? If I met her, I don't recall anything unusual."

"You wouldn't happen to know what she did there?" Stern asked. "What kind of tasks was she assigned?"

David thought for a moment, then shook his head. "I don't get involved in day-to-day operations. Not since we moved 737 to this campus."

Stern nodded. "Sure. It must be a big adjustment. That older place to this one... to this... what would you call this?"

"A church," David said evenly.

Stern gave a small smile. "Yeah. It's just different from what folks would expect."

"Well," David said through polite teeth, "it's not your grandfather's church. We do things a little differently here."

"Feels like you're about to launch a tech startup."

David smiled again. "Ministry evolves. The message doesn't change, but the methods can."

"Right," Stern said. "So, where are all the crosses? I didn't see any. I'm guessing the marketing team—"

"We're trying to meet people where they are," David said, his smile thinning.

"I don't know much about Christianity," Stern continued, "but I also didn't sleep in Sunday School. Isn't the cross kind of important to your message? Isn't it all about where God meets us?"

David leaned back, steepling his fingers. "I think we're both too seasoned for cheap shots."

"I'm not throwing them," Stern said. "Just observing."

Then he spoke plainly. "This doesn't look like the kind of place where the sinners get fed."

"On the contrary," David replied. "We have multiple ministries that help plenty. Plenty of people get what they're starving for here."

Stern let that hang.

David pressed his fingertips together more firmly. Stern could see the color leaving David's digits.

"What exactly are you here for, Chief? I'm not guessing you came here to insult me or this church."

"I'm not here for anything," Stern said. "I'm just asking questions."

"Questions about what?"

"Parallels," Stern said. "Ms. Madsen. Harbor. Some of the volunteers. Just things like that."

"You think Claire's death is somehow related to 737?"

"I didn't say that."

"You're implying it, and rather sternly."

The Chief shrugged. "Well, that is my name."

The joke fell flat.

"Like I said," Stern continued, "I'm just asking questions."

David paused, then asked, "Hopefully, you've visited other pastors in the community with the same insulting ambiguities. Reverend Michaels, too, I hope."

Stern smiled faintly. "Isn't that what you're hoping I've done?"

David offered a polite chuckle. "You might find the heart is deceitful above all things," he said, "and desperately sick. Who can understand it?"

Stern tilted his head. "Is that a confession?"

"It's a proverb," David said. "And Proverbs are still in the Bible, even if you haven't opened it in a while."

Stern glanced around at David's shelves. Still no Bible in sight. Just branding manuals and leadership jargon in hardcover.

"Can you show me?"

David shifted in his seat. "Get the app."

Stern chuckled. "I never claimed to be holy. That's supposed to be your job."

David's voice cooled. "No. My job is to help people find their purpose. What they do with it, that's on them."

"Then you'll understand why I'm here," Stern said. "Facts are my purpose. And they have a way of showing the way to everyone else's purposes."

David stood again, walking slowly toward the bookshelf. "You came here without a warrant. Without a partner. Without a call. And since I'm listing facts, I might as well remind you that you're beyond your jurisdiction in the investigation."

"Last I checked, I'm still Linden's Chief of Police. And besides, I told you. I'm just pulling at threads."

David faced the books but didn't read the titles. "But sometimes when we pull at threads, we're the ones who unravel."

Stern leaned back. "I usually find what I need."

David turned, arms crossed. "If you want to continue your fact-finding mission here at 737, you should probably speak with our legal counsel."

"But he's dead, isn't he?" Stern asked pointedly, referring to Dennis Anderson. He thought about listing the other victims who'd circled in 737's orbit, but didn't.

David didn't blink. "We've brought someone else on."

Stern gave a dry smile. "Of course you have. In places like this, it's easy enough to swap out the old for the new."

That was the moment David closed the door—figuratively.

"Isaiah wrote, 'Woe to those who draw iniquity with cords of falsehood.'"

Stern recognized the signal. He stood.

"You know what I've always wondered?"

David waited.

"How men like you," Stern said, "can talk about Jesus, maybe even wear his cross around your neck, and yet hide him from everyone around you."

David smiled coldly. "And I've always wondered how men like you—men carrying the badge of worldly authority—can be so powerless, how you can still end up being the loneliest man in the room."

The two stood silently.

"I'm going to go out on a limb," David said. "I'm betting you're a guy with an ex-wife. I'm betting she took the kids, too. Tell me something, Chief. When was the last time you spoke to them?"

David knew his audience's weak spots. And years of practiced manipulation paved an easy road.

Stern turned to leave.

At the door, he paused. "One more thing."

David said nothing.

"Harbor," Stern said. "When does the city take it off your hands? Officially, I mean."

David's voice was annoyed and low. "We sign on November 1st. But we've already given the city permission to start renovations. They begin next week."

"That deal came together pretty quickly," Stern noted. "It's good to have friends on the council."

"It's good to have friends," David replied, offering a final jab.

Stern nodded before stepping into the hallway and letting the door whisper shut behind him.

David stared at the closed door for a long time before finally sitting down. He didn't have another meeting. Instead, he reached into his coat, pulled out his phone, and stared at the black screen. Then he set it face down on the desk.

A moment passed. He unlocked the phone and pulled up a recent contact. He let it ring twice before Topel answered.

"Yeah."

David's voice was measured. "Chief Stern was just here."

"Stern?"

"Yes."

"What'd he want?"

"His words—'Pulling at threads.'"

There was quiet.

"Whoever that was at Pineview," David said, "he made a real mess of things. Too many roads leading back to—"

He interrupted his own thoughts.

"He opened a door I already closed."

"Torrence told you she was digging. He found her laptop. The stupid girl."

David's mouth tensed. "She was archiving, Steve. She was going to give it all to the police. She thought she was doing the Lord's work."

Topel remained silent.

"I tried to talk with her. I did."

David sounded like a man trying to convince himself.

"I didn't want what happened."

"What did you expect, David?" Topel asked rhetorically. "Keenan and I said we should have more help from the outside. We both knew Claire wouldn't be the end of this."

David said nothing.

"You want me to—"

"No," David cut in. "Just… keep your eyes open. And don't assume we've got time before closing up Harbor for good. Stern's going to go there and look around. I'm certain of it."

"I'll move some guys from my Faussett Road site. I'll make sure someone's there to keep an eye on the place."

Topel hesitated, then added, "You think Stern's—"

"He's circling," David interrupted, his voice lowering. "I have things sorted out with the State Police. Things aren't going anywhere. But if Stern starts asking the right people the wrong questions…"

The line went quiet.

"Just keep an eye on him," David concluded.

"Got it," Topel replied.

"And remember," David lobbed before the line went dead, "we're all in this together. If Bill goes down, if you go down, if I go down, we all go down."

David hung up without another word.

He sat still for a moment, then reached for a drawer. Inside was a manila folder with a thin blue tab. It was a volunteer record. Claire's name was written across the top in faded ink. He didn't open it. He just stared—not with remorse, but with anger. Beneath the folder, partially obscured by a glossy stack of laminated vision statements, rested Claire's old laptop and a scuffed external hard drive, their cables loosely coiled like sleeping serpents.

He closed the drawer gently and reached for his desk phone.

"Jenna—"

"Yes, Pastor D."

"Could you find a number for Reverend Daniel Michaels in Linden? Saint John Lutheran. The church office will do."

"Sure. I'll look for it and call you right back."

"Thanks."

CHAPTER TWENTY-SEVEN

David Graves arrived right on time.

Daniel saw his car from the window of the sacristy—a black Escalade that looked like it belonged to a celebrity. It pulled into the lot and parked neatly near the ramp entrance.

By the time Daniel stepped into the office hallway, David was already being shown in by Gloria, one of the older women who volunteered a few mornings each week. She looked flustered in the presence of someone who, even if only by appearances, felt important.

David smiled at her, then looked around.

"This place is… charming. Really. A proper parish. Almost reminds me of my first internship church in Ohio."

Daniel offered a small, polite nod. "We like it."

"It was a little place," David continued. "Like this. Not like the multi-campuses I'm managing now. It can be a nightmare by comparison sometimes."

Daniel offered another polite nod. "Let's go sit in my office."

They passed Jeane, and Daniel introduced them.

"Can I get you anything, Pastor David?" Jeane asked. "A coffee… or water, maybe?"

"A water would be nice," he replied, and then thanked her almost too exuberantly.

David followed Daniel into the office.

"And here we are," he said, stepping inside. He looked around slowly. "Now this is a study. Books everywhere. My

Lord, I forgot these even existed." He chuckled. "I always suspected you were sharp, but I didn't know you were this well read."

Daniel motioned to a wooden chair across from his desk. "Have a seat."

David did, crossing one leg over the other with the ease of a man who sat in meetings all day.

Jeane arrived with his water. "Let me know if you need anything else."

"Thanks, Jeane," Daniel said as she closed the door behind her.

"She's a real gem," David said. "Oh, the ones who hold up the arms of the prophet."

"Don't be fooled," Daniel said jokingly. "She runs the place."

"I appreciate you making time," David said, as if he'd not heard a word Daniel said. "I've been meaning to stop by. It's been a long season for everyone in Linden."

Daniel nodded once. "What brings you to Saint John?"

David's eyes wandered the room as if still taking stock. "Well, you, actually. I wanted to check in. With everything going on. With Claire Madsen's passing—she was one of your members, right?—I thought I might reach out. One shepherd to another."

Daniel folded his hands in his lap. "Claire died six months ago."

"I know. And I'm sorry. Things are always humming at 737. Time gets away."

"Yes, it does."

David smiled again, this one a little tighter. "Chief Stern stopped by 737 earlier this week. He asked about Claire. It caught me off guard, but it reminded me that I needed to reach out… to see how you're doing."

"I appreciate it," Daniel said. "Claire was a good girl. She was quiet. Kept to herself, mostly. But she helped people. She was one of the faithful here at Saint John's."

David nodded slowly, thoughtfully. "That's what we need more of. The faithful."

"She volunteered at Harbor, right?"

"Yes, she did. I regret I didn't know her very well. Or maybe I did in passing, but the faces blur together when there are so many volunteers. That's the challenge with scale. Sometimes people's lives slip past you."

Daniel said nothing. He simply waited.

"I wish I could've gotten to know her. I'm sure she was nice."

David uncrossed his legs and leaned forward slightly. "That's something I admire about Saint John, actually. It's small enough to see everyone. To know their stories. I imagine that's a comfort to the grieving."

"It can be."

"I think about that a lot," David said, shifting in the chair. "You know, how different our ministries are. 737 is… well, it's big. There's a lot going on. A lot of moving parts. A lot of gears shifting. A lot of momentum. Yours is quiet and steady. I don't mean that as a criticism."

Daniel offered a calm look. "I didn't take it as one."

David chuckled lightly. "Of course not. I just think churches take on different shapes depending on the vision. Ours was built to reach as many as possible. Yours seems built to sit still. Both have their place."

Daniel absorbed the comment. "I figure the Gospel is

fixed. When it's stretched, it gets too thin. And then it's nothing."

David smiled again, but only a little. "Maybe that's true. But light does find its way through even the thinnest cracks."

A moment passed. Daniel watched him, still giving away nothing.

David cleared his throat. "So, I suppose since I already mentioned it, Chief Stern came by 737 with some… well… implied theories. I'm concerned he's looking in the wrong places, and I don't want him wasting his time. If he comes by here, since you were so close to Claire, I'd hate for you to accidentally lend credibility to a false narrative."

"If he comes by, I'll talk with him about whatever he wants to talk about."

"What I mean is that—"

"The truth is rarely the wrong narrative," Daniel inserted. He wasn't sure he'd say it. But he did anyway.

David raised his hands in mock surrender. "No offense meant. I'm just trying to maintain something good. We're doing good things at 737, and it doesn't take much to soil a reputation. You and I—we don't want that for either of us."

Daniel shifted a little.

"Whether it's 737 or Saint John's, people need to be able to come to us with their grief, with their confusion. They need us to steady the ground. You and I should support one another in these things. Especially now. Especially when the people of Linden need us the most. We're in this community together."

Daniel tilted his head, voice even. "Is that why you're here? To ensure we support one another?"

"I'm here," David said carefully, "because even though we may not spend much time together, I'd hope you'd consider me a friend. And sometimes a conversation between friends can prevent a misunderstanding."

Daniel said nothing. His stillness was beginning to unsettle his visitor.

David glanced toward the hallway. "I've always respected your ministry, Daniel. You've kept this place going without taking a single step into the culture, toward the inevitability of the church's broader waters. That takes a kind of commitment to a church's identity that most people don't understand. I certainly don't."

Daniel met his eyes. "We have very different vessels, you and me."

David didn't blink. "Yes, I suppose we do. But we're both sailing. And right now, the water's choppy. If I can help you, I will. I'd hope for the same from you."

Daniel let the silence dominate.

David looked at his watch and then rose to his feet. "I won't take any more of your time. I just wanted to say— you're not alone. And if questions arise, I hope you'll think of me as a friend. And that you can call me if you need me."

Daniel stood as well.

David extended a hand. Daniel took it briefly. He could feel the slight pressure of David's grip—a performance, not a gesture. The man's skin was moisturized and smooth.

As David turned to leave, he paused at the door and glanced back at the bookshelves one last time.

"I wasn't kidding," he said. "You really are more than I gave you credit for. I'll bet after a few beers and a round of golf, we'd be brothers."

Daniel offered a polite smile. "I'm glad you stopped by."

David opened the door and stepped into the hall with

Daniel just behind him.

As they passed the front office, Jeane looked up from her desk. "Thank you for coming by, Pastor David," she said cheerfully. "It was nice to meet you."

David gave her a practiced smile. "The pleasure was mine. You keep a lovely church running, Jeane. Don't let Pastor Michaels fool you—he'd be lost without you."

She laughed politely, brushing her hand over her desk as if tidying it for his approval.

They continued toward the entrance. The carpet muffled their steps, laid tight over the old cement slab that had settled decades ago. The hallway smelled faintly of dust and distant altar flowers—Saint John's subtle signature, lived-in and familiar, unlike 737's antiseptic gleam.

In the narthex, Gloria was vacuuming. She glanced up when she saw them, her face brightening. She chirped something neither could hear and waved. Realizing, she silenced the vacuum and scuttled over.

David layered the easy charm of a salesman who'd shaken thousands of hands. "Sister Gloria," he said smoothly, "the heart of the whole operation, I'm sure."

She smiled, bashful and flattered.

Daniel opened the front door and stood aside as David stepped through. A gust of autumn wind slipped into the entry, scattering a few dry leaves across the worn tile.

"It really is a beautiful place," David said, glancing back through the narthex glass to the nave's windows. "Places like this... they have a kind of soul to them. Don't ever lose that."

Daniel gave a quiet nod. "We do our best to maintain. God is good to us."

David adjusted the lapel of his coat and offered one final

smile. "Be well, Daniel. And remember what I said—we're in this community together. Call on me if you need me."

"I'll remember," Daniel said. "And I will."

Very soon, Daniel thought.

David turned and made his way into the lot, the Escalade blinking open at his approach. As he pulled away, Daniel watched through the cracked glass of the church door. He waited until the vehicle disappeared beyond the maple trees lining the road, then quietly closed the door and slid the bolt into place.

The hallway behind him was still. Jeane hummed softly to herself as she returned to her paperwork. Gloria disappeared into the fellowship hall, carrying a stack of folded bulletins.

Daniel stood in the entry a moment longer, hands resting at his sides. The cold from outside clung to his sleeves. Then he turned, walked back toward his office, and sat in the wooden chair across from his desk—the chair David had occupied.

"I'm going to head home for some lunch," he called down the hallway to Jeane.

"Okay, Pastor," he heard.

He couldn't think as well, not with so many theology books shouting his hypocrisy. He needed the list. Even as it pestered him, it was getting quieter.

He needed the Colt. It only shouted when working. And only in short bursts.

CHAPTER TWENTY-EIGHT

The wind pressed against the side of the house in tired gusts. It had started just after sunset. Occasionally, the clap of a loose siding snapped somewhere beyond the kitchen window like a warning. The rest of the neighborhood was relatively quiet, nestled into the strange peace of late October in Michigan.

Leaves rustled down the street like voices too soft to understand. The air smelled wet, even though the heavier fall rains were yet to come.

Daniel sat at his desk with a three-fingered dram of Auchentoshan's 18-year-old.

The hallway light kept the room dim but usable. His hands were steepled beneath his mouth, the tips of his fingers resting against his upper lip. He stared at nothing. He hadn't moved for the better part of an hour.

Eventually, he shifted forward to his laptop and pressed play.

The first recording began with a hiss. Then came ambient sounds—distant traffic and the low murmur of male voices, still indistinct. Finally, the sound of a door sliding open—metal and familiar. Its dry slide and final clack were distinctive. He'd heard it in others of Claire's recordings and knew, even before she narrated, it was the kind of door you only heard on a van.

The Harbor supply van. The one Wexler had driven.

A moment passed. The voices were still speaking, but

crisper now with the door open.

Then there were footsteps—boots crunching gravel. It wasn't a recording in the Harbor parking lot. It was somewhere else. Perhaps the lot behind Pineview, where Daniel had parked? But there were no traffic sounds in the distance, only cicadas and wind.

But then came a voice that betrayed both the actors and the location.

It was Steve Topel casually explaining to Keenan the dimensions of an add-on his crew had started that day. It was a Topel & Sons construction site.

Daniel closed his eyes. He wanted to imagine Topel's face. He imagined Keenan's, too. He'd seen them in photos. He saw them at the city council meeting, tag-teaming the real estate whitewashing. Now he envisioned their faces' animation, bent and criminal.

The conversation was half-mumbled at first. Still, the recorder, wherever Claire had placed it, caught everything. Every syllable. Every slurred breath. Every thud against the van floor.

Topel went first.

The van door slid and clanged shut. Daniel could hear movement. There was a whimper, weak and gagged. There was no conversation with the girl. Just orders. Then impacts.

A slap to the face. Then a fist. Then a choked breath.

Daniel's fingers curled around the base of his glass, but he didn't lift it.

She moaned, but not in any way that suggested she was present. She was too drugged to fight. Maybe too drugged even to cry.

Topel kept going. At one point, he laughed. Not loud. Just

enough to let whoever was waiting nearby know it was going well for him.

Then Keenan's muffled voice again.

There was a pause. Some clinking, like a belt being refastened.

Then the sliding van door.

Topel said, "She's all yours." A few seconds later, the thumping of someone climbing in, followed by the van door sliding shut.

Daniel didn't need to hear what happened next. But he listened anyway. The girl had no choice. He'd leave himself choiceless, too.

Keenan didn't say much. But he didn't need to. The audio file spoke for him, picking up every gross detail—the movements, the breathless grunts, the coughing girl. Keenan hit her once. And then again. He told her not to look at him. Then he went quiet.

Daniel's jaw was locked. Not clenched with frustration—but set, with a stillness that felt volcanic. His thoughts didn't race. They formed slowly, with sharp edges. These weren't men pulling strings from far-off offices. These were monsters who enjoyed the filth—who fed off of the suffering.

Minutes passed. Maybe ten or twelve. Daniel listened to all of it, his stomach aching, and tears forming.

A final grunt of effort, a belt buckle, and the van door opened again. The audio fell silent except for the girl's labored breathing. Then, eventually, a casualness between Topel and Keenan.

The recording ended without any kind of signature or closing. Just the long, hopeless silence that came after a violation too great to describe.

Daniel opened his eyes.

He hadn't moved in the last thirty minutes.

He closed the file and opened another.

The file began the same way—doors, muffled motion, dreadfulness.

This time, the location was different. There was no crunching gravel. It was pavement. And there was traffic in the background. Like the previous recording, the location was betrayed.

It was the parking lot at Harbor.

Wexler's voice spoke. "Just bring her out. I'll pull over to the kitchen doors."

The engine hummed, and eventually the brakes squeaked to a halt.

"Don't take too long, guys," Wexler said, closing the driver's door and sliding open the cargo door. "I have to get her up to Pineview within the hour. Krill said Manny's complaining about lines forming in the office."

Topel's voice spoke again. It was clipped. He said something about closing the door behind him.

Then the movement. The girl seemed awake enough to protest. Not clearly. Not loudly. But enough to be heard.

There was a strike.

Then silence, followed by the same routine.

The door opened. Keenan would be next.

But then, shockingly, another voice.

And just like the first time he heard this recording, Daniel sat up straighter.

It was David.

He wasn't in the van. Not right away. His voice was filtered by distance—likely calling through the kitchen door.

Either way, his tenor was unmistakable. He was annoyed, maybe even disgusted. But not necessarily at them.

He heard a call to keep it down, followed by "and you didn't clean up the van last time. We cart food in that thing, you know."

That's what he said.

Daniel blinked.

Of all the things, this absurd managerial critique was the worst. Not because it was loud, but because it was real. It was the voice of a man, a pastor, not bothered by the sin, but by the stain it might leave on his property.

Then something else. David's voice became clearer. He'd moved closer, but now noticeably hushed. Daniel guessed he'd spoken while leaning in through the van's sliding door.

"She's barely in high school. And you're—"

Daniel stopped the recording. His gut clenched.

There was no reprimand from David. No command to stop. No threats of exposure.

He pressed play again.

"—going to wear her out before Cameron gets her to Pineview."

Again, that was it. He wasn't trying to stop it. He was just trying to pace it. He was trying to keep the products fresh and on schedule.

The van's frame creaked as someone climbed out. Probably Keenan forfeiting his turn.

More motion followed by instructions to Wexler concerning payments.

Daniel sat back in his chair and closed his eyes. He'd had the thoughts before. Too many times, in fact. He wondered how often scenarios like these had played out. How many girls like the ones in these particular recordings. Or the ones who weren't recorded at all. How many never got even this much of a memory?

He thought about Claire's journal. The care she took to document what no one would ever imagine. And then he thought about what they'd done to her when they found out.

Had he only come when she asked.

Had he not brushed her off. Had he not deferred her quiet pleas to a later time that never came. He was tired. He figured it could wait. He was wrong.

So terribly wrong.

And now she was gone.

The recording was still playing as he thought. It came to an end on its own. The muffled sounds of highway driving and occasional moans were the last of it.

Daniel closed his laptop.

He stood but didn't move.

A moment later, he found himself at the living room window. The neighborhood was dim and still. The neighbor's porch light swayed a little in the breeze. It made the Halloween decorations in the yard—zombies reaching up from behind plastic headstones—seem to move. A dog somewhere down the street barked. Everything else was still.

By this same time tomorrow night, front doors would be open and the sidewalks would be busy with trick-or-treaters. The neighborhood would be filled with laughter.

Daniel took a long breath.

Topel and Keenan weren't just making sure the operation was protected and orderly. They were celebrants in its desecration.

And David Graves. The pastor at 737.

He was neither disgusted nor distant. He was in charge. He knew everything. He knew the calendar. The logistics. The routes. The fees. He knew everything but the color of the girls' eyes. Although Daniel suspected even that wasn't beyond him.

Daniel whispered something from memory.

"Deliver me, O Lord, from the evil man: preserve me from the violent man; who imagine mischiefs in their heart; continually are they gathered together for war..."

The whisky glass still in his hand, he sipped and walked back to the desk.

He pulled his notebook from the drawer and scanned a few pages, tapping methodically.

The plan.

But tonight, he would sleep. Probably not very long. But enough to function. Hopefully.

And when he woke, he would finally dig into the bin of Halloween decorations he'd been too occupied to retrieve from the garage. There was something in there he needed.

A darker vestment.

CHAPTER TWENTY-NINE

Daniel fell asleep on the living room couch with a blanket over his chest and one hand resting lightly on his ribs. He hadn't meant to fall asleep there, but sometime after revisiting his notebook pages—and another scotch—his body had given up.

Daniel rarely dreamed. And even when he did, he could never remember it the next morning. But not this time.

The room was dark but warm. The hallway light still offered its dull glow. It wasn't enough to fully illuminate anything in the living room. Only the outlines of furniture and the fading, yawning black beyond.

Outside, the world had gone quiet. For Daniel, so did everything else.

† † †

He was walking through a field of snow.

Except it wasn't snow.

It was ash.

A fine, gray powder clung to his shoes and pants, filling the creases of his steps until he could no longer tell where he had walked or how far he'd come.

The sky was the kind of blue seen just after midnight, when the world is turning toward dawn. And yet, it seemed an unnatural twilight. Something was wrong. The sky was relatively clear, and yet there were no stars. The few clouds that drifted overhead churned in unnatural spirals.

He sensed a heavy pulsing from some place he couldn't see.

A church steeple jutted from the ground nearby. But only the top third of it, snapped like a matchstick, and half-buried in the ash. Its bell still hung, cracked and still.

He recognized the steeple, and yet, couldn't place it.

Daniel walked forward.

No footsteps followed him. The ash muffled and consumed everything about his presence. There was no sound at all. Not even breath.

He walked anyway.

At the edge of the field was a door.

Just a door. Not connected to anything. It stood upright, supported by nothing, painted red and slightly ajar. Its frame was clean. The handle glinted.

Both behind and around the door, a cornfield stretched in every direction. Daniel expected to open the door and enter the rows.

He reached for the knob, but it opened on its own.

The hinges made no noise.

Inside was a room—the church basement, tiled in the same pale green linoleum that had been there since the 70s. The room buzzed, lit by fluorescent tubes. Folding chairs were arranged in a sloppy circle. Coffee urns sat cold and half-empty on a nearby table. The kind of space used for Lenten soup suppers. Or a grief counseling session.

It smelled like damp paper and wax.

At the center of the room sat a girl. Her back was to him. She wore a familiar gray cardigan and dark jeans. Her hair was tucked behind one ear.

Daniel didn't have to see her face to know who she was.

"Claire," he said.

She didn't turn around.

He stepped forward slowly, his feet making no sound on the tile. The ash from outside followed him in. Everywhere he stepped, he left a fully formed footprint of grit. It never thinned with his steps. It was always full.

He circled the chairs. When he finally reached her side, she looked up.

It was her.

But not entirely.

Her eyes were too dark. Almost black. Her skin was pale—drained of all color—but not dead. She was still pretty, but only in the way statues are pretty.

Her mouth opened, but he could not hear her.

Then her lips moved again, slower this time. He could just make it out: "Why?"

Daniel tried to speak, but his throat burned instead. He swallowed and tried again.

"Because the world won't clean itself."

Claire blinked. Once. And then again.

Then she looked at the folding chairs around them.

Each one now held a figure.

All girls.

They sat still, their heads bowed. Some were bloodied. Some bruised. One wore a torn sundress. Another had one shoe.

He turned to look at them all.

One girl—not much older than twelve—stared directly at him. Her eyes were white. Not rolled back. Just… gone.

Claire rose to her feet.

"You're not helping them," she said. Her voice came hollow and echoing, like it was filtered through a pipe. "You're not healing anything."

Daniel's hand instinctively brushed at his waistband.

The Colt was there.

He felt it.

Claire saw the movement.

"You brought that here?" she asked, her voice gravelly and sharp. "Even now?"

Daniel looked at the gun but didn't answer.

One of the other girls started crying. It was faint, like the memory of crying. It didn't echo. It just filled the air like fog.

Claire stepped closer.

"Don't do this," she said. "You can't do this."

"No," Daniel replied, his voice sour, like he'd swallowed vomit.

"You're angry," she said.

"I'm faithful."

"You're afraid."

"I'm called."

"You're lying."

She placed a hand on his chest. He expected it to be cold. But it wasn't. It was warm.

"Beloved, never avenge yourselves," she said. "But leave it to the wrath of God, for it is written, 'Vengeance is mine, I will repay, says the Lord.'"

Daniel didn't move.

Claire's eyes shimmered. Not with tears. With something sharper. Something hollow.

The room shook.

One of the ceiling tiles fell. The sound was dull, like a

body hitting carpet.

The chairs clattered. The girls did not move.

Claire looked toward them and then back to Daniel.

"They're not asking for this."

"They can't."

"You do not speak for them."

"I'm not speaking," Daniel said. "I'm acting."

"You're breaking."

Daniel looked away. His breath caught.

He looked back. She stepped forward—not as an accuser, but as someone who once trusted him. For a moment, just a moment, he felt like a boy again, like someone who had wandered too far from home.

The Colt suddenly felt heavier.

Claire took another step forward. She was close enough to touch his face. Daniel saw her eyes go pale.

"I can't see you, Pastor," she whispered and reached toward him. "Where are you?"

Terror washed over Daniel. He took a step back. The girls in the chairs were gone now. All of them. Just empty seats, stained with something dark and glistening.

The room pulsed.

Claire started crying. There was blood on her cheeks instead of tears, as if something had spattered. It didn't drip. It just slid, thick and slow.

She reached out toward him again.

"Where are you, Pastor?" she cried. "Where are you?!"

Daniel gritted his teeth and stepped back even further.

He couldn't stand the pleading in her face. He couldn't take the heat of her grief.

Then her cries quieted, and her arms lowered to her side.

Her voice changed.

It was cold.

She lifted her hand with a pointed finger.

"Repent."

The room darkened.

Claire's skin began to flake.

It fell off in pale gray pieces, crumbling like ash. Her form flickered like an old TV losing its signal.

† † †

Daniel woke.

His shirt was damp with sweat. The glass on the side table was empty. Its benefactor, this time a bottle of Four Roses, was half empty.

The clock on the wall read 6:17 AM.

Daniel sat up slowly, pressing the heels of his hands into his eyes.

The dream still clung to him. Claire's voice echoed through his skull, scraping at the walls of his resolve.

He rose to his feet and walked to the window.

The street was still. The sun was struggling to rise. He shivered when he noticed the clouds slowly spiraling. It was strangely familiar.

He walked to the bathroom sink and turned on the faucet. The water was cold and sharp. He splashed it across his face and then stared at his reflection.

"Repent," he said to the man before him.

A minute passed.

He took a shower and then made some breakfast—two eggs, some toast, and a cup of coffee.

He sat in silence. He didn't taste the eggs. Or the toast. Or the coffee. He wasn't eating for flavor. He was just filling the machine.

After he was done eating, he cleaned the frying pan, his plate, and all the used utensils. Next, he spun the bread bag closed, tucking the opening beneath it in the small pantry beside the refrigerator. He returned the toaster to its place in the floor cabinet to the left of the sink.

He wiped down the counter.

When the kitchen was clean, he poured the rest of his coffee into the sink and rinsed the mug. He dried his hands, folded the towel, and hung it neatly on the oven handle.

Then he went to his desk.

The room was still dim. The sun didn't rise in Michigan this time of year until closer to 8:00 AM.

He reached for his notebook where it always was—in the drawer with the Colt.

He picked it up and opened it to the last page he had written.

A few pages of scribblings.

A strategy.

He stared for a moment. Then, slowly, he began tearing. One page. Then another.

He shredded each into smaller pieces that he dropped into the nearby trash can like its own private snowfall.

A blank page now stared up at him.

He tapped his pencil against the paper.

In a moment, he was writing. Not quickly or erratically, but smoothly.

A few lines. Then a few more. Steps. The beginnings of something new. A different strategy. Far different than what he had planned before.

The other would've happened tonight. Besides the Colt, it would've required something from his Halloween bin in the overhead attic in the garage.

But not anymore.

Now it required some shopping a few towns over, in the city of Brighton.

CHAPTER THIRTY

Brighton was thirty-five minutes from Linden if you didn't take the expressway. Daniel didn't. He took Argentine Road south to M-59, then Lahser, then Grand River. He drove the whole way with the window cracked just an inch, letting the cold October air sting his knuckles as it slipped in around the side mirror. The hum of the tires on pavement gave rhythm to his thoughts, keeping them steady and controlled.

This was not improvisation.

He parked at a strip mall off Grand River. Inside the Office Depot, the overhead lights beamed their cold artificial light. The aisles were well-stocked. Early Christmas décor was already elbowing in beside Halloween's already months-old presence.

He walked with purpose. Padded mailers and USB drives.

He saw a manual typewriter locked behind a glass display case. He didn't need it. But it gave him an idea. And he already had one in the closet at home. It was his sister's.

He went back to the paper aisle for a ream of résumé stock.

Daniel paid for everything in cash. No credit cards. No email receipts.

A few storefronts down, at the Best Buy, he purchased a prepaid flip phone and the cheapest laptop on display. Barely $300 on sale. A piece of junk meant only to get a student through college.

He paid in the same way. All cash.

From there, he drove to a Leo's Coney Island at the far end of town and ordered black coffee to go. He didn't need it. But he needed the receipt. More importantly, he needed the timestamp and the alibi. He needed the randomness of it.

He made one more stop. It was a grocery store in Whitmore Lake. He bought three manila file folders and a pack of fine-tip Sharpies. Another cash transaction. He passed a man selling pumpkins in front of the store and nodded politely. The man didn't nod back.

By the time he returned to Linden, driving past Saint John's toward his house, the church bells had already rung the eleventh hour.

Daniel's desk was clean. Before opening the packages, he'd already retrieved a pair of black nitrile gloves from below the kitchen sink. Snapping them on stirred a brief reminder of the struggle with Dennis earlier that summer.

He blinked the memory away.

He laid everything out on the desk with the precision of ritual. The laptop whirred to life with a stuttering click. After a few minutes of required setup—a fake name, a nothing email address, and whatever else Microsoft required—he inserted Claire's flash drive and waited as the contents populated the screen.

He copied only what mattered—journals, audio files, photos, spreadsheets, scanned documents. He dropped all of it into a new folder labeled "HARBOR IN LINDEN – CONFIDENTIAL."

Next, he created a summary sheet. He typed it meticulously on the new paper using his sister's old typewriter:

This contains detailed evidence regarding human

trafficking, corruption, and criminal activity associated with Harbor Ministries, 737, and Pastor David Graves. Review immediately.

No fingerprints. No personal files. No metadata.

He transferred the digital evidence onto three separate USB drives. Each was sealed in its own padded mailer, along with a typed summary sheet.

He addressed the envelopes by hand with a Sharpie:

Regional Office – Michigan State Police
Field Bureau – Federal Bureau of Investigation
News Desk – Detroit Free Press
            Attn: Investigations

They sat in a neat row on the edge of his desk. Ready to be mailed.

"I'm sorry, Claire," he said. "I should have done this a long—"

The knock at the front door startled him.

He sat frozen for half a second. His eyes glanced toward the envelopes. Out in the open. Exposed and on his desk, down a very short hallway, and around the corner from his front door.

He scattered a few *Logia* journals across the envelopes before crossing the room and traveling the hallway to the door. He opened it only a crack.

It was Stern.

He was never in uniform. This time, he wore an old Carhartt coat, not unlike the one Daniel owned, dark jeans, and a weary look, as if he'd been up late thinking too long and sleeping very little.

Daniel opened the door wider.

"Hey," Stern said.

"Hey," Daniel replied, the word slow in his throat.

"You had lunch yet?"

Daniel hesitated. "Not yet."

Stern gestured with a tilt of his head. "Come on. I was heading over to Shirley's. I could use some company and figured I'd ask you."

Daniel glanced back at the desk, then back to Stern. "Yeah," he said. "Sure. Let me grab my coat. I'll follow you there."

† † †

The diner was half full. Regulars. Older couples, mostly. One mother with a toddler flicking creamer containers off the edge of the table like stones into a pond. The air smelled of thick coffee and grilled onions. It was comforting. It was tired and honest.

They took a small table near the back, the same one Stern had sat in with Kress a dozen times before. The waitress knew him by name. "The usual?" she asked. Stern nodded.

Daniel ordered a grilled cheese and water. He didn't plan to eat most of it.

They sat in silence for a minute, the kind that grows between two people who have seen too much, had a lot to say, and yet didn't. They kept it contained. Dangerously so, sometimes. Enough to result in a divorce. Or much worse things.

Finally, Stern said, "I've been thinking about motives."

Daniel didn't answer.

Stern stirred his coffee slowly. "I mean, you look at the

trail, the order of it all—the killings. The way each played out. None of it's random. Whoever's doing it, they're not crazy. At least not in the way we usually mean."

Still, Daniel said nothing.

Stern went on. "It feels like someone is trying to send a message. Not to the world. Not even to the media. But to the people involved."

Stern paused and sipped.

"Who knows," he said with a strange finality, setting his cup on the table. "Maybe even to God."

He didn't give space before his next words.

"There's a sense to all of this. Each killing was…"

He paused.

"I think the killer sees himself as… necessary."

Daniel finally looked up and spoke.

"Necessary?" he asked.

Stern nodded. "Yeah. Like he's filling in the cracks that the system won't. Maybe someone close to the victims. Or to the people behind all this. Someone religious, maybe. Or someone who used to be."

Daniel's mouth was dry. He drank half his water and said nothing.

Stern didn't press. He just sipped his coffee and leaned back, stretching his legs beneath the table. "I'm not here as the chief today," he said. "Not really. I'm here as a guy who's just as tired as the next guy. Who wants to see something good come from all this… for once."

The waitress delivered their food. The grilled cheese was warm. Daniel didn't touch it.

Stern took a bite, wiped his mouth with a paper napkin, and asked, "Did you always want to be a pastor?"

Daniel didn't answer right away. "No," he said eventually. "I wanted to fly fighter jets."

"So, what changed?"

"One day, the Bible meant more to me than anything else."

Stern nodded, chewing slowly. Daniel finally reached toward his plate.

"The Gospel of Matthew became a favorite book. The way it begins—with broken people in the lineage of Christ."

He made the sign of the cross and then said a silent table prayer. He took a bite and swallowed.

He settled for a moment, then added, "Matthew doesn't sanitize anything. It's Abraham the liar. Jacob the deceiver. David the adulterer. Rahab, a prostitute. All in the line that leads to Jesus. People who failed God miserably, and yet, he still ended up using them in his plan. And then how Matthew ends the Gospel with Jesus saying, 'I am with you always, even to the end of the age.'"

There was a pause.

"As a kid, that meant something to me."

Then Stern said it. The thing that changed everything.

"We found a body in a dumpster in Grand Blanc last year," he said, voice lowering.

At first, Stern's words startled Daniel. They were abrupt. And yet, he immediately remembered the story. He had prayed for the victim's family in the Prayer of the Church during worship. He remembered Marcie Durham asking him beforehand to pray, but also how Brett tried to shepherd her away as if she were bothering Daniel.

"Her name was Mary. Michigan-born. From Grand Rapids. She was in foster care most of her life. She ended up on the street."

Stern took a bite of his usual—a gyro buried in onions.

"About a year ago," he continued, his mouth somewhat subdued, "she ended up in a halfway house in Lowell. She was getting clean. Doing better, it sounds. She made her way to our side of the State. She had family in Redford. Apparently, they wanted nothing to do with her."

Stern took a sip to wash down the bite.

"It wasn't anything a guy like me would've cared about. Not at all."

He took another bite.

"But then I learned she'd been in Linden. Turns out she was part of a special wellness retreat that Harbor offered up in Saginaw. You had to sign liability waivers and NDAs. The whole package. Some of the attendees ended up in Linden. Mary was one of them."

Daniel's hands tightened in his lap.

"I didn't have to look into it," Stern continued and chewed. "But I did. I spent the better part of last fall pulling at threads. I never really got anywhere."

Daniel's grip loosened. He took a bite of his sandwich, finally.

"Like I said, they found her in a dumpster. She'd been raped and beaten so badly that they could barely identify her. MSP only figured out who she was after they found some of her teeth at the bottom of the dumpster."

Stern motioned for the waitress. She didn't see him.

"Why was she killed?"

"Don't know," Stern replied. "My guess is she couldn't perform."

"What do you mean?"

"Toxicology said she'd been pumped full of Midazolam. That's a drug we sometimes found in girls' bodies in Detroit. Girls who had been trafficked. My guess is Mary was already headed for an overdose. She was likely so drugged she couldn't move. Whoever paid for some time with her, he probably beat her all the way through it."

Daniel didn't speak.

Stern leaned in. "This isn't about revenge anymore," he said, turning the conversation back to where it began. "I know it."

Daniel stared.

"We're going to catch whoever is killing folks around here," Stern said.

Daniel simmered in Stern's words. "Why are you telling me these things?"

Stern took another bite. He was speaking casually, as if all along, the conversation had been about something no more important than changing a light bulb.

"I have two daughters," Stern said. "I know what I'd do if I ever found one of them in a dumpster."

He took another bite.

"I'd find and kill the SOBs who did it. I'd pray for their souls later. Anything less would make me a rotten father."

Below the table, Daniel's trigger finger scratched at his leg.

"I'll admit," Stern continued, taking the last sip his coffee cup had to offer, "I hope whoever's doing it… well… I hope they finish it before we get to him."

He motioned again to the waitress.

"And we will get to him. We always do."

Daniel drove home in silence. He didn't go back to the

desk. Not yet. The three envelopes were still there beneath the journals.

Something in him had changed.

Or maybe something had returned. It settled on him, heavy and cold.

He leaned against the doorframe, thinking.

Stern's voice hadn't been filled with suspicion. Not exactly. It was something worse. Understanding. Sympathy, even. And that was what rattled Daniel the most. If Stern knew it was him, he wasn't trying to stop him. Not really. He was waiting to see if he would stop himself.

And while Daniel was sure he would before he left the house that morning, he wasn't sure anymore.

His hands flexed. He looked down at his fingers, the ones that had folded so precisely over the envelopes, the same hands that had served the Lord's Supper, baptized babies, buried the dead, held the hands of the grieving, prayed with shut-ins. They no longer shook. That worried him.

Because the part of him that had come home prepared to stop—to instead mail the truth and let the world deal with it—that part was fading.

What had happened to Mary—what had happened to so many others—wasn't an abstract evil. It had a face. Several, in fact. Daniel knew them. And three were still living. When the authorities step in, what if the system fails? What if Topel gets high-priced lawyers? What if Keenan and David do, too? What if they all go free?

Daniel took a breath and then exhaled steadily.

He turned from the doorframe and walked down the length of the house. Past the kitchen. Past the laundry nook. Into the garage.

He flipped on the light. The overhead bulb hummed to life.

He crossed the concrete floor, each step echoing in the boxed-in air.

Against the side wall, beside a stack of old drop cloths and a leaning snow shovel, was the aluminum ladder. It had been there since spring, untouched. The plastic feet scraped as he dragged it across the cement.

Daniel positioned the ladder and climbed, one rung at a time, until his head passed above and into the overhead storage's dusty space.

He slid the Halloween bin out from among several others. Navigating carefully, he descended the ladder to the floor below.

He did not carry the bin inside. He snapped the bin open and rummaged through it.

CHAPTER THIRTY-ONE

Halloween in Linden was a community favorite—children laughing, leaves rustling, porch lights glowing in rhythmic pulses along the streets. The sidewalks were teeming with miniature witches and pirates, Avengers and princesses, many carrying plastic pumpkins or cheap grocery totes overflowing with sugar. From every direction came the sound of happiness, of shouted thanks, of doors opening and closing in warm succession. It was the kind of night that made a town feel like a family.

Keenan stepped out from his office into the cool air, frowning at the wind. He wasn't in costume. But he would be soon. A brown trench coat over khakis, and his grandfather's fedora perched on his head. He'd told his wife, who was already at their daughter's house helping with the grandchildren, that he was going to be an old-school detective. But she knew he just didn't want to wear anything that required effort.

He had only stopped home briefly, long enough to change and check emails. When he came out, he found a note tucked under his wiper blade. It was handwritten.

> Bill, I stopped by, but you didn't answer the door.
> We need to chat. Come by the chambers before
> going to Donna's. If I'm not there, just wait. I'll be
> right back. Something came up. We need to talk
> about the Harbor deal. —Steve

The note was strange. Steve usually just walked into his

house when he stopped by. But he also knew better than to do anything other than what Steve asked. He was a powerful man in the county, and as a councilman, Keenan always kept him close.

He examined the note again. Just "something came up." That was it. No elaboration. He reached for his phone, intending to text Steve, but it wasn't in his pocket. He checked the front seat, then the floorboard. He went back inside the house.

Nowhere.

He tried calling it from the landline, but it went straight to voicemail.

This was odd. He never mislaid it.

But Steve's note seemed legitimate. And the timing made sense. The signing was next week. Maybe he had hit a snag, or the title company had pushed up the paperwork. Maybe there was something else. Whatever it was, Steve didn't want to talk about it with anyone around.

It was probably bad.

Keenan turned left out of his driveway instead of right. He'd get to Donna's soon enough. He had a sense this couldn't wait.

No one noticed Keenan's silver F-150 as it eased into a parking spot beside the old Linden Mill. He went in through the main doors and climbed the stairs to the Council chambers.

The main door was locked, as expected, but he had his key. Every elected council member had one. He slid it into the old brass lock and turned it.

The bolt gave with a dry thunk.

The building was dim and lifeless. Most of Linden's Halloween was happening in the surrounding subdivisions. Here at the Mill building, no staff, no janitor, no one. The library windows below were dark, and any noise from outside seemed to hush behind the heavy wooden door.

The second floor smelled like old books and lemon oil, the scent of the library below it wafting upward through the vents.

He stepped inside the Council chamber. Only two of the overhead lights were on.

The long wooden table sat in its usual place at the center of the room. Wooden chairs with faded cushions lined both sides. The flags in the corner drooped in still air. His name-plate was still in its place, the second chair from the left.

William Keenan, Councilman.

He walked to it on instinct and sat.

The room was quiet.

He waited.

A few minutes passed.

Then he heard rustling in the corner. A shadow stood.

At first, he wasn't sure what he was looking at.

A man stepped from the shadows palling the room's fur-thest rows.

He was taller and dressed in black.

And over his face, a pale and emotionless mask.

Michael Myers.

Keenan stood, startled and half-laughing. "What the hell, Steve? You really scared me."

The figure said nothing.

Keenan took a step back. "Okay, Topel. The mask's a nice touch. Halloween and all. But seriously—what's going on?"

Still no answer.

Then the figure raised a hand and slowly removed the

mask.

Underneath it, Daniel Michaels, no different in expression than the mask. And now, his collar, stark against his black shirt.

Keenan's face drained of color.

"Reverend Michaels," he said. "What—what're you doing here?"

Daniel stepped forward and placed something on the table in front of him.

Keenan's flip phone.

He stared at it.

"Wha—?"

"I needed you to be unreachable," Daniel said quietly.

He pulled something else from inside his coat.

The Colt.

Heavy and familiar to Daniel, it startled Keenan when he chambered the first round.

Keenan raised both hands, trembling. "Look, I don't know what this is, but if you think I—"

"You're going to call Steve Topel," Daniel said.

Keenan blinked.

"You're going to tell him to come here. You're going to tell him you need to talk to him now."

Keenan's lips parted, but nothing came out.

"If anyone other than Mr. Topel shows up... well... I think you know."

Daniel tapped the barrel on the table near the phone with a soft knock.

"Do it now."

Keenan picked up the phone with shaking hands. His fingers trembled so violently he nearly dropped it.

He dialed.

The phone rang twice before Steve answered. "Yello."

Keenan swallowed. "Steve, it's Bill. Yeah, um, we need to meet. Right now."

There was a pause.

"I can't meet you now. I'm on my way to Harbor to get the file cabinets. I'm trying to get stuff moved out before—"

Daniel motioned with the Colt for Keenan to continue.

"That can wait, Steve. Something came up. We need to talk."

"About what?"

"I can't talk about it over the phone. Just come over to the Council chambers. I'm already here."

"Someone has to get everything out of those file cabinets tonight, Bill."

"Call Pastor D. Have him go. We need to talk. Now."

Another pause.

"Alright," Topel said. "I'll be there in ten. I'll call David on the way."

The line went dead.

Everything in Linden was only ten minutes away.

Daniel took the phone back and sat in the front row. He crossed his right leg over his left and set the mask in the chair beside him. He motioned for Keenan to sit.

Keenan did as he was told, easing himself back into his chair, hands still trembling. The Colt never strayed from Daniel's grip.

Ten minutes. That's what Topel had said.

Daniel closed his eyes. He didn't move. He didn't speak. He didn't even shift his weight. The only signs that he was alive were the slow rise and fall of his chest and the way his head remained angled ever so slightly in Keenan's direction. He was listening. But also humming something. A Johnny Cash song.

Keenan tried, cautiously, to negotiate.

"Look, if this is about Claire, I didn't—I mean, I didn't even know her. And whatever you think I was part of, I swear—"

No reaction.

"I've got a wife. Grandkids. They're at my daughter's house right now. We go there every year for Halloween." He took a breath. "I serve this town. I don't know what you're planning to do, but…"

Still nothing.

Keenan shifted uncomfortably. "We can work something out. Really. What do you want? Whatever it is, I can get it."

Daniel didn't even open his eyes.

After a while, Keenan stopped talking.

There was nothing else to say.

The Colt stayed out.

Eventually, they both heard footsteps echoing up the stairs. Daniel stood and looked to Keenan. Putting the Colt to his lips, he whispered a drawn, "*Shhh*," and faded back into the shadows engulfing the room's last few rows.

The door opened, and Topel entered. He saw Keenan in his chair at the table.

"You alone?" he called, making his way toward the table.

Daniel could hear the song. He spoke aloud from the darkness what he heard.

"And I heard a voice in the midst of the four beasts. And I looked, and behold, a pale horse."

Topel froze. But only momentarily. He turned to see

Daniel emerging from the shadowed space. His eyes darted back to Keenan, who was visibly shaking.

"And his name that sat on him was death."

"What's going on?"

"And hell followed with him."

Daniel stepped forward, the Colt raised. "I'm here for your confession."

Topel went pale.

He waved his hands. "No! No! No! Don't!"

Daniel's steps were swift. He stopped just short of Topel's face.

Keenan cried out, "Don't do it! Please!"

Daniel fired.

The bullet went through Topel's forehead. His skull cracked open with a wet snap, like it had crashed into a concrete wall. A deep red mist burst backward and painted the council table and Keenan in a fan of arterial spray.

Topel staggered, not collapsing right away—just standing there as though death needed a moment to catch up. His eyes, glassy and wide, flickered once before he dropped to his knees. It was only a moment before his body fell forward with a thud so loud it seemed to shake dust from the ceiling tiles.

His face hit the hardwood floor at an angle, one cheekbone crunching audibly as it caved against the surface. Blood pooled around his head with unnatural speed, leaking into the grains of the wood, curling around the base of the table like ink in water.

Keenan gasped and pushed away from the table, his hands shaking more violently than before.

Daniel turned to him.

Keenan backed into the wall, his hands up again.

"Don't—please, I'm begging you. Please don't. I didn't—"

Daniel raised the Colt again.

Keenan tried to scream, but no sound came.

The first shot caught him in the same way it caught Webber. It went through his neck, taking some of his jaw in the process. As it did, his teeth exploded like shattered porcelain, ricocheting in every direction. His tongue, half-severed, lolled grotesquely from the side of his mouth as he gurgled and stumbled. He slammed backward into the wall and dropped to the floor, blood pouring from the lower half of his face.

Daniel watched from above.

Keenan tried to crawl.

Daniel fired again. He didn't have to. But he did, anyway.

This one entered the back of the skull and exited through the right eye socket, taking the eyeball with it. The bullet would be found the next day, halfway through a Grisham paperback on the first floor.

Keenan went limp, spasms jerking his limbs against the floor. A leg kicked once. Then again. Then no more.

Daniel's eyes were steady. He took a breath through his nose. The room stank of gunpowder—and maybe something more primal, like butchered meat left too long in the heat.

He put the Colt in his waistline.

"Kyrie eleison," he said before reaching down to collect the shell casings, putting them into his pocket.

He rose to his feet and closed his eyes.

He opened them again and looked down at the bodies. Then to Keenan's phone.

He flipped it open and dialed a number he knew by heart.

Stern answered on the second ring. "Yeah, Stern."

Daniel spoke plainly, his voice low and mechanical. "Go

to Harbor. David Graves is on his way there. He's going to take things you need."

There was a pause. "Who is this?"

"Just go. I won't make it in time."

"Reverend?" Stern's digital voice buzzed.

He didn't respond.

"Reverend… what are you—"

Daniel ended the call.

Turning, he retrieved the Michael Myers mask he'd left on the front row seat.

He descended the wooden stairs swiftly but carefully, his shoes treading heavily on each step. Before leaving, he slipped the mask back over his face. Through the door, he made his way home. He needed to get there soon. He needed the Wrangler. He was going to Harbor, too.

Outside, he blended with the dark, eventually merging with the bustling trick-or-treaters. A much bigger kid, to be sure, and yet barely noticed. Parents smiled and waved as he passed. Some shepherded their little ones a step or two away.

Nevertheless, Daniel was just another costumed man on Halloween.

Just another monster in a town full of them.

CHAPTER THIRTY-TWO

David stood hunched inside the narrow back closet at Harbor, sweat gathering along the edge of his neatly trimmed hairline.

The air was damp and paper-heavy. Around him, manila folders sagged in steel file cabinet drawers labeled in various letter ranges. The metal cabinets smelled of mildew and toner.

He cursed a few times while working. He didn't do this kind of work. Others did.

He worked quietly, but also methodically, transferring documents into a plastic tote at his feet. Some files he opened and skimmed before setting them aside. Others he tore in half and stuffed into a nearby bin for destruction. He didn't touch the third pile. Those were the ones they'd need cleaned.

The more he worked, the more frequently he cursed. This wasn't how he planned to spend his evening.

Two hours earlier, he'd been in the parking lot of 737, smiling and waving to parents, tossing candy into cartoon-themed buckets, and posing with kids in Paw Patrol costumes. He wore khakis, polished shoes, and a navy quarter-zip sweater—the approachable uniform of a man who built a church from nothing into a spiritual powerhouse with satellite campuses all around the county.

That was when the call came in.

He remembered while he worked.

✝ ✝ ✝

Plastic swords and Nerf axes. Spider-Man masks and bumblebee wings. Neon pumpkin buckets overflowing with Smarties, Mambas, and crumpled Kit Kat wrappers. He smiled through all of it, the parking lot pulsing with hundreds of tiny feet and countless adult hands snapping photos of princesses and pirates. Church volunteers handing out candy from the backs of festively decorated cars. The inflatable bounce house leaning to one side but holding. Someone had connected a Bluetooth speaker to a playlist of Halloween favorites. *Monster Mash* had already played more times than it should've.

His phone had buzzed in his pocket.

He glanced at the screen. It was Topel.

He stepped back toward the office wing, the phone already pressed to his ear before the first ring ended.

"Steve," he said.

Topel's voice came low and tight. "Bill just called. I was getting ready to head over to Harbor to clean out the closet. But he said he needed to see me right away. He couldn't tell me what it was about. Said he couldn't say anything over the phone."

"He didn't say?"

"No. But it sounds like there's a problem."

"I'll leave now and meet you there."

"No, Pastor D. Somebody needs to get those files out of Harbor tonight. We need that place cleaned up, and fast. We shouldn't have waited this long."

David ducked into the building. "That was your job," he whispered angrily. David didn't take orders. He gave them.

"I know," Topel said, "and I was on my way to do it. I

need you to do it."

"I'm not going to leave right in the middle of—"

"You can get your hands a little dirty tonight, Pastor D."

There was a moment of silence. David didn't like what was happening. Topel always had a way of slipping away when real risk emerged.

"Just go and get started," Topel said. "I'll stop by after I connect with Bill. Even better, I'll make Bill come along and help, too."

"What do you think he wants?"

"I don't know. He was acting weird, though. He said he'd tell me in person. Whatever it is, it has him spooked."

David's brow furrowed. "I thought I told you two just to burn everything in those cabinets."

"You did. But after I looked at what's there, I realized we needed some of it. We have some time before the signing, but in the meantime, we need to sort through it. And we have to make sure any of the bad stuff—anything Webber put in there that could be problematic—we have to get it out tonight."

"Why tonight?"

"Because the state called the construction office today to remind us that they're sending someone over," Topel hissed. "Tomorrow at 9:00 AM."

"Why'd they call you? They should have called me. It's not the city's building yet."

"Well, they called City Hall before they even called me. The Mayor told them that Topel Construction was already pretty much handling the place, that I had all the keys to the site. Bill heard rumblings about a visit earlier in the week, but nothing concrete. We didn't tell you because you didn't need to know. We were handling it."

"Well, now it appears I'm handling it."

"I thought we had more time, Pastor D. Look, there's no use in arguing about it now. They're doing a walk-through before the building is signed over."

"I still don't understand why this matters."

"Remember when I told you not to accept grants from the state?"

"Yes, I remember the disagreement."

"Remember the spreadsheets you got from Claire's laptop?"

David didn't say anything. He didn't know who else might be listening.

"Well, not only did she find the funds we moved, but she found things she didn't even realize were problematic. Harbor accepted state grants. Those grants had requirements. Some of them were based on how many girls were being served by the place. This morning's message said some discrepancies were found in the intake-to-exit ratios. Now they want our documentation. They want to verify from our side. If they find irregularities there, they're likely to find the other problems."

David closed his eyes.

"You see the problem?" Topel asked rhetorically. "But, I'm telling you, it's an easy fix, as long as we get on it."

David exhaled sharply while nodding, even though Topel couldn't see. "I'll head over there now. What exactly am I looking for?"

"It's simple," Topel said. "Everything in the cabinet closest to the door can burn. It's the stuff in the second cabinet we need to worry about. Webber and I shared that cabinet. There are really only three kinds of files in there. Anything that looks facilities-related, keep it. Those are fine. Anything that looks financial, or like routine intake—name, date, referral, place-ment—put that stuff in a bin. We need to look through that stuff."

"You were supposed to handle this a long time ago."

"Yes, Pastor D, I'm on it."

"Okay." David was already thinking ahead. "What about the documents I'm not sure about?"

"Put them in the bin, too. Bill and I can go through all of it tomorrow at my office. We don't have time for you to play detective tonight."

"Is there a lot?"

"Not for two," Topel said. "Besides, I've done my fair share of document tweaking at Topel Construction over the years. Hell, remember that little office I built in Byron two summers ago—the one for the dentist who, if I remember right, ended up joining 737?"

"Yes."

"Do you remember the collapsed ceiling repair in the kitchen at Harbor?"

"Yes."

"Let's just say that your dentist friend bought more dry-wall, insulation, and ceiling tiles than he needed. If I can fix that, I can fix this."

David didn't flinch at the dishonesty. "But the folks from Lansing," he asked. "They'll want to see everything tomorrow morning—and we won't have it."

"I know," Topel replied. "They'll have to wait until to-morrow night. Or maybe the next day. We'll just say it was misplaced. They'll give us time to fix it. Of course, they won't wait long. But they won't have to. We'll have it turned around in no time."

David rubbed his forehead. "Anything else?"

"Just don't read more than you have to," Topel added. "Just scan and sort. That's it. I'll go back through what you leave behind when I get there. That'll make things easier."

David remembered ending the call and stepping back out into the night. Children were still screaming with joy. A little boy dressed as a ninja ran past him. The plastic sword hit his shin. David didn't flinch.

He remembered waving to Kristin Dearden, the preschool teacher, asking her to let anyone who asked that he was heading inside to grab extra candy from his office. She nodded, distracted by a parent with a wagon full of toddlers.

That's when David left. He'd gotten to the back lot in under two minutes, his Escalade humming within moments.

† † †

Like everything else in Linden, Harbor was less than ten minutes away.

David had turned off the headlights as he approached, coasting the last block under the soft light of a quarter moon. Harbor stood like a forgotten chapel—dark windows, pulled shades in the front doors, several streetlamps casting long shadows across the lot.

David had parked behind the building, in the narrow service lane where Wexler usually parked the supply van. The place was quiet. Nothing moved.

Harbor had been empty for some time. A mere seven days after the Council vote, every resident and volunteer was already resettled at The Well in Grand Blanc. The move had been swift—an army of volunteers from 737 loaded up the beds, boxed the kitchen supplies, and dismantled every last piece of office furniture. Of course, not everything made the trip. A garage sale-style event had unfolded in the 737 parking lot, with staff and congregants selling off the leftovers: mismatched chairs, worn cookware, lamps with flickering bulbs. What remained inside Harbor now was mostly trash, scraps, and things no one wanted. But the file cabinets Topel wanted—they had stayed. They were safe at Harbor until the sale.

At least, they were.

He reached into the glove compartment and retrieved a key ring. Two brass, one black, one silver. He'd used them all a thousand times. The black one opened the back service entrance. The silver unlocked the interior closet door. The smaller of the two brass keys opened the cabinet inside the closet that only he, Topel, and Webber ever used.

The back door creaked as it opened, the hinges swollen from years of Michigan humidity and salt. He closed it behind him quickly and moved without turning on any overhead lights. He didn't need to. He knew the place well.

Through the narrow corridor. Past the walk-in pantry. Down the tiled service hall to the old utility room. Inside was a mop sink, shelving with leftover hygiene kits, and a rusted industrial hand dryer that hadn't worked since 2020.

To the left, the supply closet. It was deadbolt locked.

He turned the silver key.

The closet opened with a groan. Inside were the usual—cases of toilet paper, paper towels, unopened packs of sanitary wipes, bins of first-aid items. A broken vacuum sat in the corner.

Near the rear of the closet was a second door.

Flush with the wall. It was marked "Electrical." The same closet key opened it.

The label had been hung three years ago, back when the staff lounge was repurposed for Webber's sessions with the girls. It wasn't the real electrical room—any technician would know where that was. This one had been renamed on purpose. It looked official, boring, and forgettable. And that was exactly the point.

Unlike the other doors, the closet opened inward, revealing a short, narrow space no larger than a walk-in refrigerator. Inside were two tall metal filing cabinets.

Each's drawers were locked.

David turned the smaller brass key in the first cabinet. Then the second.

And now he was knee-deep in files—skeptical of Topel's dramatics, yet unable to shake the truth beneath them. If he was right, and even a single record was out of place, an auditor would find it. And that could bury them.

He didn't know everything Webber had tucked into the second cabinet, but he recognized some of the names. Girls who had come in and never officially left. No transfer records. No aftercare notes. No explanation. Just gone.

If even one of those files ended up in the wrong hands— if someone in Lansing concerned with grants started asking why a few minors here and there disappeared without paper trails—it would all unravel. And no amount of charm or invocation of religious liberty protections would be able to stop it.

He muttered something foul beneath his breath. The kind of language he would've chastised from the stage podium at 737.

Then he heard a sound.

It sounded distant. He waited and listened but didn't hear it again.

Minutes passed, and he continued working.

Then a voice came, not from afar, but from behind him. It was calm and familiar.

David spun around, dropping a few pages from his hand as he did.

"You left the back door unlocked," Stern said casually.

He stood in the outer doorway, hand in his jacket pocket, but not threatening. His tone was cool, and his expression unreadable.

"I didn't think anybody'd be home," he added.

"Now you have really crossed the line, Chief," David barked. "You can't just go wandering through places whenever you feel like it. Even if you are the law. You can't be in here."

"Well," he said, "I was in the neighborhood and just thought I'd check and make sure Harbor was locked up nice and tight. I wouldn't want anything happening to the place before the big sale. This deal cost me a few new patrol cars."

Stern kept his hand in his jacket and moved to the inner door. Scanning the room, "What's going on in here?" he asked.

David blinked. His mind scrambled for something to say.

"Looks like you're sorting some things," Stern said. "Need some help? I'm pretty good at sorting things out."

CHAPTER THIRTY-THREE

Daniel walked among the ghosts, vampires, and superheroes.

No one knew just how out of place he was. Or perhaps, how he actually embodied the night's terrors.

He was still wearing the mask. The pale, emotionless face of Michael Myers stared blankly ahead as he moved through the crowds. His black coat, tall frame, and silent gait made him seem like any other adult playing along. A little overzealous, maybe. But harmless. Another Halloween Dad on patrol.

He passed a trio of teenagers, all dressed like Art the Clown, each with his own variation. One pretended to size him up with mock suspicion, cocking a spiked toy bat over his shoulder. Another leaned in and whispered something to his friend, who made a low, guttural growl for show.

Daniel, much taller, slowed for just a second and tilted his masked head to the side in the character's menacing way. He was in a hurry, but he played the part.

The clowns laughed and moved on.

He kept walking.

The sidewalk shimmered in patches of orange light, cast by jack-o'-lanterns with slanted eyes and cruel smiles. The smell of firepits lingered in the air.

Daniel kept walking. His pace was increasing.

His black shoes struck the pavement with a steady rhythm, the same way they had in the council chamber, just before he pulled the trigger. A few pops that no one heard.

Then silence.

Not a flinch. Not a tremor.

But the smell of gunpowder and blood lingered. It held onto him every time, phantom-like. But this time, it was as though it had soaked into the seams of his coat. Every step he took away from the chamber felt like dragging the scent's specter behind him.

Still, he didn't know what disturbed him more—how easily he'd killed them, or how little of himself he lost doing it.

But he debated the concerns as he walked.

They deserved it. Every breath they took beyond Claire, beyond all the girls, had been borrowed. They were merchants of suffering—godless men who dealt in ruin.

He hadn't struck them down out of rage. It wasn't even fury.

He was setting things in order. He was administering justice.

As he finally turned onto his street, his thoughts turned to something else.

Stern.

The call had been impulsive. The number dialed from Keenan's flip phone, his own voice flat and unmasked. He hadn't even tried to disguise it.

Why did he call Stern? He barely remembered doing it.

He replayed Stern's story. The girl in the dumpster. Mary.

He heard Stern's words, "I hope they finish it before we get to him."

What had happened? He was ready to quit. But then, suddenly, he was in the garage digging through the Halloween bin, as if his body moved on orders his conscience never gave. After lunch with Stern, suddenly, he was recommitted to his original plan.

Had Stern given him permission? Was it sympathy? Was it a cop trick of some sort? Something meant to set him up?

Or had it been something worse? An absolution for Stern.

Had Daniel given Stern permission?

Daniel didn't know.

And yet, in a deeper, quieter place, Daniel had the sense that whatever it was, Stern could finish what he started in a way he no longer could. That maybe, when the dust finally settled and everything came to an end—if it ever did—someone decent would be left standing. Someone who'd always been willing to name things for what they were, and yet, remained clean along the way.

He climbed the front steps of his house. The porch light was off and the hallway light was on, just as he'd left them. No trick-or-treaters had been welcomed there.

He turned the knob and slipped inside, removing the mask and locking the door behind him in a combined motion. The latex clung slightly to his skin, as if it didn't want to let go. In that moment, he wondered how the mask had felt more honest than the man underneath.

The house was warmer than before. Not physically, but spiritually. It was as if the walls had inhaled his decision to continue and were, even now, accepting it.

He turned off the hallway light. He no longer felt comfortable in it. He moved in darkness. The house left no obstacles in his way.

He moved to his study. As far as he could tell, the desk was just as he'd left it.

He uncovered the envelopes from beneath the stack of *Logia* journals. He reached into his desk for stamps. He didn't care how many the packages actually needed. He simply peeled and placed eight on each. The rhythm of it reminded him of Communion wafers on tongues. Or maybe of dirt handfuls thrown onto a baby bird's grave.

There's no way these weren't going to make it to their intended destinations.

He turned without touching them further, walked past the kitchen, and stepped into the garage. The Colt's reinforcements were there. He ejected the magazine and refilled the spaces made empty by Topel and Keenan. Each round snapped into the magazine with surgical precision.

He dropped a few strays into his pocket before tucking the pistol back into his waistband.

He zipped up his coat.

Passing back through the house and into his study, he grabbed the envelopes and dropped them into his old backpack from seminary, the same one he used to carry his Greek New Testament and Book of Concord. It hung in the same closet where he'd kept Annie's typewriter. A few seconds later, he was back out in the cold.

The crowds were already thinning. Fewer children were on the streets now. Most of them were home, faces sticky with sugar, tucked under blankets. Some watched old black-and-white creature features. Others were probably watching the film that inspired Daniel's mask.

The Wrangler was in the driveway. He'd been home all night. Or so his fading alibi assumed. He opened the passenger door and climbed in, tossing the backpack in the passenger seat.

He drove without the radio. He was in a hurry. But he couldn't drive hurriedly. There were still children running in and out of parked cars on each of the neighborhood streets. Not as many as before, but some.

Into the center of town, the roads gleamed faintly beneath the streetlights. He passed Broad Street and turned toward the post office.

He parked a block away, just off a residential street shadowed by tall trees.

The mailbox was visible under the harsh white beam of a tall street lamp.

Daniel hesitated.

He could walk to the mailbox and drop the packages, keeping his face obscured from the building's cameras. It was dark. He could do this in a matter of minutes. It was only a block. He could get there and get back. He could finally let someone else take over.

But the moment passed.

Every minute mattered. And what was currently happening—spreading out from Daniel like seeping oil from a leaky tanker—didn't need more participants. It needed an ending.

His right hand already inside the unzipped backpack, he put it back on the wheel and turned the Jeep back toward the center of town.

Every minute mattered.

At the stoplight near the corner gas station, he caught the cross atop Saint John's steeple. It glinted like a blade. He turned right.

He passed the Mill building, Topel and Keenan likely still bleeding out on its second floor. He passed the used bookstore. He passed the car wash.

This part of town was quiet. Daniel didn't slow. For a moment, he felt like this would be the last time he'd ever see the town—the last time he'd ever come back this way.

Harbor was waiting. Stern would likely be there. David, too. Beyond those things, he just didn't know.

CHAPTER THIRTY-FOUR

David needed to collect himself, and he knew it. His mouth twitched, but he didn't smile. He crouched slowly and began gathering the papers he'd dropped, stacking them deliberately, giving his hands something to do while his mind spun behind his eyes.

"You're not exactly dressed for a break-in." Stern's gaze dropped briefly to the navy quarter-zip and slacks. "Then again, this isn't your usual kind of cleanup, is it?"

David stayed cool. "We've got a walkthrough tomorrow with the state. I'm just trying to make things presentable. It's not a crime to organize old files."

"In the middle of the night?"

"It's not the middle of the night. It's barely nine o'clock. And I always work late."

Stern scratched his head, his hand still inside his jacket.

"No," Stern agreed. "I suppose it isn't a crime to organize old files." He looked down at the tote beside David. "Although I suppose it depends on the files."

He moved a little deeper into the room, each step casual but purposeful. The space was tight. The mop sink. The metal shelves. Two garbage bins—one for trash, the other beginning to fill with papers that had been hand-shredded. And the tote still open on the floor.

"Is this Harbor's lost-and-found room?" Stern asked.

David's demeanor remained. But his tone hardened slightly. "I already told you, you can't be in here."

Stern attempted to look around David to the open file cabinet.

David took a step sideways, as if adjusting his posture, attempting to angle his body between Stern and the files. "You're here unofficially. I suggest you turn around and go. I don't know what you think you're doing, but—"

"I'm just watching," Stern interrupted. "Just watching a pastor do the work of a janitor."

He paused, then added, "You're sweating."

David wiped his brow instinctively, annoyed with himself for it. Again, he didn't do this kind of work. Others did it for him.

"I'm warm," he said. "That's all."

Stern didn't answer. His eyes scanned the cabinet behind David.

"Say, Pastor D," he said, poking. "Do you remember that conversation we had about the Madsen girl a few weeks back?"

David said nothing. He crouched again, placing a file into the bin beside him.

Stern continued. "The house was clean. I mean that in a forensic sense. No signs of forced entry. No DNA. No fingerprints. No struggle. Nothing wiped down. Whoever did it was relatively careful."

Another pause.

"It was personal, too," he said, as if to himself. "Not the kind of thing a stranger does. You could tell from how the body was left. Not posed, not hidden. Just dropped. Blunt force to the head, then the fall finished it. Snapped her neck clean."

David stood slowly.

"Why are you telling me this?"

"No reason."

David tilted his head. "Then what do you want from me?"

Stern took a small step forward. "There's something that's been bothering me. Just a detail, really."

David waited.

Stern took another half step. "The thing is, most people who walked into that house didn't notice much. Not even the other officers. It was early morning. The body was by the stairs."

David's face was blank as Stern described the scene.

"There was this little statue," Stern said. "Thick porcelain, shaped like a bird. It was on the floor near the wall. Its normal spot was the side table near the stairs. The dust print gave it away. Just about the right weight to do the kind of damage we saw."

"Yes, I read about it in the Tri-County Times," David said too quickly. "The police thought it might be the murder weapon."

Stern didn't blink. "That wasn't in the papers, Pastor D."

David's jaw worked slightly, grinding his back teeth. Stern could see his facial muscles flex.

"Didn't you tell me about it during our conversation?" he asked nervously and shifting. "I thought I remembered hearing it mentioned. At some point. You know, I talk with folks in Linden all the time. Maybe someone at City Hall."

Stern waited, not interrupting. He never interrupted a person's self-burial.

Eventually, David went silent, a thin veil of sweat gathering just beneath his eyes.

Stern let the silence grow again. He knew what he'd do

next.

Then, casually, he added, "Well, whatever," as if dismissing David's rambling. "You know what's funny? That statue—it wasn't just used. It was left behind. Like I said, a few feet from the stairs against the wall. It had her blood on it. And a little bit of Reverend Michaels' scalp."

David swallowed. He remembered the moment, of course. He'd hidden himself in the coat closet behind where Daniel was seated. He'd already taken the bird from beside the staircase before Claire came down for breakfast. He didn't know why. It just felt sturdy.

"Now that," Stern said, almost amused, "was the strange part. Most perps, even the stupid ones, are smart enough to dispose of the weapon."

David breathed slowly through his nose.

"Apparently," Stern continued, "this guy wasn't too bright."

David stiffened.

"I don't think the guy who killed Claire was much of a thinker. Probably didn't do well in school. He definitely wasn't very controlled. I think he panicked and chased her. About the only thing he got right was the gloves he was probably wearing. Beyond that, I'm guessing he didn't realize what actually goes into a crime scene investigation."

David took another breath.

"Either way, we'll get him. He's definitely not smart enough to get away with it."

David didn't speak. He didn't blink. He shifted his stance rigidly.

Stern stepped forward once more. But he didn't speak just yet. He let silence dominate.

Then, finally, another prod.

"You ever seen a man pretend to be composed, but inside, he's unraveling?" Stern asked. "They stop blinking. They breathe through their nose. They try to stand taller. Just like you're doing now."

David's voice came at last, low and bitter. "I know what you're trying to do."

Stern raised an eyebrow. "Do you? Are you clever enough to read me?"

A long, stifling silence followed.

Then came David's voice—plain and leisurely.

"She chose her path."

Stern's stomach turned. It was all he needed.

"You twisted son of a—"

David's voice was still plain. "You sound like you have proof, but you don't. Not really."

"You just gave me what I needed," Stern replied.

He moved to his left, positioning himself nearer to David and the cabinet.

David shifted slightly, too, causing Stern to pause. He examined David carefully, watching his lips curling faintly toward speech.

"Do you believe in God, Chief Stern?"

Stern blinked. "Is this a sermon?"

"Do you believe in spiritual forces?" David pressed. "In demons? In the principalities and powers. The things unseen?"

Stern was quiet for a moment. "I believe in evil. And I believe it has hands. Sometimes, those hands steer Escalades and crack young women over the head with porcelain birds."

David gave a confident half-smile.

"Did you ever open your Bible?" he asked, recalling their previous conversation in his office.

"No," Stern replied. "I've heard enough of it twisted by SOBs like you."

David chuckled, and for a moment, it was almost real.

"Then let me help you," he said. "Do you know what happened when Saul disobeyed? When he let his enemy live?"

Stern said nothing.

"God took his kingdom," David continued. "Tore it from him. And gave it to someone else."

"But not before he sent Samuel to confront him," Stern said, betraying a better knowledge of the Bible than David expected. "I came here to confront you," he continued. "And now I'm here to take you in."

David's head tilted. "I'm not coming with you."

"Yes, you are," Stern said. "You just gave me probable cause, and now you're out of options."

"No," David whispered. "You are."

He stepped in fast, not gracefully—just suddenly.

Stern reached for him, but the space was too tight. They bumped shoulders, legs tangling. Stern grabbed for David's arm but missed.

Stern reached inside his jacket—too slow. David lunged, catching his forearm and twisting. The two men slammed against the cabinet, jostling violently.

The Glock slipped from its holster during the scuffle and hit the tile.

Both saw it at once. Stern dove low—

But David got there first.

A single shot rang out, shattering the ceiling tile. Dust rained down. Stern froze, then reached.

Another shot. This one found him.

Stern gasped. His knees buckled.

This time, startled by the recoil, David dropped the gun. It clattered to the floor. He kicked it away accidentally, his chest heaving.

Stern slumped against the wall, his hand pressed to his side. Blood was already darkening his shirt.

"You... you shot me," he muttered. "You actually shot me."

David stood over him, flushed and panting.

"I can't let you leave here," he said.

Stern groaned, trying to sit up, but the pain drove him down again.

"You have no idea what you're doing," David said. "None."

He turned and stepped around the tote. He knelt and retrieved the pistol. He wasn't worried about prints. Not anymore.

Standing up, but only partially, he shifted toward Stern and crouched.

"I don't even really know for sure how you ended up here," he said. "And yet, here you are. Just like Daniel was there that day."

Stern's breathing was uneven. He glared through the haze of pain.

Pressing the barrel to Stern's head, David checked his pockets. No phone. But he did have keys, which David jingled mockingly in Stern's face. "You're not going anywhere," he said, before pocketing them.

He scanned the closet's shelves. A can of degreaser.

He saw an unopened three-pack of Cartwright matches on

another shelf of paper towels. He tore open the pack, keeping one box.

"I shouldn't need all three hundred," he whispered, shaking the box as he shook the keys.

He dropped to one knee beside Stern. "You should know, I didn't kill Daniel that day at Claire's out of professional courtesy. One pastor to another."

He pressed the barrel to Stern's head again. This time, a little harder.

"You will not get the same courtesy."

Stern coughed up red.

"A walk-through is happening tomorrow, Chief Stern," David continued. "Well, at least, it was."

He examined Stern's shirt as it grew darker and wetter.

"But now, there's going to be a fire. It's going to be a total loss for 737."

He tapped the gun against Stern's head.

"They're going to find the arsonist burnt beyond recognition in the ashes. He messed up. Made a mistake. Something happened. Insurance will cover it. Maybe I'll convince the board to use the money to build an addition onto the Grand Blanc campus. We have twelve acres there. Plenty of room."

Just then, they both heard a sound.

David lowered the gun. Stern was too weak to make a move.

Outside, in the lot, Daniel had just arrived. David's Escalade was parked ahead of him. And next to it—a Linden police cruiser.

In a moment, he was at the rear service door. His hand was still on the handle when he heard the muffled pops inside. As a man who'd killed before, they were familiar.

Inside, David stood perfectly still, the gun still pointed, but his eyes locked through the doorway toward the hall.

Stern's breathing was shallow. He coughed up a little more blood. A string of it spattered to the floor beside him.

CHAPTER THIRTY-FIVE

David moved with purpose.

He walked the central corridor of Harbor with the same practiced confidence he had used for years while giving tours and offering comfort to new residents. But tonight, there were no information packets or folded hands.

Tonight there was fire.

He had lit it only a few minutes ago in the northeast administrative office—far enough from where he intended to go next to create a delay, but close enough to the document closet to do the damage he needed, regardless. A dozen folders he'd been carrying were now soaked in degreaser and already curling black from the flame. The box of matches would soon ignite in sulfuric rage. He hadn't waited to watch. It would take time, but it would spread. The particleboard desk was doused, too. The room's carpet was old and thin. Before setting the fire, he'd killed the fire alarm panel entirely, flipping the master switch inside the security cabinet near the maintenance stairwell. No lights, no alerts. Nothing would signal for help.

This fire didn't need help, anyway. It just needed room to breathe.

As he passed the small breakroom near the northeast wing, he caught a flicker of movement—a figure stepping out from the adjoining hall, far down and nearly out of sight. Taller. Dark clothes. The man turned a corner, and then he was gone.

David stopped. His fingers tightened on the Glock's grip

at his side.

He couldn't see who it was. The light was bad. And the person was moving too quickly.

There's no way it was Stern. Had Topel arrived? Maybe Keenen?

David stepped backward into the shadows and waited.

Nothing.

No return steps. No voices. No sound, except the fire's crackling, growing louder behind him. It had a language of its own. Its words popped and danced and whispered its threatening resolve. David listened to it speak. It told him that whoever was down the hall didn't matter. He didn't have time to chase shadows. He had work to do.

He turned again, walking quickly now. Past some resident rooms. Past the stairs. Toward the kitchen.

He would open the gas lines. That would finish things for good.

Meanwhile, Daniel moved quietly along the corridor near the copy room, careful with each step. The security lights provided just enough light to see.

He crept past the staff lounge, keeping against the wall. The Colt was raised.

From somewhere ahead, he heard coughing. A wet rasp. He followed it.

Two turns and he found the source.

Stern sat half-slumped against the wall just outside the narrow supply closet, his face pale and wet with sweat, his shirt soaked through with blood. The blood wasn't spurting—it was spreading, dark and steady. Somehow, he'd managed to crawl, leaving a smear behind him. His breathing was labored, but he was conscious. His dull eyes found Daniel almost immediately.

"Reverend," he muttered.

Daniel dropped to his knees, tucking the Colt in his belt. "You don't look so good," he said.

"I'm not good," Stern replied, shaking his head weakly and struggling for breath. "A little… below the… collarbone. Top of… my lung… I think."

"We need to move," Daniel said, pressing his hand to Stern's side and assessing the wound.

Stern winced, then grabbed Daniel's wrist. "It's David… He took my gun… You gotta stop him… He's going… He's going to burn it all down."

The space was starting to darken with smoke. Light flickered from the far end. The fire's voice was getting louder.

"I'm going to get you out first," Daniel said.

"No," Stern spoke in a gurgled whisper. "Go after him… You don't have time."

"I'm not leaving you here."

"Leave me," Stern growled and coughed blood. But Daniel didn't listen. Instead, he crouched and braced his arms under Stern's to drag him. The pain made Stern's breathing ragged, but he didn't cry out.

Each of Daniel's backward movements was careful. Still, each bump along the rough floor elicited a fresh stab of agony from Stern through gritted teeth.

Turning a sharp corner into the wider expanse of the kitchen, every jolt along the uneven floor caused Stern to cry out silently, his broken breaths punctuating the chaos. Daniel could feel the weight of Stern's pain in every strained muscle and every shuddering step. Blood painted a trail behind them, and Daniel's shoulder burned from the strain.

"Hang in there," Daniel said. "We're almost there." The words were for both of them.

Finally, they reached the rear exit. Daniel shoved it open with his shoulder. A cool night air burst against them. Its autumn wind stung his cheeks, carrying oxygen, and for a moment, hope. He kept dragging until Stern was leaning against the wheel of David's Escalade.

Daniel dropped beside him to rest. But only for a moment.

"Where's your phone?" he asked.

"It's… in the cruiser… in the cup holder."

"I'll get it."

"You can't," Stern said. "It's locked… And David took… my keys."

"Never mind," Daniel said. He reached into his jacket and pulled out Keenan's phone.

"Call for help," he said, tapping 9-1-1 on the flip phone without dialing it. He put the phone into Stern's hand.

Catching his breath, Daniel stood to make his way back inside.

"David killed Claire," Stern wheezed from behind him.

The words grabbed Daniel, stopping him abruptly at the door. He didn't look back but only turned his head.

The Colt in his hand again, he opened the door. The heated air inside hit him, but not as hard as Stern's words. He would find David, even if it killed him.

He crouched low through the door. The smoke clung to his skin and clawed down his throat. His nostrils flared at the acrid stench of melting plastic and scorched wood. The fire was no longer distant. It was breathing, advancing, murmuring its crackles from the north wing. He couldn't see it yet, but he knew it was already consuming room after room. Its voice was preaching now, shouting its gospel of ruin from the rafters.

He moved forward, one cautious step at a time.

Then, just past the prep table, he saw into the hallway. Not the fire, but its flicker. Amber and red reflections danced across the hallway walls. Daniel paused, listening. Somewhere deep in the building, something cracked and crashed loudly—part of the ceiling giving way.

But above the fire's voice, there was another sound. The hollow report of a door slamming against its frame.

He saw David. He was coming straight toward the kitchen in a jog, keys clinking in one hand as he put them into a pocket. He had Stern's weapon in the other.

Their eyes met for the first time.

Surprise. Then recognition.

In that moment, David knew. It had been Daniel, the quiet clergyman he never suspected. He was the one who'd torn open men's chests and shattered their skulls.

Both guns went up.

David's was first, but his shot missed, biting into the walk-in freezer door behind Daniel.

He fired again—wild, panicked—three more shots, each ringing like nails he intended for Daniel's coffin. One hit the prep counter. Another shattered a light overhead. The last clipped the edge of a storage rack, sending a spray of metal and sparks.

Daniel moved through it, staring.

He didn't panic. He didn't flinch. He didn't care. Let the bullets come. Let them tear through his body and soul. He would finish this.

And yet, the air between each shot seemed to bend, each

round veering just enough to miss—as though the space itself had taken his side. As if God really was... *maybe.*

The song played. He could hear it. It played so loudly. He could feel it booming in his middle.

Whoever is unjust, let him be unjust still. Whoever is righteous, let him be righteous still.

David charged through the doorway. He fired again.

Whoever is filthy, let him be filthy still.

Daniel aimed low and steady.

Cash's words echoed in him, inscribed long ago in the Revelation to Saint John.

He fired once. The Colt thundered.

David spun and dropped behind the prep table. The first bullet hit his thigh—a crimson bloom spraying from his slacks.

Daniel stepped forward. He didn't crouch for cover. He didn't take shelter.

He was invincible, even if he wasn't. And he was hunting.

David scrambled, kicking a metal bowl across the floor. He crawled fast toward the industrial stove, grunting as he went, dragging Stern's Glock behind him.

Daniel followed at an angle, not letting the stainless-steel counters block his view.

"You killed Claire," he said, leveling the Colt.

David answered with another round.

This one pinged off a pipe overhead. Still, Daniel walked.

David moved again, this time toward the prep station. If he could get around it, he could get away.

Daniel followed.

Watching David's movement, he crossed back around. He would meet him in the serving line on the other side. But the fire had reached the furthest edge of the small dining room, and the hallway beyond the kitchen was already being consumed. Soon, the kitchen would be a maze of flames and shimmering steel.

Daniel caught sight of David's foot disappearing behind the deep fryer station.

He moved to cut the distance.

Another shot came—ricocheting off the edge of the counter. But David had run out of room.

Cornered between the stove and the dish basin, David slammed the stove knobs into the "on" position.

Gas hissed like a serpent. Flames hadn't reached this far yet, but they were coming. The whole place was one drifting cinder away from annihilation.

Daniel circled an overturned bin of utensils. He rested his left hand on the edge of the serving tray rail as he approached. The Colt was still in his grip and pointed.

David pulled the Glock's trigger. But nothing happened. Only a clack. He tried again. Nothing.

Nervously, he threw the gun at Daniel. It hit his leg and skidded out of sight beneath the sink. He threw a pan next. Then another.

Daniel closed the distance. He didn't fire. Instead, he reached to the stove and shut off the valves.

David slumped to one side, propping himself with one hand while raising the other.

A sick, mocking grin painted his features.

"You," he rasped. "It was you."

Daniel's chest heaved. His black shirt was drenched from the heat.

He said nothing as he leveled the Colt.

David's hand trembled at his side, but the grin on his face didn't fade.

"You should be dead," he said. "At Claire's."

His chest rose and fell, the pain now in every breath.

"You were right there. I could've finished it."

He coughed. The smoke was getting worse.

"But I didn't."

Daniel said nothing.

"Do you know why?" David asked. "It was mercy."

He leaned against the counter, smearing it red.

"It was respect. One shepherd to another."

He paused.

"I know you, Daniel," David coughed, the smoke wafting into the kitchen in thickening billows.

"You killed Claire," Daniel said. "You turned girls into ghosts."

"And you think what you're doing is bringing justice?"

Daniel didn't blink.

"I've come to hear your confession, David."

David's grin faltered.

"Do you think—"

Daniel fired once into David's chest.

The bullet pierced the sternum, cracking through bone and punching into the heart's edge. David gasped—a wet, rattling sound—his body jolting backward. Clutching his chest, blood pouring through his fingers in thick, ruby ropes.

"You should have killed me that day," Daniel said and fired another shot.

Then another.

One shattered David's shoulder, jerking his body sideways with a grunt. The next took his hand—the same hand that had once gripped a Bible while also abusing girls—splintering it into meat and shards. Fingers snapped like twigs.

He crumpled fully now, writhing onto his side, trying to crawl with his elbow. He went nowhere, his legs kicking uselessly behind him. Mucus and blood mixed at the corners of his mouth.

Daniel stepped forward, the Colt still raised.

He looked down. There'd be no mercy. Not in these flames.

He fired once more.

The round struck near the temple. The skull cracked sideways. His spine twitched. One leg kicked out involuntarily.

Then nothing.

A bloom of light behind Daniel's back.

The fire had reached the doorway.

"Kyrie eleison," he said above the body before him.

Daniel took Stern's gun and put it into his rear waistline before reaching to turn the stove's knobs back to full. Then he retreated.

Once outside, he saw that Stern had already crawled as far as his Jeep.

Within seconds, the fire reached out to touch the gas, as if whispering, "It's time."

The explosion was like God's own hammer. It ripped through the kitchen, blew out the rear wall, and sent a blossom of fire skyward. The heat was instant and flattening, the flames crowning the building with a halo of wrath. Its fury cast shadows a mile wide.

The Escalade caught first.

Then the patrol car.

Metal warped and screamed. Tires burst. Shattered glass

rained like crystal hail.

Daniel shielded his face as the flames roared behind him, licking into the sky in a funnel of orange and black.

He turned back toward the flames.

The Colt was still in his grip. His breathing was ragged, hot in his throat.

Before him, the twisted husk of the kitchen glowed like a furnace. What remained of David lay just inside the rim of its smoldering char.

Daniel went to his knees near the front bumper of the Jeep. Its windshield was spiderwebbed and pocked from debris. The hood was dented. A long scar from shrapnel ran along the hood. But the rest was untouched. It was drivable.

Stern watched from a few feet away, one hand gripping a tire and the other clutching his wound.

They both heard sirens now—rising and racing, getting nearer.

Daniel looked toward Stern.

"You should go," Stern said, his voice straining and low.

Daniel didn't answer.

"It's over," Stern said finally. "But... if you stay... it ends very differently."

Daniel looked toward the blaze and then back at Stern.

"I have nowhere to go," he said. "And I deserve what's coming."

"Is that... a... confession?"

Daniel almost nodded—but then he reached into his coat. He pulled out his keyring. Prying its overlap apart, his thumb nudged his house key free. He placed it in Stern's hand.

"Go to my house," he said.

Stern was weary but listening.

"There are two flash drives," Daniel continued. "One is in a book. *Luther's Works*. Volume 25. The other, a backup, is tucked into *The Conservative Reformation and Its Theology*. If it's not there, it's in the top drawer of my desk. Under a notebook." He paused. "Take the notebook and the drives. Everything's there. All of it."

Stern looked at him, a new awareness creeping across his face.

Daniel stared straight ahead.

"Claire gave the drive to me the morning she died," he said. "She slipped it into my coat."

He glanced toward Stern.

"She gave it to me, but I think it was really meant for you."

The wind shifted, pushing smoke and sparks across the parking lot. Stern winced, coughing again, gripping the key in his hand.

Daniel's voice softened, nearly lost beneath the rising roar. "I wasn't supposed to be the one who did this," he said.

Stern clenched his jaw. "You'll never—"

"I know," Daniel replied.

Stern grimaced, pain tightening every muscle. "I'll say I did it… Self-defense… I caught him with the files… Tried to stop him… He shot me… I shot him."

Daniel didn't move. He didn't speak.

"All of this," Stern added through complicated breaths, "as far as I'm concerned… it's enough."

Daniel lingered a moment longer. Then he shifted Stern gently away from the Wrangler's tire, laying him flat. He tucked his jacket beneath Stern's head, tucking the chief's gun in between its folds. He climbed into the Jeep. The engine groaned, coughed once, then turned over.

He looked through the window at Stern one last time.

They spoke—but not with words.

Stern ended the conversation with an exhausted nod, ultimately shooing him away with a bloody hand.

Daniel shifted into gear and rolled slowly toward the back access lane that led out toward the surrounding farmlands. Gravel popped beneath his tires.

In his rearview mirror, the world burned.

By the time the first fire engine crested the hill, lights flashing red and blue against the black sky, Daniel Michaels was gone—swallowed by the Michigan darkness, and by something he would never be able to outrun.

CHAPTER THIRTY-SIX

It had been weeks since the fire. Only ruin remained.

The smoldering wreckage of Harbor Ministries had been cleared away. In its place was a flat expanse of blackened dirt and bulldozed concrete. The sale never went through. The walkthrough never happened. The official story cited a gas explosion—an accidental ignition from an electrical fire that started in the administrative wing. No signs of arson could be definitively proven. And the body found inside—burned beyond recognition, with dental records and height estimates matching Pastor David Graves—the investigators were satisfied, and the file was closed for good.

Two others had died that same night: Bill Keenan, a councilman, and Steve Topel, a contractor and county commissioner. Both were found executed at the Mill building.

Like the other murders, it shook the town.

The local tri-county newspaper spun stories.

The whispers never stopped.

But the headlines eventually did.

The story lost oxygen once the narrative coalesced—gritty, shocking, and, more importantly, self-contained. David Graves had orchestrated a criminal operation under the guise of ministry, protected by doctors, lawyers, accountants, former law enforcement, and local elites. When it fell apart, he snapped. He killed his coconspirators, attempted to destroy the evidence, and died in the fire.

The murders of Keenan and Topel had occurred earlier

that night. With no cameras, witnesses, or reliable timestamps, the official timeline fit the version Stern submitted. No one wanted to dig deeper.

It was all clean. Neat and digestible.

Stern had made sure of that.

He sat alone now, in his living room, the lights off, the TV silent, a bowl of soup on the end table, still untouched. A bandage wrapped his chest where the bullet had entered—clean through the top of his lung, missing the heart by centimeters. He'd been out of the hospital for ten days. The doctor said he was lucky. He didn't feel lucky. He felt like a man who wanted to hug his daughters, to kiss his ex-wife.

Daniel's notebook sat on the coffee table. He hadn't burned it yet. But he would soon. His service weapon rested on top of it. He hadn't touched it since the night he'd returned from the hospital. It felt heavier than it used to. He could still feel the heat of it against his temple, the slight depression in the skin of his forehead where David had pressed the barrel.

He would've died then if it hadn't been for Daniel.

He leaned back into the cushions and watched the light on the wall shift as a neighbor's headlights passed by the front of his house.

The paperwork was done.

He had signed it himself that morning, and the State Police weren't asking any more questions.

The official report named David Graves as the primary perpetrator behind the trafficking network tied to Harbor. The deaths of Topel and Keenan were attributed to Graves, citing motive and opportunity. It was a stretch, but Stern wrote with conviction.

His own shooting was framed as an ambush during a late-night check of the building. Stern had supposedly interrupted Graves while destroying files, and a struggle ensued. Graves shot him, but Stern returned fire. The body couldn't be conclusively identified through DNA—too damaged—but no one questioned it. The dental records matched. And David had not only left the Trunk-or-Treat event at 737, but after lying to Kristin Dearden, he never returned.

No one was questioning David's guilt.

But there was a sadness for Reverend Daniel Michaels.

His congregation at Saint John mourned him quietly but deeply. Two Sundays of frantic concern went by before authorities finally decided that Daniel may have been one of David's victims after giving the flash drive to Chief Stern.

As far as anyone knew, Daniel had been silenced for his courage.

The congregation, his district and synod, the town, no one spoke ill of him. No one dared. Whatever secrets the drive held, they believed he'd carried them with integrity. And for that, they thought he'd died.

Stern exhaled, his breath tired from the damaged lung. He coughed once, then again, and reached for the soup. He didn't eat it. Just held it, letting the warmth seep into his fingers.

He thought about Claire. He thought about Mary—and about the others he'd seen in files that no longer existed. They were buried now—some literally, some metaphorically—but their stories had finally been told. Or at least, someone had tried to tell them. That was something. Maybe not enough. But something.

And Daniel?

Stern didn't know where he'd gone. He hadn't asked. He hadn't looked. He could have. But some things don't need to be found.

Daniel had done what the system wouldn't, what it couldn't. Maybe that made him a monster. Perhaps it made him something else entirely.

Stern sipped the soup. It burned his lip. He sipped anyway.

✝ ✝ ✝

Daniel had driven through five states.

Michigan. Ohio. Kentucky. Tennessee. Mississippi.

The further south he went, the warmer the air became. The road no longer crackled beneath autumn leaves. The sun beat hotter through the fractured windshield, and the trees—more cypress now than maple—lined the highway like tired old men tipping their hats as he passed.

He had discarded the envelopes in his front seat—and pieces of himself—along the way.

His driver's license was the first to go. He stopped at a rest stop in northern Kentucky, walked out onto a wooden overlook above a lazy river, and dropped the laminated card over the railing. It tumbled in the air like a dead leaf and vanished beneath the water's surface without a sound.

A few towns later, he left the collar at the entrance to an old cemetery.

He found a small Lutheran Church—Missouri Synod church in a suburb outside Memphis. He parked behind the building, near the fellowship hall, and waited until no one was around. Then he stepped inside through the unlocked side door and left his alb and several clerical shirts folded on the altar rail. He stood there for a moment, watching the red eternal flame lamp flicker in its glass.

He whispered the Kyrie one last time, then turned and left.

Later, on a two-lane road hugging the Mississippi River, he tossed his old seminary class ring into the current. By the time he reached Louisiana, Daniel Michaels was gone.

Somewhere past the southernmost highway sign, under heat-thick skies and with nothing in his pockets but folded bills, a man without a name kept driving. He didn't know what town he'd stop in. He only knew he'd know it when he saw it.

✝ ✝ ✝

Stern submitted for retirement after Christmas. He didn't plan to at first. But then again, everyone knew he wouldn't be in the office much longer. He moved slower now, talked a little softer, and left more paperwork unfinished than he used to. He'd already turned down two media interviews and ignored an out-of-state number that kept calling. What was left to say? He'd done what he could. The truth had been buried in a way the town could live with. The rest, well, that was someone else's burden now.

In the weeks that followed, he heard from his oldest daughter for the first time in years. She attributed the surprising phone call to an anonymous letter she'd received—beautifully written, describing the man her father really was. It spoke of second chances and ultimately convinced her to reach out. Stern's younger daughter was still keeping her distance, but the oldest wanted to try. She wanted to make something real between them, if possible. Stern wanted it, too. He needed it. More than air. And he took her up on it, spending more time with her, her young husband, and the infant son he'd only ever heard about but never met.

EPILOGUE

The church was small, barely more than a corner store-front.

It stood at the intersection of Claiborne and Elysian Fields, a flat-faced brick building with a peeling sign in the window that read: "Christ Redeems. Sundays at 10." A second sign taped beneath it read: "Food Pantry Open Tuesdays, 1–4 PM."

He had found it the week he arrived. The doors were unlocked. The pews—mismatched and wobbling—had been pushed to the walls. Folding chairs had replaced them. There was no altar. Just a music stand. The air smelled of old coffee and hymnals.

An elder, Silas, had kept things going after the last minister left, but no one really filled the role. No one wanted to, not in that neighborhood.

And so, they just gathered, prayed, and waited.

The congregation was tiny. A dozen souls, maybe less. Most were older women who lived nearby, or single mothers with restless toddlers.

No one asked where he'd come from. And he avoided giving his name.

Soon, he just started showing up. First to sweep the sidewalk. Then, to clean out the gutters. He replaced a cracked lightbulb in the women's bathroom. And when the Wednesday Bible study leader failed to show, he offered to read the passage.

No one stopped him. He read slowly and clearly.

Psalm 34.

"The Lord is close to the brokenhearted and saves those who are crushed in spirit."

It came out hollow at first. But his voice steadied as the verse continued.

A woman in the front row nodded. A man with a twisted cane whispered, "Amen."

Later, he helped unload canned goods from a battered Ford pickup and organized them on dusty pantry shelves. Silas asked if he was looking for work. He just shrugged.

Silas handed him a small envelope anyway. "We don't have much," he said, "but we believe in honoring a man who serves. A worker is worth his wages."

He tucked it in his back pocket. He didn't count it. He just said thank you. He wasn't rude. He was reverent.

He'd been staying in a small apartment over a corner market. He paid cash. Money he'd made from helping in the market. The landlord didn't ask for a name. Only a handshake and a promise to keep quiet after 10.

He agreed.

He kept the shades drawn. The windows were cracked. The walls were bare.

Sometimes, in the early morning, he sat on the fire escape with a cup of gas station coffee and watched the sun rise over the rooftops. The haze above the Mississippi turned orange, then gold. The sounds of jazz and garbage trucks drifted through the alleyways. A boy on a bike delivered newspapers with a crate on the front. A man with a saxophone played beneath the overpass.

The city was loud. But his mind was quiet.

He heard screams in his sleep. He saw blood in his dreams. But they no longer chased him. Not really.

They walked beside him. Not haunting him—but bearing witness.

They weren't ghosts.

They were saints.

He didn't know how long he would stay in New Orleans. He didn't make plans. But every Sunday, he stood behind the music stand and read the Scriptures to the handful of people who came. He didn't impose himself. They asked him to do it. There was something about him, and they wanted more of it.

He spoke simply. He didn't raise his voice or build to flourishes. He just opened the Bible, turned the pages slowly, and said what the text said. Some days it sounded like mercy. Other days, it sounded like judgment. But whatever it was, he spoke it like someone who had been through fire and come out burned—but not consumed.

They started calling him "Pastor." He let them. Even Silas. He never introduced himself that way.

A few began arriving earlier on Sundays. Others stayed longer after the closing prayer. The folding chairs filled out slowly. A new mother with two children started bringing coffee in a travel dispenser. Someone donated a pulpit. The music stand became a lectern. Another added a plastic cross to the front of the new pulpit.

He tried not to notice when the changes happened. But he always did. And deep down, he knew he wasn't just filling in anymore. He was leading.

He grew a beard. It changed his face more than he expected. A few of the kids in the neighborhood started calling him "Preacher." The name stuck. The past loosened its grip.

Still, at night, he sometimes heard his former life's sounds, following him like a shadow with a hymnbook. He never spoke of them. But when he stood at the music stand each week and read the appointed readings, they were there. Every word he spoke was a counterweight to the voices. Every line of Scripture was a rebuke to the part of him that still remembered.

Then one bright Sunday morning, he saw him.

The man came in quietly, just as the sermon began. He stood near the back for a time, watching. When no one moved to stop him, he took a seat in the last folding chair along the back wall, his arms crossed loosely, his eyes fixed forward—not skeptical, not hostile, just resting. And watching.

The man in the pulpit preaching, his faded Geneva gown hung heavily on his narrower frame. He felt the shift in the room. His voice caught for just a moment, not enough for anyone else to notice, but enough for him to feel it. He looked up and saw him.

Stern.

Older now. A little thinner. The wound had aged him in ways that were more than physical. But it was him. Of course it was. He was a good detective. He was good at what he did.

They locked eyes for only a moment.

There was no panic. No fear. Only a silent exchange—an agreement to leave the past where it belonged.

When the service ended, Stern waited until the last congregant had shuffled out. He didn't approach right away. He just stood near the back, giving the room its silence. Then, finally, he stepped forward.

The pastor didn't flinch. He was scooping up his

handwritten sermon and folding his Bible closed. The two men faced one another again, this time without blood or smoke between them.

Stern reached out. "I'm Jeff."

The pastor took it. His grip was firm but gentle.

"I'm Matthew," he replied.

A moment passed.

"I had a friend once. His favorite book of the Bible was Matthew." And then, once again, Stern betrayed his knowledge of the source. "The tax collector turned apostle. The record-keeper turned witness. A man who had once profited from suffering but ended up writing about mercy."

Another moment passed before Stern turned to leave.

Looking back, "Looks like you're doing good work here," he said, like a man sealing a confession for good.

Matthew nodded. "Trying to."

Stern added in the same quiet voice, "My oldest called me a few months back. First time in years. She's got a husband now. Little boy, too. Said she got a letter. We're... trying again. Been going to church with them."

"That's good," Matthew replied, offering a reserved smile. "You're a blessed man."

And then Stern was gone.

† † †

That night, after locking the church and walking the three blocks home beneath a purple sky, Matthew ate a quiet dinner at his small kitchen table. Leftover beans and rice. An orange. A cup of water. He sat with the window cracked, the sound of a trumpet off in the distance—someone practicing scales against the hum of the street.

He turned on the TV.

It was already on the local news.

The anchor's voice was steady and practiced.

"Two men were found dead late last night in the Algiers Point neighborhood, both with execution-style gunshot wounds to the head. Police are calling the deaths 'targeted' and say they may be connected to ongoing gang activity. Detectives on the scene say the investigation is still in its early stages."

The broadcast cut to grainy night footage—yellow tape, flashing red and blue lights, sheet-covered bodies near a graffitied alley. A reporter spoke to a nervous neighbor. Then back to the anchor.

Matthew muted the volume. He stared at the screen for a long time before glancing toward a noticeably loose floorboard beside him.

Eventually, he reached forward and turned the TV off.

In the quiet, the only sound was the buzzing of the kitchen light and the distant music from down the block.

He stood, crossed to his makeshift desk made from milk crates and plywood, and sat.

An open notebook waited. A few lines were already written across the top of the page in his compact, even handwriting. It was a funeral sermon of sorts for a boy in his congregation.

Travis. He was nine years old.

He'd been caught in gang-related crossfire at the school bus stop. His mother, Lorraine, had called Matthew the day it happened, her voice shaking. He went to be with her at the hospital. He held the dying boy's hand.

He prayed.

He read the Psalms aloud.

He did these things for hours.

When the nurses finally crept through the room, silencing the monitors and turning off the life support machines, Matthew recalled something familiar. A stillness. It felt like it might crush the air out of the walls.

He'd been there before.

In another life.

Lorraine, her fingers gently tangled in her son's hair, eventually turned to Matthew. Her voice was almost gone when she asked if he would say a few words at the funeral home—maybe even lead a service.

He wouldn't say no. He might even do more.

A lot more.

Matthew resumed where he had left off, whispering "Kyrie eleison" as his pen scratched against the page.

Visit *ChristopherThoma.com* for more information.